Praise for
Randal Greenwood

"Writing with passion and power, Green-wood tells the story of the Civil War in the Western states of Missouri, Kansas, and Arkansas. His characters are compelling and his research impeccable. I'm already looking forward to his next novel."

—**James Reasoner,** author of *Rivers Of Gold*, *The Healer's Road*, and *Wind River* on *Burn, Missouri, Burn!*

Forge books by Randal L. Greenwood

Burn, Missouri, Burn
Kansas, Bloody Kansas
Ride, Rebels, Ride

RIDE, REBELS, RIDE

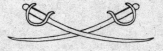

RANDAL L. GREENWOOD

A TOM DOHERTY ASSOCIATES BOOK
NEW YORK

This is a work of fiction. All the characters and events portrayed in this novel are either products of the author's imagination or are used fictitiously.

RIDE, REBELS, RIDE

Copyright © 1996 by Randal L. Greenwood

A Forge Book
Published by Tom Doherty Associates, Inc.
175 Fifth Avenue
New York, NY 10010

Forge® is a registered trademark of Tom Doherty Associates, Inc.

ISBN: 0-812-53457-3

First edition: February 1996

Printed in the United States of America

0 9 8 7 6 5 4 3 2 1

Lovingly dedicated to my father, Kenneth M. Greenwood. From the time he read me stories as a little boy until now, he has been my dad, my hero, and my best friend. He instilled in me a love for books and a curiosity about life, and taught me that anything can be achieved if you believe. Thanks, Dad, I love you.

Acknowledgments

I want to give special thanks to our Lord, who has granted me the experiences, abilities, and life that I might write. I want to thank my editor, Harriett McDougal, Nadya Birnholz, and the rest of the staff at Tor Books for the work they have put into my books and for their continued support. Thanks to Charles Keegan for the cover art. Heather Gillingham, Pat LoBrutto, Tara Padykula, and Carrie Smith for editing my books, and my agent, Nancy Yost of the Lowenstein Agency in New York, for her continued efforts on my behalf. Thanks to Linda Quinton, Ralph Arnote, and Larry Yoder of Tor Books and the rest of the sales department.

A very special thanks to my dad, Kenneth Greenwood. Dad has proofread all of my books and is good at catching the little mistakes or errors I don't see. He has made all the copies of the original so I could concentrate on writing and has traveled with me to all the Western Writers Conferences. Thanks to Mom, Midge Greenwood, for her faith in my writing.

Thanks to Vance Farrar, my computer expert, for fixing all the problems. Special thanks to Larry Bradford, who helped make the wedding ceremonies correct. A big thank you to Gayle Claggett for keeping my studio running smoothly so I could concentrate on writing.

Aunt Evelyn Prather made sure I had the finances to attend all the writers' conferences that made this book possible. Thanks to my wife, Rebecca, for seeing to it I had the time to write and for all the things big and small a wife does for her family and her husband. To my children, Evan, Amber, and Ciara, who understand when Daddy has to write.

Thanks to Cynthia Coker, Chet Coker, Johnny and Wendy Quarles, Kevin Scott Woolverton, William K. Dyer, Jr., Billy and Kieth Farrar, and John and Lois Harvey for their encouragement.

I wish to thank Wilson Powell of Batesville, Arkansas, for his historical information and descriptions of the area. Lynne Pace Rowland of The Book and Frame Shop, Laura Findley, and Ken Davis for helping me find information on Camden and Chidester House during the Civil War. Thanks to Marion Meyer of Sante Fe, New Mexico, for information gained from her book, *Mary Donoho, New First Lady of the Sante Fe Trail* for information on Clarksville, Texas, during the Civil War.

I'd like to thank Elmer Kelton, Johnny Quarles, and James Reasoner for taking the time to read my book and for their help and encouragement. It's wonderful when your heros become your friends.

I used a number of books and sources for authentic information about Jo Shelby's cavalry and the guerilla war in the Trans-Mississippi region: *Shelby and His Men, or the War in the West* by John Newman Edwards, published in 1867; *General Jo Shelby, Undefeated Rebel* by Daniel O'Flaherty, published in 1954; *William Clarke Quantrill, His Life and Times* by Albert Castel, published in 1962; *Gray Ghosts of the Confederacy* by Richard S. Brownlee, published in 1958; *Quantrill and the Border Wars* by

William Elsey Connelley, published in 1909; *Action Before Westport* by Howard N. Monnett, published in 1964; *Civil War on Western Waters* by Fletcher Pratt, published in 1956; *The Battle of Mine Creek* by Lumir F. Buresh, published in 1977; *Steele's Retreat from Camden* by Edwin C. Bearss, published in 1967; *Patterns, A Social History of Camden, Volume II* by Camden School Writing Project, published in 1988; *Units of the Confederate States Army* by Joseph H. Crute, Jr., published in 1987; *Official Records of Union and Confederate Navies, Volume 26: A Compendium of the War of the Rebellion* by Frederick H. Dyer, published in 1979; *Jessie James Was His Name* by William A. Settle, Jr., published in 1966; *Confederate Indians* by Frank Cunningham, published in 1959; and, last but not least, *Capture of the Gunboat Queen City* by Coleman Smith, *Confederate Veterans Magazine*, Volume XXII. Coleman Smith was a member of Collins's battery during Shelby's capture of the "Queen City." His real-life adventures during this engagement became the basis for Calvin Kimbrough's actions during this battle.

Contents

Foreword

This book is a historical novel. General Jo Shelby and his Iron Brigade were real. All the campaigns and battles in this book actually happened. My characters are fiction and are not made to represent anyone truly, living or dead. The Kimbrough, Bartok, Cahill, Stryker, Farnsworth, Covington, Lightfoot, Burke, Mayes, Farley, McKerrow, and Thomas families, as well as all the slaves, are fictional. There was never a Third Kansas Cavalry during the war, and all the men assigned to it are, of course, fictional, as are General Kessington and Major Kenton Doyle.

Briarwood and all the plantations except the Lightfoot Plantation are works of fiction, but the events that happened there really happened on plantations in Missouri, Arkansas, and throughout the South. The homes and businesses listed in Camden and Clarksville are real.

It is my hope to give an impression of the effects of the war on people from Missouri and Arkansas. The Trans-Mississippi region, located west of the Mississippi River, has largely been ignored by history books and writers in general. The bloody border conflict between Missouri and Kansas erupted into a fiery war unequaled in the history of the United States; homes were burned and whole towns destroyed.

The Union ordered entire counties emptied of Southerners; their homes and property were stolen or destroyed. Roving bands of guerrillas, Bushwhackers, and freebooters worked for both sides, and some just stole for themselves. Through all this, there were men of honor and courage who fought in regular army units, on both Union and Confederate sides. They fought for what they believed in. Most of the incidents here did occur in the Trans-Mississippi region during the Civil War.

Quantrill and the other guerrillas are largely condemned, but I think it is important to understand their motivation. It is time the Jayhawkers and the Kansas Red Legs are recognized as just as evil if not worse than the Bushwhackers. It is my hope that history will come alive to the reader, and that he or she will gain a greater sympathy for the southern people.

1

Unwelcome Guests

Katlin studied Cassandra as the buggy bounced along the lane on the way home to Farnsworth House. Twenty-year-old blonde Cassandra was a classic beauty even when her long hair was tied up tightly in a bun. Katlin envied her sister-in-law's high cheekbones and eyes which were the color of the morning sky. They had often depended on Cassandra, strong willed and not easily intimidated, to pull them through the tough circumstances of the last year and a half. The destruction of her home and death of her parents only served to make Cassandra stronger, melded in the fiery crucible of war.

Katlin heard Jethro, the former slave who now worked for the Kimbroughs, yell at the horses, urging them forward. It was the day after Christmas and the weather was unseasonably warm. Happy at the outcome of the trip to Andrew Covington's plantation, Katlin wondered why Cassandra was lost in thought. "Cassie, why are you so quiet? I don't think you've said ten words since we left Covington Manor."

Cassandra jumped, startled. She saw the concern in Katlin's eyes. Just a year younger than Cassandra, Katlin was into her eighth month of pregnancy, but she remained active and vibrant. Her flowing brown tresses caressed her shoulders and her blue eyes sparkled and danced in the late afternoon light. "Sorry, Kat, I was just thinking about the future. You know with Little Rock in Union control it won't be long until the Yankees take Batesville. I don't want to live near Yankee soldiers again. When the Yankees arrive we must leave."

"Please don't let what has happened in the past spoil the day for us. We should be happy! We managed to buy Jeremiah from Andrew Covington. I can't wait to tell Becca. It's the best Christmas present she'll ever have. Even if it is a day late."

"I know you're happy about it, Kat, and I'm glad for Becca, but now isn't the time to be spending money. Who knows how long this war will last? We might need every cent before it is over. It just hasn't seemed like Christmas, and, to be honest, I'm glad it's over." Cassandra pulled her coat more tightly around her neck as she continued to brood.

"I promised Becca I'd get Jeremiah and I kept my word. Don't you understand, Cassandra? Becca loves him and she doesn't want to risk losing him. When he was a slave belonging to someone else, there was always the chance he would be taken away or sold. Now Becca will have peace of mind, and so will I. Besides, Jeremiah is a good man, and we'll need his help if we ever do leave here," Katlin said.

Secretly Katlin was glad she didn't need to elaborate further. She had recently read a letter from her father that was supposed to be opened only upon his death. Curiosity had gotten the best of her, and she discovered a terrible family secret. Her personal slave, Becca, was her half-sister, child of her father's longtime affair with one of his slaves named Callie, who was now deceased.

Shocked by her discovery, Katlin went to Becca with

the news. They decided to keep their discovery a secret: Katlin would arrange the purchase of Becca's suitor, Jeremiah, who belonged to Andrew Covington, and Becca would get her freedom papers.

The girls had grown up together—Becca was just a year younger—and Katlin couldn't remember a time when they hadn't been together. Becca was startlingly beautiful, her skin the color of liberally creamed coffee. She had a fine, slender nose, dark eyes sparkling with life, and straight, dark hair. To some degree, Katlin even envied Becca's voluptuous figure and well-shaped legs. Yet there was a barrier between them, an unspoken rift caused by the fact that one was a slave and the other a master.

Pulling herself back from her own reflections, Katlin responded, "Well, it's foolish to argue about it now; it's already settled and I have purchased him." The carriage wheeled into the lane leading to the portico of Farnsworth House.

Cassandra said, "I've heard rumors from Andrew's servants that Union troops are heading this way. I talked to Andrew and he says he will leave with us if the Yankees come. He has already prepared three wagons and started selecting what they will take with them."

Katlin looked sternly at Cassandra, as if searching her very soul. "You've already decided we'll go, haven't you, Cassie? Even if it's the middle of winter and I haven't had my baby yet."

"It was pretty much decided for us when Little Rock fell. The Yankees will come, and I won't live near them again—even if we have to leave in the middle of winter. Evan told us to go to Texas, and I think he's right. Last time we were too crowded, but this time we'll take a second wagon and team. You'll need to lie down for most of the trip. We could even put you in this carriage. It has springs and will ride gently compared to the wagons."

"The Yankees might take all our stock if they come. We might not have any horses left to pull the wagons when they're done with us."

"I've made up my mind, Katlin. If they come we'll leave the next day. I'm not going to stick around here and watch them destroy this home like they did Briarwood." Cassandra paused. "Last we heard our boys were in Southwest Arkansas. Maybe we could find them if we were to head in that direction."

The carriage pulled up alongside the steps leading to the portico of Farnsworth House. Jethro hopped down and helped Katlin ease herself down the carriage step. Eight months into her pregnancy, Katlin's slender frame made her look even farther along. She walked with a wide stance for balance, and moved awkwardly. This was her first pregnancy, and she was doing her best to adjust to the experience. Cassandra was glad that so far Katlin had handled it with relative ease.

It concerned Cassandra greatly, the possibility of Katlin having to travel when she was so close to having the baby. Taking to the road again in the middle of winter with a pregnant woman was something Cassandra didn't relish, but she would do it if necessary. She prayed the Yankees wouldn't come until after the baby was born.

"Jethro, take the carriage to the barn. Have Jeremiah put the horses away and feed them. Then return to the house. I might have further chores for you," Cassandra said.

"Yes, Miz Cassie, I'll see to it right away. Miz Katlin, you get some rest. You done too much today with that baby a comin'." Despite his size and broad, burly shoulders, Jethro carried a kindly expression. His dark eyes shone with intelligence and perfectly matched the deep mahogany color of his skin. Years of hard work on Briarwood Plantation had honed his aura of strength and vigor.

Katlin smiled at Jethro's genuine concern. "I'll rest, but first I want to share the good news with Becca. Thanks for driving us today, Jethro. You drove as smooth as you could, and I appreciate it."

He smiled as he tipped his hat and climbed into the carriage. He snapped the reins and drove the buggy toward the barn.

Cassandra located Becca, busy cleaning in the study, and sent her to talk to Katlin. Becca's eyes were full of questions as she entered the room. In a nearly breathless voice she asked, "Well, Miz Katlin, would he sell?"

Katlin tried to remain serious to play the drama for all it was worth, but in the end she was unsuccessful. Despite her intentions, a wide smile broke across her face. "He didn't want to sell, but we convinced him."

Relief followed by joy flooded Becca's face. She let out a little scream followed by a giggle. "Let me see it," she said.

Katlin reached into her handbag and extracted the signed papers. "This is the bill of sale, and now it is yours. All you have to do is sign the paper and he will have his freedom."

Becca pulled Katlin close as she could over the swelling of Katlin's belly and gave her a hug. When she pulled back, Katlin could see the tears of joy in Becca's eyes. "Thank you, Katlin. This is the best present I've ever had."

"I'm glad I could help," Katlin said. "When will you tell him?"

"He's down at the barn now, working on horse tack. If ya don't mind, I'll run down and tell him now."

Katlin smiled. "I think it would be wonderful to surprise him with the news. I'm sure you'll want to celebrate." Katlin looked down at her swelling belly and rubbed it gently with one hand, placing the other hand on her lower back. "The baby is tellin' me it's time to rest. I think I'll go on upstairs."

Within moments of Katlin's departure for the bedroom, Jethro plunged through the front door. He found Cassandra in the hallway. "Miz Cassie, we got company headin' up the drive an' it ain't good. I seen four Yankee riders comin'."

Cassandra's smile faded quickly. She had been enjoying the day, but now only thoughts of danger pressed upon her. She hurried down the hall to the study, stepped quickly to the desk, opened the drawer, and removed a revolver. She checked to confirm that it was loaded and primed, then slipped it quickly into her handbag.

Cassandra was grateful for those days spent with her father and brothers back at Briarwood Plantation when she was growing up. Often she went down near the river with them to practice target shooting for pleasure. Even then the times were dangerous, what with the border war raging between Bleeding Kansas and Missouri. Her father wanted her to know how to protect herself, and she'd taken a liking to shooting a handgun. There was something satisfying about hitting a target when you aimed at it.

It wasn't until the trip south that she killed her first man. A Yankee deserter named Sergeant Barnes led a small band of renegades on an attack against their wagon. By luck her family all managed to escape, except for Becca, who was raped by her captors. Cassandra and Jethro rescued Becca and, in the process, Cassandra killed Sergeant Barnes. She knew she could do it again if necessary.

Cassandra slipped into her coat. "Jethro, come with me and we'll see what they want."

As Cassandra, Jethro, and Becca reached the porch, the riders drew rein in front of the house. Though they were mounted they wore Union infantry uniforms, and their cavalry gear looked new and fresh. Three privates and a corporal faced them. It was clear by the corporal's manner that he was the one in charge. He was small and wiry looking, with a mustache and heavy muttonchop sideburns. Cassandra found herself wondering how so small a man could grow so much thick hair. He tipped his hat at her and smiled in appreciation of her good looks. "Good day, ma'am, I'm Corporal Stivers of the First Nebraska Cavalry. I'm here to inform you that Colonel Robert Livingston will have his command post set up in Batesville at the Cox mansion should you have business with him. We've come to rescue you from the Rebels."

Cassandra studied him with cool aloofness. "I'm sorry

to hear your command is planning on stayin' in Batesville. If you're protecting us from the Rebels, who will protect us from you?"

The smile quickly faded from the corporal's face. "Just what are you trying to suggest, ma'am?"

"Every time we've been near Union soldiers we've suffered. I'd be much happier if you weren't here."

A rail-thin soldier sitting beside the corporal spat tobacco, then growled out, "Damn, Bob, we got us a bunch of Rebel sympathizers livin' here."

"Shut up, Murray, I'll do the talkin' here." The corporal looked back at Cassandra. "I ain't interested in your opinions, lady. Like it or not, we're here. The colonel wants us to gather provisions for our troops. Order your man here to fetch us some food so we don't have to help ourselves. We can be kinda messy, if you know what I mean."

"I think I understand perfectly, Corporal." She turned to Jethro, who was standing behind her. "Jethro, go down to the smokehouse and fetch these gentlemen a couple of hams. See if Fanny can spare other goods from the kitchen."

Jethro looked at the men with distrust. "Yes, Miz Cassie."

He turned, and as he entered the house, Becca stepped onto the porch and moved to Cassandra. "If you don't need me, Miz Cassie, I'll head down to the barn. I want to give Jeremiah the good news."

"Go ahead, Becca. I think we can handle this just fine." Cassandra turned to face the riders. "If you gentlemen will wait here, I'll see that the food is properly gathered." Cassandra spun on her heels and strolled into the house.

As Becca walked to the barn, the soldiers watched her go. "Damn, Bob, that's one fine lookin' nigger gal if I ever seen one. I'd damn sure like to roll in the hay with that."

"Damn you, Murray! Call me Corporal Stivers or call me Corporal, but don't call me Bob."

"I don't mean nothin' by it, Bob . . . I mean, Corporal.

You ain't had that extra stripe three days, an' I been callin' ya Bob as long as I know'd ya."

Corporal Stivers was listening, but his eyes were still on Becca's swinging skirts. "Just the same, Murray, give it a try." He licked his lips. "I reckon from the looks of her that black gal has got some white blood in her from somewheres. Some of these slave owners like to breed some of their slaves themselves. What kids come along still nothin' but nigger slaves, but they get all the fun of makin' 'em." Stivers winked at the others. "I think that one owes us a little pleasure for all the trouble we been through to free her and her people."

"Leave the girl alone, Stivers. She hasn't done anything to you."

"Shut up, Bannon, I give the orders around here. Them Rebs ain't any better than we are. They can diddle these gals all they want and no one says a word. You stay here with the horses if you don't have the stomach for it. You probably prefer sheep anyway!"

The others laughed at Bannon as they swung down from their saddles, then tied their mounts to the hitching rail.

"Don't do it, Stivers. The captain won't like it."

"What the captain don't know ain't gonna hurt him any. You damn sure ain't gonna tell him nothin'. If you do, Bannon, so help me God, you'll wish you was dead."

Tom Bannon tried to hold his gaze with Corporal Stivers, but his fear won out and he diverted his eyes. Stivers laughed as the three men walked toward the barn, leaving Bannon behind with the horses.

The Devil's Death Dance

The Union soldiers led by Corporal Stivers stood ominously silhouetted in the doorway, hesitating while their eyes adjusted from the bright sunlight to the dim light filtering into the stable. Jeremiah released Becca from his embrace and whispered in her ear, nodding toward the intruders.

Jeremiah was a tall dark man with rugged good looks and a heavily muscled frame. Despite his size and strength, he tried to look meek and friendly. "Can I help you, gentlemen?"

Stivers growled, "You sure as hell can, nigger. Get your ass outa here and find yourself something else to do for a while, if you know what I mean."

"Sure, massa, whatever you want." He turned toward Becca and motioned for her to come with him.

Stivers grabbed her arm as she tried to slip by. "Not her, boy. You go on. She's gonna keep us company for awhile."

Becca's eyes widened in fear. Jeremiah interposed himself between Corporal Stivers and Becca while trying to loosen Stivers's grip on the girl. A burly soldier punched Jeremiah in the gut, doubling him up and sending him to the ground, gasping for breath.

"Nice work, Oates. Nigger seems kinda pushy." Stivers laughed as he viciously kicked Jeremiah in the mouth. Blood sprayed from Jeremiah's crushed lips as his teeth cracked. "Now get out of here, boy, like I told ya."

Jeremiah drew up his knees, his forehead still pressed to the ground. He crawled painfully away, inching toward the back of the barn, eyes blurred by pain-induced tears and breath coming in ragged little volleys. After a couple of yards, Jeremiah slowly rose to his feet and, with his hands holding his stomach, staggered toward the shadows near the back of the barn.

The men immediately turned their attention to Becca. Murray and Harvey Oates each held Becca by an arm, while Stivers stood facing her. "Hows about a little kiss, honey?"

Becca shook her head and twisted her face away from Stivers. He reached out and grabbed her roughly as he squeezed his fingers into her cheeks, forcing her to look at him. "Now you be real nice an' we'll show you a fine time. You give us any trouble an' I'll make these masters of yours look like Sunday school teachers. You got it?"

Becca spit into the corporal's face. His lips began to twitch as his eyes flashed fire. He backhanded her hard, snapping her head around. "Ah, you're a feisty one, ain't ya? Well, you just go ahead and fight us 'cause it ain't gonna make any difference. I like it rough."

Becca tried to shake herself free, but the soldiers held her firmly, laughing at her efforts. Stivers reached for her dress and grabbed it at the neck. He yanked hard, nearly pulling her free from the other soldiers' grasp. The material in the dress remained intact, tearing only slightly. Stivers glowered angrily. More determined, he yanked again and this time the dress ripped away; the sound of tearing cloth echoed in the hollow of the empty stables. All eyes stared at Becca's exposed breasts standing firm and round, the nipples a dusty tan.

Becca, her arms restrained by the soldiers, stared defiantly at Stivers. Suddenly, Stivers arched his back, and his eyes went wide in terror. He staggered a half step toward Becca, his eyes bulging in pain. Blood gurgled and rattled in his throat as he tried to suck in air. Horrified, Becca saw four iron tines protruding through Stivers's chest, his shirt soaked with blood. He tottered for a moment, then half turned to look behind him, his fingers clutching at the bloody tines of the pitchfork. He fell onto his face at Becca's feet. Little clouds of dust and straw lingered in the air above the fallen body and Becca watched the pitchfork twitch with the dying beat of Stivers's heart.

The other soldiers stood momentarily stunned by the horrifying and sudden attack on their comrade. When they lifted their eyes from Stivers's body, they stared into the angry face of Jeremiah. He turned to run as the soldiers released Becca and reached for their guns. Becca remained in place, frozen by shock.

"Je . . . sus Christ, Harv, why didn't ya stop him?"

"Hell, I didn't see him until it was too late. I was lookin' at the girl."

Both men held their guns at the ready. Murray yelled in a high-pitched voice, "We can't let that nigger get away with killin' Bob. Let's go get him."

"What about the girl?"

"Yeah, that's a good idea. Maybe we can use her." He grabbed Becca and held the gun to her head. "Come on back here, boy, or I'll kill the girl. I'm gonna hunt you down an' kill ya anyway, so ya might as well turn yourself in and save the girl." Harvey couldn't resist fondling one of Becca's exposed breasts, the fingers of one hand teasing her nipple as the other hand held the gun to her head. He whispered in her ear as he pressed himself tightly against her body, "Can't let the corporal die for nothin'. I still intend on havin' you, gal." He yelled loudly, "Hurry up, boy! I ain't in the mood to wait. You know you gotta pay for killin' a white man.". He paused, then said, "Come on, nigger!"

Jeremiah hesitated, not knowing what to do. Finally resigned, he stepped out quietly into the dim light of the barn. He held his hands up where they could be seen. "I'm here, let her go."

Harvey smiled wickedly. "I ain't gonna let her go till we're done with her and you're dead." He pivoted the pistol away from Becca and shoved her down on the floor. He stepped forward and aimed his revolver at Jeremiah, who dove for the shadows and slid belly-first into an open horse stall. Muzzle blasts flared from the barrels of the soldier's guns, illuminating the murky shadows in the barn. They missed and splinters flew from the stall wall above him. Jeremiah felt his hands slide through the slick, sticky horse dung, the pungent odor filling his nostrils. He rolled against the wall, expecting the men to appear at any moment to shoot him at point-blank range.

The two Union soldiers stood at the ready facing the stall. "What do we do now, Harv?"

"Well don't just stand there, Murray, go on up there an' shoot him!"

The soldiers had their backs to Becca as they focused their attention on Jeremiah. She looked around quickly for a weapon and spotted a hay hook hanging over the lip of the stall divider. She edged closer to it and wrapped her fingers tightly around the handle. She heard the sound of running feet approaching the barn. It was now or never. She stepped forward and with a hard, overhand thrust drove the hook deep into the back of Harvey Oates. Oates screamed in pain as the revolver fell through his fingers. He spun around and slammed Becca hard into the barn wall. Becca slid to the floor, the wind crushed from her by the collision with the wall.

Murray, who had nearly reached the stall where Jeremiah was hiding, spun to face Harvey's horrendous scream.

At the same instant, a man with a gun burst through the

open doorway and stood silhouetted against the winter sky. Murray swung his revolver, pointed it at the intruder standing in the doorway and squeezed the trigger. Flame leapt from the barrel and the slug tore home; the outlined figure staggered and dipped his pistol barrel. Murray thumbed back the hammer and fired again; the second shot hammered the man through the doorway and pitched him onto his back. As the sunlight illuminated the body, Murray realized his mistake. "Son-of-a-bitch, I just shot Bannon!"

Jeremiah rushed from the stall, grabbed for the still-hot revolver in Murray's hand. Meanwhile, Harvey Oates struggled in vain to reach the hay hook stuck in his back. Finally, he gave up to watch Jeremiah and Murray struggle for the gun. Realizing his danger, he began to search for his pistol in the gloomy shadows and loose straw covering the barn floor around him. Harvey spotted the partially straw-covered revolver and stepped forward as he bent down to grab it.

Becca, recovered from being slammed into the wall, edged toward Harvey Oates. As he bent over to reach his gun, Becca loosed a vicious kick from behind that hit home with a solid thud between Harvey's legs. The man grunted in pain as his hands went involuntarily to his crotch. He fell heavily onto his face and rolled over onto his side, driving the hay hook even deeper into his back as he let forth a blood curdling scream.

Murray, still struggling with Jeremiah for control of the gun, slowly managed to twist it toward Jeremiah. The gun roared again and the bullet seared Jeremiah's side. Reeling from the shock of the bullet passing his ribs, Jeremiah slipped his grip from Murray's wrist and stepped away. In a low growl Murray said, "Now you're gonna die, boy."

As Murray again aimed his Colt revolver, a bullet ripped into his back from the direction of the doorway. The unexpected blow staggered Murray as his fingers involuntarily jerked the trigger of his gun. His errant shot plowed into the dirt and straw of the barn floor at his feet.

He turned slowly in amazement to see a woman standing in the doorway; a smoking pistol in her hands. The gun roared again and a second shot ripped through Murray's belly. A third shot to the chest toppled the soldier onto his back. His blood turned the straw beneath him bright crimson.

Jeremiah strained to recognize the silhouetted figure with the smoking gun. At her first words he knew his guess was correct.

"Becca! Jeremiah! Are you all right?" Cassandra asked.

Becca began to sob, released from the tension of the confrontation. "I guess I'm okay."

"I think I'm okay too, Miz Cassie," Jeremiah said thickly through his bloody and swollen lips. "That one is still alive. What are we gonna do about him?"

Cassandra stepped forward and stared at Harvey Oates. He was lying on his side; the handle of the hay hook still protruded from his back. His hands still gripped his crotch. His voice pleaded as he looked up at her through pain-glazed eyes. "You gotta help me. I . . . I can't get it outa my back."

Cassandra still held the warm pistol in her hand. "I'll help you, just as I would any wounded animal beyond help. I'll put you out of your misery." She lifted the gun and pointed it at his face. Harvey's eyes widened. The shot reverberated in the confines of the barn as the pistol ball ripped through Harvey's head and lodged into the earthen floor beneath him.

Jeremiah was shocked by Cassandra's brutality. "Lordy, Miz Cassie, why did ya kill him?"

She glanced at Jeremiah and in that brief moment, he saw the bitterness in her eyes. "He would have gladly done the same to you or me." She paused as she looked around the room at the scattered corpses of the four Yankees. "Once the first one died they all had to die. We can't let them bring other soldiers here."

"They'll send more lookin' for them. What are we gonna do, Miz Cassie?"

"We're gonna get rid of the bodies and leave here as soon as possible. We don't have any other choice."

"What if other soldiers come before we get rid of the bodies?"

"Just pray they don't." Cassandra paused. "Hide the horses in the barn for now. I'll tell the others and send Jethro to help you. Load the bodies in a wagon and then hide them in the woods. Clean up any bloody straw you find and scatter fresh straw and dirt on the floor to hide any signs of struggle. Don't forget to clean up the pitchfork and hay hook, and keep the guns. You'll have to hide their saddles and equipment with the bodies. I'd scatter their horses a good distance away from the bodies. Move quickly. We haven't got time to waste, Jeremiah!"

Becca stood shivering in the cold, trying to cover her nakedness with the tattered remains of her dress. Her light coat lay on the floor where the men had thrown it. She stared at the corpses of the Union soldiers. "Why is it every damn Yankee thinks he's got the right to use me any way he wants 'cause I'm black? I keep hearin' how they fightin' to free us. Well, if this is their freedom, I don't want it! They think they have the right to just pleasure themselves anytime they want, an' we oughta be grateful. Massa Thomas treats me better than this. At least he never tried to rape me."

Cassandra suddenly looked very tired. "War changes everything. When you are fighting for your very existence, for survival, there are no rules. Values get twisted, and what normally might look wrong suddenly is justified." Cassandra looked at Becca sadly. "Becca, you'd better go to the house with me and put on another dress. Then you can help Jethro and Jeremiah clean up this mess." She watched Jeremiah drag Murray's body toward the door. "We'll all work late tonight. Then I'll ride over to Covington Manor and tell Andrew what happened. I'll see if he wants to come with us." Cassandra slipped the gun back into her handbag, guided Becca through the door, and started for the house.

3

Along the Ouachita

By December 1863 the war between the states was entering its third winter. Jo Shelby and his brigade had just completed their great Missouri raid when General Holmes ordered them to set up winter camp along the Ouachita River in Southwest Arkansas, eight miles south of the city of Camden. Colonel Shelby's cavalry brigade had suffered through another year of heavy campaigning and was in dire need of rest.

In just six days the brigade built their winter camp: a small town laid out with streets in neat rows. The green cottonwood planks used to make the small cabins were cut at a nearby sawmill. Each individual cabin was made to house from eight to twenty men, although the majority were smaller. Fireplaces were fashioned from mud, brick, and adobe and attached to the rough structures for heat. Doors were hung on leather hinges. Crude bunk beds lined the walls; stumps or roughed-out chairs and tables were built for the comfort of the men. The floors were of packed dirt, and the men were required to walk to the edge of camp to do their personal latrine duties.

Captain Ross Allen Kimbrough sat playing solitaire at a crude table. The athletically built, broad-shouldered Missourian stood six foot one and looked older than his twenty-five years. He supposed that living outdoors for most of the last three years was as much to blame for his aging as anything else, but he knew there was more. Stress was an everyday part of his life—Ross Kimbrough was in charge of Colonel Jo Shelby's scouts, responsible for keeping the brigade well-informed of enemy movements and ensuring they didn't stumble into ambushes. Jo Shelby's Iron Brigade was battle-hardened and led by the best commander in the region. With this respect came awesome responsibilities—Shelby's cavalry brigade constantly found themselves thrust into the forefront of nearly every action. After months of hard fighting, Ross was glad for a chance to rest.

Only his love for Valissa Covington gave him any hope for the future. He met the green-eyed Arkansas belle at the Lightfoot Plantation in 1862 and immediately lost his heart to her. In December of that year, after Ross was wounded at the battle of Prairie Grove, his brother Jessie took him to Covington Manor, where he was nursed back to health under Valissa's loving care. When he closed his eyes he could still picture her in his mind.

She had lovely auburn hair that hung to her shoulders in long, thick waves, but her eyes intrigued him most. They were the color of new bluegrass in the spring, mostly green with just a hint of blue. He felt a tingle in his groin as he remembered how she came to him in the night and filled him with love and pleasure during his stay at Covington Manor.

Only one thing bothered him. She had refused his offer of marriage until the war was ended. It had hurt him deeply, but made him resolve to do everything possible to speed the end of this destruction. He would fight like a tiger to drive the enemy from his beloved Missouri.

Andrew Covington, Valissa's father, was against their
relationship from the start, hoping his daughter would instead marry the wealthy and widowed shipping magnate
Joseph Farnsworth. Farnsworth had gone to England and
was busily engaged in operating his fleet of blockade runners. Ross found it odd that his two sisters, Cassandra and
Elizabeth, now occupied Joseph Farnsworth's house near
Batesville, Arkansas, while Farnsworth was overseas. He
at least owed this kindness to Andrew Covington, assigned
the task of taking care of the home in Farnsworth's absence. Ross supposed that when the war was over Farnsworth would return. Still, he remained confident—in the
end he would gain Valissa's hand in marriage.

Ross stopped shuffling his cards and studied his face in
the small shaving mirror hanging near the door. Squint
lines were beginning to form at the corner of his pale blue
eyes. He rubbed his hand through his thick blond beard
knowing it needed to be trimmed. He guessed most would
call him ruggedly handsome. He returned to his deck of
cards as he reshuffled and dealt himself out yet another
hand of solitaire.

It was now late December 1863 and another blustering
day was on hand, the frigid air pouring in from the north.
The light from the small fire in the primitive fireplace was
weak at best, and the occasional shift in the wind sent
smoke into the room, making his eyes water. As Ross
strained to study the cards in the dimness of the cabin, he
listened to the discordant music of the snores of Jonas
Starke in the top bunk near him.

"Danged if Jonas doesn't sound as loud as the saw
down at the sawmill," Ross told the empty room. He
reached for his tin cup to take another sip of the erstwhile
tea. The bitter taste of the amber liquid made him wince.
"Sometimes I'd rather do without than drink this crap.
Tastes little better than river mud," he thought. "God, what
I'd give for a fresh cup of real coffee."

It was times like these that made Ross wonder about his
decision to stay with his old friends in this cabin rather

than with the other officers of the brigade. At least there would be a better chance of finding some coffee now and then with the officers. Still, he had fought alongside these scouts all over Missouri and Arkansas. They were more than just men he could trust, they were his friends—worth the minor irritations of the life they brought with them. He glanced up at the door just as Rube Anderson slipped the latch. A cold wind poured through the open doorway, scattering the cards onto the floor.

Ross frowned. The rough former backwoods farmer reminded Ross of a grizzly bear. Rube's full beard and long straggly dark brown hair coupled with his amazing strength only added to the comparison. "Damn it, Rube, don't hold the door open so wide. You just ruined my game," Ross said as he bent down to pick up his scattered cards.

Rube smiled broadly from underneath his battered slouch hat. He spit a stream of tobacco in the direction of the fireplace and it sizzled on the burning log. "Sorry, Capt'n, about your cards, but I got a couple of fellers with me I think ya might want to see."

Ross looked up. In the dim light he saw two familiar faces smiling back at him. "Well, I'll be danged if it isn't William Gregg and Billy Cahill. What are you two doin' here?" Before they had a chance to respond Ross said, "Are Quantrill's men joining us in camp?"

Bill Gregg stepped forward and offered his hand for a hearty handshake. "Nah, I'm afraid Capt'n Quantrill won't join up with the army this winter. Him and a bunch of the boys are winterin' over northwest of Sherman, Texas, along Mineral Creek." Ross shook Gregg's hand firmly before settling into the chair and placing the deck of cards on the table.

"So are you boys here to socialize?" Ross asked. Rube Anderson flopped onto his bunk as Billy Cahill stepped forward to shake hands with Ross. He was glad to see Billy in good health.

He had first met sixteen-year-old Billy in 1862 when

they found him trying to defend his burned-out homestead. As luck would have it, Shelby's men stumbled along too late to save the farm from a raid by Jennison's Kansas Jayhawkers. The Yankees tortured the boy's father before forcing Billy and his mother to watch him hang. The Jayhawkers burned everything to the ground that they didn't think worth stealing and rode out leaving a young and deadly enemy behind in Billy Cahill. Just a few weeks later the boy joined William Clarke Quantrill's Raiders.

Ross quickly snapped back to the present as Bill Gregg responded, "Nope, we up and quit the outfit. We rode here directly from Shreveport. General Kirby Smith is runnin' the whole damn Trans-Mississippi department from down there. Busy as he is, he took time to see a couple of ole Bushwackers like us." Gregg's smile widened. "We got what we came for. Smith assigned us to Shelby's Brigade. We're both members of Colonel Shanks's Twelfth Missouri Regiment, Company H." Gregg looked over at his young partner. "We signed the muster papers just 'fore we came to see ya. We'll ride with the brigade till the end of the war or until a bullet catches up with us, whichever comes first."

Ross studied Gregg. His hair was thinning a bit and his forehead was high; his thick mustache drooped at the ends. He was friendly and sincere, a man you could depend on in a good fight. "Come on, Bill, how are those Yankees ever gonna catch a bead on a couple of Missouri backwoods Bushwackers? Hell, you're too slippery for a musket ball to track down and too darn cussed ornery to let it," Ross joked.

Ross turned toward Billy and smiled at the blond-headed boy with the freckles sprinkled lightly across his nose. He figured the boy must have grown two inches since he had seen him last. Despite his youthful look there was something in those cold brown eyes that hinted at the deadly killer lurking inside. In battle Billy Cahill lit up with a fiery ferociousness that reminded Ross of himself.

Ross studied the boy's guerrilla shirt: It was long

sleeved and made from heavy cotton; a deep V was cut into the front and bordered by a large embroidered rosette. The shirt was covered with bright and colorful hand embroidery laid over its burgundy color. Four deep slash pockets were arranged on the shirt and from each pocket protruded the butt of a revolver, making the shirt heavy indeed. These shirts were a sort of uniform for Quantrill's men, each unique in color and design, all highly functional—a clear sign that they, the Missouri Bushwackers, were some of the most deadly men on earth. Bill Gregg's shirt was similar, but a russett brown.

"Glad to see you remain healthy, Billy. Liz will be pleased to hear you've joined the brigade for good. She asks me in every letter if I've heard anything about Quantrill's boys or if I've seen you. She's nearly worn me ragged with questions." Ross motioned for Billy to seat himself alongside the crude table. "Liz has nearly worried herself sick over you."

"She doesn't need to worry about me. I can take care of myself."

"We know that, Billy, but she knows what would happen if the Yankees ever cornered you. We all know they don't take prisoners when they catch Quantrill's men."

Billy nodded his head in agreement. He leaned back in his chair and said, "I've done a powerful lot of thinkin' about Elizabeth too. I'm afraid I'm in love with your sister."

"I've known it for some time. No one that's watched the two of you could think otherwise. You looked as if you were the only two people in the whole world while you were smack dab in the middle of a crowded dance floor."

"Yeah, those were the times. If I live through this damn war I hope I'll share more good times with her. She's a mighty fine woman."

William Gregg moved near the crude fireplace and began to load his meerschaum pipe. Ross shifted his weight in the chair and looked at Billy questioningly. "So how has it been, Billy?"

Billy rocked his chair onto its two back legs. "It's been pretty rough, Ross. The Lawrence raid was the worst. Much of what we did there was wrong. In the past we felt like we were there to stop the wrongs done by the Jay-hawkers, the Yankees, and the Red Leg scum. You know, even things out a little and give them a taste of their own medicine." Billy paused as he straightened out a kink in his leg.

He continued. "Somewhere down the line, things got all twisted. At Lawrence both Bill and I realized we were be-coming like the very scum we hated. When I first joined Quantrill it was like we were avenging angels, repayin' with an eye for an eye. Now somehow it's different. The guerrilla bands are fightin' among themselves like packs of wolves. Use to be we tried to defend southern people and give some back of what was stolen from them by the Yankees. Now it seems greed has seized many of the boys by the throat. All they care about before they plan a raid is how much plunder is in it for them."

Billy eased the chair back down and leaned his arm on the table. "Once Quantrill could control all the various guerrilla bands, but he's losin' it. He's lost faith in a Southern victory, and the boys can sense his loss of heart. Hell, he's more interested in his girlfriend, Kate King from up near Blue Springs than anything else. He just isn't bloodthirsty enough to suit the likes of Bloody Bill Ander-son, George Todd, Archie Clements, Fletch Taylor, Jesse James, Riley Crawford, and others. They don't care any-more about right or wrong, or anything except what they might gain. Some of them just live for the sheer joy of killing."

William Gregg had a good glow going in his pipe as he puffed out a small cloud of tobacco smoke. He pulled the pipe from his lips and said, "Billy is right. Why, ol' Bloody Bill Anderson just goes plain loco when he gets up his blood fever. He gets a real strange glow in his eyes, like he's staring right through you. I heard him say once he loved lookin' in a man's eyes and seeing the fear there when a man knows he's gonna die. Bloody Bill says he never feels more powerful than when he has a man's life in his hands. One shot and they're on their way to hell, courtesy of Bloody Bill."

Cahill continued, "Riley Crawford and Jesse James have been ridin' with Bloody Bill and follow his lead. He sets a mean example for those two sixteen-year-olds." Billy shook his head in disgust. Ross thought it strange that Billy seemed to think of himself as older than Riley and Jesse when in fact they were the same age.

William Gregg said, "There's still a few good men with Quantrill, but they're gettin' fewer every day. Quantrill's band is down to eighty-five men. Several have gone into regular service, others have just quit the war."

Ross saw the sadness crowding in on Gregg. Bill took another puff on the meerschaum before he continued, "Cole Younger left too. We saw him at Shreveport. General Smith is sending him to New Mexico to do some recruiting for the Confederacy. Cole told me he thinks Quantrill's command is gone to the wind. He says Capt'n Billy has lost control and it's nearly as dangerous from your ranks as it is from the enemy. It's rule by the strongest, and a man's life ain't worth more than a dog—and just as easily shot."

Billy Cahill listened quietly, now and then nodding his head in agreement. He dug his boot back and forth in the dirt-covered floor, forming a little heel-shaped hole, until William Gregg stopped talking. "Well, I think Cole's right," said Billy. "When men as strong and brave as Bill Gregg here and Cole Younger think it's time to get out, I know it's time for me too. I just can't ride under the black flag anymore. It all seems kinda dirty now and I don't like it. Do ya know what I mean, Ross?"

"Yeah, I think I do. The more killin' you do the easier it gets. You get hardened to it after awhile, and there are some that get where they like it. Then suddenly, you see a child or a woman grieving over the body of some man you shot, and you begin to question yourself. When you start thinkin' too much, you wonder . . ."

Gregg nodded his head in agreement. "I know I can't forget the faces of the men I've gunned down who wanted to surrender. I was angry and I had my blood up at the time, but now I see those scared faces sometimes in my sleep. I need to return to a more civilized form of warfare than fighting from the bush. That's why we're here. I've always found pride ridin' under the stars-and-bars for Jo Shelby."

"I know we can use you both in this outfit. I've fought alongside some good men in my day, but none better than the two of you."

Both men smiled in response. "What are ya drinkin' in that cup, Ross?" asked Bill Gregg.

"It's some mighty poor excuse for tea is what it is. I wish I had a good hot cup of coffee."

Bill Gregg smiled at Billy Cahill before he turned to Ross with a wry grin. "I 'spect we could help ya a mite with that problem." He reached into his stained and dusty haversack and pulled out a large drawstring bag. Bill loosed the string and poured a few coffee beans into the palm of his hand. "If you start grindin' these beans, I'll have Billy fetch us a fresh pot of water, an' we'll have hot coffee."

Ross stared in astonishment as he saw the bag of coffee beans. "Where did you find those? Coffee beans are more scarce than hen's teeth in these parts. Why, I haven't had a good cup of hot coffee since we got back from the Missouri raid."

Bill Gregg poured the beans into Ross's hands. "How we come to have these beans is a long story, but if ya got the time I don't mind tellin' ya."

"Around here any fresh news would be appreciated. With the weather like it is, I've got nowhere else to go, so tell it."

After slipping on a pair of leather gloves to protect his

hands, Billy Cahill took the pot from the hearth. "I'll go get the water and Bill can tell the story."

"I'll do it, youngun. It won't take long to smash these beans, so hurry."

Bill Gregg watched as Ross began to grind the beans on the table with the butt of his Sharp's carbine. "You might say these beans are a gift from that old Free-Stater, General Blunt. When we were headin' south for the winter we ran into his personal baggage-train near Baxter Springs, Kansas. We killed most of his men including his whole regimental headquarters band. We captured most of his personal belongings, including his general's commission and his sword, but the old devil got away from us thanks to a fast horse and a handy ravine he managed to jump. It was John Jarrette, Dick Yeager, and Frank Smith that danged near caught him."

"Why did Quantrill kill Blunt's band? Wouldn't seem they'd be a threat to anybody."

"They probably would've been fine except for one blame fool amongst them. A member of the band riding in the wagon pulled a gun and killed Bill Bledsoe when he asked them to surrender. That got the boy's blood up real quick, and they didn't stop shooting till every man jack of them was dead. Hell, they even killed the young drummer boy. That was the part I couldn't understand. He wasn't more than twelve, I'd say, and too young to die for what someone else did. We piled the bodies in the wagon belonging to the band and set fire to it." He paused as tears came into his eyes. "I wasn't there when it happened and neither was Billy. We were busy chasing after the soldiers still on the run."

Bill Gregg paused before he continued. "I saw some things near Baxter Springs that made me ashamed. Some of the boys stripped and mutilated a few of the bodies for sport. That was all for me. I knew then I had to get out of the outfit. It's bad enough to ride down a man and kill him, but it's plain sick to find pleasure in torturing his corpse. Man crazy enough to do that is likely to do most anything. Well, we killed everyone we could catch, and we caught a heap of 'em. Among the dead was Major Henry Curtis, Blunt's chief of staff and son of General Sam Curtis."

"The boys caught James O'Neal, the artist-correspondent, and killed him too. Seems he was sent out here from back east to cover the war for *Leslie's Weekly*. I guess he's drawn the last picture he's gonna do of the noble lads in blue routing the frightened Rebels. I got a picture he drew that I found when we went through the plunder. I'll dig it out and show it to ya sometime. All together, I figure we killed eighty men."

"So you got the coffee beans from the plunder you captured from Blunt's headquarters?"

"Not exactly. I told ya it was a long story, didn't I?" Bill said as he rubbed his whiskered chin. "Well, what we did was capture a wagon and some mules from Blunt's boys. We used it to haul the body of Bill Bledsoe, and John Koger, who was wounded." Bill watched as Ross continued to crush the beans. "Hey, that one over there needs to be a mite smaller." Then Bill Gregg continued his story.

"Well, we headed on down through Indian territory and Koger got to complaining about Bledsoe's body stinkin'. We stopped awhile and made a slave we captured from Blunt's command named Jack Mann dig a couple of graves. We put Bill in one, and Quantrill had Mann shot an' put in the other one. I guess the man couldn't complain about how deep it was. Hell, he dug it himself!" Bill Gregg laughed at his own joke. "Capt'n Billy said it was the best place for a nigger caught workin' for an abolitionist like General Blunt. Besides, he killed and stole from white folk in Missouri before he slipped away to Kansas."

Ross didn't find humor in the story. He thought about the fear a man must feel knowing he's digging his own grave. Ross, forcing a smile, tried not to let his disgust show. "So, how did ya get the coffee beans?"

"Don't be in such an all fired hurry, boy, I'm gettin' to it. Well, anyway we continued on south to Texas, and when we got to a town called Sherman, Quantrill traded the captured wagons and mules for four one-hundred-pound bags of quality coffee beans. When we left Quantrill, Billy and I helped ourselves to about ten pounds of coffee beans apiece. If we're careful and don't get too generous they ought to last us awhile. Be glad to share some of 'em with ya, Ross."

"That's mighty nice of you, Bill. A man needs a good cup of hot coffee now and then to comfort him."

Billy Cahill fumbled with the door latch and kicked the door open with his toe. A gust of frigid air poured into the room. Billy balanced the filled coffee pot in his hand.

"Shut the door, Billy, before we freeze!" shouted Jonas Starke as he sat upright in his longjohns in bed.

"Ya can't go fetch a pot of fresh water without opening the door, old man. Keep your longjohns on and you might get a cup of hot brew." He looked at Gregg and Kimbrough as he talked. "Sorry I took so long. The river is frozen. I had to chop a hole in the ice before I could dip for water."

Jonas, who had slept through Bill Gregg's whole story, rubbed his eyes as he asked. "You got some coffee? Where did ya get coffee? I haven't had any coffee since the Missouri raid."

Ross shot a stern look at Jonas. "Don't even ask. It's a long story and Bill doesn't want to tell it again."

Bill Gregg watched as Ross carefully swept the ground beans from the table into his hand and put them into the pot. Billy Cahill set the filled coffee pot near the fire to brew. "I don't mind telling him the story, Ross."

Ross rolled his eyes at the news. "I guess I can sit through it again if I can wrap my hands around a cup of fresh coffee pretty soon." But Ross wished that Jonas hadn't asked.

Minutes later, as the aroma of fresh brewed coffee filled his senses, Ross gratefully took his first sip. The rich taste and the comforting warmth from the cup took his mind back to other times and places. He thought of home and what the war had cost him. His mind shut out the sounds of Bill Gregg rambling on with his story that grew a little at each telling. Ross thought about his brothers and sisters. They were all he had left. He only hoped the army could bring a southern victory and a swift end to the war before he lost any more family. "I wish I were at Farnsworth House again like last winter, and close to Valissa and my sisters," he thought.

4

Under Suspicion

Cassandra grabbed the pile of blankets from her bedroom and hurried downstairs. She walked briskly toward the front entrance and exited Farnsworth House. As she left, she nervously scanned the road leading to the Great House. Her stomach felt as if it were tied in knots, and a great sense of dread hung over her like a black cloud on the horizon. Yesterday the shootout in the barn with the Yankee soldiers shattered any illusions she might have held for a peaceful exit from Batesville. All morning she had nervously expected the arrival of Union troops.

Driven by her uneasiness and understanding the need for urgency, she had relentlessly driven everyone to prepare for an immediate departure. She stepped quickly to the back of the wagon and handed the blankets to Fanny so she could pack them away.

She heard it then, the rolling, staccato beat of horses' hoofs against hard-packed earth. She turned her eyes warily toward the sound and caught her first glimpse of

soldiers dressed in Union blue riding into the courtyard.
The Union patrol pulled their horses to a halt near the
wagon. A boyish-faced lieutenant guided his sorrel horse a
few steps in front of his men and stopped abruptly. Soft
clouds of dust floated in the air around the spirited horse's
dancing hoofs as the young man smiled and tipped his fingers to his hat in a loose salute. "Good day, ma'am, I'm
Lieutenant Harker of the First Nebraska Cavalry. I'd like
to ask you a few questions if I might?"

Cassandra tried to put on her friendliest smile as she
greeted the young officer. She replied, "Of course, Lieutenant Harker, I'll be glad to help you if I can." She recognized the outfit's name from her encounter the day
before with Corporal Stivers and his men. These men
would be well acquainted with Stivers, and the knowledge
gave her a sinking feeling in the pit of her stomach. She
hoped her fear wasn't apparent to the young officer.

The lieutenant smiled at her as he used his leather-
gantleted hand to brush away the dust from his uniform
jacket as he spoke. "I sent a detail led by Corporal Stivers
to gather food for our regiment from your plantation. I'm
sorry to say Stivers and his squad are missing. Not one of
them reported to our camp last night. I was wondering if
you could shed a little light on this situation for me? Do
you recall seeing any of my men yesterday?" His smile relaxed into tight set lips as his eyes seemed to bore into her.

Cassandra wondered if he could see right into her mind
and read her thoughts. She gave him one of her best
smiles, hoping her beauty would sway his judgment.
"Why yes, of course, Corporal Stivers and three other men
did stop by here yesterday. They weren't here more than
half an hour. Fanny, our cook, gathered a couple of hams
and some bread for them to take back to your command.
I'm sorry to hear your men are missing." She hoped her
voice sounded convincing.

"Pardon me, ma'am, if this seems rude, but doesn't it
seem strange that my men disappeared after visiting your

place? Where do you suppose they went or what do you think might have happened to them?"

"I'm certainly no expert on military matters, and it isn't my concern to keep track of Union soldiers." She paused a moment before adding, "However, I did overhear your men talking. I believe the one called Murray said something to the effect that the food should feed them several days. I got the impression he wasn't happy in the military and the four of them seemed distracted."

Lieutenant Harker fixed her with an icy stare. "Are you suggesting, ma'am, my men might have deserted?"

"I'm not suggesting anything, Lieutenant, I'm just telling you what I overheard. I wouldn't presume to think for you, as I'm sure you are intelligent enough to gather your own conclusions."

Anger burned in the lieutenant's eyes as he replied, "Corporal Stivers has served with me since this regiment was formed over a year ago. He is a little gruff and can be crude at times, but he is a good soldier who has always seen to his duties. I don't believe he is a deserter, and it leads me to wonder if you are being truthful with me."

Cassandra balled her hands into fists and placed them on her hips. She tried her best to look indignant. "Are you suggesting I would lie to you? I only told you what I heard! You have the nerve to doubt my word?"

Her sudden anger seemed to startle the young lieutenant, who seemed surprised by her response. "I'm just saying that what you're suggesting doesn't fit the soldier I know. It seems suspicious."

Cassandra considered walking away angrily with the hope the lieutenant wouldn't further pursue the matter. Intuitively, she knew he wasn't convinced by her story. She decided to take another tack. "Murray wasn't talking to Corporal Stivers at the time, but to another soldier. I'm sorry I don't know his name. Stivers was assisting my cook in gathering the food."

Lieutenant Harker swung down from the saddle and stood stiffly by his horse. When he looked up, his smile suggested he might be amused by her story. "Then you aren't suggesting Stivers went with the men who presumably deserted. It still doesn't explain why none of the squad returned to camp last night."

"Lieutenant, I repeat, it is not my responsibility to explain or figure out what happened to your men. I'm only telling you what I heard. Maybe the other soldiers overpowered Corporal Stivers and made good their escape, or perhaps they didn't desert at all, but ran into a Southern patrol or guerrillas. There are many possible reasons why they might not have returned, and I haven't got all day to stand here and discuss each of them with you. I have my own problems and if you don't mind I'd like to return to loading our wagons."

"I'm sorry, ma'am, but I'm afraid I do mind. First off, we took the most direct route here from our camp and we didn't see any signs of a fight or struggle along the way. Secondly, my pickets didn't report any shots fired either today or last night. It might be possible for my men to be captured without shots being fired, or they might have been too far away for us to hear. It seems reasonable we would have seen some signs of a struggle, but we didn't find any. It seems to me there's more going on here than meets the eye. You don't mind if my men have a look around, do you?" Without waiting for a reply, Harker turned toward his men. "Sergeant Rodale, have the men search the grounds. I want a thorough search made, and then have the men reassemble here. If you find anything of interest I want it brought to my attention immediately."

The middle-aged sergeant was ruddy faced with a drooping walrus mustache. He nodded to acknowledge the lieutenant's instructions. He turned in his saddle and issued his orders. In a matter of moments the soldiers were dismounted, and while some looked after the horses, the rest began their search.

Cassandra eyed the situation anxiously. She secretly prayed that Jeremiah and Jethro had done a thorough job of cleaning up the stable and disposing of the soldiers and their equipment. While she watched, the men searched the wagon and carriage parked in front of the Great House. The lieutenant assisted in the search, peering into the wagon and studying the items collected there. He studied her smugly. "It appears you are planning a trip. Might I inquire where you intend to go in such a hurry?"

Cassandra was prepared for this question. Indeed, she had planned this story after the shootout had ended. "Yesterday, before your men arrived, we received word my mother is seriously ill in Little Rock. I'm afraid her condition is quite poor, so we must leave immediately."

The lieutenant leaned back against the wagon. "Funny, isn't it, that my men disappeared just as you decided to take a trip." He scratched his chin thoughtfully. "And just how did this word of your mother's illness reach you yesterday?"

"A traveler stopped by before your men came. He brought the letter from my mother."

"Did this stranger have a name? And where is he now?"

Cassandra paused for a moment as her mind raced. She hadn't dreamed up a name for the fictional traveler, although she had thought ahead enough to have Katlin write a letter that was supposed to be from her sick mother, in case they would need something to support their story. "I . . . believe his name was Jacobs, Ben Jacobs. I have the letter he brought, if you'd like to read it." She hoped it would convince this stubborn lieutenant.

The lieutenant smiled slyly as if he believed he had caught her in a lie. "You seemed to have trouble recalling the traveler's name. Maybe he didn't exist. How did he arrive, when did he leave, and where did he say he was going?"

Cassandra's lip quivered just a moment and her stomach seemed to move into her throat. She said, "I'm not particularly good with names and the man was a stranger. You see, the news he brought to us was so distressing I could think of little else than to prepare for the trip to my mother's side."

"I asked you how John arrived, when he left, and where was he going. Maybe he saw something that will help resolve this whole issue."

Cassandra caught the change of name by the Union officer. "I told you his name was Ben. He rode in on a bay horse. He was so anxious to be on his way that he only stayed an hour or so, just time enough to feed and water his horse and have a bite to eat. I recall something about heading for Tennessee. He didn't say why."

"I see," the young officer said. "If you don't mind, I would like to see the letter from your mother. If you wouldn't object."

"It is rather personal, but if it will help convince you I'm telling you the truth then it will be worthwhile. Please follow me to the house."

Just then a terrified scream came from the portico. Everyone by the wagon turned to look in the direction of the screams. Two Union soldiers were dragging Becca out of the house.

Cassandra hiked her skirts in her hands and began to run toward the house as she screamed, "Let her go! Let her go immediately!"

Lieutenant Harker followed on her heels as his cavalry sword jangled along beside him. He stopped before the men. One of the two soldiers, a dark-haired man with greasy hair and a pock-marked face, said, "Lieutenant, we found this woman hiding in a linen closet. She went nuts when we ordered her out."

Cassandra tried to get between the soldier and pry his fingers loose from Becca's arm. "Let her go! She's one of my maids."

"Why was she hiding, ma'am?" asked the lieutenant.

"Can't you see she's terrified? She's been raped before by Union deserters. The sight of your uniforms is enough to frighten her. For God's sake, please call off your soldiers."

"Release her, men." The soldiers let her go and Becca collapsed into Cassandra's arms. Becca sobbed in ragged little gasps as she clung tightly to Cassandra. Cassandra, who could feel the trembling of Becca's body, turned to face the lieutenant while still comforting the woman in her arms. "Thank you, Lieutenant. She is no threat to you, she's just frightened out of her mind." The lieutenant looked a little embarrassed by this whole scene. "Private Hawthorne, did you find anyone else in there?"

"Yes, sir! We found a pregnant woman. She's upstairs in bed."

The lieutenant turned to Cassandra. "Who is the woman upstairs?"

"She is my sister, Katlin. She is expecting a baby in another month or so."

"I see," said Lieutenant Harker. "There's no sense in bothering her. May I see the letter now?"

"Yes, of course." Cassandra hurried into the house and up the stairs. In minutes she returned with the faked letter, which the lieutenant took and examined. It appeared to be soiled, with addresses printed on the outside. He read it, carefully folded it, and returned it to the envelope before handing it back to Cassandra. "Thank you for letting me see it. Your mother has very pretty penmanship. I'm sorry she is so ill. I hope our visit hasn't caused you too much distress. I'll check back with you if any new leads turn up. If you'll excuse me, I'll see to my command."

The lieutenant bowed deeply from the waist before spinning on his heel and walking down the steps. At the base of the stairs Sergeant Rodale approached him. Cassandra watched their animated discussion. The sergeant motioned in the direction of the stable and both men walked briskly away. Cassandra wondered what the sergeant might have found. Was there anything still in there that might incriminate them? Her heart beat faster as she clung even more tightly to Becca. "Perhaps we should go in the house," she said softly.

Lieutenant Harker followed Sergeant Rodale into the barn. It took him a minute as his eyes adjusted to the dim light in the stable. "Show me what you found, Sergeant."

The sergeant led the lieutenant to a stall holding a black mare. He pointed at some splintered wood near the top of the stall wall. "It appears to me to be a bullet hole in the stall, Lieutenant. I thought you'd want to see it for yourself."

"Lead that horse out of the stall and bring a lantern over here so we can examine the wall more closely."

In moments a lantern was lit and brought to the lieutenant while a private led the horse out of the stall. Harker noticed a powerful looking black man standing near the door. He was guarded by two troopers. Once the horse was removed, Harker stepped into the stall and held the lantern near the wall. In the amber glow of the lantern light he found what appeared to be two fresh bullet holes in the wood. He took out his knife and dug a deformed forty-four-caliber roundball from a bullet hole. The other shot had penetrated the wood and probably buried itself in the floor. He examined the bullet carefully and gave a knowing wink to the sergeant. "Thank you, Sergeant. Have you talked to the stable hand?"

"No sir, we haven't. Would you like to have a word with him, sir?"

"Yes, bring him over." Seconds later the soldiers shoved Jeremiah before the boyish Union officer. "I dug this round out of the stall wall over there. The hole looks very fresh and the ball is still shiny. Can you tell me how those holes got there?"

Jeremiah drew himself up proudly. "Yes suh, I can. Dem holes was put there by Yankee soldiers jus' yesterday, suh."

Interest flickered in Harker's eyes. "You say they were put there yesterday by Union soldiers?"

"Yes suh, that's what I said. Them soldiers come in here and didn't think I moved fast enough to suit 'em. They made me dance while they shot at my feet, 'fore they shouted, 'Run for your life, nigger.' I done as they said an' they shot at me an' hit the wall yonder. I scooted out the door an' hid in the woods till they was gone. That big one, he smelled like he was liquored up, suh."

The lieutenant stepped nearer the black man. "You wouldn't lie to me, would you, boy? After all we're risking our necks to free your people. Least you can do is help us. Isn't that right?"

"Pardon me, suh, but I can't see how bein' free gonna help me none if some Yankee boy kills me."

Lieutenant Harker smiled at the truth of Jeremiah's statement. "I suppose you have a point there. I want you to know, my soldiers aren't authorized to take shots at coloreds for sport. I would like to reprimand these men for what they did to you. Can you tell me where I can find them?"

"No suh, I surely can't. Like I done tol' ya, I went an' hid in the woods till I was sure they was gone. Ain't worth gettin' killed over to see where them Yankee boys went. Ain't no one gonna care if some boy gets himself killed along the way, so's I stayed away."

"I can't say as I blame you. I still don't know why they would come down here and shoot at you."

"When soldier boys been drinkin' they likes to have some fun. Guess they just like to see us colored folk dance. I ain't hurt none, but I sure don't want to see them again. You folks ain't gonna hurt me, are ya, suh?"

"No, we won't hurt you, and I'm sorry for what my men did to you. If I catch them and I can prove they did this, I'll bring charges against them." He turned to his men. "Let him go and have the men mount up, Sergeant. Something just doesn't add up, but I don't think we'll find Corporal Stivers and his men here. We best get on with looking elsewhere." He turned and strolled casually toward the door. Minutes later, Lieutenant Harker led his company down the lane away from Farnsworth house.

Cassandra pulled the coat collar up more tightly around her face as she rode beside Jethro in the wagon. Her eyes scanned the bleak winter landscape before her as Jethro

urged the horses forward. Slate gray skies cast a dismal
pall upon the world and drove a chill wind through her
blankets and clothing. She shivered a little and adjusted
the comforter across her legs. Patches and skiffs of still-
white snow lay crusted in the shadows of the fence and the
trees that lined the road. As the wagon rocked back and
forth to the motion of the team and the bumps in the road,
she thought about how far they had come.

It was now January 6, 1864. They left Farnsworth
House two days after killing the Yankee soldiers. She
hated leaving to face an uncertain future, but they could
not remain behind. Sooner or later, someone would find
the murdered Union soldiers, and there would be hell to
pay if the Kimbroughs were linked to the shootout. She
wondered how long it would take before Farnsworth
House lay pillaged and in ruins, or set to the torch by
Union soldiers or sympathizers. Still, it wasn't really any
of her concern. She didn't own Farnsworth House and the
man who did could buy a dozen more like it when the war
was over. Those in the blockade-running business stood to
make huge profits.

She recalled how Lieutenant Harker had brought his
company in to search for his missing men. Somehow they
had convinced him their story was true. Fortunately, Jeremiah had done a good job of hiding the bodies, the equipment, and the horses in the woods away from the White
River, and no one had discovered anything before their departure.

She had gone to the Covingtons, but they needed a couple more days to be ready to travel. They agreed to meet
at Searcy, a town a little more than forty miles to the
south. The trip had been smooth, and as they had said they
would, Andrew and his group met them in Searcy. Now
they had left that town behind and continued south toward
Brownsville, Arkansas—due east of Little Rock where
they would intersect the Little Rock and Memphis Railroad running between Little Rock and Duvall's Bluff. She
hoped they would not run into too many Union patrols

guarding the captured line. They planned to continue to move south toward Pine Bluff, then swing southwest toward Mt. Elba, Camden, and eventually East Texas.

She leaned out from the wagon and looked behind her to make sure everyone was keeping up. Jeremiah guided the second wagon and Fanny drove the carriage carrying the very pregnant Katlin, who spent most of her time lying in a bed they had fashioned.

Behind the carriage came three wagons belonging to Andrew Covington and his family. He had been somewhat reluctant to leave Covington Manor with Batesville in Union hands, but feared staying more. After all, Union people would be likely to single out a Confederate legislator for special harassment or even imprisonment if captured. Andrew felt it wise to leave before it got that far. Even if he lost Covington Manor he was in a far more enviable position than most Southerners. He was still partners with Joe Farnsworth in the blockade-running business and he already had accumulated a fortune to last a lifetime. Staying wasn't worth the risk to a man who took few chances to his personal safety.

Cassandra wasn't sure how she felt about Andrew Covington. She, like Ross, resented the fact he was indirectly getting rich off the war while most of the people in the South were losing everything. Andrew Covington could be in the field fighting with the soldiers, but he always seemed to find ways around endangering himself. Still she was glad for their company.

Cassandra, satisfied that all the wagons were in position, turned her eyes to the front. "How far do you guess we've come from Searcy, Jethro?"

The broad-shouldered black man smiled at Cassandra. "I reckon we came maybe ten mile since we left town, Miz Cassie."

"I was guessing about the same. The cold makes it seem we've been traveling longer."

"Yes, ma'am, it surely does."

Before more could be said, she heard the sound of galloping horses and a fast-approaching wagon. Cassandra turned quickly to see the carriage driven by Fanny pulling alongside.

"Whoa up there, Jethro!" Fanny pulled in the horses near Cassandra's wagon. "Miz Cassie, we gots to find somewhere to hole up for the night an' real soon. Miz Katlin fixin' to have her baby. Her water done broke an' we got to get her in somewhere proper and more warm to have her birthin' a baby."

Cassandra was surprised. "Are you sure, Fanny?"

Fanny gave Cassandra a look of reproach. "Yeah, I'm sure. I seen a heap a babies born before, an' when the water breaks that baby ain't gonna be long in comin'."

"Jethro, I'll ride ahead with Katlin and Fanny. You bring the wagons up as fast as possible. We'll try to find a place in out of the weather."

"Yes, ma'am, we'll be along directly. You sure you'll be all right?"

"We'll manage, Jethro, just hurry."

In seconds Cassandra jumped in the back with Katlin, and the carriage was rapidly rolling along behind the galloping horses. Cassandra looked at Katlin, whose face was twisted by the pain of a contraction. "How are you, Kat?"

As the contraction eased and the tension flowed out of her belly, Katlin glanced up at Cassandra. "How does it look like I'm doing? It hurts like hell!" Katlin tried to relax and her expression became more gentle. "I'm sorry. It just hurts worse than I ever hurt before. I didn't mean to take it out on you."

"That's okay. You can yell at me all you want. Today you're entitled. You just hang in there. We're gonna try to find a place for you to have your baby."

For another two miles the carriage raced along the road. "Miz Cassie, I can't keep pushin' these horses this hard, it might kill them."

"I know, Fanny, just a little farther. If we don't see a house at the top of the next hill we'll slow down and give them a chance to cool down."

"Whatever you say, Miz Cassie."

Katlin's contractions were coming closer together now. Even Cassandra could tell, and she had never seen a baby being born before.

"God, Cassandra, you've got to find me someplace now or stop this carriage. I can't take much more of this," yelled Katlin.

"One way or another we'll quit after this next rise." Cassandra silently cursed herself for pushing the group to leave Searcy. She knew Katlin was getting close to her time, but she had been afraid Lieutenant Harker would discover the dead soldiers and come after them.

The wagon topped the next rise and they saw a small cabin set back into the trees near where the hill leveled off into the flats. "There's a cabin, Fanny. Drive for there," shouted Cassandra.

They approached the cabin quickly and as they neared, it was apparent that it was unoccupied. Inside on a crude table they found a note written in ink and left under the edge of a rock.

It read: *We ain't home as you can see. My husband died in '63 while fighting in the army. Food is gone and most of the livestock, so we left too. We've gone to Benton to stay with my sister. If you want to use the cabin you are welcome to it. I hope you'll leave it in good shape for the next traveler and restock the firewood. Please leave our home as you found it. Someday when the war is over we hope to come home. Thanks, stranger . . . Emma Tarbert.*

It was a two-room cabin with a fireplace on both ends. In the smaller of the two rooms, which sat on the south side of the house, they found a double-sized bed frame with interlaced ropes forming the foundation for the bedding. Fanny and Cassandra worked quickly to make a bed for Katlin.

After they moved Katlin inside, Fanny saw to her while Cassandra started a fire in the fireplace. They had Katlin settled in before the rest of the caravan reached the cabin.

"You all just stay in the other room and out from underfoot. I can handle this birthin' without any more help."

"Fanny, I'd feel better if you'd let Cassandra stay with me."

"Honey chile, it's you that's havin' this baby an' if you want her here, or anyone else, you just say so an' it'll be all right with me."

Three hours later Katlin held her new baby son in her arms. Blue eyes squinted out at his new world and studied his mother for the first time. His skin tones were beginning to pink up a bit as Katlin lovingly looked on. "You don't have much hair on the top of your head yet, but that'll come later. Your daddy is gonna be proud when he first lays eyes on you. He didn't say so, but I know he was hoping for a boy, so I know he's gonna be happy." She ran her fingers along the softness of her baby's arm, and as she touched his cheek he turned his head toward her finger.

"You see what he's doin' there, chile. That baby is tellin' you he's ready to eat. You don't feed him pretty soon and he'll howl to the world about it." Fanny smiled at the young mother and son.

Cassandra sat near the head of the bed where she had held Katlin's hand throughout the ordeal. During the birth Cassandra thought Katlin would break her hand she had squeezed it so hard. Even now her hands felt wrung out. The birth of her nephew was both terrifying and exciting at the same time. At Briarwood Cassandra had watched new foals entering the world, but never before had she witnessed a human birth. The wonders of nature astounded her. She felt proud that she had played even a small role in bringing the new baby into the world.

"I wish Jessie were here to see his son. I know he'll be so excited." Cassandra paused, then continued. "Have you got a name picked out for the baby?"

"Yes, I do. Jessie and I talked about it on our honeymoon, and after he left with the brigade, we also discussed names in our letters. We decided if we had a boy we'd call him Glen Alan Kimbrough in honor of his grandfather. I've always thought it was a beautiful name and I know it makes Jessie happy."

Cassandra smiled as she blinked away tears. "I know his grandma and grandpa would be real proud. I wish they were alive to see him."

Katlin looked up at Cassandra. "I believe in heaven they can see him, but my folks are gonna have to wait a while. It's a long way back to Missouri and who knows how long the war will continue."

"I'm going to tell everyone the good news. You feed that baby and get some rest. This caravan isn't moving until you and little Glen feel up to traveling again." Cassandra watched as the new mother tentatively offered her breast for the first time to the newborn. Then she turned and left to share the joy with the others.

5

Brownsville Dilemma

Worried, Cassandra scanned the road ahead of her as a town came into view. If her calculations were correct, this town should be Brownsville, Arkansas. Normally such a sight would be welcome after a long and tedious journey, but this time the town on the horizon looked ominous.

Brownsville straddled the tracks of the Little Rock and Memphis Railroad that connected Little Rock and Duvall's Bluff. With the fall of Little Rock to the Union armies, this railroad would be an important link and a source of supply for the Federal troops. It was only logical that Brownsville would have Yankee soldiers on patrol to protect the strategic lifeline to General Steele's Union Army, which now held Little Rock. It was facing the Union troops that Cassandra dreaded, not the town itself. She felt a cold shudder at the thought.

She wondered if the bodies of Stivers and his men had been discovered. If so, Colonel Robert Livingston or Lieutenant Harker of the First Nebraska Cavalry at Batesville might be looking for them. She told Lieutenant Harker they were going to see her mother—they would be looking in the wrong direction if they were looking for them at all. She knew if they wanted her found badly enough, the Union forces could dispatch telegrams to their armies in the field. She only hoped they had more pressing matters to worry about than the fate of four missing soldiers.

Cassandra wished they had put more distance between Batesville and themselves, but the birth of her nephew Glen Adam Kimbrough had altered their plans. They spent nearly a week at Emma Talbert's two-room cabin before continuing their journey. They left the cabin in better shape than they found it, as the note had requested. Time was slipping away from them, and the middle of January 1864 had already passed as they approached Brownsville.

Cassandra held on tightly to the handle beside the seat as the wagon rocked through the rutted road and splashed through the thawing mud holes. The rough jolts and bumps jarred her and her back ached from the rough ride's constant beating. She knew she wasn't the only one suffering and wondered how Katlin and the new baby were holding up. Despite her misgivings, maybe a stop—if even a brief one—would be a welcome respite from their travels. She promised herself she would try to check her anger and be courteous when she confronted Union soldiers. Now would not be the time to evoke their anger.

As they drew closer to the edge of town, Cassandra saw armed Union soldiers standing guard and walking their beat near the train station. She tried to look unconcerned as the group crossed the tracks and led their wagon train toward the town square. The party led by Cassandra and Andrew Covington reached a local hotel before being stopped by Union soldiers. The sergeant in charge located an officer to speak with the party, and after a short wait, Andrew and Cassandra were ushered in to visit with an officer inside the hotel.

The two walked in softly, as if they were visiting a funeral home and afraid to wake the dead. They stood quietly before the officer's desk while long, slow moments passed. Cassandra became aware of the constant and repetitive ticking of the clock on the wall. The officer seemed lost in thought as he studied the ledgers on the desk in front of him. Finally, the major wearily lifted his eyes from his paperwork to the intruders. His glance at Andrew Covington was quick and precursory. His eyes were narrowed from studying ledgers and he wrinkled his forehead at the interruption. As the officer's eyes turned toward Cassandra his irritable expression faded. His eyes opened wide, his forehead wrinkles disappeared, and for a moment his mouth hung open in astonishment.

It took him just a moment to recover as he shouted, "Orderly, bring this lovely lady a chair immediately. She must be tired after her long journey." He didn't take his eyes off of her even for a moment as he slid back his chair and rose to his feet. In a few swift strides he was around the desk and offering Cassandra his hand. "Allow me to introduce myself. My name is Colonel Vincent Barclay in command of the First Indiana Cavalry. How may I be of assistance to you?"

Cassandra was astounded by Colonel Barclay's swift change of deportment. He stood holding her hand for longer than necessary and grinning at her as if she were a goddess. She looked into his chocolate brown eyes for a moment before her eyes wandered up from his bushy eyebrows to stare at his high forehead. Barclay had his thin hair carefully arranged over his balding pate as if those scant few strands could somehow diminish or conceal his certain slide toward total baldness. She guessed him to be in his mid-forties, and he stood only slightly taller than herself.

She recovered quickly after a shocked momentary delay. "I thought we were summoned here by you, Colonel."

Colonel Barclay stared at her as if he were afraid that if he blinked she might mysteriously disappear. "Yes, of course, you caught me off guard. I never expected to see someone of your rare beauty walk into my office." He hesitated a moment as he looked into her eyes before continuing. "We are on temporary duty here, and as part of our orders it is necessary for us to check on travelers passing through town. Would you mind if I ask you a few questions?"

While they talked a young orderly appeared with a chair and set it near Cassandra. The colonel motioned for her to be seated as he eased himself down on the corner of his desk. Cassandra adjusted herself in the seat before she replied, "I suppose so, Colonel, since it is your duty. Just don't make your questions too personal." She smiled coyly.

"Fine, let's start with your names and where you are going." He smiled again, letting his eyes roam down her trim figure as she crossed her legs in her full-skirted traveling dress.

Cassandra studied Barclay's eyes and knew he was lustfully imagining what she must look like under her dress. Being a beautiful woman she had long ago learned when a man was ripe to be manipulated, and she intended to take full advantage of this situation. With any luck at all they would slide through this with minimal delay. "My name is Cassandra Kimbrough and this is Andrew Covington." She motioned toward Andrew who was still standing awkwardly beside her chair.

Andrew recognized that the colonel wasn't interested in anything he might have to say, and for once he remained quiet, offering the colonel his hand. The officer reluctantly glanced at Andrew as if acknowledging him would interfere with his appreciation of Cassandra. He shook Andrew's hand quickly, then turned his back on him.

"We are traveling toward Texas," Cassandra continued. "I'm afraid the war has made us refugees and forced us from our homes in Missouri. We only hope to escape the fighting and find refuge there."

A concerned and sympathetic expression crossed Vincent Barclay's face. "I'm sorry to hear of your loss. This war is a terrible business. Indeed I find it so unfortunate we must fight at all. Do you have family or a place to stay in Texas?"

"No, we don't have family in Texas that I am aware of, but anywhere away from this fighting has to be an improvement."

"I see," said the colonel as he rubbed his chin thoughtfully. "How many are traveling in your party?"

Cassandra replied, "I have two other women and a baby, and four domestics traveling in my wagon and buggy. Andrew has two women and three servants traveling in his two wagons." She took the liberty of speaking for Andrew, and the former Confederate congressman had the good sense to let her do it, remaining as silent and inconspicuous as possible.

"Are you carrying any contraband or illegal weapons intended for the Confederate army?"

"Certainly not," Cassandra said. She hoped she sounded authentically indignant enough. "We wouldn't be foolish enough to invite arrest by carrying weapons or supplies for the army. We are merely refugees wishing to aid no one. We only hope to escape this terrible war." She hoped Colonel Barclay wouldn't doubt her word. The guns taken from Stivers's men were hidden in a secret compartment beneath the floor of one of the wagons. A careful search might discover the hiding place. She hoped the Lord would forgive her for her lies.

Cassandra's statement seemed to appease the colonel, who desperately wanted to stay friendly with her. He turned toward Andrew. "You, sir! Why aren't you serving in the army?"

"My health won't permit it. I am too sickly to stand the rigors of living in the outdoors under primitive conditions. Because I have been loyal to the Union, my neighbors drove me out," Andrew lied. He would be imprisoned immediately if the Union soldiers discovered he had once been a member of the Arkansas Confederate congress.

The colonel seemed anxious to accept Andrew's explanation. He once again turned his attention to Cassandra.

"It would be wonderful if you could stay in this area for a while. I'd love to share your company and get to know you a little better. I'm sure there must be much we share in common."

Cassandra knew there was nothing more she wanted to know about Colonel Barclay. She only wanted to get through enemy lines and on her way as swiftly as possible. Still, she had the good sense to know better than to offend him. "I'm sure I would enjoy your company, Colonel, but we must be on our way. This is winter and we must take advantage of this break in the weather to make all the progress we can if we hope to reach Texas by spring. I'm sure you understand I must think of the others in my party and not give in to the temptation to seek my own comfort." She tried to smile sweetly, while secretly hoping it didn't come across as insincere.

"I understand, but I must admit I'm disappointed." He sighed softly as he shifted his weight on the desk. "Have you selected your route to Texas?"

"Why yes, we intend to travel toward Pine Bluff, head south toward Mt. Elba, then southwest toward Camden. From Camden we will angle southwest until we reach Texas." As she spoke, Cassandra noticed the colonel's expression brighten and she hoped she hadn't made some kind of error.

"Excellent!" He clapped his hands, rubbing them together in delight. "I am so glad to hear you are going to Pine Bluff. We received orders this morning to rejoin our brigade there. Tomorrow we march. We will be glad to escort you safely to Pine Bluff, and it will give us more time to share your company." The colonel beamed at the prospect of spending more time with Cassandra. He turned toward Andrew, who still stood awkwardly near them. "You, sir, are welcome to join us as well."

Andrew shot a nervous glance at Cassandra before he gave a slight smile in return. "Thank you, Colonel Barclay. I'm sure we'll be much safer in your company."

The colonel dismissed Andrew quickly by glancing

away from him and returning his gaze to Cassandra. "Please accept my invitation to join me for supper tonight in the hotel."

"I certainly appreciate your kind invitation, Colonel, but I can't leave my family to dine alone."

Colonel Barclay looked disappointed, then his face brightened. "I'll invite you all to join me for dinner. Will that be satisfactory?"

Cassandra felt trapped but realized she must go along. She only hoped she could get through the meal without any slip-ups and escape the colonel's company as quickly as possible. "Then, of course, we would be honored to join you for supper. Would seven o'clock be suitable?"

Colonel Barclay smiled happily. "I am delighted. Seven o'clock will be fine. Well, I'm sure you will need time to freshen up a bit before supper. I think we've answered the appropriate questions. Let's see to arranging for rooms for your party in the hotel and finding a place to park your wagons. Your servants can prepare the wagons for our departure to Pine Bluff in the morning."

With that the colonel rose to his feet and offered Cassandra his hand. She took it and he assisted her from her chair. He led her to the hotel lobby where they made arrangements for rooms for the night. When the other young ladies entered the hotel, Colonel Barclay was pleasantly surprised. Not only would he dine with the beautiful Cassandra, but three other beautiful women as well. As his eyes swept over Katlin, Elizabeth, and finally Valissa Covington, he smiled delightedly. Cassandra wondered if the colonel would ever be able to remove the silly grin from his face. From all appearances, Colonel Vincent Barclay must have thought he had entered heaven. For Cassandra, the opposite was closer to the truth.

6

Chidester House

Cassandra released a sigh of relief as her wagon led the small caravan out of Mt. Elba, Arkansas. It felt good knowing they were leaving the last of the Yankee cavalry behind her. She planned to lead her party in a southwesterly direction toward Camden, Arkansas.

At first Cassandra was surprised when Andrew Covington let her assume unofficial leadership of the group upon joining them at Searcy. Since he was both a man and a former congressman she assumed he would want to be in control. She realized he declined only because he was reluctant to draw attention to himself. By letting Cassandra assume leadership, he could keep a low profile: If the Yankees were to learn he was a former Confederate legislator his fate would surely be arrest and prison. Facing such fearful measures, he acquiesced. Cassandra was secretly pleased. She found she enjoyed being in charge and this built additional confidence in her abilities. After the destruction of Briarwood, Cassandra was forced into a leadership role for the first time and it had frightened her. With time, the mantle of responsibility became more comfortable and helped strengthen her through adversity. She knew the others depended on her clear thinking, and she responded to the challenge.

On the trip south from Brownsville with Colonel Barclay and the First Indiana Cavalry, Cassandra kept her ears open for any information she or the Confederacy might find useful. She learned much by listening to the officers talk, but had yet to hear any mention of Jo Shelby or his troops.

Finally, in the hotel lobby at Pine Bluff, Arkansas, a young Yankee captain gave her the information she needed. Colonel Shelby's men were camped south of Camden, Arkansas, along the Ouachita River. The young officer, who was drinking far too heavily, bragged about how his brigade would whip the tar out of Shelby and his men come spring. She smiled secretly to herself, knowing the information she carried could help the Southern cause.

Cassandra recalled how difficult the last two and half weeks had been for her and her companions. The supper in Brownsville with Colonel Barclay had gone well enough. They slipped away early in the evening, claiming they would need their rest for the journey in the morning. Colonel Barclay had tried his best to be charming. When he sensed he was making little progress in seducing Cassandra, he redirected his efforts toward Valissa. The stately, blue-eyed blonde played him along skillfully. The evening ended far too swiftly for the Union officer, and his disappointment was evident.

The trip south toward Pine Bluff was accomplished through harsh winter weather. The winds howled in chilled protest and whipped against them unmercifully as the procession advanced slowly along the rutted trail. Every few miles, it seemed, the wagons would have to leave the road as supply trains or Union troops plodded past. Evenings were spent huddled around a campfire, trying to stay warm. Only on one evening between Brownsville and Pine Bluff did the colonel have his tent erected for evening meal. Even Cassandra appreciated the one evening spent away from the wagons.

When they reached the banks of the Arkansas River, further delays occurred as they waited for passage on a river ferry. Finally, Valissa's charms won out as Colonel Barclay pulled rank to move them up in the line of wagons and troops awaiting a spot on the ferry. It would cost them another evening of dining with the colonel, but getting across was worth the sacrifice.

Pine Bluff was a beehive of activity. Located near the Arkansas River, it was an important link of defense protecting the waterway to Little Rock. Supplies were shipped up the White River to Duvall's Bluff and by train to Little Rock as a back-up to the main route of riverboats, gunboats, and steamers plying the waters of the Arkansas. Pine Bluff was situated nearly halfway between Little Rock and the junction of the Arkansas River and the waters of the mighty Mississippi. At least a brigade of Union cavalry surrounded the town.

Cassandra was disappointed by the overflow of Union troops. The officers of the various commands filled all the available hotel rooms and boarding houses. Forced to camp in their wagons at the outskirts of town, they nevertheless kept their word and dined once more with Colonel Barclay. It was during that evening that she met the drunken and talkative Union captain. The lack of accommodations in Pine Bluff gave Cassandra the excuse she needed to continue their journey. Still, they didn't see the last of Union troops until they passed through Mt. Elba. It troubled her to see just how deep the Federals had penetrated.

Cassandra shifted in the seat and glanced behind her. One good look was all she needed to reassure her that the other wagons were still keeping pace. Finally, they were in Rebel territory. For the first time in weeks she could relax. Everyone in the traveling party remained in good health despite the rugged weather. Even baby Glen and mother Katlin were doing well.

Cassandra marveled at their luck. It was a miracle the Yankees hadn't arrested them. They had been allowed to roam freely through Union lines unmolested. Indeed, they were fortunate enough to enjoy a cavalry escort of sorts. She wondered why the Yankees still hadn't discovered the bodies of Stivers's men. If they had, the news hadn't caught up with them. It seemed no one was looking for Cassandra and her party, and for that she was grateful. Soon they would be in Camden and she would send word to her brothers. She smiled as she thought about the possibility of a family reunion, but her thoughts were more on seeing her fiancé, Captain Evan Stryker. She felt the heat rise in her cheeks and her heart beat a little faster at the mere thought of the bold Texan.

Cassandra pulled herself from her thoughts as her wagon crested the rise, her eyes gazing for the first time upon the rolling, green waters of the Ouachita River. She lifted her eyes and studied the far shore. A ferry boat was working its way slowly across the current toward the eastern side. Her eyes followed the winding road leading up the steep riverbank until it disappeared behind a fortified hill across the way. Farther north as she looked upriver she glimpsed what appeared to be more fortifications astride a taller hill, standing guard over the river. Between the two hills she caught her first look at Camden, Arkansas. Cassandra studied the river wharfs and docks and the buildings beyond and guessed the town held nearly twenty-five-hundred citizens, not counting Rebel soldiers.

Cassandra's heart soared as she realized they had finally reached their destination. Ever since they had heard Shelby and his men were stationed near Camden, they looked forward to this moment. At least for a time their travels might be ended, and perhaps soon they would be reunited with their loved ones.

It didn't take long to negotiate passage on Bradley's Ferry and in two trips all were landed safely on the western shore. The ferry boat crew was very helpful and gave directions to Camden. Cassandra and her party departed at once.

They followed the Bradley Ferry Road around Fort Diamond, the fortification on the hill, until they reached Washington Street. They turned onto this main thoroughfare and began their search for a place to stay. The ferry boat operator suggested they might find room and board at the Chidester House, a stop on the local stage line. His only other suggestion was to try Major Graham's Grand Mansion. After two more stops to ask directions, they finally pulled their wagons onto a short path leading to a large combination barn and carriage house situated behind a stately home. Painted on the barn Cassandra read CHIDESTER & RAPLEY AND COMPANY, STAGE LINE. Scattered about the grounds were an outhouse, a smokehouse, and another structure that appeared to be slave quarters. A slave working in the barn led them to the house, itself constructed of lumber planed and painted white. Cassandra noticed that it had recently been expanded by the addition of wings to the west and east. A detached kitchen sat directly behind the house, and the smoke curling upward from the many chimneys offered hope of warmth. They were ushered into a large living room, a cheery fire glowing in its large fireplace.

"Y'all please be seated. Miz Leah be down directly to see you." The housemaid disappeared and they settled happily into the plush chairs near the fire. It had been a while since Cassandra had felt the simple pleasure of a soft seat. After a short time, an attractive woman in her thirties appeared and as she entered the room, Cassandra rose to greet her. As they shook hands the woman said, "Allow me to introduce myself. My name is Leah Minerva Chidester and my husband is Colonel John Chidester. I'm sorry my husband isn't here, but I'm afraid he's temporarily away on business."

Cassandra nodded, released the woman's hand, and motioned toward the others. "I'd like to introduce you to the members of my party. This is Andrew Covington, his wife,

Caroline, and their daughter, Valissa." She motioned toward Katlin. "This is my sister-in-law Katlin Kimbrough and her son, Glen." Katlin nodded sweetly, remaining seated as she cuddled the baby. Elizabeth stepped forward and Cassandra put an arm around her. "This is my sister, Elizabeth, and my name is Cassandra Kimbrough. My family is originally from Missouri, but the Covingtons are from Batesville. We intend to stay in the area for a few weeks. We've heard we might find rooms here. Do you have any available?"

Leah said quietly, "We have rooms available upstairs occasionally when they aren't in use by our drivers. I only have one room available currently. I could house a few of you for awhile, but there simply isn't enough room for your entire party. Perhaps the rest of you could find space at Major Graham's mansion. I know they take boarders on occasion, although I'm not sure they'll have an opening. I'm sure you understand, housing is tight with the war going on." Leah looked inquisitive. "May I inquire why you have come to Camden?"

Cassandra smiled. "We have heard Colonel Jo Shelby's Confederate cavalry is in winter camp near here. My three brothers and my fiancé are serving with the brigade, and so is Katlin's brother. We want to spend some time with our family before we continue our trip to Texas."

Leah smiled. "It's always nice when a family can be reunited, and I'm sure you'll enjoy your stay here. The area is positively a beehive of activity and the Yankees wouldn't dare attack the fortifications surrounding our fair city. Did you say you are from Missouri?"

"Yes, we were until the Yankees killed my father and burned us out. Now, like so many others, we are refugees."

Leah wrinkled her forehead. "I'm sorry to hear of your loss, but I'm glad you reached our lines safely. I do hope we can keep the damn Yankees away from Camden." A look of concern crossed her face. "I hate to ask, you understand, but I have to consider my family. Do you have money to pay for a room?"

Cassandra nodded. "We have sufficient funds if your rates aren't too high."

"The room is a dollar a day and board is fifty cents a day per person. I won't count the baby. Is that acceptable?"

Andrew Covington stepped forward. "Cassandra, if they have a room, why don't you take it. I'll take my family and people down to the Graham mansion if Mrs. Chidester will be so kind to give us directions."

"Thank you, Andrew, you're very thoughtful," Cassandra said. She turned to Leah.

"The Graham mansion is just down the street from here. It is a large home and you can't miss it."

"Then good day, ma'am," Andrew replied as he motioned to his family. "Valissa, Caroline, let's be on our way. You ladies can catch up on all the latest news after we find a place to stay." The Covingtons all shook hands with Leah Chidester before they left the house and returned to their wagons. When they were gone Cassandra asked, "Do you have room for our servants?"

"Yes, I believe we have room in the slave quarters, and you may park your wagons near the barn. How many slaves do you have traveling with you?"

"We have four."

"I believe we have enough space to house them. If not, we'll have space in the loft above the barn. I'll only charge you a dollar a day for their lodging and twenty-five cents a head a day for their meals."

"I suppose your price is fair under current conditions. We'll take the room." She reached in her purse and extracted a twenty-dollar gold piece. "Here, you can use this toward our bill," Cassandra said.

Leah's expression brightened. "Good, I'm glad to have you as our guests. You know, we had General Sterling Price from your fair state staying with us for a while. We were honored he chose our home for his headquarters until he left recently for Louisiana." She sighed and her smile took on a dreamy look. "We found him to be quite dashing and a fine Southern gentleman."

Cassandra nodded dutifully. "All Missouri is proud of General Price, and his victories for the Southern cause are legendary. We are indeed honored to be your guests."

"Fine, I'll have my girl show you up to your room and you can have your people bring in your things. We only have one bed in the room, but there is adequate space to lay a pallet or two on the floor. We'll let you choose sleeping arrangements among yourselves. I'm sure you'll want to clean up and rest. Supper is at six. Now if you'll excuse me, I'll see my people are aware we'll have additional company for supper." Leah Chidester took a mental count of her new guests before she left the room. Moments later, Cassandra and her sisters followed the maid up the stairs to their room.

After supper Cassandra and the others followed Leah Chidester from the dining room into the living room. The meal was heavenly. They dined on sweet potatoes and smoked ham. Cassandra noticed during the meal that Leah kept a key on a chain around her waist. Curious, she asked Leah what the key was for and the woman told her it was the key to the smokehouse. With the war going on and food supplies at a premium, she was taking every precaution to protect the family's food supply. After enjoying the delicious meal, Cassandra understood completely.

They settled in the chairs around the fireplace and Cassandra watched with amusement as two of Leah's boys, six-year-old Will and four-year-old Frank, played with their marbles. Both boys were on the thin side and had the same narrow, slender faces and haircolor as their mother.

Cassandra felt the cares of the world slip away from her shoulders as she sipped at the china cup filled with fresh-brewed coffee from the kitchen. It was like a slice of heaven to enjoy fresh coffee again. Earlier in the day at the urging of Leah Chidester, Cassandra had visited the kitchen. Leah was justifiably proud of her kitchen. It con-

tained a fine iron stove—the first in the area—and she
wanted her guests to see it. Cassandra was impressed by
the array of shiny utensils hanging near the wood-burning
stove. Indeed, the stove was every bit as nice as the stove
they had owned at Briarwood.

"Would you care for some more coffee?" Leah asked.

Cassandra replied, "I still have half a cup, but I suppose
I could stand to have it warmed." The Chidester maid
stepped forward, filling her cup to the brim, and Cassandra
eased the cup to her saucer to let it cool a bit. "You have
a lovely home. When did you build it?"

Leah smiled at the compliment. "We didn't build the
house. The house was originally built by Peter McCollum
and his slaves in 1847, or so we've been told. My husband
purchased the home from him two years ago and we added
the wings to the house. When we first came to this area
four years ago we decided this would be the perfect place
to establish our home. Camden is so lovely. My husband
operates the Butterfield stagecoach and mail routes in this
area."

"It is such a lovely home. I'm surprised anyone would
want to part with it."

"Mr. McCollum really didn't want to sell the house at
first, but my husband was determined to own it. When
John tendered an offer for ten thousand dollars in gold, Peter accepted. It was a large sum, but we've never regretted
spending the money. John added the stables and barn. A
business like ours requires a good barn and stable to keep
our livestock and equipment."

Cassandra was startled when Leah told her how much
the house cost. Usually such things were of a private nature, but she felt Leah wanted her to know to demonstrate
how successful her husband had become. "I can certainly
see why you would be proud. The furnishings are beautiful."

Leah smiled as she shifted herself in her seat. "Thank
you, we had most of it brought up from New Orleans by
steamboat before the war."

Katlin Kimbrough, sitting to Cassandra's left, said, "I'm very impressed with Camden. I noticed the beauty of the buildings and stores along the wharves and docks. Judging by what we saw, Camden must do a brisk business along the river."

Leah Chidester looked pensive for a moment as if lost in thoughts of yesterday. "Yes, before the war much of the region's agriculture was brought here to be shipped to New Orleans by river steamer. We shipped cotton bales out of here by the thousands."

Leah smiled as she recalled happier days. "We had riverboats of every size and description visit here, and when the water level was high the stores were absolutely brimming with the choicest goods." She took another sip of her coffee before continuing. "In the summers, the steamboats would bring all kinds of pleasant diversions. One of my favorite times before the war was right after we arrived in town. The steamboat *Banjo* tied up at the docks and put on a minstrel show. Oh, what a night. The darkies sang and danced and the calliope played by the light of the moon under the glow of lamps. I remember they called the show 'The Wood's Mind Music,' and over a thousand people gathered for the show."

Leah's thoughts stirred Cassandra's memories. "We grew up along the Missouri River, and I can recall many happy days when the riverboats came to town. When Jo Shelby married his wife, Betty, I was pretty young, but I can still recall cruising up and down the river after the wedding. Jo owned the steamboat and the band played and we danced until the wee hours of morning." Cassandra smiled.

Leah returned her smile. "The river has always supplied us with special entertainment. My husband use to love it when the *Juda Laura* came to town. He tried to hide his excursions to the riverboat from me, but I knew where he was going. The *Juda Laura* offered dancing girls, casinos, and open bars, and I suppose he thought it was unfit for a lady. It sure didn't keep him away from gentlemanly pleasures."

Leah smiled knowingly. "There were so many fine occasions. I recall the time Captain Cannon challenged Captain Tobin to a steamboat race. Captain Cannon piloted his steamer, the *R. W. McRae*, against Captain Tobin's *Lizzie Simmons* during the race. The whole town got excited and great amounts of money were wagered on the winner. It was a close race, but the *R. W. McRae* won.

"I think the finest riverboat ever to come up the Ouachita was the *J. F. Pargoud*. She was the most elegant sidewheel packet I ever saw." Leah looked sad. "I heard the ship was burned in the Yazoo River last year to keep her from being captured by the Yankees. It is such a tragic waste. Now that the Yankees control the Mississippi the river trade has come to a halt.

"Well, I suppose it does absolutely no good to live in the past. We can only look and hope for the future. Tomorrow we must send word of your arrival to Jo Shelby's camp. I'm sure you're anxious to see your loved ones."

Cassandra's heart soared at the thought. "Yes, we're quite excited to see them again. I hope they will be granted leave."

"Judging from what I've seen around here, I don't think it will be a problem. We see soldiers visiting town often, and it is not all for business."

The conversation drifted on for a while longer as Elizabeth and Katlin talked, but Cassandra's thoughts were no longer on Chidester House. They were on a bold Texas captain named Evan Stryker.

7

Hay Fever

Becca slipped out of the kitchen door and walked briskly toward the barn. She enjoyed the sunshine bathing the yard in its warmth and gently caressing her hair and shoulders. The air was still, and a cloudless blue sky lent a feeling of more warmth than one would expect for this time of year.

The weight of the tin pail swinging in her hand felt reassuring. Beneath the soft folds of the checkered cloth were several pieces of fried chicken and cornbread muffins for Jeremiah and herself for lunch. Jeremiah was working on tack in the barn and still hadn't taken time to eat. Becca planned to surprise him.

Becca was pleased when Katlin returned to breastfeed the baby. It freed Becca from her duties, at least until Katlin and the baby finished their nap. The ritual of feeding the baby at midday followed by a nap had become the standard routine since their arrival in Camden. Freed from her duties temporarily, Becca decided to spend time with Jeremiah.

She stepped from the bright sunlight into the dimly lit shadows of the open barn door. She paused to let her eyes become accustomed to her new surroundings. She heard a hammering to her left and, following the sound, stepped through another door to find Jeremiah bent over a workbench. He was putting the finishing touches on a bridle and had just driven the final rivet.

The smell of fresh hay, mixed with the odor of oiled leather and the more musky scent of horse dung still lying in the stalls, made for a familiar yet potent mixture. She liked the way sweat glistened on Jeremiah's bare biceps and the shape of his tall, lean torso, taut muscles rippling under his cotton linsey shirt. She studied the chiseled features of his face. Those large, dark eyes contrasted nicely against his deep-tanned skin. Like herself, he was lighter than most of the field hands she had met, but his skin was still a couple of shades darker than hers.

He looked up, and seeing her enter, gave her a big smile. "What are you doin' out here, girl?" He laid his hammer and bridle down and stepped over to greet her.

"Everybody's done with eatin' up at the big house. They said you hadn't eaten, and I haven't either. I thought I'd bring you your lunch. We can share it."

"I just finished repairing this piece, so I guess I can spare the time." He stopped to admire his work, holding it up to the light before pulling her close. He hugged her, his hands sliding down and softly squeezing her hips beneath her dress.

"Stop that now," Becca said as she pushed teasingly against his chest. Her voice seemed to lack sincerity. "Your hands are dirty an' you're gonna soil my dress. What Katlin gonna say if she sees me with your handprints on my butt?"

"Lordy, I don't know what she gonna think, but I sure like how you feel, gal." He gave her a soft pat and another squeeze as he held her.

Becca gave him a quick kiss on his lips and then twirled

herself out of his embrace. "There'll be plenty of time for
that later. Wash your hands and we'll eat."

Jeremiah stood and watched Becca for a moment as she
removed the red-and-white checkered cloth from the pail
and spread it over a hay bale. From the bucket she removed pieces of golden brown chicken and cornbread
muffins and laid them on the cloth.

Jeremiah let his eyes roam over her fine features and
dark eyes. Those eyes always seemed to captivate him.
Her skin was light, like liberally creamed coffee. He'd
seen white men with skin tanned by the sun that was
darker than hers. He was truly fortunate that she was half
black and therefore considered tainted by most white
Southerners. Otherwise he knew white men would swarm
like bees to honey around her striking and voluptuous
beauty. He noticed how their eyes lingered on her despite
her standing as a servant, and as a man he understood how
they would find it hard to resist her obvious charms. Today she wore her straight black hair pulled up at the nape
of her neck into a ponytail. He liked it better when she let
it hang loose and free.

As he watched her work he admired how the dress
hugged and outlined her every curve as she bent over the
bale. He felt a warm surge in his crotch as he saw how
the cloth of her skirt clung to her hips. In that moment he
knew he wanted her more than the fried chicken, even if
it was his favorite food.

Reluctantly, Jeremiah left the barn and walked toward
the well in the yard near the porch. He lowered the bucket
until he heard the container splash as it settled into the water. A tug on the line told him it was filled and he pulled
hard on the rope. He dipped out a ladle full of cool water
and drank greedily. Then he poured the rest into his work
bucket. Returning to the barn, he washed the grime of the
morning's work off his face and arms, then poured the remainder of the water on the ground.

When Jeremiah returned to the dimly lit tack room he
found Becca waiting patiently. His first urge was to say to

hell with the chicken and carry her off to the loft, but he knew better than to risk her anger by ignoring the lunch she had brought. Dutifully he sat beside her, and after a whispered prayer, dug hungrily into a chicken breast. The chicken was still warm and succulent. He eyed Becca's beauty with the same gusto he used to polish off his meal.

Becca enjoyed his attentions and ate seductively, enjoying wielding this power over her man as she teased and flirted with him. Becca knew every move she made only increased his desire for her.

She watched him finish his last muffin and stand and walk around behind her. She felt him tug at the ribbon in her hair and felt the bow release as her hair fell free about her shoulders. She pulled forward and gave him a reproachful look. "Now see what you've done."

He stepped closer and ran his fingers softly through her hair. "You know I like it better when you wear your hair full and on your shoulders. It ain't hurtin' nuthin', is it?"

She saw the passion in his eyes and she softened. "I suppose not, but I'll have to tie it back before I go back to the house. Miz Katlin don't think it looks proper to wear your hair down when you're workin'."

"Well, she don't own you no more," he said rebelliously.

She looked at him with an ornery glint in her eyes. "No she doesn't, but she's still my boss. Free or a slave you still have to follow the rules. Even a man as stubborn as yourself ought to know that."

"Yeah I know," he said softly and shyly.

She turned away from him as he rubbed his hands softly on her upper shoulders. She relaxed and enjoyed his massaging fingers. She tensed as she felt his fingers undo her top two buttons on her dress. "What are you doin'?" she asked.

"What do you think I'm doin'? I'm undoing your dress, gal. I can give you a better back rub without all this in the way." He continued to work at her buttons despite her protest.

"You've got more in mind than givin' me a back rub, Jeremiah. I haven't got the time, and besides, what if someone was to come to the barn? I'd be so embarrassed if we got caught."

Jeremiah felt his passion rising. He glanced upward conspiratorially. "We could go up in the hayloft. It'd be much more comfortable, and no one would look for us up there."

She felt the last of her buttons down to her waist give way and his warm hands slip the straps of her camisole and sleeves down her arms. She resisted him, fighting to keep herself covered. "Not here, Jeremiah," she protested. "It's not safe."

His breathing was more rapid now and she felt a slight tremor in his hands. "Will you go to the loft with me?" he asked, hope edging into his voice.

She turned as she held her dress together and looked into his face. She could read his passion and love for her in his eyes. In that instant she knew she would not, could not deny him. "Yes, I'll go. Where is the ladder?" she asked softly.

Jeremiah smiled so widely she thought his face might burst. "Over here, I'll show you." He took her to the ladder and she started up the rungs. Jeremiah watched her climb and took a glance up her dress. His quick glimpse of her exposed calves beneath her knee-length bloomers as she moved up the ladder only intensified his need.

Becca reached the top and pulled herself into the loft. Dim light filtered through the cracks around the loft door, and some light spilled upward from the barn floor. Around her were stacks of hay arranged so that it could be forked over the edge to fall below into the stalls. As she stood and studied her surroundings, Jeremiah reached the top and moved behind her. She felt his hands peel her sleeves down her arms until her dress hung at her waist, his hot breath blowing warm on the nape of her neck. He grabbed the bottom edge of her camisole and lifted it above her head in one fluid motion, leaving her naked above the waist.

Becca felt his arms come under hers; his hands caressed her full breasts as he cupped and squeezed them. She felt her aureolas, exposed to the cool air, begin to harden as her nipples tightened and jutted out. She felt his fingers close over her nipples and pinch them until she felt a tightening in her belly and a moistness building between her legs. His lips worked along her neck, tonguing and licking her into a frenzy of desire. He moved his attention to the side of her neck, and she felt his tongue dart into her ear for a second before he started sucking and nibbling at her earlobes. She laid her head back against him as a soft moan escaped her lips.

Before she knew what was happening, Jeremiah's hands left her breasts and he dropped to his knees and clutched at her dress gathered at her waist. With a rough, jerking motion he peeled her dress, bloomers and all, to her ankles, where the clothes clung to her hightop shoes. Becca swayed for a moment, fighting for balance on unsteady feet.

She felt Jeremiah's hands slide up her thighs until they reached her buttocks. He slid his hands inward until he cupped and squeezed her hips. She heard him moan in pleasure as he slid one hand inside her thigh and moved it upward with probing fingers. Jeremiah's rough treatment and his lustful actions set Becca's belly swirling in turmoil, her muscles tightening. The rising heat she felt earlier was gone, and in its place fear swelled within her, threatening to make her scream in distress. She felt his moist lips nibbling at her supple hips as his fingers worked deeper, and suddenly she jerked forward, trying to escape him as she fought to stifle a scream.

Her feet caught in the tangle of clothing gathered at her ankles, and she tumbled forward and pulled free of Jeremiah's grasp. She landed on her face in the hay and rolled to face him. "Leave me alone," she hissed in a low, menacing growl as she held her hands in front of her, her long fingernails resembling a cat's claws drawn and ready for battle.

Jeremiah looked confused at her unexpected reaction. "What the hell's gotten in to you, Becca?"

She pulled at her clothes and tried to cover herself as she pulled away from him. Hay clung to her hair, giving her a wild look to match her eyes. "Don't you ever treat me rough like that, Jeremiah, or I swear to God I'll cut you and feed it to the hogs!" she shrieked at him.

Jeremiah's gaze faltered and his face looked puzzled as he tried to understand the sudden change that had swept over Becca. He held his hands up before him as if to show her he meant no harm. "What's gotten into you, girl? You know I wouldn't do anything to hurt you. Don't you know I love you? I want you but if you don't want me, it can wait for another time," Jeremiah said softly and reassuringly. "I wouldn't do anything to upset you." The sudden hostility he faced, where moments before there had only been passion, confused him. Becca saw the conflict of shame and need in his eyes.

Like a sudden thunderstorm her emotions broke and tears spilled from her eyes and glistened wet against her cheeks. Deep sobs overcame her as she curled herself into a ball and hugged her knees to her chest. Lost as to understanding what he had done wrong, Jeremiah edged closer. "Let me hold you, Becca."

At first she pulled away from him, but when she looked into his eyes she no longer saw passion, but genuine concern. She wrapped her arms around his neck, burying her face in his shoulder. Her bare breast pushed against his shirt and he felt sobs rack her body. Hot, wet tears soaked his shirt as he held her close, gently rocking back and forth like a mother comforting a hurt child. She cried softly for a long while as he stroked her hair and back. The rocking motion and his tender touch combined evenly with his soft voice whispering, "Now, now, it's gonna be all right. You just cry it out. I've got ya, honey-chile."

After a while the tears stopped and Becca felt more

calm. She felt so safe and warm in his loving embrace. She knew now how foolish her fears were, for Jeremiah could no more harm her than he could a child. She knew he was a kind and gentle man and she realized it was the reason she loved him so deeply. Shame and the burn of blood flowed in her cheeks. She blushed in embarrassment. "Forgive me, Jeremiah, I'm sorry for the way I've acted."

"Don't matter none, gal, long as you know I'd never hurt you."

"It wasn't you, Jeremiah. When you grabbed at my dress so roughly it caught me by surprise. Suddenly I recalled that fat, ugly Yankee, Sergeant Barnes, and his men clawing at me and ripping away my clothes. They forced me down and beat me when they raped me. They made me do unspeakable things for them. I felt that fear flood over me, like it was happening again." The words seemed to catch in her throat as she fought to talk through the rising sobs. He felt her tremble and convulse in waves as the tears began again.

Jeremiah eased the two of them on to their sides in the sweet-smelling hay as he cradled her head to his chest. "Cry it out, darlin'. Don't you worry none. I ain't ever gonna let it happen again. Remember how I stopped Stivers and his men at Farnsworth House? I'll kill any man that tries to force himself on you, even if it costs me my life." His voice softened more. "My life wouldn't be worth livin' if it weren't for you, so you just cry it all out." He stroked her hair gently and ran his fingers in soft, gentle circles across her back.

Becca felt the anguish slipping away from her as she lay protected in Jeremiah's strong arms. The warmth of his chest seeped through his shirt to her body. She knew then he would never take her against her will even though his need for her was strong.

She felt a rising tide of guilt for her actions, for Jeremiah had proven his love. She felt a deeper tenderness building for this tough but amazingly gentle man. As she

listened to the beat of his heart pounding in his chest she
became aware of his throbbing member straining his pants
as it pushed against her tummy. She felt it pulse with each
beat of his heart.

She knew then how uncomfortable he must be in his
need, and yet despite his desires his concern still was for
her. Overwhelmed by this realization, she felt a fresh surge
of desire glowing low beneath her belly. She pushed him
gently on his back and undid two buttons on his shirt as
he watched with a puzzled expression. Becca slid her fingers through his opened shirt and ran her hand through the
curly hair of his chest to feel the sinewy muscle hidden
under his warm skin. Her fingers teased at his nipples.

She leaned over him and pressed her eager lips to his.
He returned her kiss tenderly. She felt a rising tide of lust
building strength and propelled by her love as her kisses
became more ardent. She opened her mouth and she felt
him respond. She probed his mouth with her tongue, and
his met hers. Her breathing became more ragged, matching
his in intensity. She moved her hand lower over his pants
until she covered his manhood with her cupped hand. She
squeezed gently and felt it twinge in response as it strained
against the material. She tugged at his belt and, while still
maintaining her passionate kisses, felt the belt slip free.
She carefully worked her hands down his fly, undoing the
buttons. Gingerly, her fingers worked their way through
the front of his longjohns. When at last her fingers
wrapped themselves around his throbbing manhood, she
knew this time she would be all right.

Surprising Arrival

Becca lay exhausted on Jeremiah's chest, still breathing heavily from her exertions. Their perspiration mingled freely as Jeremiah clung to her with a deep-throated groan. Becca, still feeling the ecstasy of her orgasm, knew he was tottering on heaven's blissful edge. She gave one last effort as she swayed her hips and thrust against him. It felt so good it almost hurt as he stiffened his back and released his pent up tension. His hands still clung tightly to her buttocks as if trying to keep her from moving. She stayed still for a couple of minutes as spasms hit his muscles in waves.

She felt Jeremiah relax as his muscles released the last of the stored tension gathered during their lovemaking. Becca felt totally spent and deeply relaxed as she lay on his chest, her knees still astride him. After a couple of minutes, she rolled slowly to her side, exhaling deeply as she lay on her back beside him. With great effort, she slid her hand up and brushed a lock of hair from her eyes. The hay prickled and poked at her uncomfortably, making her itchy. Becca panted as she fought to refill her lungs with fresh air.

Beside her she heard Jeremiah moan softly and felt one last tremble as his muscles continued to unwind. "Thank you, Becca," he said giddily. "I think I just saw heaven." His soft chuckling interrupted his words for a moment. "It's like I'm floatin' on a big ol' fluffy cloud on a warm summer's day without a care in the world." He turned toward her. "When I'm with you nothing else matters."

Becca saw the contentment written all over his face and in that moment her love for him deepened. She ran her fingers softly down his cheek until she stopped beneath his chin. She felt complete and whole as her body basked in the afterglow. For a fleeting moment she worried about becoming pregnant, but then she realized she would welcome his child. Although they still were not formally united in marriage, everyone knew they were a couple. Katlin had promised to see them properly wed once they reached Texas, and that was good enough for Becca.

Suddenly, she heard the creak of the barn door on its hinges. A voice rang out in the stillness of the barn and echoed off the rafters, startling the two lovers lying in the hayloft. "Hey, is anyone here?" The voice was deep and unmistakably male.

Jeremiah whispered harshly under his breath, "Oh, shit, not now!" He scrambled to his feet and searched for his longjohns. "Yes, I'm in the hayloft. You stay right there an' I'll be down in a minute."

Jeremiah hurriedly tugged on his longjohns. Still naked and afraid of being discovered, Becca nevertheless kept her head. She reached for a pitchfork standing nearby, and careful to keep away from the edge where she might be seen, forked over a portion of hay to fall in the stall below.

Jeremiah smiled as he saw what she was doing. He yelled loudly, "I'll be down directly. I just need to finish throwin' down some hay." As Becca sent down yet another forkful of hay, he slid into his pants and buttoned them. Next came his shirt, and after tucking in his shirttail, he fastened his belt. He slipped his feet back into his brogans and tied them as more hay continued to fall.

"Listen, up there in the hayloft. I haven't got all day to wait," the voice said impatiently. "If you're going to be a while, we'll leave the horses here for you to feed and put away."

Another voice drifted up from below, "Can you hear us?"

"Hold on, suh, just hold your horses. I'm coming!" He gave one final glance at Becca standing naked in the hay, the pitchfork gripped tightly in her hands. He couldn't remember seeing a lovelier sight as his eyes viewed her from head to toe. He admired her full breasts, flat tummy, and shapely legs. He motioned for her to stop dropping hay and she set down the pitchfork. Just before his head disappeared below floor level he gave her a sly wink.

He climbed down the ladder, hay clinging to his hair and his clothes. When he reached the floor Jeremiah turned toward the men.

A smile creased his face as he recognized the two young gentlemen standing before him. "Well, if it ain't Capt'n Stryker and young Massa Jessie. Lordy, the women sure will be excited to see you. They been more nervous than a cat on a hot stove since we got here. Every day they wonder if'n this gonna be the day you come."

Both men smiled as they recognized Jeremiah. They hadn't seen him since better times back at Farnsworth House. It seemed like a lifetime ago. Captain Stryker said, "We sure didn't expect to find you working in the barn. Don't the Chidesters have slaves?"

"Yes, suh, they do, but the colonel leased his men out to the army until the trenches and forts around the city get dug. Figured I'd make myself useful since they been good enough to let us stay." He looked thoughtful for a moment before he said, "I guess you musta got the letter the ladies sent?"

"Yes, and we were pleased y'all reached here safely. Are Cassandra and Katlin here?"

"Nobody's taken a wagon or carriage out today, so I bet they'll be in the big house waitin' for ya."

Jessie glanced up at the floor of the hayloft as he heard a board squeak above him. "Is there someone else up there, Jeremiah?"

A sheepish look crossed Jeremiah's face as he said, "No, suh, probably it's just a pigeon or a rat. You know these old buildings, sometimes they kinda creak and groan as the day heats up."

Both soldiers were now staring up at the loft floor, and conversation died away as they listened. Jeremiah swallowed hard, hoping he wouldn't be discovered in his lie.

Just then, Fanny waddled in through the door. Blinded by the sunshine outside she said, "Jeremiah, have you seen Becca? Katlin's awake from her nap, an' she wants Becca to watch the baby." Without waiting for his response she said, "Miz Lizzie says she thought she seen two riders come up to the barn. She wants to know who's here."

Jeremiah blushed red as he heard Fanny's words. Before he could respond he heard Jessie say, "Fanny, you look as lovely as ever. You got a hug for me?"

The large black woman strained her eyes in the dim light as she studied the faces of the two men standing before her. "Is that you, Massa Jessie?"

"It's me, Fanny," he said as he swept into her arms and swung the rotund woman. Fanny had been like a second mother to Jessie and his siblings as they were growing up. She was their nanny for as long as he could remember, and after the children got older she became the family cook. Fanny was like family, and he loved her dearly.

"My, my, Massa Jessie, you ain't nuthin' but skin and bones. Ain't they feedin' you in the army?" Her dark ebony face glowed with happiness. "Land sakes, the gals gonna be pleased to lay eyes on you."

"Are they up at the house, Fanny?" Jessie asked as he continued to hug her tightly.

"Yes, suh, and I know they're anxious to see you." She glanced over his shoulder and saw Captain Stryker stand-

ing nearby, smiling at her. "Capt'n Stryker, Lord be
praised, Miz Cassie gonna be happy as a lark to see you
again. She been missin' you somethin' awful."

Jessie let her go as Fanny greeted Evan Stryker, then
glanced over at Jeremiah and in that instant she recalled
why she had come to the barn. In a stern voice indicating
she would not tolerate anything but a clear answer she
said, "Jeremiah, I asked you if you know where Becca is?"

Jeremiah shrugged his shoulders. "No ma'am, I ain't
see her since she brought some chicken out for me to eat.
I reckon she done gone to the outhouse or maybe to her
room." He pointed in the direction of the slave cabins.

"Ain't like that gal to run off and leave the bucket and
cloth behind after she ate lunch with you." She eyed Jeremiah suspiciously. "You better find that gal an' get her on
up to the house, you hear?"

"Yes ma'am, I'll get right to it after I take care of these
horses for the gentlemen. I'm sure she'll show up directly,
an' if she don't I'll find her."

"You see that you do, Jeremiah. Here it is in the middle
of the day and she's disappeared. I haven't got time for
your foolishness." She turned back to the two soldiers and
with a much more cheerful tone said, "Come on up to the
house. Jeremiah will take care of your horses." She looked
puzzled as if she just remembered something. "Where's
Massa Ross and Calvin?"

"Calvin is back at camp on guard duty, and Ross is on
a scout. Calvin is trying to get leave and Ross will come
in when he returns. I suspect they'll join us in a couple of
days. We can talk about it in the house. Lead the way,
Fanny."

Fanny turned for the barn door and the men followed
her. As they left, Jeremiah released a deep sigh of relief.
He stepped to the ladder and shouted in low tones, "It's
safe now. You can come on down."

Becca, fully clothed, peered down on him. "Jeremiah, I
knew we were gonna get caught."

"They didn't catch nothin', gal. Come on down and I'll

help brush off the hay. You've got it all over you." Jeremiah smiled at her as she carefully climbed down the ladder. When she reached the ground he began picking and brushing at the hay hanging on her clothes. His smile was wide with good humor. "What's the matter with you, girl? You look like you done rolled in the hay."

Becca couldn't maintain her stern expression and joined in Jeremiah's mirth. Both were soon laughing nearly uncontrollably, partly because of the humor of the situation and partly from relief at not having been caught. Becca slapped at his arm as if to tell him to stop. "I'd better get up to the house and see about the baby."

Jeremiah stopped picking at her clothes long enough to run over and fold the red-and-white-checkered material they had used as a tablecloth. He set the folded material in the dinner pail and handed it to Becca. "Don't forget this, gal, or they be askin' you where it went." He slapped her playfully on the rump as she headed for the door. "You know, I never saw anyone look as good as you did holdin' a pitchfork."

Becca glanced over her shoulder and smiled as she watched him untie the first horse and move toward the stalls. Becca fussed and slapped at her skirt as she walked toward the house, worrying the hay might still be clinging to her dress. She hoped Fanny wouldn't be too full of questions.

As Fanny, Evan, and Jessie approached the porch, Elizabeth Kimbrough stood in the shade of a square-shaped pillar. Liz squealed in excitement, gathered her skirt in her hands, and bounded down the steps to greet them. Jessie opened his arms to her and her momentum nearly knocked him off his feet. Liz hugged him tightly around the neck and while still holding on to her brother, held out a hand to greet Evan. "Captain, it's good to see you again." She winked at him. "Cassie is in the house." Evan gently kissed the back of her hand as Jessie eased her down. Liz smiled shyly at Evan's gentlemanly gesture.

Jessie released his sister and took the steps two at a

time. Fanny, moving ahead of him, held the door open as he stepped through. Elizabeth was caught off guard by Jessie's sudden departure, but she was determined that Captain Stryker would not slip by her as well. She stepped in front of him, blocking his path. "Captain, have you heard any news of Quantrill and his men?"

Evan smiled at her question and decided to tease her a bit. "Why, yes I have, but I don't think you'll be interested in them any longer."

"And pray tell, what is that supposed to mean? Billy is all right, isn't he?"

Evan stopped walking for a moment and tried to look genuinely concerned as he crossed his arms across his chest. "No, I'm worried about him. You see, that poor boy is so lovesick for a freckle-faced, blue-eyed girl from Missouri that he can hardly keep his mind on his duties. I'm surprised he hasn't deserted and come looking for you. If he doesn't recover soon I fear he'll be little help to our brigade."

Elizabeth's eyes widened in amazement at Evan's declaration. "Did you say Billy is with Shelby's brigade?"

Evan could no longer maintain his little charade. His face broke into a wide smile. "Yes, Billy quit Quantrill's band and he and William Gregg enlisted for the duration of the war with our brigade. He is now a private in Company H, Twelfth Missouri Cavalry of Jo Shelby's brigade."

Elizabeth hesitated a moment as the words slowly sunk into her consciousness. She felt a sudden surge of joy as she realized that the danger to Billy's safety, while not totally removed, had been lessened. Riding with Quantrill or fighting from the bush with any of the guerrilla bands was a dangerous undertaking, full of risks. She knew the Yankees didn't bother taking Bushwhackers prisoner, and those who were captured were usually summarily executed.

How many nights, she wondered, had she lain awake worrying about Billy being captured? Too numerous to count. Although he still faced all the dangers of battle and

camp life there was now at least the hope of survival
should he be captured by the enemy, as both sides in the
regular armies kept captive soldiers as prisoners of war.

Elizabeth's joy overcame her as tears glistened in her
eyes. She smiled as she pulled Evan Stryker into her
arms and hugged him tightly, grateful for this wonderful
news. "Thank God he has come to his senses." Liz leaned
away, still clinging to Evan's arms, and looked him in the
eye. "Does Billy know I'm here? When will I see him?"

Evan stared into those youthful blue eyes and saw the
genuine concern revealed there. "He's on picket duty now,
but he'll be off in two days. I've secured a few days' leave
for Billy. I know soon as he is released from duty, nothing
will keep him from seeing you."

Evan saw the relief and happiness on her face and he
was glad he had such good news. However, he felt impa-
tient over the delays the young beauty was causing him.
He was anxious to see Cassandra. He held Liz by the
shoulders and spun her around so she was no longer between him and the steps. "Now if you'll excuse me, I'm
anxious to see your sister."

Elizabeth, though dazed and a little giddy from the good
news, understood. "Thank you," she managed to whisper
as she watched him bound up the steps toward the house.

While Evan Stryker was detained by Elizabeth in the
front yard, Jessie had entered the house. He stopped as he
entered the unfamiliar entranceway, letting his eyes grow
accustomed to the new surroundings. From the stairway he
heard Katlin cry out as she saw him standing there. She
held her hand to her mouth and tears gleamed in her eyes.
She fell eagerly into his arms at the foot of the stairs. Jessie felt Kat tremble in his arms as tears of joy soaked his
shoulder. He heard her whisper in his ear, "Thank God He
has brought you safely home to me. I was afraid I might
never see you again."

Jessie fought back his tears as he held his wife tightly.
He had spent so many lonely nights far from her side,
dreaming of this moment. Now his emotions threatened to

sweep his composure away like a leaf in a whirlwind. He kissed her hungrily, not caring who might be watching, and Katlin responded. She regained her composure and pulled herself free of Jessie's embrace. Still holding his hand she turned and said, "Mrs. Chidester, I'd like to introduce you to my husband, Jessie Kimbrough. Jessie, this is Mrs. Leah Chidester. She has been kind enough to rent us a room in her home."

Leah had risen from her rocker when she saw Katlin rush into the stranger's arms. She smiled now as she studied this young man for the first time. His piercing gray eyes shone with intelligence. She guessed him to be a little under six feet tall, with wavy, light brown hair. His body looked taut and trim from his service in the army. "I'm pleased to meet you, Jessie. Since your family arrived they've spoken of you often."

Jessie smiled. "I hope what you've heard has been positive."

"Yes, I assure you, they have told me how proud they are of you. You should know how deeply they care for you."

Jessie looked lovingly at his young wife again, as if he were worried that should he take his eyes off her for a moment, she might disappear like a wisp of smoke on the wind. "I know how lucky I am, Mrs. Chidester, and I'm grateful for your kindness to my family."

"Not at all, it has been my pleasure, and I have to admit I've enjoyed having some women for company. My husband is gone on business, and they have helped fill the void." She hesitated for a moment before she continued. "I think it would be nice if you could share the room with your wife tonight. I'm sure you have some catching up to do." She gave Jessie a knowing wink that both embarrassed and reassured him equally. "We are short on rooms here, but we might persuade Elizabeth and Cassandra to sleep on pallets in my room for a couple of nights so you can be together. A man and wife need time alone if their marriage is to remain strong."

Jessie smiled as he looked at Leah. "It is so kind of you to make such a generous offer, Mrs. Chidester, but I hate to impose on your hospitality."

"Nonsense, it is my pleasure. In these terrible times we should hang on to any happiness we can find. One look at you and any fool can see how deeply in love you are. I admit I feel a little envious of you. I only wish my husband was as eager to see me as you are to see your wife. I'm sure Cassandra and Elizabeth won't mind." She stopped and turned to look at Cassandra. "You don't mind, do you, Cassandra?"

Cassandra wasn't really hearing what Leah Chidester had to say. Captain Evan Stryker had stepped quietly through the open door and stood framed in the light that streamed through the entrance. She stood there for a moment as if she didn't really believe her eyes, as if blinking might cause him to disappear. She moved forward slowly until she reached Evan's side and took both of his hands in hers. She looked into his hazel eyes, his brown hair now hanging in uncut waves to his shoulders. She gazed at the flowing brown mustache, at the way it curled up on the ends by the deep dimples in his cheeks. Reluctantly she turned to the others and without answering Leah's question said, "Leah, I'd like to introduce you to my fiancé, Captain Evan Stryker of Shelby's brigade. Evan, this is Leah Chidester."

Evan was reluctant to take his eyes off Cassandra, but he made the effort. "Pleased to meet you, Mrs. Chidester."

"The pleasure is mine, Captain Stryker. We don't have any rooms to spare, but you are welcome to spread your bedroll here in the living room near the fire during your visit. I hope you'll accept an invitation to supper tonight."

"Thank you for your kind offer, and if Cassandra doesn't mind I'd be pleased to accept."

Cassandra gave him a look that plainly showed it was foolish even to have asked. "Thank you, Leah, I really appreciate your offer, and Evan will be pleased to accept your kind hospitality." She looked back into Evan's eyes.

"Would you please excuse us? I'd like to take a stroll with Evan and show him some of Camden. We have much to discuss."

Leah smiled knowingly. "Of course, I understand. We won't eat until five, so take your time. Cassandra, I'll have a pallet made up in my room for you."

The young couple smiled and nodded their understanding. Cassandra took Evan's arm and guided him through the door and onto the porch.

After the two had parted, Jessie said, "Kat, I want to see my son. Where is he?"

Katlin smiled proudly and replied, "He's upstairs asleep. I just finished feeding him. Come, let me show you." Katlin took her husband's arm and guided him up the stairs to see for the first time his two-month-old son, Glen Adam Kimbrough.

Becca stood just inside the doorway, near Fanny. She had entered the house after Captain Stryker and had stood by quietly. Now that both couples were leaving, Fanny turned to face her with a look of disapproval. "Where you been, gal?"

"I ate dinner with Jeremiah like I told you I would, then I went to my room. I got me an awful headache, so I lay down for a little bit."

Fanny looked at her as if she didn't believe a word of it. "Well, you dilly-dallied around so long the baby don't need watchin'. I suspect they might want a baby-sitter later, so they can be alone for a while. You can help in the kitchen until after supper, then we'll see." Fanny fished a piece of hay off the back of Becca's dress before leading the way to the kitchen.

9

Exploring Camden

Jessie eagerly followed his wife up the Chidester House stairs to the second floor. When the letter reached him in camp informing him of the birth of his son, it was a dream come true. In the days that followed, he often wondered if the baby would favor him, or Katlin. Jessie tried time and again to conjure an image of his son, but he was never successful. Try as he might, he couldn't guess how his son would look. Now he was moments away from solving the mystery.

Katlin paused at the door and motioned for Jessie to be quiet. She opened the door slowly and silently like a thief in the night. She tiptoed into the room and rounded the edge of the bed, with Jessie staying close. Next to the bed in a cradle loaned to her by the Chidesters, little Glen Adam Kimbrough lay soundly asleep.

Jessie stared in awe at the rounded little face with pink-toned skin. The baby wore a cream-colored cotton nightshift. He had kicked off the light blanket and Jessie stared at the tiny, stocking-covered feet. Jessie studied the thin brown hair curled on the top of his son's head and gingerly touched his son's hand with his forefinger. The baby's tiny hand gripped the finger. In that moment Jessie felt a swelling of pride. This was his son.

Katlin beamed as she watched Jessie's expression at seeing his son for the first time. She sensed the beginnings of a bond forming between them. Filled to nearly overflowing with love for the two of them she moved behind her husband. She hugged him from behind and he straightened as he turned to face her. He held her tightly, rocking her gently side to side. When she lifted her chin his lips met hers.

Katlin pulled herself free from his arms and tugged at his jacket. When she had it removed she shoved him gently, urging him to sit on the bed. She grabbed his boot and tugged it off, and then reached for the other one. Once his boots were removed she slid quietly onto the bed beside him. As Jessie leaned his head back onto a pillow, he felt Katlin lay her head gently on his chest and he smelled her sweet perfume. He stroked her hair lovingly as they lay together, enjoying the warmth of each other's body seeping through their clothes. Jessie felt contented and wished this moment would last forever as he held his wife in his arms while his son slept quietly nearby.

Cassandra and Evan left the Chidester House and, on a whim, turned east on Washington Street toward the Ouachita River. Although it remained unspoken, both desperately wanted to share time alone, and a rambling stroll with no set purpose suited them perfectly.

Cassandra pulled her knitted shawl tighter around her arms as they leisurely strolled along. She slipped her hands around Evan's arm and laid her head softly against his shoulder as she kept an even pace with his stride. Evan felt warmed inside with a soft inner glow. His contentment was growing and he smiled to himself, thinking that if he were a cat, he surely would be purring. "God, how I've missed you," he said softly.

Cassandra didn't look up, but found comfort in his words. "I've missed you, too, although I shouldn't admit it. It might go to your head and you'll take me for granted."

Evan smiled at her response. "I'd have to be quite a fool ever to take you for granted." They walked on in silence down the tree-shaded lane. Washington Street was a main and important thoroughfare through Camden and, as such, many fine homes lined the street. Many houses stood above the street level, accessed by climbing steps to reach the higher ground. After a while, the couple simply held hands as they ambled along and talked. Soon they reached the town's main business district.

As they passed by the courthouse, Evan studied the imposing brick structure. The large, two-story building covered most of the square bounded by Washington, Adams, Jefferson, and Madison streets. Evan admired the artistry adorning the cupola, perched high atop the hipped roof. An entryway from each street led into the building, and windows on both levels and every side provided the interior with natural light during the day. It was an impressive structure and an integral part of the local government.

They left Washington and moved along Jefferson Street east toward the river. There they stopped on the high bluff standing guard over the Ouachita River. They glanced to the south where the bluff extended several hundred feet before them. A cliff hung over the greenish-brown waters of the river, giving them a good view of the bluff, the town, and the Ouachita spreading out before them in a spectacular panorama. Fort Lookout, covering a good-sized portion of the bluff, was still under construction. They watched, somehow oddly detached, as the slaves toiled to dig and haul dirt from the trenches and rifle pits to the earthworks and ramparts protecting the city. Their white overseers were mostly older men, unsuitable for duty with the army. The slave drivers sat or stood in a relaxed fashion as they watched the slaves work. They seemed as intent on soaking in the sun's warmth on this early March day as they were in keeping the workers busy.

Cassandra was fascinated by the work on the military defenses circling the city, but Major Stryker had seen enough of war. Instead he found solace in watching the lapping, rippling waters of the river as birds darted and dived over its rolling, flowing waters. His eyes studied the shoreline down past the docks and quays, working south past the city to Bradley's Ferry, standing almost in the shadows of Fort Diamond. He held Cassandra tightly around her waist as he watched the ferry boat fight its way across the current to the other shore. From the bluff the town spilled out before them, displaying all her magic and charms. After resting for nearly half an hour while they talked about their mutual dreams for the future, Evan led Cassandra from the bluff toward the city's wharfs.

As they left the bluff they passed by the Nunns's home. It was a beautiful large log home, covered with planed wood and perched on the bluff above the street. Steep steps led to the house and the couple admired it as they watched children playing in the yard.

They continued their conversation as they meandered along the city streets. Cassandra talked of growing up in Missouri along the banks of the Missouri River and the carefree life she enjoyed before the war. She talked for a while about their trip from Batesville and how much she had missed him. Evan talked of his childhood days and about his trip by wagon train from Mississippi's Water Valley to Bastrop, Texas, and finally to the high prairie near San Marcos. He told of the long, empty days spent in winter camp and the suffering endured there in the midst of winter.

When they reached the quays they walked out over the river on the wooden planks covering the docks. From these river wharfs, mostly empty since the war ended river-steamer commerce, he could examine the river more carefully and feel a part of its timeless ebb and flow.

The swampy, mossy smell of the river filled Evan's nostrils, mixing with the tar-and-pitch smell of the main pilings and ropes that supported the docks. As they walked, the sound of their footsteps reverberated off the planking and seemed unnaturally loud. Evan listened to the lapping sound of the river beneath them as it splashed against the pilings. The constant, rhythmic beat of the water's flow somehow soothed the tensions away from Major Stryker as they stood on Coker's Landing. It amazed him how much tension from living through life's everyday problems, compounded by the uncertainties of war, could intensify emotions even when action wasn't eminent.

As he stood near the end of the dock and gazed out over the river to the distant shore, he felt more certain than ever before of what he truly wanted. He turned toward Cassandra and looked deep in her eyes. "Cassandra, I don't want to wait any longer, let's get married right away." As he stood there holding the woman he loved, Evan felt a sudden urgency. If he waited, she might never share his life. He recalled a store they had passed on their way to the wharfs, Stinson's jewelry store. Although it was closed, he had noticed a note attached to the window telling potential customers how to contact the family if they needed the shop opened for business. "I can contact Stinson's and buy a wedding band. We'll find the minister of that Baptist church we passed, or someone from another church to marry us. Will you do it? Will you marry me right away?" he asked as his eyes anxiously studied her face, hoping she would agree.

Cassandra knew she loved this bold Texan and wanted nothing more than to spend the rest of her life with him. Still, inside she knew the time wasn't right. As much as she wanted to be with him, she somehow understood it would be better to wait. She couldn't bear to look in his eyes and say what must be said, so she pulled him close and clung to him as she spoke. "I love you, Evan Stryker, more than life itself, but I don't want to rush into this. There is so much to consider."

Evan pushed her away from him so he could study her

face. He felt a sinking feeling in the pit of his stomach, and his wounded pride welled to the surface. He felt the sting of rejection and was startled because she had not eagerly accepted his proposal to marry him immediately. "Why not now?" he pleaded. "Don't you want me as much as I want you?"

She could read the hurt in his eyes and watched him fight to retain control of his wounded pride. Cassandra tried to remain calm and cool as she said softly, "Don't you see? It's not that I don't want you, it's just not the proper time. The war is still going on, you might be called back to duty at any moment, and there is no place for us to stay. Every available room in the city is filled. We were lucky enough to find room and board with the Chidesters, but we are forced by circumstances to share our rooms. Where could we honeymoon?"

"I don't care where we go, as long as I am with you. Maybe we could go into the country while I'm still on leave and find a place for a few days. Maybe we could go toward Poison Springs."

"Please, Evan, try to be practical. The family is counting on me to lead them. If I should become pregnant or distracted it could prove disastrous. You know it isn't safe here. You told me yourself as we walked near the courthouse, General Steele is expected to lead his Union army on an expedition this spring. You said they'll likely move against Southwest Arkansas. It is entirely possible we'll have to continue our travels until we reach Texas. My family is counting on me. For the time being, I must put their needs and their safety first, no matter how much I would rather do otherwise."

Evan could read it clearly in her eyes. This stubborn daughter of Missouri had made up her mind and nothing he could say would alter her decision one whit. He sighed deeply, releasing his disappointment in one low, slow whoosh. He wanted to be angry, to shout, scream, and release his pent-up frustration and anger at the world, but he knew this girl expected him to show strength and wisdom.

He would not, could not let her down. He grabbed her by the shoulders. "Just answer one question: Do you love me?" he asked, slowly and deliberately.

He saw her lip begin to tremble and he gently brushed the first tear away from her eyes as she said, "Yes! Yes, I love you with all my heart and I want to be the mother of your children. I want to feel you lying beside me in the dark every night, and I want to share your life." She stopped for a moment as she fought back the tears. "You know I love you, but we must wait. Tell me you understand. Tell me you will wait for me, Evan, please?"

Inside he wanted to continue to argue for his point of view—to declare that life owed him nothing and at any time he could die of illness contracted in the brigade's camp or of a Yankee bullet in battle. Waiting offered no guarantee there would ever be a time for them, and yet, he found himself unwilling to take a stand against her. He loved her enough to wait for her if he must. "I understand, Cassie, and I'll wait, but you must know I do it under protest. War changes everything and the temptation is to live for today because there is no guarantee of a tomorrow. I guess I envy your faith in the future. I'll wait for you, and if God is willing, we will have that wedding day in Texas."

She hugged him tightly on that lonely, windswept wharf. Their kisses fueled Evan's heated passion. He wanted her so bad he ached deep in his groin. He would endure it rather than forsake her company.

They walked hand in hand away from the docks and past a large, imposing two-story brick warehouse standing near the docks. The building still had a new look about it and painted on the side they read J. M. BROOKS, GENERAL SUPPLY.

"It is a beautiful building, don't you think?" Evan asked as they passed the structure.

"I've heard Mrs. Chidester call the building the Old Star Warehouse, although it isn't old." They cut west and walked past other stores, including Peter McCollum's Mercantile.

As they moved near the edge of the business district they saw a peculiar sight. There on an empty lot sat a wagon with the words M. E. GREENWOOD'S TRAVELING PHOTO GALLERY painted in bright vermillion on the canvas cover. In front of the wagon sat an open-sided three-wall tent of white muslin. The tent faced north, and its roof slanted upward at a forty-five-degree angle, enough to put the one end in shade, yet bounce diffused light into the tent. They stood and watched curiously as the photographer worked to arrange his subjects before his camera. Three Confederate soldiers were posing with their unit's battle flag and appeared to be members of their regiment's color guard. The other two men held their muskets at the ready, bayonets mounted as if ready to defend the flag at all costs. The photographer fussed with them a bit, arranging everything to his satisfaction before slipping under the black cloth attached to the camera. The boxy contraption sat atop a three-legged, heavy tripod. He yelled to the soldiers to hold still as his hand moved around and removed the cap covering the lens. "Hold it, hold it, okay!" he shouted as he replaced the cap. He slid a glass plate holder from the back of the camera and inserted another one. "Did any of you want an individual portrait?" He asked with a hopeful lilt to his voice. The men shook their heads no, and although he looked slightly disappointed he said, "Very well, come back in a couple of hours and I'll have your portrait completed. I'll hold your deposit until your return, and then we'll settle up proper, gentlemen."

The soldiers smiled and chatted among themselves as they carefully sheathed their flag and trotted off toward the nearest saloon, laughing and joking as they went.

The photographer noticed the couple standing nearby and approached them with a wide grin. "Allow me to introduce myself. My name is Melvin Greenwood, and as you can see I'm a photographer. Would you and this beautiful young lady like to have your likeness made?"

Evan studied the man standing before him. The man was oval faced with a luxuriant beard and mustache. He stood around five feet seven inches tall with wide shoulders and a very stocky build; long through the body, but short in the legs. He was stout and compact, but he carried his weight well. Evan had known other men built like this and all had been deceptively stout for their size. In a way the man reminded him of a human bulldog, lacking the ugly bulldog face. His age was hard to guess, but Evan, staring into the man's kindly pale-blue eyes, figured him to be in his thirties or early forties.

Evan turned to Cassandra. "Should we have our image made together?"

Cassandra smiled excitedly. "I would love to. In fact, I'd like to bring my whole family down for portraits." She looked inquisitive. "How long will you be in town?"

Melvin smiled at the prospect of more business. "I intend to stay till the end of the week, but if business is good, I may stay longer. As you can imagine, with the uncertainties of war, many people are choosing to preserve their likeness, should they fall in battle. Most are shipping their images home to their families." The man rocked back and forth on his feet as if proud of the role he was taking to preserve family memories.

"What kind of images do you make?" Evan asked.

"I can offer tintypes and the latest carte vistas in a variety of sizes. I also offer a few frames and mounts to protect your treasured heirlooms," he said pompously.

Cassandra tugged on Evan's sleeve. "Why don't we wait until Ross and Billy can join us. When we have the whole family together we can have our portraits done."

"Only if you will do images with just the two of us, so I can carry it with me when I'm away from you."

Before Cassandra could respond, Melvin interrupted, "Your lady is very beautiful, Major. I'd be honored to do individual shots of her, and I would present one of those to you free of charge just for the honor of capturing her beauty on my photographic plates."

Cassandra blushed slightly from the compliment. "I'd be honored, sir, to pose for you. When all my family arrives we will make arrangements then. It shouldn't be more than a couple of days."

Melvin smiled as he offered his hand. "I'll look forward to the day and I'll be happy to be of service." He kissed her knuckles charmingly as he held her hand lightly and bowed from the waist. He straightened and shook hands heartily with Evan. "If you'll excuse me, I'd best see to developing and making my prints for my customers. Good-day." He pivoted on his heels and returned to his wagon.

As the couple turned west on Washington Street Cassandra was bubbling with excitement. "You know, Evan, of all the possessions I own, I treasure most the family photos Fanny saved from Briarwood. Those portraits are all I have to keep the images of my parents fresh in my mind. I wouldn't trade them for anything in the world."

"I suppose you still have the images from Jessie and Katlin's wedding?"

"Yes I do, and it'll be fun to dig them out and see them again. I know Jessie and Katlin will want to have another sitting done with little Glen." She squeezed·him excitedly as they sauntered along. "I'm so excited to have my family together again." She only wished her parents could be here to join them.

10

Oakland Picnic

Jessie woke slowly from sleep as the morning sun, tracking across the sky, spilled light through the window and glared harshly in his face. Gradually his mind cleared away the cobwebs of dream-laced sleep. This was the morning of the fourth day of his leave at the Chidester House with his wife, son, and family. The first three days had been a healing salve for his war-torn mind. During these days he had renewed his relationship with his wife and gotten acquainted with his son.

He remembered holding his son for the first time, almost afraid to touch him at all, believing his son to be as fragile as glass. Katlin had laughed at his timid first attempts but as the days rolled along he gradually became more accustomed to holding his child. Now he had reached the point where he would hold his boy above his head as if the boy were a hawk soaring and diving at his prey. Little Glen would laugh and coo and seemed to enjoy being bounced in the air. The boisterous rough play acted to bond father and son.

Perhaps the proudest moment of Jessie's life came when photographer M. E. Greenwood posed Jessie, Katlin, and little Glen in their first family portrait. They ordered an individual image of baby Glen, made tiny enough to fit into the small locket Jessie always wore. The locket was a gift to Jessie from Katlin the day Shelby's brigade rode away from Lafayette County. Jessie felt his good luck talisman was only enhanced by the addition of little Glen's likeness.

The morning hours were spent sitting for a portrait of the Kimbrough siblings. A second family shot included Captain Stryker, Billy Cahill, Valissa Covington, Katlin, and baby Glen. The men had their photos individually done in uniform, while the ladies donned their finest fashions. It seemed the photographer, ever enamored with Cassandra, would never finish taking shots of her. He also showed considerable interest in capturing Valissa on film—so much so that Elizabeth and Katlin began to feel slighted. They finished the session with shots of the couples before payments were made and images were ordered. Today they would have their photographs. Jessie was anxious to see the work firsthand and hoped he wouldn't look too stern and stiff. All in all, Jessie couldn't recall a happier three days in his young life.

He felt the soft heat of his naked wife lying next to him and it drew him from his reminiscences to the present. Katlin's hair spilled across the pillow near his face, her arm loose across his chest. She lay on her belly with her right leg halfway across his legs. He recalled their lovemaking the night before and how they slipped into deep sleep from their efforts, neither taking the time to slip into nightclothes.

He vaguely recalled Katlin waking up sometime in the night to baby Glen's urgent demands. She must have fed him and returned the baby to his crib before she again snuggled up against her husband. He felt a deep contentment and enduring love for his wife as they lay side by side.

He let his free hand slide gently around the curve of her

calf, through the hollow behind her knee, and traverse her thigh, inching ever inching toward her hips. Her skin felt cool and smooth as satin in spots as it warmed to his touch. He thrilled to the sensation of his fingers dancing lightly over her skin. His hand reached her hips and he lingered there slowly, squeezing and caressing his favorite part of her anatomy. His fingers slipped between her legs as he gently probed her warm and downy softness. His attentions began to arouse her and she rolled over turning her back to him, not so much to deny his probing, but to delay leaving the blissful state of sleep.

Jessie grinned as he studied her back. He loved looking at the graceful line of her shoulders tapering down her back as it narrowed at the waist, then rounded and swelling into those gorgeous, shapely hips. His eyes continued their journey as he studied her slender but athletic legs. He loved the way her well-muscled thighs tapered from knee to hip, and the shape of her calves, curving to end at her graceful ankles.

Jessie marveled at his luck. The pregnancy and the birth had not left a telling mark on Katlin's figure. He was amazed at how quickly she had regained her figure, as if she were never pregnant. In that moment, as he had since the very first time he had laid eyes on her nude body on their wedding day, he marveled at the Good Lord's gift. He could not imagine anything more beautiful or awe-inspiring than a woman's body. Nothing in his life had offered him such joy or pleasure. When they made love he felt more vibrant, more alive than at any other time in his life. He felt it was a shame that God's masterpiece, the peak of his artistry, must remain covered and hidden from view for so much of the time.

Although he had made love to her at bedtime, he wanted her again, but he wasn't in a hurry. He gently massaged her shoulders and back, kneading and rubbing in little circles until he heard her moan softly in pleasure. He continued working lower, including her hips and thighs into his massaging, and moving down until he reached her ankles. After fifteen minutes of this concerted attention, Katlin rolled over slowly and teased him with a sultry grin. "You can't stop until you do this side," she whispered in breathy, passionate tones.

He smiled, as he was only too happy to oblige. His hands worked their way across the swelling of her breasts. He lingered there, teasing her nipples until they arose taut and firm against his fingers. He loved how they tickled against his palm as he massaged gently in a circular motion. He brought his hand down across her ribs and the flat valley of her belly, pausing at her belly button. He slid his hand eagerly down the gentle slope below, through her soft down to her beckoning heat. She opened her thighs to him and he answered her need as he stroked her legs and felt her seething passion as her intensity increased.

Jessie sought to kiss his wife and found her lips warm and inviting as they locked in amorous embrace. His lips found her throat and he kissed and teased the nape of her neck. His mouth sought her earlobe, and he sucked and nipped at it before he let his mouth seek her breasts. As Katlin arched her back with mounting lust, the sudden reverberating cry from the crib brought a crashing end to their lovemaking.

Little Glen was ready for a new day and he wanted breakfast immediately. Both looked at the screaming interruption in the crib beside them with solemn expressions of deep disappointment. Glen's cries quickly built to a crescendo, threatening to disturb the entire household. The parents sighed heavily as Jessie rolled away from Katlin. She sat up at the edge of the bed and smiled at Jessie with an ornery twinkle in her eye. "Welcome to fatherhood, Daddy!" Jessie smiled back weakly, secretly cursing his son's poor timing. Still he did his best to handle his disappointment as Katlin lifted the squalling baby from the crib. He realized then that parenthood indeed had its price.

As Valissa Covington settled into the buggy seat next to Ross Kimbrough, he flicked the whip above the two-horse

team. Stirred out of their doldrums by the crack and pop
of the whip, the horses perked up and the team surged into
a walk along the driveway. Ross guided the team expertly
from the driveway of the Graham mansion onto Washington Street. He held one hand lightly on the reins; the other
encircled Val at the waist. She responded by snuggling
into him, and Ross smiled in delight. The world couldn't
have looked brighter to Ross Kimbrough as they rode past
the houses on Camden's main thoroughfare with his girl at
his side. They were finally on their way to a picnic, in a
buggy he had borrowed from the Chidesters.

Ross welcomed the opportunity to be alone with Val. It
had been a struggle ever since he had arrived in town on
leave. First his sister had plans for the family to have photographs taken, and that had taken a big chunk out the first
full day. Next came a round of juggling interference from
Valissa's father, who wasn't particularly happy to have
Ross around his daughter again. Ross thought if he heard
any more praise for Joseph Farnsworth and how much
wealth he was accumulating, Ross himself would explode
in rage. Andrew hurled Farnsworth's successes and wealth
in his face, taunting him, as if to show his daughter that
this young man could never offer her Farnsworth's secu-
rity. Ross was proud that Val paid little heed to her father's
antics and spoke up for him. Still, the building animosity
between himself and Andrew only deepened as the week
wore along. At least for awhile he would be free from
the pompous former Arkansas congressman.

They turned north on Adams Street and passed by the
large two-story courthouse. He watched proudly as the
banner of the Confederacy atop the courthouse cupola rippled and billowed in the gentle breeze. They continued
through the business district and rode toward the outskirts
of town. Adams turned gently toward the west and, if followed long enough, would turn into Maul Road. As they
passed near the hills of Oakland Cemetery, Valissa put her
hand on his arm. "Stop for a moment, would you, Ross?"

Ross pulled the buggy to the edge of the road and halted

the team. From their position they watched soldiers milling about two Confederate wagons that were stopped near freshly dug graves. As the couple observed them, the detail carried the rough wood caskets and lowered them one at a time into the graves. The scene seemed to touch some nerve in Valissa and she watched the proceedings intently. After a few minutes of observation, Valissa turned toward Ross and asked, "Were those men killed in battle, Ross?"

"No, I doubt it. I haven't heard about any skirmishes or battles lately. Besides, those wagons belong to our brigade. Those men died in camp of illness or disease."

Valissa looked shocked at his words: "So many are dying of illness? Is most of it brought on by wounds suffered in battle?"

"No, most of the ones who would die from wounds passed away earlier in the winter."

Val looked surprised by his response. "I never realized the losses were so high."

"No one likes to talk about it much. The truth of the matter is we lose two men from disease for every one we lose in battle. Seldom a week passes when we don't have burial details at work."

"How tragic it must be for their families," Valissa said softly.

"Yes, it seems such a waste. If a man dies of wounds suffered in battle, his loss is mourned and it is a dreadful loss to his friends and family, but his death is seen as heroic. Everyone can say he gave his life nobly for the cause, however much they mourn his passing. It's hard to explain, but I guess death is expected in battle—it doesn't come as a surprise. But to die in camp from a disease without facing the enemy seems useless and without value. No one can look at their passing and say it was for any worthwhile purpose. Does that make any sense?"

"Yes, I guess it does. We do value the loss of life differently, although I suppose few are aware of it." Valissa sighed deeply before continuing. "We didn't come out here to be melancholy. We came out here to share a picnic and the wonders of nature. I refuse to let things we have no control over ruin my day." She smiled invitingly at Ross. Beyond the cemetery, on the far side of the hill, it was lovely and green. "Let's drive over there."

Ross pulled hard on the reins, but the horses were reluctant to give up nibbling the patch of grass beside the road. He urged them on with a pop of the buggy whip above their heads. A short distance later they pulled into a cozy glade. Ross picketed the team near lush grass while Val spread a quilt on the ground.

By the time Ross joined her, Val already had the food prepared. She handed Ross a plate of cold pork-and-beans, sweetened with a portion of dark molasses. A thick slab of smoked ham lay across the beans for the main fare. A slice of mild cheddar cheese and a thick slice of fresh bread with butter garnished the plate.

Ross smiled happily. The food in winter camp along the Ouachita was monotonous and scarce. This was the best he'd eaten in a long time, and to top it off he shared the company of a beautiful woman. He could think of only one thing that would give him more joy, and with any luck he would enjoy that later. He dug in to the food ravenously while Valissa poured him a glass of apple brandy.

Valissa laughed at the obvious delight Ross was taking in the sumptuous repast. It pleased her to see him so happy. Ross noticed her smile and he glowed with satisfaction. Light, fluffy clouds drifted through an azure blue sky, and the sun felt comforting as it warmed into a mild March day.

He studied Valissa as he ate. She wore a scoop-necked blue gingham day dress that accented the blue-green color of her eyes. He had never seen eyes so beautiful. They were the color of new bluegrass, green with just a hint of blue in them. Her hair hung loose about her shoulders and emphasized her light complexion. Her hair often varied in hue and tone under different kinds of light. Sometimes it was nearly strawberry blonde and other times it was auburn. The dress clung to her nicely, accenting her curves and capturing his undivided attention.

She watched Ross as he ate and thrilled to his admiring glances. She had to admit he was ruggedly handsome and, when he smiled and showed those deep dimples, shivers of delight coursed through her. She liked his deep blue eyes and thick blond hair, but most of all she loved his wide-shouldered, narrow-hipped athletic build. He had shaved for her since coming to town and the skin where his winter beard had been was pale in comparison.

Val knew he was head over heels in love with her and she reveled in the mastery she had over him. Despite her fears of commitment and of ending up a lonely widow before the war was ended, she still delighted in entertaining the idea of accepting his proposal of marriage.

Still, she didn't voice these thoughts to him, because she sensed that once she admitted such things, he would pounce on the opening and accept nothing short of immediate marriage. This frightened her—she knew her father would be furious.

The war was not over and soon Ross would return to action. She would be left behind alone to face her father's wrath. The mere thought that he might cast her out to take care of herself while Ross was away frightened her. Despite her misgivings she loved her father and was reluctant to disappoint him. Even before the war began and shortly after the passing of Joseph Farnsworth's first wife, Andrew Covington had cast lustful eyes on Farnsworth's wealth. Andrew figured having his daughter marry a man of wealth and power could only enhance his political aspirations and coincidentally assure his daughter an opportunity to live a life of wealth and luxury. Valissa could understand his interest, but knew one vital element was lacking.

Despite all other considerations, Valissa knew she didn't love Joseph Farnsworth. A prim and proper man, he lacked the fire and zest for life she found in Ross Kimbrough. Joseph was several years her senior, and although he was still relatively young, there was a decided difference in temperament. She supposed it might be different if she had time to know Joseph more thoroughly, but it wasn't possible. He was often gone, seeing to his steamboat company and now off operating his blockade running business. Somehow, deep inside, she understood that with Joseph Farnsworth she would always take a second seat to business. For a woman of her beauty and pride it was difficult to accept.

Her thoughts were interrupted as Ross lowered his empty plate. He moved near her, slipped her plate out of her hands, and with quick, catlike moves eased himself on his back with his head resting in her lap. She smiled down on his triumphant face. "Are you sure you're comfortable?" she asked as she ran her hand through his hair.

Ross asked, "What were you thinking?"

Not wanting to reveal her true thoughts, Val tried to sidestep the question. "Oh, nothing in particular. I guess I was just thinking about the war and those men buried over there."

If Ross didn't believe her it wasn't apparent. "I thought we weren't going to let things we can't control ruin our day." He smiled at her as he stroked her arm, which was still stroking his hair.

His touch was warm on her skin and it sent electric tingles of pleasure up her arm. "How long do you think it will be until the brigade is called into action again?"

Ross grimaced. He didn't want to think about war and duty with such pleasant distractions so near at hand. "I don't know. I have some of my men on long scouts near Little Rock. Our spies tell us Steele is getting itchy about starting a spring campaign. Most seem to think they will try to capture the remainder of Arkansas. They already have most of it under their control, as you've seen for yourself. Camden and Washington are important to the Confederacy, so I only think it logical the attack will come, and soon."

She knew what his words meant. If Union general

Steele was ready to begin his campaign, then the Confederate army must respond. "Then you'll be leaving soon?"

He nodded. "It is my best guess we'll leave soon."

She looked at him with sad eyes. "How long do we have before your stay is over?"

"Shelby said he wanted to march at the start of the week and interpose our army between Camden and the Union army." Ross looked grim. "Two more days and I must return to duty. The others must return then as well. I've talked to Cassandra, but I want you to promise me you'll encourage her to continue to East Texas."

"If we stay here we'll be closer to our army. Won't I have a better chance of seeing you more often?"

"I don't want you to risk it. Cassandra might be wanted for the killing of those Yankee soldiers, and it is too dangerous for her to take a chance of being caught behind enemy lines again. You'll find more safety in Texas, and I'll rest better knowing you are out of danger."

Valissa felt warm inside as she looked down at him. He was genuinely concerned for her safety—a clear indication of the depth of his love for her. She shifted slightly, trying to restore some circulation in her leg. "Lift up a minute, my leg is asleep."

Ross lifted his head. She moved her legs out from under him and rolled on her back beside him. Ross moved alongside her and smoothed her hair with his hand. He bent forward and gently kissed her on the lips.

Valissa's response was eager and ardent. She whispered in husky, low tones, "Are you ready for dessert?"

Ross, certain of her meaning, smiled brightly as he kissed her again, letting his tongue probe against hers. The meal was good, but the memory of what was to come would overshadow his future recollections.

11

Marching to a Brass Band

Calvin Kimbrough lifted the warm mug of beer to his lips and took a tug of the amber-colored liquid. It slid down his throat in two gulps, leaving behind a slightly bitter tang in his mouth. The smell of stale beer, tobacco spittle–soaked sawdust, and cheap cigar smoke assailed his nostrils. He glanced across the dimly lit table at his companion, Captain Gilbert Thomas.

Gilbert looked tall even slumped in his chair. He stood six feet two inches tall when he chose to carry himself upright. Gilbert's gray eyes were glazed from the whiskey; his brown hair remained unruly and hung across his forehead into his eyes. Tonight, Calvin thought, Gil looked much older than his twenty years.

Gilbert remained surly as he stared into his bottle of bourbon as if it were a crystal ball with the answers to all his problems. All the answers were hidden somewhere inside the bottle and he would find them if only he studied it long enough, or absorbed its contents. Gilbert rubbed out the stub of his burnt cigar in the ash tray and then pitched another shot-glassful of sour mash down his throat.

"You better slow down, Gil, or I'll have to carry you out of here," Calvin said softly, not wishing to draw further attention to their table. He had already pulled Gilbert out of a confrontation with a Texan that had threatened to turn into a nasty knife fight. Gil needed no better reason to pick a fight than overhearing the soldier say he was from Texas.

Ever since Evan Stryker had won Calvin's sister's heart, Gilbert hated anything and anyone from Texas. Still, there were others insulted by Gilbert's behavior, and in a rundown bar like this one, a drunken soldier was fair game.

Gilbert looked up at Calvin with bloodshot eyes. "Don't tell me what to do, Corporal. You know I outrank you and I can damn sure outfight you."

Calvin knew it was the whiskey talking, so he ignored Gil's posturing. They had grown up together in Missouri, and Gilbert had served for a time with the Missouri Home Guards before he returned home. He knew it was his sister, Cassandra, who drew Gilbert home again. Gil had had a crush on Cassie since their childhood days. To Cassandra it was another matter, for she considered him nothing more than a good friend. Gilbert wasn't satisfied with that arrangement and continued to pursue her affections.

When Cassandra met the handsome Texan Evan Stryker, she quickly fell in love. And with that, Gilbert had turned bitter and increasingly turned to rotgut whiskey and Kentucky-style sour mash to drown his emotions.

Despite all this, Gilbert and Calvin remained friends. When he was sober, there was no better leader in a stiff fight than Captain Gilbert Thomas. "Say, Gil, why don't we leave here? There have to be friendlier places in town than this one."

Gilbert banged his hand down hard on the table and heads turned all throughout the bar. His voice rose above the din in the saloon. "I'll leave when I'm damn good and ready. If you're in such a damn hurry, take off! See if I care."

Calvin sat back in his chair, angry at Gilbert's aggressive behavior. One glance around this rundown Jefferson Street bar and he knew he couldn't abandon his old friend, even if he was being obnoxious.

Gil returned his attention to refilling his tumbler and as he did, Calvin thought sullenly about how he had come to the point of wasting his evening touring the bars of Camden in the company of Gilbert Thomas.

He received leave and accompanied Billy Cahill, Gilbert Thomas, and his brother Ross to town just a few days ago for a family reunion. The first night went well, except for Gilbert, who stormed off in a fit of anger to the Graham mansion to see his parents. The next day the Kimbrough family went to have their portraits made, and Calvin joined them.

It was there he first felt the odd one out. The rest of his family now were couples—Cassandra and Evan, Elizabeth and Billy, Jessie and Katlin, and Ross and Valissa. He alone remained unattached. As the day wore on, he began to feel like a fifth wheel. It had seemed like this most of his life, for Calvin was always the shy, introverted member of the family. He had kept company with a few young women while attending the University of Missouri before the outbreak of war, but none of the relationships had gone very far.

This time he felt more alone than ever before in his life. He supposed it had to do with the loss of his parents. Maybe it reflected the dangers of war. Living with the knowledge that each day could be your last made life seem all the more dear. Seeing his brothers and sisters so happily paired, engaged, or married left him feeling as if he were missing out on something vitally important.

These melancholy thoughts flooded him now as he recalled how uncomfortable he had felt around the couples at the reunion. In the end, he floundered around searching for an excuse to leave the gathering. He left to locate Gilbert and together they sought to drown their troubles in alcohol.

Calvin shifted his weight in his chair and took another sip of the tepidly bitter beer. His mind turned fondly toward Dee Ann Farley. He remembered how surprised he had been when he awoke from a concussion received at the battle of Helena to find himself in bed with Dee Ann.

It turned out that Ross had taken him there to be nursed back to health. Earlier in the war, Ross had saved Dee Ann from a group of renegades who were raping her. Recalling her debt, she offered to take care of Calvin. He smiled shyly as he laughed a little under his breath, recalling how well she had truly taken care of him.

Dee Ann's husband was killed in battle and she was left alone on her farm to raise two small children. The war had left her lonely and she needed Calvin as much as he needed her. Although she was plain and nothing more than a backwoods girl from the hill country, there was something about her that made her special. He recalled her work-hardened, curvy figure and how she used it to give him more joy than he had ever known before. He found her to be naive in so many things, yet earthy and honest about her desires and expectations. Dee Ann was far different from any woman he had encountered, and she taught him much about the simple pleasures of life.

As their time together drew to a close, he found himself struggling with the thought of introducing the plain farmgirl to his circle of wealthy friends. Calvin couldn't picture her fitting into that society. There was also the nagging question of whether he could accept the mantle of responsibility of helping to raise someone else's children. Since Dee Ann was his first real experience with a woman, it raised new questions. What would it be like with another woman?

In the end he rode off to rejoin Collins's battery with no firm promise to return. He remembered how guilty he felt as he rode away—guilty for taking advantage of her trusting nature and then leaving her with little hope he would ever return.

The time since had given him space to reflect, and now, as he sat nursemaiding a friend through a drunken binge, he wished for all he was worth that he could be with Dee Ann again. Gilbert slumped over, his shot glass spilling its contents across the table.

Calvin knew Gilbert had finally succumbed to the war with whiskey and had passed out. Calvin slipped some change out of his pocket and left it on the table, then slung his friend's considerable weight across his shoulders and toted him from the saloon. As he walked heavily down the street, his burden on his back, Calvin slanted toward Washington Street and the Graham mansion. He stayed close to the shadows so he would draw the least attention.

Elizabeth Kimbrough laughed in glee as Billy Cahill spun her across the floor in step to a lively waltz. He spun her in tight circles and with such speed that she was afraid she might succumb to dizziness. As they neared the fiddler's stand the number ended, and the two of them stood breathlessly on the dance floor. Elizabeth said, "I don't know about you, but I could use a drink."

"Lead the way to the punch bowl," Billy said.

The young couple made their way across the crowded dance floor. The news had swept through the town and military commands like a whirlwind: The army would soon be on the march. Shelby's command had orders to leave tomorrow, so this would be the last night Elizabeth would spend with Billy for quite a while. The town of Camden rose to the occasion, offering a hastily planned grand ball at the Graham mansion. It seemed half the town had turned out, including all the soldiers who could secure passes for leave.

Elizabeth and Billy reached the punch bowl and he scooped up two glasses of lemonade. They greedily gulped the contents and refilled their glasses. Billy stood close to Liz and held her hand in his. He felt hot and sticky in his clothes from dancing several numbers in a row. Eyeing Elizabeth under the soft light of candles and lamps strung around the dance floor, he thought how much he loved the light dusting of freckles spilling across her nose. As he studied this pert strawberry blonde with the pale blue eyes, it occurred to him how good it would feel to slip out into the night air and cool down. "It's very muggy in here," he began. "Would you like to stroll through the garden in the moonlight? We might cool down before we hit the dance floor again."

Liz smiled teasingly. She too was overheated from their dancing and she had gone through two glasses of lemonade as if they were nothing. She looked into Billy's brown eyes and said, "I'd love to walk in the garden with you, if you'll promise to dance with me again."

"Nothing could keep me away," he answered.

They strolled out onto the veranda and down the walk to admire the beautifully trimmed hedges outlined by the light of a nearly full moon. The fragrance of fresh spring flowers drifted softly on the southerly breeze. The couple stopped in the shadows of a large oak tree. Billy ran his fingers through the soft waves of her hair and gently wrapped his hand around the nape of her neck as he drew her to him. She met his lips with hers in an impassioned kiss. After a long moment, she pulled away and buried her head into his chest while wrapping her arms tightly around him. He felt her then as she began to sob and shudder in his arms. The tears came fast and wet, and he felt the soggy trace of them against his shirt.

He lifted her face in his hands and studied her tear-streaked face in the weak light. "What's wrong, Liz?" he asked worriedly.

Her lips quivered before she could speak, but with effort she said, "These last few days with you have been incredible. I've never been so happy in my life, but tomorrow you ride off to war and I'm afraid I might never see you again."

Billy had the same fears, but he knew better than to express them to Elizabeth. "Nonsense, this isn't half as dangerous as ridin' with Quantrill. Now that I'm ridin' in the regular army, ain't no one gonna keep me from comin' back to you."

"I only wish I was as confident as you. I worry about you and wonder how you're doing. I lay awake at night afraid something dreadful will happen to you. Don't you see I feel so helpless? There is nothing I can do but worry."

"If you want to help me, then pray for me. Ask God to bring me home to you in one piece, and his angels will look over me."

Elizabeth looked at him curiously. "Do you really believe in the power of prayer, Billy?"

He looked deep into her eyes. "Yes, I do. I admit I didn't early in the war. I blamed God for most of my problems and I couldn't see how he could let Jennison's Jayhawkers come and pay us a call like they done. I figured he coulda stopped it somehow. The war has helped me see the light. I've seen many men die, and I killed a lot of them too. When a battle starts only a fool wouldn't stop to pray. I've seen miracles on the field of battle I could only say were heaven-sent. You pray for me, and I'll have just that much better chance of comin' home to you."

His words seemed to comfort her and she smiled up at him. "I'll pray for you, Billy, and when the war is over I'll be waiting for you, if you want me."

He felt a joy that nearly overpowered him as he pressed her to him again. "You're the only thing I've got to live for, Liz. My family is gone, and all my hopes and plans are with you. When I know you want me, I've got a reason to survive and a purpose to my life."

He kissed her again and he felt her eagerly respond. Her tongue pressed against his and a shiver of delight ran through him. He wanted her badly, but she was a lady, and as such he respected her. No matter how much he wanted to make love to her, he would wait until they could be properly married. He wanted nothing to taint their relationship in any respect. Reluctantly, he pushed her to arm's length. "I promised you another dance."

She looked at him and her expression clearly showed her confusion. "Don't you want me, Billy?"

"More than anything in the world, but we should wait until we're married."

"I don't care, Billy. I love you with all my heart and you are all that matters. I would just die if something should happen to you and we never made love. I've dreamed about it so often and wondered how it would be to lie with the man I love. Aren't you curious? Are you sure you won't slip away with me and make love to me tonight?"

Billy swallowed hard and grimaced as if in pain. Never in his life had he wanted anything more than he wanted her now, his breathing growing ragged and rapid. He could almost picture her naked loveliness spread out in the moonlight eager for his attention. How often had he dreamed of such an opportunity?

Still, he had never made love to a woman and he wasn't exactly sure how he was supposed to go about it. The problems of his youth and inexperience plagued him. He worried about what would happen if they should be discovered, and how embarrassing it would be if she became pregnant before they were married.

No, despite how much he lusted to explore the wonders of love he would not be seduced by his desires. He loved this Missouri belle and he would show her the proper respect and the war be damned. "I love you, Liz, but I want our first time to be special. I know it sounds stupid and old fashioned, but I want to wait for our wedding day."

Elizabeth hugged him tightly and gave him a tender kiss before she said, "All right, Billy, we'll wait. And I promise you I'll give you a night you'll never forget." She turned, took his hand, and led him back toward the mansion and the dance floor.

On the twenty-third of March, newly promoted General Jo Shelby marched his brigade through Camden toward

Princeton. It would be their duty to guard the crossings along the Saline River and all roads leading to Camden.

The last night was a melancholy affair for the Kimbroughs as they said their final good-byes to their loved ones. Each knew their time together would be short, but the time had passed by much too swiftly. All wondered how many would still be alive when next they met.

The men were reluctant to leave the ladies and pleasures of Camden behind but were tired of the monotonous camp along the Ouachita. After a winter of endless training, drilling, and dress parades, they were eager to get on with bringing the war to a conclusion.

So it was with mixed emotions that the columns of Jo Shelby's Iron Brigade rode four abreast through the streets of Camden. The uniforms were patched and cleaned to their best appearance. The weapons glistened in the sun and the leather saddles, bridles, belts, and scabbards were polished to a shine. The brigade looked to be as solid and battle-hardened as any cavalry ever seen in the West. The citizens of Camden lined the streets to watch the army pass in revue.

As Jessie's company passed to the stirring sounds of the brass band of General Marmaduke's personal headquarters he spotted Katlin holding his son in the crowd along the street. He fought to retain his military bearing as he sat ramrod stiff in his saddle, but his heart betrayed him. He turned his head and took one last, longing glance at his wife as the company paraded by. He bit his lip and clenched his teeth tightly to keep from crying. Tears streaked down his sullen cheeks anyway as he swore under his breath, "God damn this stinkin' war!" He would have given anything in that moment to be with his wife and son and have the war at an end.

Jessie knew a soldier's duty, and despite his emotions he knew what he must do, no matter the hurt. Winter was over and a brand new spring of fire and fury awaited those blind enough to face war and spit in its eye.

12

To the Victor Go the Spoils

Ross Kimbrough stood in the deep shadows of a pine at the crest of the hill. From his high position overlooking the winding valley below, he watched the road for movement. As a cool breeze moaned softly through the boughs of pine and laurel scattered about him, Ross involuntarily shivered against the cool air. Though he felt the cold in the wind, he knew spring was on its way by the fragrance of new life budding on the trees and borne on the wind. He sniffed deeply of the pleasant aroma as his eyes scanned the road below in the valley.

It had been several days since he had said good-bye to Valissa and his family, and those thoughts intruded upon him. The parting had been bittersweet, for none could know who of them would live to meet again. He felt a hollowness in the pit of his stomach, as if something vital had been snatched away. Leaving the lovely Val behind was one of the hardest things he had ever done. As he rode mile after mile away from her, his distress was increased. He was desperately in love and there was no escaping it.

Ross knew the contents of General Shelby's orders when the brigade marched through Camden. As they rode through town to the martial sounds of General Marmaduke's brass band and the cheers of the people, Ross already knew the depth of the challenges facing them. Union general Steele was planning a campaign against Southern Arkansas, and Shelby's brigade was to be the first line of defense. It would be one patrol after another as they sought to fight and delay Steele's progress.

Their first order of business would be to determine when and where the campaign would begin. His best guess was that Camden lay squarely in the middle of Steele's planned route. The thought sent chills down Ross's spine—he thought about the possible danger looming on the horizon for his family and the citizens of Camden. As the brigade trailed out of town, he hoped fervently the women would heed his words and leave for the safety of Texas.

Jo Shelby led his men to the banks of the Saline and posted them near Princeton, Arkansas. From Princeton he sent patrols and scouts to look for enemy movement along the roads leading south from Little Rock. Today, Ross was leading one of those patrols.

A glint of sunshine and movement along the road tore Ross from his thoughts and brought his attention back to the present. "Sergeant Starke, bring me the field glasses!"

"Yes sir!" the wiry little scout responded as he reached into the saddle wallet and extracted the binocular case. He left the horses held by Bill Corbin and moved up to the crest. He stepped briskly until he reached Captain Kimbrough. "Here ya go, Capt'n," said Jonas Starke as he handed the field glasses to Ross.

Jonas squinted his eyes as he peered at the valley and the road below. "Hell, sir, what cha need field glasses for? I can see wagons from here without 'em."

Ross swung the binoculars on the wagons moving around a bend in the road. A couple of twists on the knobs and his view came sharply into focus. He studied the lead wagon and read the garishly painted red lettering on the canvas cover spread over the hoops: BEN HANKINS, SUT-LER. As Ross scanned the next wagon in line, he observed the driver. The man wore a brightly colored vest, a shirt with long white sleeves, and a bowler hat cocked on the side of his head; in the corner of his mouth the man held the butt of a well-chewed cigar. He noticed the Union cavalry escort and concluded the caravan and their provisions were on their way to pay a visit to local Federal regiments wintering in the area.

Ross replied, "I'm well aware they are wagons, Sergeant, but I want to know what kind of wagons and who owns them." He paused a moment to lower the glasses and look at his old comrade and friend, Jonas. "Looks like Union sutlers are headed our way."

A smile of delight quickly spread across the gaunt cheeks of the heavily whiskered sergeant. "Now that is good news, sir. Shall I tell the men?"

Ross pointed his finger farther down the valley, near their present position—from that location, his men would be hidden from the view of the sutlers and their escorts. A turn in the road would mask their movement to the unsuspecting wagon train. "I want the men positioned in the woods along the side of the road there."

Sergeant Starke nodded his acknowledgment of the order.

Ross bent down and with a stick sketched a rough drawing in the dirt. "Place thirty men to block the road here, Sergeant. When they make this bend, they'll be squarely in our trap."

"They won't even know what hit 'em, sir," Jonas said as he glanced up from the crudely drawn plan. Jonas stood, moved toward the waiting horses, and swung into his saddle. With a quick application of his spurs he moved down the back of the hill to the men waiting below.

Ross counted the sutler wagons and men winding their way unknowingly into his trap. He counted eleven wagons and a patrol of approximately seventy-five Union soldiers.

He knew there would be far fewer in a matter of minutes. Ross smiled to himself, thinking about the goodies possibly held in those wagons.

During their winter encampment along the Ouachita River Ross's men had been on a bland and repetitive diet. Good food was scarce, and his men had often dreamed of capturing a well-stocked sutler's wagon. Now eleven were rolling his way. He licked his lips in anticipation as he considered their good fortune.

When Ross reached his troops, the men were already in place. From the bushes he watched as the wagons rolled around the bend and moved steadily toward them. At his signal, his thirty men spurred out into the road and lined up in ranks of ten men, three lines deep. Ross nudged his horse forward until he was in front of his men. The Yankee cavalry accompanying the sutlers reined in their horses, surprised by the Rebels spilling onto the road before them. A few near the front of the column tried to bring their carbines to bear while their horses pranced, danced, and skittered. A young lieutenant shouted a warning to the lead wagon, which halted in the middle of the road.

Ross had selected this ambush site carefully. Where the wagons were now halted, one side dropped away down steep and rocky banks to a stream. On the other side, thick trees lined the road making it impossible to turn the wagons around. Ross smiled as he watched the confusion. The lead wagon tried to turn but as the team jammed against the edge of the narrow road, they could go no farther. The other wagons hopelessly stacked up behind, with no place to go.

Puffs of smoke blossomed from the barrels of the Yankee carbines in a ragged volley. Most of the shots went high, but Ross felt one tug at his sleeve as it tore through his jacket, somehow miraculously missing his arm. One cavalry mount two horses away from Ross dropped in his tracks, hit in the head by Union fire. The rider uttered a curse as his mount went down like a ton of bricks and threw him under the prancing feet of the neighboring horse. The horse, nervous from this sudden burden rolling under his feet, let loose a shrill whinny. As calm as if his men were on parade, Ross ordered, "Forward at a walk, ho!" The men followed in perfect order, their revolvers held at the ready. When the soldiers had cleared the downed horse, the man in the rank behind filled the empty slot.

Ahead, the Union soldiers were beginning to panic; a few were dismounting and struggling to reload. The gap narrowed until fewer than thirty yards separated the Confederates from the confused Union troopers. "Front rank, fire!" shouted Ross. With a sound like a string of fire-crackers, the pistol shots rang down the line as his men responded.

The driver on the lead wagon clutched at his chest before pitching forward onto his team of horses. The team, in their panic, bolted forward until the wagon rolled against them. Trapped by their forward surge and inertia, the horses tumbled down the embankment, taking the wagon with them. Ross watched in despair as the wagon tumbled, spilling its cargo and rolling over the helpless team on its wild descent, throwing the animals about as if they were no more than toys.

Union saddles were emptied by the first volley, and other soldiers ran for cover amid the Rebel barrage. Ross turned his attention to the next wagon in line. A gray-bearded man with a prominent paunch threw his hands in the air and shouted, "Don't shoot! I surrender." The Union troopers who were still standing looked shaken and glanced nervously over their shoulders looking for a route of retreat.

The Rebel charge moved forward as Ross shouted, "Forward at a trot, ho. Fire at will!" The men responded as they spurred their horses to a trot. All around him the constant popping of pistols rang in his ears, and powder smoke stung his eyes.

Then the woods beside the Union wagons exploded in a

rolling barrage. Powder smoke, dark gray and dense, boiled from the woods like a deadly fog as Union drivers and troopers fell as though cut down by a giant scythe. Rebel yells filled the air as Southern troopers hidden in the woods opened up with flanking fire on the unsuspecting wagon train.

In a matter of seconds all resistance was shattered, and those troopers still standing or mounted dropped their weapons and surrendered. A few at the rear of the train abandoned their comrades and bolted. The pell-mell gallop of their hasty retreat left only clouds of dust lingering along the road.

Ross turned his attention to his whooping and hollering men, organizing the roundup of the Union prisoners and posting a guard over them. His losses were light, with only one man and two horses killed and one horse wounded. A lone shot echoed sharply across the valley as the injured animal was destroyed. Ross wondered why he felt worse about killing a loyal steed than he did about the loss of human life scattered across the rutted road.

They had captured ten stout wagons, seventeen prisoners, and twenty-nine cavalry mounts courtesy of good old Uncle Sam. He counted nearly thirty bodies in Union blue, lying like so many busted rag dolls. Already his men were searching the bodies and removing the canteens, haversacks, weapons, ammo, and cap boxes from the Union dead.

Jonas bent over a burly Yankee body wearing sergeant stripes. As he dug through the pockets he pulled out a worn deck of cards and a thick roll of Union greenbacks. "Will ya look at this, Capt'n, looks like this one was lucky at cards." Out of the next pocket onto the hard-packed dirt beside the body rolled a pair of dice, landing with seven showing. Jonas laughed as he pointed at the pair. "Good Lord, the sum-bitch can roll sevens even when he's dead."

Ross swung out of his saddle and studied the dead man. The dead man's mouth hung open, and his eyes stared vacant and unseeing. "Appears to me his luck ran out, Jonas." On a hunch, Ross bent down and picked up the pair of dice from the dirt. He hurled them against the ground and they bounced off the dead man's leg before spinning and settling to a stop. Again seven appeared on the dice. Ross smiled knowingly. "The dice are loaded. Our friend here wasn't above cheating his friends out of their money. No wonder he had such a large wad of bills."

Jonas smiled as he scooped up the dice and studied them closely for a moment before he slipped them into his pocket. He shook his head in amazement. "I'll be damned!"

"You'll be more than that if I see you trying to use those loaded dice around camp."

Jonas tried his best to look as if his feelings were hurt. "Come on, Capt'n, you don't think I'd try to cheat my friends, do ya?"

Ross smiled. "I've seen the best of men do worse for a chance at money. Give them here, Jonas."

"Ah, Capt'n, why do ya have to be such a prude? I could make a killin' back at camp with these here dice," he pleaded. Reluctantly, he dug them out of his pocket and handed them to Ross.

"You can keep the money, Jonas, but not these." Ross hurled the dice as hard as he could toward the stream. Jonas grimaced as the dice disappeared under the swift current. "Ah, Capt'n, you can be a hard man at times."

Near the closest wagon, Rube Anderson was removing the shoes from a dead Yank. Disappointment flickered across his face as he realized the shoes were the wrong size. He shrugged his shoulders and pitched them into the wagon, then proceeded to the next body.

Ross watched as Rube spit an amber stream of tobacco juice into the dusty road and continued the ritual. This time his face broke into an excited smile. He shucked off his worn-out shoes, the sole of one hanging loose and a hole through the sole of the other. He replaced them with the shoes taken from the dead soldier. His smile grew even wider as he tried them out with a few tentative steps. He let loose a whoop of joy and shouted, "Danged if they don't fit. Darn near new shoes and they're already broken in."

Ross smiled to himself as he walked down the line. His men were busily engaged in examining the cargo in each wagon and calculating their take. Terrell Fletcher leaned out over the tailgate of a wagon and motioned for Ross, who quickened his pace and approached the young soldier. "We've struck it rich, Captain! There's nineteen boxes of first-class cognac in here."

Ross Kimbrough's eyes widened upon hearing those words. He felt his heart skip a beat—fine French brandy. His mouth almost watered in anticipation. "Are you sure, Fletch?"

"Yes sir, I've already opened a box and it's the real thing, Captain. Look for yourself, sir." Fletch handed him a bottle of cognac, and Ross studied it carefully. It seemed such a shame to have to turn this over to headquarters, but he promised himself a bottle or two before they gave up those boxes. He handed the bottle back to Fletch.

"Keep the others out of this wagon. I don't want anyone touching this liquor. All we need is to have the men sloppy drunk while we're still behind enemy lines. Do I make myself clear, Fletch?"

"Yes sir, perfectly clear, Captain. I'll drive this wagon and guard it personally, sir." He hesitated for just a moment. "Capt'n is there any chance I can have a bottle when we reach camp, seeing as how I discovered it?"

"You keep the others out of the cognac, and a bottle is yours, Fletch."

Terrell Fletcher smiled brightly as he slid the bottle back into the box and hammered the lid closed with the butt of his revolver. "Then consider it done, Captain. I'll guard this here wagon with my life."

"I'm sure you will, Fletch, I'm sure you will," Ross said as he walked toward the next wagon. Ross stopped at each and made the same inquiry: "What's inside?" He was pleased by the answers he received. The wagons were well-stocked with all the delicacies a soldier might desire—candy, tobacco, coffee, eggs, maple syrup, molasses, sugar, flour, cornmeal, stationery, canned fruit, tinned sardines, salted pork, bottles of fine bourbon, sweet potatoes. Nearly anything that might pry a soldier loose from his cash was safely packed in the wagons. Now it all belonged to the brigade.

Ross sent a few of his men down the embankment to put the last of the wrecked wagon's team out of their misery and salvage what they could from the wagon's remains. Before an hour had passed the wagons were on the road again, only this time under new ownership.

When they reached brigade headquarters at Princeton, Captain Ross Kimbrough reported to his commanding officer, General Jo Shelby. When Ross completed his report and listed the captured supplies, he stared into the jubilant face of his commander. One question lingered in the captain's mind and he knew he must ask. "Sir, are we sending the wagons and their supplies back to headquarters?"

Jo Shelby let an amused smile cross his face as he stroked his beard thoughtfully. "Do you think we should, Captain?"

Ross drew himself to a tighter stance before responding, "No, sir! The men fought hard to capture these wagons, and they deserve a share of the spoils." Ross studied Jo Shelby carefully, wondering how his commander would respond to his bold declaration.

Jo Shelby leaned forward and said, "I can't agree with you more, Captain. Distribute the food and supplies to our brigade—including the cognac—except, of course, to those still standing guard. Save their share for when they are off duty. In the morning send the prisoners, empty wagons, mules, and horses to Camden under guard. Make sure it isn't your men, Captain. I need them leading raiding parties for me."

Ross smiled joyously as he turned to go. Before he could exit the tent, the general said, "Oh, Captain Kimbrough, I want two dozen bottles of cognac sent back to

General Price at Camden by someone you can trust. Tell Old Pap they are a gift from me with my compliments. Will you see to it, Captain?"

"Yes sir, I'll send it with our courier carrying despatches to command headquarters. Is there anything else, sir?"

"Yes, Captain, have half a dozen bottles of that cognac delivered to me and pick out something special for officer's mess. I expect Billy, my manservant, will fix us a rare treat for supper tonight, and I want you to join me and my staff. Tell your men Captain Wilkerson crossed the Saline and captured eighteen Federals and two hundred prime, fat steers. They'll all have fresh beef to eat tonight with their other goodies."

"Yes sir! The men will be pleased. This will be like Christmas to them, maybe even better."

"Our soldiers have suffered, and there is much yet to come. They deserve to enjoy the fruits of their labor. To the victor goes the spoils, Captain. You are dismissed." Jo Shelby gave Ross a wink as the captain exited the house that served as temporary headquarters. As Ross walked away he felt a glow of satisfaction and contentment he hadn't felt since he had been with Valissa. Today was a good day, a very good day.

13

Riding Through the Swirling Mist

Ross galloped the heavily lathered Prince of Heaven through the streets of Princeton at breakneck speed. He rounded the last corner and slid the big black stallion to a halt in the loose gravel of the street, sending a shower of small stones skittering across the ground. Ross swung down and hastily handed the reins to a sentry standing duty in front of the house that served as General Jo Shelby's headquarters. "Corporal, see that my horse is walked, rubbed down proper, watered, and fed. If it isn't done right there'll be hell to pay when I lay my hands on you. Is that understood?"

One look into the intense eyes of Ross Kimbrough left little doubt to the sincerity of his words. The rail-thin soldier quickly replied, "Yes sir, I'll make sure your horse is properly cared for, Captain."

Ross gave his trusted mount a loving pat and flicked white, lathered foam from the horse's neck. It pained Ross to see the horse so winded and spent. He paused for a moment and listened to the animal fighting to drag fresh air into its lungs. He had nearly used up Prince of Heaven—a lesser horse would have died on the trail. Only the importance of the reports he carried for General Shelby could force him to take such a risk. The information he carried concerning the movements of the Union army demanded immediate action and with it could lie the future of the war west of the Mississippi.

Ross reluctantly turned away from his horse and trotted toward the door of the temporary headquarters. In short order he was ushered into the living room where General Shelby stood waiting for his report.

Without waiting for Shelby to speak, Ross said breathily, "General Steele is on the move, General. I have his exact numbers and location."

General Shelby stepped urgently toward a table that dominated the center of the room; on it were spread various maps of the area, with the best and largest map lying in the center. "Give me their position and numbers, Captain Kimbrough."

In two quick steps Ross stood beside his commanding officer. Ross bent over the map and stabbed his finger brusquely at the current location of the Union army. "They're here, sir." He pointed at the town of Rockport and the road leading southwest. Ross looked earnestly into the eyes of his commander. "My scouts and I counted thirteen thousand soldiers of all arms and forty-eight pieces of artillery crossing a pontoon bridge erected across the Ouachita River. They are marching down the Wire Road toward Arkadelphia."

Jo Shelby was quick to grasp the significance of this latest intelligence. "They've already moved past us. Now there is nothing between them and Southwestern Arkansas but Marmaduke and Fagan's cavalry brigades." General Shelby studied the map carefully and slid his finger along its surface. "We can move here and cross the brigade eight miles below Arkadelphia at this ford. Then we can strike the Wire Road and hit them from behind."

Ross looked surprised. "Pardon me, General, but we've

only got twelve hundred men in our brigade. How can we take on an army of thirteen thousand supported by strong artillery?"

General Shelby walked away from the table toward the fireplace. He stared into the flames as he spoke. "I received a dispatch from General Sterling Price while you were out trying to locate General Steele's army. Union general Nathaniel Banks is moving along the Red River with an army of thirty thousand men. He is accompanied by a strong fleet of Union ironclads and gunboats, led by Admiral David D. Porter. It looks like their immediate objective is to capture Shreveport."

Jo Shelby looked away from the dancing flames that licked at the burning log and turned to face Captain Kimbrough. "General Kirby Smith, our commander of the Trans-Mississippi region, has ordered General Price to send our army's infantry to aid General Richard Taylor's Rebel army in Louisiana. Our infantry is now marching toward Shreveport under the command of General Thomas H. Churchill to fight against Banks's Yankees. General Price is with generals Marmaduke and Fagan and their cavalry brigades in the vicinity of Camden. Our orders are to keep General Steele from linking up with General Banks's army in an attack on Shreveport."

"Excuse me, General, but if we sent our infantry off to Louisiana to fight Banks, how are we supposed to stop Steele's army?"

"General Price has retained our artillery and cavalry and we must do the best we can with what we have. I hope we can delay Steele's advance until we are reinforced. I'm sure you understand how important holding Shreveport is to the cause. If we don't stop them, all of Arkansas and Louisiana will be in Union hands, and Texas will be wide open for invasion." Shelby slammed his fist into the table. "We have no choice, we must do all we can to stop Steele from joining Banks's army in the attack." General Shelby cleared his dry throat with a hacking cough, and once the bout of coughing ceased, he leaned both hands heavily on the desk as he studied the maps.

"General Holmes has been replaced by General Sterling Price. Price now commands Arkansas and our brigade. This is the only good news I have received of late. You know how little faith I held in the abilities of Granny Holmes. I am confident General Price will respond quickly to our aid."

Ross Kimbrough was awestruck by the task facing them. Even with Marmaduke and Fagan's brigades he knew General Price would command an army of thirty-five-hundred men against an army of thirteen thousand. He knew they were in for the fight of their lives. "What do you want me to do, General?"

"Follow Steele's army. I need to know his exact position. I'll gather the brigade and march along this route." General Shelby pointed out the route on the map, indicating the ford below Arkadelphia and the Wire Road. "I intend to hit Steele's rear guard hard and keep attacking. With luck we will disrupt his advance and his supply lines. Keep me informed and Godspeed, Captain." Shelby left the table and walked toward a door leading to another room in the house. "Major Edwards, come here immediately!" As Ross slipped out of the house he saw General Shelby gathering his staff.

A full, blood-red moon rose at midnight, and by the light of the huge orb rising through the mists, Shelby's brigade marched in pursuit of Steele's army. Major Evan Stryker rode with Captain Thorp's regiment as they moved out. General Shelby wanted a staff officer to carry out his orders and keep him informed of what was happening at the front of the brigade.

Evan pulled his coat tight about him as he rode through the chilling mists rising from the dark, dank canebrakes. The thick growth of abundant plant life crowding the lowlands was wreathed in cottony layers of fog and mist, giving the area a surreal presence. Evan looked about him and watched as the men rode through the drifting patches of fog. In the eerie moonlight the riders at times appeared as ghosts passing through the fog-shrouded mist. He shivered, thinking how many of these men would soon die in the coming battles. Would they haunt these canebrakes for eternity, swathed in clouds of white mist as they were tonight? Fear crowded in on him as he faced the web of his fears and fought to pull his thoughts away from the macabre.

They reached the Ouachita long before daylight. The river, dark and dangerous-looking by the moonlight, ran rapid and deep. With no time for hesitation the lead companies plunged into the chilling waters.

As the waters splashed up on him and then closed about his legs, Evan sucked air in deeply. The frigid, early spring flows of the river surprised him—the cold was like a slap. Wide awake now, he was keenly aware of his discomfort as the waters drained away the heat from his body. Around him the plunging and thrashing of the horses threw an icy spray of water and mist into the air. The moonlight caught these droplets and illuminated them, and they glistened like little stars falling from the skies. He listened to the labored breathing of the horses and the splashing of the men and animals through the current, the low grunts and groans of the men as they felt the shock of the frigid running waters. Then they splashed ashore on the other side. The river had been crossed safely, but Evan realized that many men would get a good, icy bath tonight.

Beyond the river they reached the broad path of the Wire Road. The signs of a passing army were clear—the road was deeply rutted, cut and marked by hundreds of wagon and cannon wheels that had run before them. The dust began to rise and clung tenaciously to the wet clothing, coating the men in layers of dust-encrusted mud from their waists down to their feet.

Suddenly, out of the deep shadows along the Wire Road, Captain Ross Kimbrough and some of his scouts blocked the column. "Major Stryker, Captain Thorp, halt!" Ross shouted. As the column stopped in the road, Ross rode alongside the officers. "Good morning, gentlemen. It is good to see you. Around the bend you'll find an infantry brigade of Union soldiers protecting Steele's rear."

"Do they know we're coming?" asked Thorp.

"It doesn't appear they have a clue. Right now all they're concerned about is filling their canteens and getting a drink from a large spring. Their officers have them drinking by files."

"Major, do you want to take command?" Thorp asked Evan.

"No, Captain, you are in command of your regiment, I'm simply here to gather information and relay it to General Shelby." Evan turned to Ross. "Is there anything more I should pass along to the General?"

"Yes indeed, Major. There are two companies of Union cavalry still in the city of Arkadelphia. They think they are guarding Steele's rear, but by taking the ford you bypassed them. If Shelby sends men after them I think he can bag the lot."

"The general will be pleased to know this, Captain. Good work! Would you send one of your men to inform headquarters? I'd like to stay here with Thorp awhile longer so I can tell Jo how much resistance we will encounter here."

"No problem, Major." Ross rose in his stirrups and yelled over his shoulder. "Rube, ride to General Shelby and report." Without further delay, Rube Anderson galloped back down the halted column toward the rear.

Major Evan Stryker turned back to Captain Thorp. "It is your call, Captain."

"Thank you, Major." The fearless young captain grinned. Moments later he had his regiment ready for battle and aligned in ranks across the road. Major Stryker took his place on the end of the first row, while Captain Thorp and his color guard rode before the regiment. Side by side, the regiment rode forward with grim determination. As they rounded the bend, Evan saw blue-uniformed shapes moving in the moonlight. The Yankee soldiers remained unprepared, waiting their turn at the spring.

With wild Rebel yells piercing the night, Captain Thorp led the charge in one mad dash down the Wire Road. The order to fire came above the roar of galloping hooves striking the hard-packed earth and the shrieking screams echoing in Evan's ears. They were running over them now, and the guns roared and boomed in the night, their flames searing and flashing in the moonlit gloom. It all became a swirling montage, as Evan glimpsed men shot out of the saddle, frightened faces exploding into bloody gore before his eyes.

The Union soldiers bolted and ran after firing one ragged volley at the charging Rebels. The Confederate cavalry rode the men down, killing them at point-blank range as they dashed down the road or stumbled through the brush that bordered it.

Here and there, a soldier stood and thrusted his bayonet at the nearest charging cavalryman. Thorp's sword flashed in the moonlight as the blade cut wickedly, slicing down on running soldiers. The Rebels broke through the scattered enemy line as the Union soldiers ran in utter rout away from the point of attack.

As the pursuing soldiers rode into a clearing, the sight that greeted them caused the attack to falter. Less than a hundred yards away and drawn up into battle ranks were fresh Union infantry, bayonets gleaming in the moonlight. Captain Thorp urged on the milling Rebels who stalled before the menacing Union ranks. He circled his sword over his head and stood tall in his stirrups, shouting above the momentary lull. "Forward, men, for the glory of Missouri!" He charged with his color guard on his heels.

The Rebel lines were no longer organized; the charge and chase along the road undid the unit's formation, until the regiment was a mob of armed and angry men. They followed Captain Thorp in a mad dash against the deadly, waiting Union line wherever they could find a space to put a horse.

The Union line did not waver, but stood calmly, guns
pointed and ready to fire at the mass of charging Rebels.
Then, as if they were on the field simply practicing a drill,
they fired as one at the Rebel mob approaching. A curtain
of flame danced from their muzzles and lit the night with
unnatural angry red flames followed by clouds of expended black powder smoke.

Captain Thorp was struck several times; his horse stumbled as minié balls tore through its flesh. When the two
stopped tumbling in the moonlit dust Thorp's dead horse
pinned the wounded captain to the ground. The front rank
disappeared as though it had melted into the ground. Soldiers catapulted from their empty saddles, struck down by
the enemy fire. Horses pitched and rolled, dying on their
feet, their momentum hurling them forward. Evan watched
in fascination as the color bearer slid from his saddle. The
flagstaff landed on the butt of the pole and stood on its
own for a moment before it began to flutter forward toward the ground. Another trooper, seeing the regimental
battle flag struck down, rode up, leaned low in the saddle,
and scooped up the staff before it could touch the ground.
He waved the banner valiantly as the remaining troopers
tried desperately to untangle themselves from the deadly
ruin of their scattered comrades. Before they could reorganize, the second rank of Union infantry stepped forward
and fired while the first rank reloaded.

The second deadly wave of leaden hail ripped through
the disorganized ranks, and the Rebels wavered. During
the Union infantry's two deadly barrages, Evan Stryker
had somehow miraculously remained untouched. He
pulled his horse to a halt and stepped down to check on
Captain Thorp, but the brave young captain was beyond
help. Evan's horse skittered sideways, frightened by the
turmoil swirling about him. His eyes rolled white and
frightened in the night as Evan fought to swing back into
the saddle.

Already the Rebels were beginning to retreat toward the
protection of the woods behind them. Evan rode toward

the trees, fearing at any moment that a minié ball would come crashing into his back. The whine of bullets whirling past his head made him duck, though he knew that in the time it took him to move it would have been too late. The bullets tore past him and slapped into the trees beyond. Moments later, as he rode into the relative safety of the trees, Evan glanced over his shoulder and counted nearly thirty Confederate bodies and as many horses lying before the enemy line.

After Major Stryker made his report, General Shelby rode forward and immediately assessed the situation. He spread the brigade into battle line as the Union soldiers pulled back into the protection of the woods. Shelby ordered his men forward, and they charged. Elliott's regiment took the worst of it, attacking across an open field. Three times they tried and three times they were bloodily repulsed.

Collins's battery unlimbered on the field and began lacing the woods with their deadly projectiles. General Shelby rode forward, urging his men on and shouting, "My gallant men, it will not do! Don't show your back to the enemy! Charge them once more! Follow me!" The reorganized ranks moved forward behind their beloved general—where he would lead they would follow, even through the very gates of hell.

The regiment rode forward at a gallop, rapidly eating up the distance as they closed in on the enemy lying in wait in the woods. Shelby's column remained tightly massed, and as dawn broke on the horizon, Shelby's charge hit the center of the Union line. Major Stryker saw the approaching woods and the Union soldiers lurking in the brush like deadly blue ghosts. Like a ragged line of firecrackers the Union line erupted in flame, again hurling their deadly, leaden missiles against the charge. Somehow, the general made it through; the Union fire was not as accurate as before.

Shelby ordered his men to fire, and their revolvers opened with terrible effect on the Union line. Shelby waved his sword, urging his men forward, and on they came, this time overrunning the center of the line. Horses fell, bayoneted through the chest by crouching Union infantry, while muzzle blasts from their riders blackened faces and punched holes through the broken bodies of the Union infantry. The line wavered and broke against the surging Rebel tide. Blue-coated Union soldiers threw down their guns and ran.

Shelby led his men through the gap and circled back against the line from the rear. Assaulted by Rebels from both sides, the line broke and withdrew in haste as Shelby reorganized his command and gathered prisoners. Shelby had his dead and wounded collected and sent to the rear. Evan Stryker rode with the general as he sought out Captain Williams, still mounted on his gray steed. "I can't compliment an officer more pointedly than by assigning him to a post of imminent danger," General Shelby said. "Take command of the advance so nobly led by Captain Thorp, and let me see you do good work today." Captain Williams drew himself up proudly and returned the general's salute. He rode off to take charge of the advance.

The Union brigade led by General Rice, though in full retreat, retained its organization. A short distance down the road he received reinforcements from another brigade and a six-gun battery. He set up a strong defensive line in the heavy woods and waited for Shelby's next move.

Major Stryker studied this new Union line through his field glasses, scanning the two Union brigades backed by the six-gun battery standing in battle line. Evan swallowed hard and felt fear clutch his throat as he fought to remain calm. Glancing at the early morning sky, he watched the steadily rising sun and wondered if he would live to see the sunset.

14

The Fires of Hell

Major Evan Stryker stayed close as General Shelby examined the new enemy position. From their observation point they had a clear panorama of the Union lines. The remnants of the first brigade, driven from the field in disarray in the skirmish fought in the dawn's prelight, rallied around a second Union brigade drawn up in a battle line. At the center stood a splendid six-gun battery, unlimbered and cleared for action. Shelby's brigade was reforming its own line of battle parallel to the enemy line.

Major Stryker panned his field glasses across the intervening distance and studied the strong enemy position. Stryker understood his commander and knew what to expect. The first skirmish had only begun the day, and Shelby would not allow this new barrier to stall him for long. The general would attack despite facing veteran infantry troops in strong positions. Being outnumbered had never discouraged Fightin' Jo Shelby, and today would be no different.

Shelby lowered his field glasses and pointed to a hill

along their lines. "Major Stryker, inform Captain Collins to advance his battery to that hill and open on the enemy artillery as soon as he is ready. I want the Yankee battery silenced and driven from the field. It is the backbone of their defense, and we'll break them if we can take them out of the fight." He gave a brisk salute to Major Stryker. "Hustle, Major, I want to attack their line within the hour."

Evan returned the salute and ran to his horse. In seconds he was threading his way through the trees and heading north on the Wire Road in search of Collins's battery. He made less than half a mile before the battery came clattering into view.

Major Stryker reined in his horse as he drew alongside Captain Collins. "Captain, I have orders for you from General Shelby. He wants you to follow me and place your battery on a site he has selected. Then, by the force of your guns, you are to drive the enemy artillery from the field."

Captain Richard A. Collins cracked a wry grin. "Lead the way, Major, and we'll get to work."

In twenty minutes Collins's battery reached the hill. Within thirty minutes, the battery was cleared and ready for action.

Calvin Kimbrough stood to his gun and sighted at the enemy artillery across the way. When Collins's battery reached the hill, the enemy artillery began shelling. So far, the Union battery fire was ineffective; the shells fell short or whined harmlessly over their heads to explode far behind the lines.

As Calvin squinted along the sight, a great gout of dirt erupted twenty feet in front of his cannon. Clods rained down on him like hail, peppering and stinging his back and shoulders. His vision was temporarily dimmed by the drifting cloud of dust; it momentarily choked away his air, and he cursed low under his breath at the damned Yankees firing away at him. In anger he purposely aimed his piece on an exposed caisson placed too close to the enemy artillery. Satisfied, he stood away from the piece. "Number two ready to fire, sir," he yelled.

"Collins's Battery, fire at will!" shouted Dick Collins, and the four Rebel artillery pieces roared as if they were one. The first volley from Collins's battery came close but did little damage. Calvin saw his first shot ricochet off a mound a short distance in front of the enemy battery and skip through without hitting anything before it exploded in the woods. The other crews fared little better. Calvin yelled at his ammo carrier to cut the fuse shorter on the next shell. As Calvin aimed his second shot, he saw smoke billowing from the woods beyond the battery. Apparently the shell explosion had set off a fire in the dry timber behind the enemy battery.

Calvin again aimed for the caisson. He watched as flame jetted ten feet from his cannon and the recoil rocked the big gun back. The concussion from the blast rang in his ears as he watched the shell arc in and hit the targeted caisson. The resulting explosion sent a concussion wave he could feel across the field. Red-hot flame exploded into a fireball hurling pieces of the caisson like deadly shrapnel in every direction, while a dark plume of smoke roiled upward. Shells began cooking off in the flames, hurling case shot and deadly missiles through the Union battery, while explosive shells shot off like fireworks into the sky and woods around the Union position.

When the smoke and confusion cleared, half the enemy battery crew was dead or wounded. The artillery piece nearest the caisson canted its barrel skyward at an awkward angle, and one wheel was splintered and gone. Not a man still stood near the destroyed gun. A whoop of joy went up from Collins's battery as they studied the result. The remainder of Collins's men continued to fire on the enemy, not stopping to enjoy the moment but anxious to score their own successes.

With no more than twelve rounds fired by their own battery, the Rebs watched what remained of the Union artillery battery crews bring up their horse teams. Frantically

they hauled away the remaining cannons as they fled from
the accurate fire. By now flame and smoke rolled from the
woods behind the enemy, and fires burned in smoky
patches between the lines.

Calvin directed a last shot at the fleeing battery. The
shell buried itself·in the ground near the Union battery and
showered them with dirt, but didn't explode. Shouts came
from the battery officers to redirect their fire on enemy
troop positions. Calvin bent over his sight, aimed at a
group of Union cavalry still mounted on the ridge, and
sent a shell hurling in their direction. The shot screamed
over their heads and exploded in the woods. Showers of
debris rained down, and great branches fell from high in
the tree tops. Calvin smiled and relaxed a little. With the
enemy battery driven from the field, his danger was lessened for the time being.

Jessie Kimbrough huddled behind the protection of a
thick oak as he peered cautiously around to study the battlefield. The rest of his company were in line beside him,
hiding in the best cover each could locate. To the rear and
below the ridge fifty yards behind them, the horse holders
held four horses apiece safe from enemy fire. Jessie secretly wished he were a horse holder crouched in relative
safety.

The day had begun auspiciously enough for Jessie's regiment. Captain Gilbert Thomas had led them on a mad
dash to capture Arkadelphia from the south. The Union
rear guard wasn't prepared for an attack from this
direction—they assumed they were still protecting the rear
of Steele's army.

Shelby's order to use the ford below Arkadelphia had
worked perfectly, cutting off unsuspecting troops from the
main body. Two full companies of cavalry and officers
surrendered with hardly a fight. Still, it took time to strip
the soldiers of their weapons and mounts and march them
to those assigned guard duty. This brought the regiment up
late to this engagement. Since they were the last to go in

line, they were ordered to the far left to overlap the Union's far right.

Jessie let his eyes scan the Rebel line. The men hunkered down behind their meager protection with grim determination, waiting for the orders that would surely come. Jessie checked his pistol loads and made sure he was ready for action. Then he heard Gilbert Thomas as he shouted above the roar of battle, "On your feet, men! Form ranks!" Jessie stepped nervously from behind the protection of the tree and joined his friends as the regimental colors advanced. Gilbert stood unafraid before his men as if he were bulletproof.

Jessie ducked at the whirring sound, like a mad bumblebee, as a minié ball sliced the air near him. It thudded into the trunk of the tree he had been hiding behind only minutes earlier. All down the line the men formed ranks, shoulder to shoulder, as if on parade. Here and there a Yankee bullet found its mark. The Confederate soldier, when struck, would crumple from the wound or fall backward from the force of the blow.

After many battles the soldiers knew what they must do. Those who fell were left where they lay and the wounded ignored. There wasn't a man to spare to take care of the fallen, who were left to the care of bandsmen, teamsters, and medical aids pressed into retrieving the wounded.

The bugles sounded the attack and the line surged forward. As they crossed the open distance between the lines, Jessie struggled to stay in step, occasionally having to pass around a tree. In front of them the orange flames of a burning patch of grass licked at the nearest tree. Acrid smoke twisted and spiraled from the ragged flames, stinging his eyes. The line parted and the men grouped up to pass around the blaze and reform on the other side. Jessie felt the searing heat of the little inferno hot on his cheeks as he passed. They were coming closer to the enemy lines now and Jessie observed that the right flank of the opposing line dangled tantalizingly in front of them. The regiment would flank the end of the Union line and, if not stopped, would sweep down the enemy line, rolling it up before them with enfilading fire. If they were successful, the entire Union line would collapse.

The enemy fire increased, and here and there a man fell from the ranks as the advance moved relentlessly forward. The Union line would soon be in range of the cavalry's pistols and then they would rake the line at close range with their superior firepower. A revolver in both hands, Jessie tightened his jaw and resolutely marched on. He saw the enemy soldiers crouching in their cover as wildfires burned just behind the Union lines. They were now so close he could make out the individual features of each man and the powder stains on each blackened face.

He spotted the Union regimental battle flag of the Ninth Wisconsin Infantry waving defiantly in the wind and framed by the flaming orange fires that flared behind it. They stood, weapons in hand, against a backdrop of swirling and dancing sheets of uncontrolled flame on the wind. The blinding smoke wreathed and wrapped its gray tendrils about the men amid a shower of falling red-hot cinders and flying sparks drifting from the dry woods blazing hot behind them. Jessie wondered if they had somehow passed through some unseen portal to the very gates of hell. Was Lucifer himself directing these devils to oppose them?

The German immigrant soldiers were shouting at one another in their native tongue, adding to the mounting confusion among the determined Rebel ranks. The unfamiliar words sounded guttural, unnatural in these surroundings. The Union flag bearer urged his fellow soldiers to make a stand while his color guard closed in to protect the silken banner.

Jessie stopped, leveled his pistol, and aimed carefully. When he squeezed the trigger he saw the sergeant boldly waving the regimental flag over his head before hesitating and clutching the silken banner to his chest. Red blood stained the banner as the soldier's knees buckled and gave way. Another Union soldier lifted the fallen flag ripped from the fingers of the dying sergeant.

Jessie felt a scream of rage and pent-up fear rip from his throat. It drifted harmlessly away on the winds, lost in the madness of the raging battle. The constant firing of weapons popped and clattered around him.

Jessie leaped forward, his guns blazing in both hands at point-blank range. He felt the recoil in his hands, thumbed the hammers back automatically, and squeezed off the next round. He continued as though he were a machine, firing at each soldier until he went down. He swung on the next target and kept firing even after no Union soldiers remained to face his blazing guns. He stood there in a stupor, still clicking his hammers down on empty cylinders, his eyes glazed by the heat of battle.

The enemy soldiers were down or running. Pink Hawkins now held the captured silken banner and danced in glee amid the bodies of the dead Union soldiers. Those Yankees who survived the charge were on the run, dodging through the racing flames of the fires that raged a short distance behind the battle line. The Rebel soldiers chased them, fired by the adrenaline surging hot through their veins.

Captain Gilbert roughly laid a hand on Jessie's shoulder and was met by Jessie's vacant stare. "They're empty partner, and the enemy is gone. Are you gonna spend all day firing those spent weapons?"

Jessie looked down stupidly as if unable to comprehend that the guns were unloaded. The message slowly seeped through the dull haze that fogged his brain. The brutality and the danger of the charge had somehow temporarily unseated his reason. Amid the noise and swirl of battle he hadn't noticed the weapons had ceased to buck in his hands. He put the guns away and drew a fresh revolver before joining in the deadly chase after the fleeing enemy.

Near the center of the line, Major Evan Stryker accompanied Jo Shelby as the general rode along, urging the advancing line. Evan ducked his head involuntarily as he heard the whistle of exploding shells fired from Collins's battery.

The lines were closing within fifty yards and the Confederate line staggered under the heavy fire of the superior numbers of the enemy troops. The advancing line stalled and wavered in the open field. General Shelby cut through the line and yelled, "Follow me, men. Show the devils how we treat those who would destroy our homes! Onward for Missouri!" General Shelby vigorously waved a loaded revolver in the direction of the enemy to emphasize his point.

The Union line fired another volley, and Evan watched in horror as he saw his commanding general exposed in front of the enemy. He saw General Shelby reel in the saddle and watched as both of the general's saddle holsters fell free to the ground, shot away by enemy bullets. His soldiers rushed past Shelby at a run as they recklessly charged the enemy lines.

Evan rode to his commander's side. Jo Shelby, his thick, full, russet-colored beard streaked gray by powder smoke, stared in wonder at his arm while talking to himself. Shelby saw the sleeve was torn. A red welt raised by a passing musketball had caused him to reel in the saddle.

"Are you all right, General?" Major Stryker asked.

"I'm okay, Major, just a near miss." He looked down at his saddle and noticed his holsters were gone. How the bullets that shot them away had missed him was an unexplained miracle. As the two officers glanced forward to observe the progress of the attack, Evan heard the general's horse let loose a hoarse groan as blood spayed from a fresh wound ripped into its throat. The horse pitched on its side, the spurting blood coating Evan's face. The general rolled from the dying sorrel as the animal crumpled to the ground, legs thrashing wildly in pain.

Evan wiped at the hot, sticky blood clinging to his face and felt his hat plucked from his head by a passing bullet. He wheeled his dancing horse around Shelby's dying mount and reined in next to General Shelby. The commander rose to his feet only to stagger suddenly and clutch at his right thigh.

"Damn!" Jo Shelby yelled as he studied the wound in his leg. In an instant Evan was out of the saddle and kneeling next to his general. He inserted two fingers into the torn pant leg and gave it a little rip. Exposed by the tear was an angry red line oozing droplets of blood from a bullet graze across the top of Shelby's thigh. When Evan saw the wound was minor he breathed a low sigh of relief. "It's only a minor wound, General. Sir, allow me to remove you from the field. You make too good a target, and our army needs your leadership. We can't afford to lose you."

"Nonsense, Major, my men face this danger without fear. How can I do less? I will stay until we know the day is won."

With the right of the Union line in disarray and the Ninth Wisconsin on the run for the second time today, the rest of the enemy line was exposed. Already lacking their artillery support, the line dissolved in hasty retreat. The Yankees ran through the heavily burning woods with the Rebel soldiers in close pursuit. The Union rear guard, smashed by this brutal attack and savaged by raging fires roaring out of control, raced toward the main body of Steele's army.

In places the wildfires were so hot that the Rebel soldiers had to maneuver toward their own lines to escape the heat. The fires weren't as bad in the center of the line, and the pursuit on the heels of the enemy continued.

As Billy Cahill raced down the hill in pursuit of the fleeing soldiers, gravity speeded his progress beyond his control. He slammed into a tree that had suddenly loomed up in his path; recoiling from the blow, he fell headfirst down the hill. The wind gushed out of him and the ground slammed into him with added fury as he slid down the ravine, vines and brush plucking at him. Finally he slid to a stop and fought to pull himself to a sitting position.

His chest ached from the fall, and he fought to suck

fresh air into his lungs. He coughed as he breathed in the smoke that swirled and collected in the bottom of the ravine. When his friends reached him, he was trying to regain a sense of his surroundings. Lieutenant William Gregg bent over him to check to see if he was all right. Once satisfied, the soldiers looked around them.

To their left they saw that the ravine widened. Near a pool of shallow water, severely wounded Union soldiers lay abandoned. Terrified, Billy saw that the racing flames were sweeping through the brush surrounding the enemy wounded. The men edged closer, but the heat of the flames made the Rebels shield their faces from the heat. Red, orange, and yellow flames seared and danced along the tree branches and flashed from bush to bush in the tender, winter-dry underbrush.

Billy watched in horror as a man stumbled toward him, clutching at a sucking, bloody chest wound and screaming at the top of his lungs. Dark clots of blood intermingled with fresh red blood oozing through the tortured soldier's fingers. Billy tore his eyes away from the awful wound and saw a more blood-curdling sight. The man's back was on fire and, as he stumbled toward Billy, his hair burst into flame. The fire spread to the sleeves of the doomed man's uniform. He slipped his hands from his chest and held his burning arms out, as if to clutch Billy in a final embrace.

The pitiful, tortured screams of the man's agony filled Billy's ears, and his eyes widened in horror. Billy stumbled backward, trying to avoid the fiery apparition approaching him. He felt his stomach sour as he watched the licking flames blacken the soldier's face as the skin scorched away and bubbled like some sort of hideous tar. The teeth, those horribly white teeth, screamed at him against the red of his gaping mouth and blackened skin. Billy fired and fired again.

The bullets struck the head of the flaming wreck of a man and hurled him backward, ending his misery as he sprawled on his back. The voracious flames continued to lick at the body as the fire spread to the chest. Billy turned away from the awful sight to see one just as lurid.

A man, his spine severed and paralyzed from the waist down, dragged himself on his belly toward the shallow water. His fingers clawed and tore at the earth as he struggled to get away from the racing flames. Although he was moving as swiftly as his tortured condition would allow, it wasn't fast enough. Flames exploded along his legs as the cloth caught fire. Still, the man inched forward.

As the flames spread to his back, the man for the first time felt the agony of his searing flesh. His screams of excruciating pain echoed through the ravine, filling Billy with horror. The man halted his forward motion and pleaded with one outstretched, pitiful hand, "Kill me, for the love of Christ, please kill me!"

Billy rushed to the man's aid, leveled his gun near the man's temple, and pulled the trigger, but the hammer fell on an empty cylinder. Billy tried twice more, but his gun clicked harmlessly on tattered, expended caps. The gun was empty, no matter how much he might wish it weren't, and he could not stop the suffering.

Billy felt a tug at his shoulder and found himself flung back from the burning man dying slowly before his eyes. Lieutenant William Gregg stepped forward, leveling his revolver between the man's eyes at point-blank range. His eyes met those of the burning soldier, and in those frightened, pain-wracked eyes he saw for just a splinter of a moment a shadow of blessed gratitude for ending his grisly anguish. William Gregg squeezed the trigger, and the gun bucked in his hand. Muzzle flash scorched the man's face, so close was the gun's muzzle to his head. The back of the soldier's head exploded, spraying fragments of blood, skull, and brain matter over the yellow flames dancing along the soldier's burning back.

Billy turned away and he felt the sour burn of stomach acid scalding his throat as he retched. The other wounded soldiers were beyond hope as they died in the searing flames. Billy felt himself pushed away from the ravine by

Bill Gregg as the Rebel soldiers began a mad dash to escape the onrushing flames. He ran on legs fueled by fear as if the devil himself were on his tail, as fast as his legs could carry him from the scorching heat and the suffocating fumes and smoke of the hastening blazes.

They didn't stop running until the fire was safely behind them. As Billy stopped near the middle of the clearing he bent over and rested his hands on his knees, sucking in lungfuls of fresh air. He looked back at the rising flames consuming the woods and watched the deadly pall of black-and-gray smoke coating the horizon with its broiling, deadly gases. In that moment Billy realized a single, solitary truth: Death had lost some of its mystery, for he had already visited hell.

15

Storm Front

The pursuit of the enemy continued until darkness ended the madness. Prisoners were brought in by the companies; the Union dead and wounded lay scattered through the woods for miles. Never before had Shelby's brigade fought so persistently and desperately for so long against infantry. It remained remarkable that cavalry had defeated veteran infantry on good, heavily timbered ground of the enemy's own choosing. The Confederates faced strong winds, a fierce firestorm, and a determined enemy, yet delivered victory. Nearly two hundred of Shelby's best men lay dead or wounded from the day's battle, but the Union army had fared far worse. More than four hundred Union prisoners captured on the field of battle were gathered to be sent to Rebel prisoner of war camps.

The fires caused by the battle still burned uncontrollably on the hillsides. The lurid flames lit the night with garish light, and the smoke obscured the line of march. The weary Rebel troopers, eager to escape the raging fires and anxious to exploit their advantage, continued their steady advance after Steele's army.

After putting the dangers of the burning fires behind them, Shelby bivouacked his men for the night. The general, though weary, was eager to resume his attack with the new dawn. During the night, Ross Kimbrough and his scouts brought in news of the remnants of Rice's shattered brigades. They had joined Steele's main column ten miles to the south. Local citizens, having tasted Federal occupation and finding it disagreeable, poured in throughout the night to offer food and to care for the wounded.

The army marched again at dawn and caught Steele's army waiting ten miles distant on good ground. The battle line was two miles long, with cavalry well in front and artillery scattered among the infantry across the crests of a series of hills. So determined had been Shelby's attack that Steele believed he faced an entire Confederate army instead of a single brigade of cavalry. Noticing that the Union cavalry were exposed and well in front of the enemy line, Shelby decided to attack. He ordered his troopers into formation on the plain to face the enemy cavalry. When all was in place, Shelby ordered the charge.

Jessie Kimbrough shifted his weight in the saddle atop Star's Pride to relieve the numbness in his hips. The day had been spent in the saddle, and the night had passed far too swiftly. Star's Pride noticed the shift in his master's weight as they stood in battle line and turned his head to look at Jessie. Jessie gave the big bay a loving pat on his neck and said softly, "Easy, Pride, I'm just a little saddle sore. I can't be any more tired than you."

Star's Pride seemed to understand and bent down to nibble on the tender new blades of spring grass trying to emerge through the dead growth left from winter. Jessie felt the old tightening in his belly as he looked around the valley. Before them, formed on the far side, were the ranks of the Union troopers. Battle was imminent and the old, familiar signs of nervousness were making themselves known. He felt his breathing increase and his palms begin to sweat.

Jessie tried to calm the fear growing inside him by studying the blue skies above him. To his dismay he noticed a dark, low line on the horizon to the west in glaring contrast to the nearly cloudless blue skies overhead. If the clouds moved this way they would surely bring a chilling spring rain and he didn't relish being soaked. It would surely affect the loads in his revolver—with wet powder he might as well throw his gun at the enemy for all the good it would do. The clouds were still far away, and he hoped they would slide around them, either to the north or south.

He tore his eyes from the threatening skyline and studied the valley. They were facing a grassy clearing which rose into a series of steep and precipitous hills to the south. Trees were thick along the side of the hills bordering the valley and on the south end beyond the Union cavalry. The trees led right up into the hills. Even from here he saw an occasional glint, a flash of light reflecting off a Union gun barrel or a bayonet belonging to the infantry situated on the crest of the hills. The enemy's location was strong, and the thought of attacking such a formidable position made Jessie shudder as if Death had touched him with an icy hand.

Star's Pride jerked his head up abruptly as Collins's battery opened the battle with the first booming salvo. Pride nervously sidestepped until he brushed the next horse in line as the cannons roared, the sound rolling and echoing across the valley. "Whoa. Easy, big fella," Jessie said as he tugged on the reins.

They stood in place for another fifteen minutes as Collins's battery softened the opposition. Then the bugle calls joined their melodic tunes to the sounds of war. Nearly a thousand seasoned Confederate troops moved forward at a walk to face the enemy. The walk increased to a trot and then to a gallop as the noise of four thousand hooves drumming against the earth sounded like rolling thunder

roaring through the valley. The cavalry rode onward, an ir-
repressible juggernaut rolling like an undulating wave
against a distant shore.

The sound surrounding Jessie nearly overwhelmed his
senses, as the pounding of the hooves, the creak of leather,
the jangle of bit chains, and rattling of sabers and canteens
mingled freely with the snorting and breathing of horses,
the shouts of men, and the snap and pop of regimental
banners flapping on the wind. All waited for gunfire to
join the noisy chorus. On they charged, low over their saddles, directly at the enemy. Jessie saw the puffs of muzzle
smoke before the sound reached his ears as the mounted
Union cavalry opened fire with their carbines. Most of the
shots went high as only a pitiful few Rebels fell from the
charge.

In front of his position, Jessie watched as the Union officers ordered their men to hold their positions. Knowing
they didn't have time to reload the single-shot weapons,
the Union officers urged their men to ready a saber charge.
Jessie smiled in grim satisfaction as he waited patiently for
the order to fire, as the Rebel line rolled on relentlessly.

Jessie knew his command, unlike the hapless Yankees,
was armed with pistols. Most carried several revolvers on
themselves or their saddles. At close range they would un-
leash a deadly barrage. A sword can't kill what it can't
touch and a pistol shot is pretty accurate under thirty
yards. The ability to fire a multitude of shots at very close
range without reloading against an enemy unable to reload
its single-shot weapons would prove to be devastating. He
wondered how long it would take for the Union army to
see how ineffective and outdated swords and single-shot
carbines were against revolvers.

The distance closed to within twenty-five yards when
the command to fire reached him. Like popcorn popping
in a pan over a hot fire, the pistol shots echoed down the
line. Great gaps opened in the Union line as saddles emptied and horses went down thrashing. The charge rolled
on, and Jessie fired three shots before he broke through.

He wheeled his horse back against what remained of the Union line, but it was already giving way under the attack. He dodged a flashing blade as a Yankee trooper sliced the air near him. He rammed Star's Pride into the Yankee horse, and the unbalanced trooper tumbled from the saddle and rolled under the flailing horse's hooves. Jessie spurred forward and fired into the back of another Yankee trooper, catapulting the hapless soldier from his saddle.

Almost as quick as it had begun, the attack was over. The Yankee cavalry, overrun and decimated by the concentrated revolver fire, broke and ran. The attack became a rout and the battle became a chase as the Rebels pursued the fleeing Yankees. The thought occurred to Jessie that it was amazingly easy to roll over the Yankee cavalry. He wished it were as simple against their veteran infantry.

The Rebels gathered, congratulating one another and whooping and hollering in celebration of their easy conquest. General Shelby allowed them little time to savor their victory. They still faced an overwhelming foe that outnumbered them more than twelve to one. He knew Steele would not stand idly by for long when he could easily flank and overwhelm this single brigade with his entire army.

The Rebels moved into the woods on the south end of the valley, dismounted, and waited for the enemy response. Steele sent forward a single brigade of infantry with a line of skirmishers deployed to the front.

Major Evan Stryker stood by General Shelby and watched the Yankee brigade advance. This move by Steele puzzled Evan. If the Yankees intended to do battle, why did they not wait in their superior positions for Shelby's attack? If they feared he wouldn't attack such a formidable position, then why on earth didn't Steele advance his entire army? The long line could easily outflank the extremely outnumbered Rebels and force them from the field with one concentrated attack as if they were nothing more than chaff on the wind.

Instead the Union troops advanced one brigade at a time.

Both men looked at each other with expressions of utter amazement. Slowly, a wide grin broke across Shelby's face as he realized his good fortune. If the Yankees weren't willing to press their advantage, then he was ready to exploit the error of their judgment. Instead of ordering a retreat, Shelby ordered the regiments to form a dismounted line of battle and deployed Collins's battery to await the attack. The Union's miscalculation of Shelby's resolve was about to explode in their faces. Seeing the exposed enemy flank on the single Union brigade, he ordered Captain Elliott to lead a regiment against the dangling line. As the order was dispatched, cold winds and strong gusts buffeted them as the squall line hit Shelby's brigade.

For the first time, Major Stryker took his eyes from the Union infantry skirmishers approaching through the trees. He let his eyes roam across the windswept skies above him. He saw a towering wall of cloud fast approaching out of the southwest, preceded by a line of gunmetal gray cumulus clouds scudding in so low it seemed that he could reach out and touch them. The clouds swirled and bubbled like a witch's cauldron gone mad, boiling up at a dizzying pace. Beyond the storm front the horizon was a deep, dark, ominous blue. He feared the thunderstorm rolling in from the west more than the Union soldiers he must face.

The enemy skirmish line was within shouting distance now, and began to pepper the Rebel line with musket fire. Evan heard the bullets whine through the trees and watched the leaves, severed by their passing, drift down to be whipped away on the rising wind. Evan held on to his hat tightly with one hand as he squeezed off his first pistol shots with the other.

The firing increased in intensity down the line until the noisy din of battle echoed across the valley. The Confederates eased ahead and drove the skirmish line back onto the advancing brigade. He heard Collins's battery open up and the big guns' shells ripped through trees, sending shards of wooden splinters hurling like shrapnel through the enemy lines. The firing grew heavier until the Yankee line gave way. It wasn't a rout—the Yankees were discouraged, but they weren't shattered. They would retreat, reform, and plan another attack. Evan yelled in triumph as he watched the Yankees backing toward their line. "Hold your positions, men!" Evan shouted encouragingly. "We've got them on the run! Save your ammunition, boys!"

Then it began, a cold stinging rain that swept across the field of battle in driving sheets, soaking everything in a matter of seconds. "Ah shit, just what we need," Evan thought as he tugged his coat collar tight around his neck.

General Shelby approached him and, turning his back to the driving rain, said, "Major, I fear I've made a grievous error. I've sent Elliott to flank the enemy brigade we just drove back." He hesitated as he looked overhead at the approaching wall of clouds rapidly closing on them. The whole sky was a dark liquid-gray now, filled with oppressive gloom. Although it was nearly midday, it looked more like late evening. "This storm is going to be a bad one, and I'm afraid Elliott might lose his way and stumble into enemy lines. I want you to ride to him and give him my orders. Tell him the attack is canceled because of the weather. He is to return immediately to our lines. Hurry, Major, we can't afford to lose any more men than absolutely necessary."

Evan saluted briskly and returned to his horse. He untied the rubberized rain poncho he had taken from a captured Union soldier long ago and slid it over his head and shoulders, tying the hood securely around his face. He slung himself into the saddle just as a deafening crack of thunder rolled overhead and lightning flashed across the sky. His horse shied from the noise, and Evan fought to regain control. He wheeled his trusted mount and spurred behind the Confederate line. Once he reached the end of the line he could ride directly toward Elliott's regiment.

Calvin Kimbrough stood behind his cannon as his crew reloaded the piece and the rain swept over them. In minutes the big guns were wet, as were the men servicing them.

The order came immediately from Captain Collins to cease fire. If the powder and fuses were wet the artillery was useless anyway and would be a mess to clean and prepare for firing again. The ammunition chests were sealed and the men sought what shelter they could in the trees near the knoll where the artillery battery stood in place.

When the hail started falling, there was nowhere to go to dodge it. It stung, leaving welts where it struck the men, as if God himself were hurling stones at them. Calvin tried to protect his face, but the icy blows pummeled against him. A large hailstone bounced off his head, and his ears rang from the blow. Delmar Pickett tugged at Calvin's sleeve and made a dash across the clearing. Calvin followed him as the two ran as fast as they could toward the ammunition wagons. Upon their arrival, they scurried under the protection of the wagon bed like rabbits seeking sanctuary from a pursuing coyote. They were not alone; a few teamsters were already beneath the wagons.

The hailstones ranged from pea- to marble-sized, and some were nearly as big as a man's fist. They tumbled to the ground in a dizzying array, bouncing off trees, the ground, and everything else on their merciless way to the earth. Twigs and leaves cut loose from the trees by the falling missiles drifted helplessly on the wind. Lightning streaked across the sky in jagged lines so bright that Calvin had to squint against the lurid glare. Deep-throated thunder rolled over the land, echoing more ominously than any artillery he had ever heard.

God seemed intent on showing his power to the puny humans who dared to wage war against his wishes. If they wanted to see power, if they wanted to see the magnitude of His fury, He would show them who ruled over this land. He unleashed the powers of Mother Nature on both armies. Neither a gun nor a cannon fired, all silenced by His power. Men huddled and curled into balls on the ground as they tried to hide from the punishing, pounding hail. Others sought sanctuary under trees or behind rocks.

Nothing seemed to help and never did soldiers feel more exposed or helpless.

The darkness increased as the storm continued to build in intensity. The skies filled with dizzying flashes and explosive rumbles as lightning cracked and jaggedly streaked across the heavens. The intensity of the loud booms shook the earth as the hailstones began to drift, collecting into icy piles and coating the ground with white.

Suddenly, as he lay beneath the wagon, Calvin began to sense the danger of their position. Here they sat, hiding under a wagon filled with black-powder charges in a lightning storm. If one bolt hit near the wagon there wouldn't be a piece of him left large enough to bury. He would be nothing more than a large, bloody, wet spot at the bottom of a huge, empty crater. He looked at his friend, and the terror showed in Calvin's eyes. "Del, you know what will happen if lightning hits near this wagon?"

The question caught Delmar off guard. Until now, he was pleased he had found a place to hide from the storm. Now the realization of their danger swept across his face. Delmar swallowed nervously as he moved to pull his knees up under him. "Let's get the hell out of here," he shouted as he ran toward the knoll, Calvin close on his heels.

As he ran, Calvin felt the hair on his head and arms begin to rise in the electricity from the air. A strong stench of sulphur and brimstone filled his nostrils as a bright, blinding light bathed him in its glow. A huge explosion hurled him up into the air, catapulting him in a head-over-heels somersault. It threw him ten feet over the crest of the knoll, and Calvin landed with a jolt, the wind knocked out of him. As he lay there in the mud and hailstones, a dark cloud descended over him and he faded into a pool of darkness.

16

Whirlwind

Calvin Kimbrough sucked in some muddy water and coughed violently as he fought to clear his lungs. He sat upright and rubbed his hand against his chest. He had landed with such force the wind had been driven from him, knocking him out cold. His faculties returned slowly as he sat upright beside a spreading pool of water. He glanced around him and saw his battery's cannons just a few yards away, still abandoned on the knoll. He spotted Delmar lying on his side a short distance away.

Calvin rose slowly and hunkered against the stinging rain that whipped against him. He struggled through the sucking mud to his friend's side. Delmar looked up at him and rubbed his forehead wearily. "I feel like I've been run over by a herd of buffalo. What the hell happened?"

Calvin looked confused. He wasn't really certain. He just remembered a huge explosion and recalled the sensation of flying through the air. After that it was all blank.

"I don't know, Del, but there's one way to find out. Come on, I'll help you up."

The two men staggered up the knoll as they leaned on one another for support. When they reached the crest they looked to where the ammunition wagon had been. Now there was nothing but a large crater surrounded by blackened and charred remnants of the wagon that had earlier given them shelter. The neighboring wagons were overturned and the teams dead in their traces. Near the crater lay bodies of men and pieces of human flesh, strewn about in smoldering disarray. Calvin stared at the destruction in disbelief. Apparently the wagon had been hit by lightning which touched off the explosion when the ammunition ignited. He didn't know if he'd been hurled through the air by the lightning strike or the explosion. He was just grateful to be alive. The two men sagged to the ground, overcome by the realization of how close death had come to claiming them.

Jessie Kimbrough hunkered down as best he could behind a large log lying in a shallow ravine. He watched the hailstones bouncing around him and was glad to have this little bit of sanctuary. The water around his knees and feet rose slowly in the continuing downpour, but he wasn't ready to abandon his meagre shelter. The rain hammered down hard, like a cow peeing against a flat rock, ricocheting into the air from the strength of its own velocity. Then he heard it, a wet, swirling, sloshing sound over his left shoulder. Jessie glanced around warily, curious about the noise. He saw a wall of water five feet high, carrying everything in its path and rushing for him.

Jessie let loose a terrified scream as he scampered desperately over the log and clawed his way up the muddy bank. He'd nearly reached the top before the water caught him and sucked him into the swirling, chocolate-brown waters. The force of the flash flood swept him along the edge of the ravine until it slammed him against a large tree.

Fighting to free himself from the force of the rapidly flowing water, he shoved his foot against the trunk with all his might. He felt the tree give as the leverage of his legs propelled him around the edge, and as he swept past he grabbed a handhold on a low-hanging branch, clinging to it desperately as the swirling waters battered against him. Slowly, he made progress, pulling himself hand over hand until he cleared the water gushing behind him.

Nearly exhausted, he crawled away from the ravine for the higher terrain. Now he understood the wisdom of most of the veterans who sought higher ground. A quick search of his equipment made him realize he had lost one of his revolvers in the flood. One pistol remained safely in his covered holster, but it was hopelessly waterlogged. A third had somehow remained tucked into his belt. One shoe was gone, lost in the flood waters. He slumped back against a large tree and slid to the ground. His body was racked with shivers from the cold as he curled himself into a ball, fighting desperately to regain some heat and hold it in his numbed body.

At the first sign of rain, Billy Cahill retrieved his rain poncho from his blanket roll wrapped across one shoulder and tied at the opposite side of his waist. He slid it on, covering his guns, blanket roll, and uniform, cinched the drawstring hood up tight, and tied it off beneath his chin. Under the rubberized surface, his accoutrements would be protected from the rain.

A few of the soldiers around him also had ponchos with them, but the vast majority did not. Many never acquired one; the Confederate army didn't issue them. Others had left their ponchos rolled up behind their saddles back with the horses. Early in the war, Billy learned to keep things handy when forced to leave his horse. In battle you never knew if the horse would still be there when you returned.

Billy suffered through the hailstorm as best he could by clinging tenaciously to a large tree trunk. The hail slanted down from the southwest, so the northeast side of the tree gave a measure of protection from the pelting stones. Billy's face was turned to the south when he heard a thundering boom that caused the earth to shake beneath his feet. A dazzling flash from the top of a tree thirty feet away nearly blinded him. He felt the concussion of the lightning strike as the tree exploded from the fury of the electricity coursing through its bark. The tree buckled and split in half with a cracking, splintering sound. As if in slow motion, the huge branches tottered earthward. They struck the ground, pointing in his direction. The impact snapped off branches and twigs and sent debris flying near him. The hair on his arms rose and a shiver of fear coursed through his body. He was spellbound by this awesome spectacle of heaven's fury as he stood clinging to another large oak just a short distance away.

As the flames flared in the twisted remains of the tree and smoke boiled from the wood, the rain sizzled against the struggling flames. In minutes the torrential rains extinguished the fire. It occurred to Billy then how lucky he was that lightning had struck a tree other than the one to which he was clinging. But there was no safe haven in a forest from an electrical storm. The sudden realization unnerved him and he felt an overpowering helplessness. He could face the enemy in battle or in hand-to-hand combat without fear, but how could he defend himself from the elements? Biting his lip, he pondered the question. In the end, finding no answer to his problem, he sought refuge behind yet another tree.

Major Evan Stryker rode through the storm and felt the relentless hammering of the hail. It took every measure of his riding skills to keep his horse under control. The animal was frightened by the raging storm and hurt by the hailstones, but Stryker had his duty to fulfill. On he rode, through the sheeting curtains of rain and the icy, clattering stones. He reached Elliott's regiment at the zenith of the electrical storm. Lightning bolts laced the sky in a tangle of brilliant and dazzling light. It reminded Evan of a giant fireworks display gone mad. The fury of the storm lashed at the beleaguered troopers. He made his report and helped lead Elliott's command toward the Confederate lines. If nothing else had gone right at least he had carried out his orders. Elliott's men would not be abandoned.

Major Stryker was surprised when he noticed a decrease in the severity of the storm. The hail had stopped, at least for the moment, although the ground was slippery with the white stones. In places the hailstones were piled like snow in drifts a foot deep. He edged his horse around a particularly large pile and ducked under a low-hanging branch in his path. The wind was dropping and the rain let up until it was nothing more than a heavy mist lit by a ghastly, flickering light whenever the lightning cracked across the sky. The clouds remained sullen and threatening, massed in intensity and whipped into fury by incarnate winds that lashed them upward into the heavens. He looked again to the southwest and saw for the first time the funnel-shaped cloud, twisting and writhing through the air like a snake of death.

Evan blanched in fear as he looked at the terrifying sight approaching, now not more than two miles away. He watched, captivated by the blood-curdling sight of its awesome power. The air seemed more dense, its pressure increasing, and then he heard the approaching twister. Its loud roar sounded like a large freight train rumbling directly at him. He felt the same helplessness he might have felt if, stuck in the tracks, he faced an onrushing train running at full tilt. He tried to get a fix on the probable path of the funnel in the hope he could avoid it.

The funnel seemed to hopscotch around as the ropy shape of the tornado whipped about like a dog chasing his tail. When the funnel touched the earth, the spot was marked by a swirling mass of flying debris. The longer it remained in contact with the ground, the higher the debris climbed. Pieces of trees and undergrowth circled the swirling mass until they floated free and fell from the skies. Huge trees were ripped from the earth and hurled upward into the spiraling vortex.

Evan figured the course quickly in his head. It looked to him like the cyclone would pass in a line between the two armies, roughly where the Union skirmishers had stood before the storm had forced them to fall back.

If they moved swiftly, Evan thought, Elliott and his men might avoid a direct hit by the funnel cloud. Captain Elliott came to the same conclusion, and both officers were soon shouting to the troopers above the roar. The men needed little urging to race away from the track of the approaching whirlwind. But as they neared their lines their path was blocked by the swift-running waters that flooded the ravine. The waters had swelled past the banks, forcing dismounted Confederate soldiers to huddle in the trees, trapped by the rising waters. One of them was Jessie Kimbrough, Cassandra's brother.

Major Stryker, seeing their escape route blocked, felt a rising tide of despair. He shouted orders for his men to lie flat on the ground. Nothing could be done for the frightened horses tied to the nearby trees.

Evan's heart hammered in his chest as he lay in the mud. He lay his forehead on his crossed arms to protect his face. This gave him a little pocket of air to breathe and allowed him to keep his face out of the cold, wet mud that oozed under his poncho and soaked through his pant legs, chilling him. He didn't know if the trembling that racked his body was caused by the cold or the fear twisting at his gut.

He heard the deafening roar of the approaching whirlwind. The crashing sound of trees being ripped from the earth, their branches shattered and scattered by the swirling death cloud cutting a path through the wooded hills, nearly overwhelmed him. The unholy sound was like nothing he had ever heard in his life, and never before had he felt as terrorized as he did now. Panic surged through him, and he prayed.

Stryker prayed more intensely than he ever had before.

He prayed for forgiveness of his sins. He prayed to be spared as the demon of death and destruction whirled so close to him. As it drew ever closer, his ears began to ache from the increased pressure, and he covered them with his hands, willing himself deeper into the mud.

Then he heard it—the crashing of debris falling around him. He tucked himself into a little ball, trying desperately to make himself as small a target as possible. He heard the screams from men around him blending with the shrill, frightened whinnying of the horses. He recoiled in shock as he felt something slam into his leg. The blow stung but his legs responded, and he changed his position as he hugged the ground. Gradually the intensity of the sound decreased and the confusion seemed to settle around him.

Warily, Evan peeked from his muddy refuge and glanced up. He looked over his shoulder and saw the tornado continuing its treacherous path to the northeast. He released a huge sigh of relief when he realized the storm was moving away from him. Somehow, by the grace of God, he had survived. A long, battered swath of denuded land marked the passing of the cyclone where everything living was either knocked down, stripped, or destroyed. The intermingled, interlaced branches of felled trees littered the area on both sides of the three-hundred-yard-wide path of the tornado. The whirlwind had passed fewer than four hundred yards from him.

Once he could control the shaking in his knees, he began to look around him. Miraculously, his horse and most of the men had survived the passing funnel cloud. Five horses were missing and three more had been killed by falling debris. Two men crushed by a falling tree lay not more than a hundred feet from Evan's position. The water continued to flow through the ravine, and they were still cut off from their lines.

The rain came again, though not as hard as before, and the sky to the west began to lighten. Evan walked around the damaged area and crossed the path the tornado had taken. He saw sights he would have never thought possible. He found a musket ramrod shoved through a small tree, protruding from both sides. The shaft remained perfectly straight as it stuck out from the trunk. He found straw embedded in the bark of trees and the body of one hapless Yank dangling upside down in the branches of a tall tree, his body distorted and impaled on a broken branch like a discarded doll thrown away by an angry child. Evan turned away from the carnage, happy it was not one of his men high in the shattered tree.

By the time Stryker finished his inspection, the water had receded from the flash flood and Shelby's troopers had crossed the ravine. The sky cleared rapidly, and two hours after the storm had stopped the battle, sunshine poked through the broken clouds. Evan saw a brilliantly colored double rainbow stretched against the skies; never had such a sight been more appreciated.

Daylight remained and General Shelby, still not content to give up the fight, ordered his men into the natural protection of the tangled debris left by the funnel cloud. The Union line remained in their positions on the far hills. General Shelby moved along the line, trying everything he knew to tempt the enemy out of their strong positions. They refused to budge.

As Shelby's staff moved down the line, he noticed a large log cabin that was spared by the tornado. The home was abandoned, probably evacuated by its inhabitants when they saw the Yankee army approaching. The substantial and stately cabin sat near a crest of a hill and was surrounded by fruit trees and shrubbery. Thinking the house would give him both a good field of view and a position to command his attack, Shelby advanced his troops in and around the house. The Yankees spotted this advance and opened with long-range artillery fire from a battery of twelve-pound howitzers.

Collins opened fire in return, hoping to silence the enemy battery fire. Evan wasn't sure why, but no one had paid much attention to the fifteen beehives positioned between the house and the Confederate troops to the north.

The hives ranged from natural gum stands to more elaborate boxes with sliding panels and caps. The fourth round from the Union battery exploded in the middle of the hives, splintering three, toppling four more, and angering the honey bees. An angry swarm rose from the damaged boxes and looked for a target on which to vent their anger.

A large cloud of the buzzing, singing, biting, and stinging insects descended on the unsuspecting Confederate soldiers. General chaos followed as the first wave of bees dove on the chosen targets of their wrath. In moments the stinging insects were swarming among the horses and attacking the men's hair and faces with a vengeance.

Unlike the Union army these newfound enemies attacked relentlessly from every angle. In minutes the men were falling out of ranks and stumbling across the field, slapping and clawing at their flying tormentors. Horses reared and bucked off their riders; others plunged and raced off in all directions, the riders fighting to regain control. The battle with the Union army was all but forgotten as the Rebels tried to deal with this latest and seemingly more dangerous threat.

Shelby, from his position at the cabin, was still uncertain of the cause of the ruckus. He stood and watched as his line of soldiers curiously scattered across the field, and cussed and swore as he saw his brigade disintegrating before his very eyes. At this distance he couldn't determine the cause.

Evan thought the general might explode he was so indignant over the disorder erupting among his veteran troopers. Below in the ranks Shelby watched his officers scurry here and there, cajoling the other men and trying to urge them back into ranks, but nothing seemed to help. Angered beyond words, General Shelby determined he would handle this disgraceful disobedience personally. "Orderly, bring me my sorrel," he yelled angrily. Shelby swung into the saddle and yelled at his staff, "Mount up, men! Something is disrupting our lines. Maybe the enemy has flanked us. By God, if my field commanders can't control their troops in the field then I'll court-martial the lot of them and replace them with my staff."

All the staff officers mounted up and followed their commander as he raced down the hill. As they closed on the scattered Rebel line and rode near the disturbed bee-hives, the command staff got its first inkling of the real problem. They came under repeated attacks as a second wave of the winged warriors descended upon the hapless officers.

General Shelby, already stung several times about the face, cursed indignantly as he raced for some bushes, plunging through the Rebel lines as he rode to escape the stinging, torturing insects. Evan tried to keep pace as the insatiable bees assaulted him in turn. As he followed General Shelby, the antics of the field commanders were met with gales of laughter from the troops.

The bravest of men flinched, dodged, twisted, and slapped as they ran from the swarm. The line was now a wreck as soldiers abandoned their positions. At every turn more bees reinforced the attack. The officers shouted orders and fought to maintain control, but their calls went unheeded.

If the stingers didn't hurt so badly, Major Stryker would have found the scene amusing. As another bee pierced his scalp he cried out in pain and plucked away the offending insect. He wanted to laugh and cry at the same time. Without an order issued, this part of the line had fled the field in full retreat. The orders were passed and the rest of the brigade joined the hasty withdrawal three miles to the north. There they set up camp for the night along good, fresh water on high ground.

As Evan sat in the camp that night daubing mud on his many swelling bee stings, he realized with a wry smile the magnitude of the situation. A Union army many times their size was unable to put Shelby's brigade in flight. They had fought through a firestorm, survived a terrible thunderstorm, and nearly been sucked up by a tornado, yet they had held their ground against all odds. But a band of winged warriors armed with deadly stingers had done what no one else had done. They had put the Iron Brigade in complete and total rout. The swelling, burning reminders of their defeat would remain with them for several days in the form of angry, red welts.

17

Prairie D'Ann

Captain Ross Kimbrough ducked his head as he entered through the tent flap. A rumpled and groggy General Shelby, still half asleep, sat at the edge of his cot with his head in his hands. The general was bathed in pale yellow light cast from a lantern tied to the ridgepole along the center of the tent. Ross felt sorry for having to wake the general in the middle of the night.

General Shelby rubbed his hands across his face and eyes and smoothed his hair back. "My orderly said you had some urgent news that couldn't wait until morning, Captain." Shelby paused as Lieutenant Jacobee entered the tent carrying tin cups of coffee for the general and Captain Kimbrough. He handed the cups to the two officers and left the tent. The general tried to take a sip, but winced at the hot coffee. He set his cup down on his folding field desk beside the cot. "Let's hear it, Captain. If I'm lucky I might still get some sleep tonight."

Ross stood awkwardly before the general as he held his own coffee cup. The coffee was very hot and the handle was beginning to burn his fingers. Ross stepped forward and set the cup at the edge of the desk. He straightened and said, "I'm sorry I had to have you awakened, General, but I have some important news. General Steele has sent nearly all his cavalry around the left side of our brigade and they appear to be headed for the Wire Road. We captured some Yankee stragglers and interrogated them. Their orders are to attack you from the rear at dawn. They hope they can crush us between their cavalry and the main body of their army."

The news startled General Shelby, and his expression became more alert. "Do you have any numbers for me? How many men are at the rear?"

"They were moving after dark, General, and it is hard to get an accurate count. I reckon they have nearly four thousand mounted troops positioned four miles behind us, sir."

General Shelby scratched at his beard thoughtfully as he asked, "What about the rest of Steele's army?"

"The Union army has moved nearly all their wagons and most of their infantry across the Little Missouri River. They still have their strong defensive line in place where we hit them yesterday." Ross paused a moment as Shelby pondered this news. "There is more, General. One of my scouts, Terrell Fletcher, brought more bad news. General Thayer, with several thousand troops, is on the road from Fort Smith, Arkansas. He should rendezvous with Steele's army in two days."

This news of additional troops didn't seem to faze General Shelby. "Does your man think it will take them two days to reach Steele?"

"Yes, sir, two full days of hard marching over muddy roads."

"Splendid, Captain. Two days will give us time to deal with Steele's cavalry and march around his army. It is time we block his progress instead of harassing the rear of his army." The general reached for his coffee and took a sip, swallowing gingerly. "Lieutenant Jacobee, come here immediately!" Jo Shelby shouted.

Lieutenant Jacobee entered the tent. "Lieutenant, wake my staff and tell them to report at once. Start rousing the brigade, Lieutenant. We are about to have guests."

Sensing the urgency of the situation, Jacobee spun on his heels and exited the tent. General Shelby returned his attention to Captain Kimbrough. "You better drink your coffee, Captain. You know how difficult it is to come by." Almost as an afterthought, Shelby said, "Get yourself something to eat. I'm afraid none of us will get any more sleep tonight. We have an ambush to prepare."

General Shelby moved his camp in the middle of the night. He withdrew his pickets to give the illusion he was retreating then set his men in ambush along the Wire Road.

Billy Cahill leaned forward in his saddle, the leather creaking beneath him. He pulled out each of his weapons one at a time and double-checked them to make sure he was ready for battle. His eyes felt red and dry, and his body still ached from the day before. Like all of Shelby's brigade he had received little sleep during the night. By three in the morning they were back in the saddle, and before sunrise they were placed in ambush.

Billy felt the sun rising behind him as the sky overhead lightened. He looked around, studied his surroundings, and saw the rest of Company H, Twelfth Missouri Cavalry, mounted and waiting in a wooded draw. The Wire Road was just a short distance to the west of their position, and when the Yankee cavalry came looking for Shelby's brigade they would find a nasty surprise waiting for them.

He heard it then, the plodding sound of a cavalry column on the move. He had heard the sound a thousand times before, and the familiarity of it made it unmistakable. He licked his lips in anticipation and adjusted his battered, wide-brimmed slough hat on his head, drawing it down tighter for the charge to come. The tables were about to turn on Steele's hapless Yankee troopers.

On the rise, a signal shot cracked and echoed off the

hills. Billy saw the riders in front of him move out and he spurred Bess forward. In minutes they cleared the draw and swept in a wide turn until they struck the Union cavalry column on the Wire Road.

A cloud of powder smoke from the first volley of the Confederate troopers, who were firing from cover, drifted along the ridge that bordered the road. The Union soldiers were utterly surprised by this unexpected attack, and many saddles were suddenly emptied. Before they had a chance to reorganize, mounted Rebel cavalry swept down on them, guns firing, screaming the Rebel yell at the top of their lungs.

Billy, riding with his reins held in his teeth, leveled his matched pair of Remington revolvers at the nearest troopers. He aimed and fired each revolver deliberately, carefully picking out his targets. Two saddles were emptied as he plunged through the shattered enemy line. The surprise assault caught the Yankees offguard, and instead of taking a stand they broke and ran. They broke in every direction, forgetting completely that they outnumbered the Rebels four to one.

Gleefully, Billy joined the chase. Most of his company pursued a large group of Yankee troopers riding south down the Wire Road. Yankees riding slower horses were easy targets as they straggled behind the others. One by one, the men were killed or captured. Billy emptied the saddles of seven horses single-handedly during the wild pursuit.

The chase continued for nearly three miles until the stampeding Yankee cavalry ran into Steele's advancing Union infantry coming to join the attack. The infantry was overwhelmed by the panicky Union cavalry fleeing over and through their ranks, disrupting their troop movements. The panic and terror evident in the Yankee cavalry quickly spread through the now disorganized and disrupted Federal infantry, who also began to flee in great numbers toward the safety of their lines. General Shelby halted his men and waited to see what Steele would try next.

Union cavalry units scattered in all directions like quail flushed from cover. Although a large portion of Steele's cavalry was driven south into his lines, it would take days for some regiments to rejoin Steele's army. Still others fled toward the safety of Little Rock. Shelby had successfully turned the tables on the would-be ambushers.

The next day, Steele and his entire army crossed the Little Missouri River. The following day several thousand troops under General Thayer's command from Fort Smith, Arkansas, joined his command.

General Shelby crossed the Little Missouri River with his army five miles south of the point of the Union army crossing. Swinging to the east of Steele's army Shelby had found good, dry roads and his brigade swiftly circled the Union troops. The way was now open for Jo Shelby to march his brigade in front of the Yankees and block their advance.

He selected his ground carefully, placing his brigade at Prairie D'Ann. It was a beautiful stretch of level land bordering the muddy bottoms and marshes of the Little Missouri River. General Steele's large army and supply train had struggled through these lowlands, fighting the mud, high water, and swarms of mosquitos, gnats, flies, and other insects that infested the swampy region.

The Union army found it necessary to cut trees and lay the logs horizontally to corduroy the roads through the mud. Otherwise the wagons would sink to their hubs. This made for a very rough ride and walk for men and horses, and the wagons chattered across the uneven surface. It was that or not cross at all. Forced to stick to this corduroy road, Steele's army was therefore limited in its movement and speed. That evened the number disadvantage considerably between the two armies.

While waiting three days for Steele to advance through the marshes, word came that generals Marmaduke and Price with their Confederate army were only five miles south of Shelby. General Price had his men digging in and fortifying to stop Steele's advance from moving farther south. General

Shelby was ordered to delay Steele for as long as possible. Meanwhile, General Gano marched his army of several regiments of Texans and Choctaw Indians out of the Indian Territories to join Marmaduke and Price's army. The combined Confederate forces set to face Steele's invading army now numbered nearly seven thousand. General Shelby patiently awaited the Union advance.

Calvin Kimbrough stood to his cannon and waited nervously. Beyond them the sounds of skirmishing erupted in the lowlands to the north. Steele was finally advancing to the attack. Powder smoke, hanging like low-flying clouds, drifted in and out of the trees and bushes. It reminded Calvin of the drifting fog he had seen occasionally in the early morning hours of summer before the sun burned off the heavy dew.

He let his eyes roam along the length of the Confederate line and he felt reassured. This was a good position on high ground. The brigade was situated on the long crest of a little narrow ridge overlooking the marshes. He watched as Steele's army drove back the Rebel skirmishers and began to form lines of battle on the plain below his position.

When the enemy first came into view, General Shelby ordered Collins's battery to engage. As if they were one, the first volley echoed across the flats. Great gouts of dirt were flung into the air by the impact of the shells among the Union regiments trying to form into battle lines. As Calvin placed the pendulum hausse sight on the bracket and aimed his cannon, he admired the coolness of the enemy falling under their fire.

Steele's men advanced slowly in blue-uniformed ranks. Unlike the Confederate army, each soldier was identically dressed and equipped. The deep navy blue of their uniform jackets worn over the sky blue of their woolen pants made them appear to be a perfect set of toy soldiers on display. Each regiment was led forward by a set of flag bearers holding the embroidered and silken banners that fluttered in the winds; their color guards marched alongside to protect the regimental colors. Light glistened off their bayonets, burnished rifle barrels, and uniform buttons, and here and there, it would sparkle and reflect off a brass belt plate or buckle shined to a brilliance as if the men were simply on parade. The roll and staccato beat of the drummer boys set the rhythm for the tramping feet, and the bugle calls ordered the change of formations.

Two magnificent six-gun batteries belonging to Steele's army advanced to the front and set up to do battle. Collins shifted his fire to the nearest enemy artillery, and the duel commenced. The fire became intense as the shells began to fall among the men of Collins's battery.

Exploding shells cut the air above them and thudded into the earth, heaving dirt and debris high. Solid shot skipped along the ground and plowed through the battery like stones skipped across a pond by a child. Sometimes these skipping cannonballs missed and other times they found their mark. The burnt powder from their muzzle blasts fired at the Yankees mixed with the dirt and confusion until Calvin's vision was nearly obscured.

Calvin felt the whoosh of a cannonball whip past him and heard a sound like a sledgehammer striking a ripe watermelon. Something hot and wet stung him and he looked down to see bright-crimson blood coating his hand. He glanced beside him and saw Moses Faye's body ripped in two at chest level and scattered about the ground not four feet away. The cannonball had caught him in the midsection and severed his body into two pieces. Calvin's eyes widened in horror as he stared into the open chest cavity and watched Faye's heart still beating. The body twitched, and Calvin stood mesmerized.

He felt a stiff shove in his back as Captain Collins tried to break the spell. "You can't do anything more for him, Calvin. Keep your gun in action!" he shouted over the deafening roar of the gun next to him.

Calvin glanced down at his sticky hand and wiggled his fingers. Satisfied that he was unhurt, he returned to his duties. A shell exploded in front of the cannon on their right. The rammer, James Lindsay, screamed in agony as his arm was ripped off above the elbow. Another crewman, John Pollack, was hit by spinning fragments that ripped into his right side and sent him sprawling. Calvin, his mind now nearly numb, heard John say to his old friend, "Jim, we've fired our last piece for ol' Jo," as men pulled the horribly wounded men away from the cannon and over the crest of the ridge.

Another battery of enemy artillery rolled into place and joined the cannonade against Collins's battery. The four-gun battery now faced eighteen large-bore artillery pieces in an unequal contest. Still, Collins's big guns held their ground.

Calvin watched in satisfaction as a solid shot from his cannon struck the carriage of a twelve-pound howitzer directly beneath the cannon barrel. Severed cleanly in two, the barrel sagged to the ground, and the crew around the destroyed cannon took serious injuries.

The cries and whinnies of dying horses reached his ears as shrapnel decimated the ranks of the horses Collins's battery used to pull their big guns. He was glad his horse remained in relative safety behind the lines with the ammunition wagons and the crew's black-bear cub, Postlewait. Most of the crew's personal mounts were safely hidden, but those necessary for moving the artillery were kept close in case the battery had to withdraw.

Yet another Union battery joined the attempt to silence Collins's guns, bringing the total still firing at the Rebels to twenty-three. The breech of Calvin's cannon was so hot from the constant firing that it scorched his hand. He finished sighting and stepped free of the carriage.

The rammer, Edward Locke, moved to his position as Delmar Pickett yanked the lanyard. The cannon recoiled in a cloud of smoke as it rolled back from the discharge. Calvin looked at Ed, automatically expecting him to step forward and sponge the barrel. Instead he saw Edward's now headless body quiver and topple backward like a tree felled in a forest. Locke's hands still clung firmly to his rammer as his lifeless body struck the ground. Calvin looked around him, but Locke's head was nowhere to be seen. It had been severed neatly and carried away by a Union solid shot.

Calvin should have been terrified by the gruesome injuries being inflicted around him, but his mind had already become numb to violence and death. His eyes saw the slaughter, but his mind would not recognize the fact. He continued on as if he were nothing more than an insensitive machine, incapable of feeling or emotion. He knew, somewhere in the deep nether regions of his brain, that if he let his mind cave in even for a second to the horrors sweeping around him, or to acknowledge the intense danger, he would topple immediately into insanity. He stayed doggedly at his post as dear friends died around him.

The mounted Rebel cavalry flanking both sides of Collins's battery's position also were taking a fearful beating. Still, they stood their ground without wavering. Great gaps were ripped in the line and the holes were silently refilled with fresh troops; nearby soldiers frequently had to dismount to remove some old friend from beneath the prancing hooves of his horse. Steele sent forth cavalry, and they were driven back with the first infantry charge.

By now, Collins's battery had withstood the barrage for well over an hour. First one, then another Union battery was withdrawn, suffering terrible losses at the hands of the Rebels' accurate cannon fire. The unequal contest continued, but Steele's legions still couldn't break out and bring his full army into play. The Rebels kept them pinned until darkness put a temporary pause to the contest.

Nearly every horse used to pull the artillery for Collins's battery lay dead among the guns. Seventeen crewmen were dead and a score more severely wounded. As the guns were withdrawn by hand to the safety of the supply wagons, Calvin realized he had somehow survived the day. To save the artillery itself, horses were taken from their duty pulling ambulance and supply wagons to replace the ones killed in battle.

At first Shelby thought night would end the contest, but

still the Union army tried to advance. Fighting flared up in the night all along the line. Collins's battery, their ammunition nearly expended, contributed little to the night fighting.

At midnight Shelby withdrew his command. Despite their efforts, the vastly superior numbers of the Union army occupied Prairie D'Ann.

18

Departure

Once Steele's army was free of the constrictions imposed by the marshy lowlands, they could spread out across the plains. General Sterling Price now realized the position he had chosen to make his stand against the onrushing Union army would not hold and could easily be flanked. Reluctantly, he abandoned his lines.

Still, the severe blows struck by Shelby served their purpose. Steele's troops were now demoralized by the repeated defeat suffered at the hands of a smaller army. They also believed they must be facing much larger numbers than were really present. This made Steele much more cautious and conservative in his movements.

Two roads now lay open to Steele's advance. One led to Camden and the other to Washington, Arkansas. At Washington, the exiled congress of Missouri and much of the Arkansas legislature were running their respective governments. General Price believed Steele wanted to capture the city, and he moved to prevent it. All Confederate troops

were removed from the road leading to Camden in anticipation of Steele's move on Washington.

General Steele, already tired of the constant battering he
had taken from General Shelby, now realized he faced a
larger and more powerful Southern army. Knowing his
mission to reach Shreveport was far behind schedule, he
saw the road to Camden open to the east and he took it.

Realizing his error and wishing to fight to save Camden
before it was lost, Confederate general Price ordered generals Shelby and Marmaduke to make a forced night
march. The movement taxed the already battle-weary soldiers of the Iron Brigade, yet they reached Poison Springs
on the Camden road ahead of Steele's army. There would
be one last try to stop the Union forces from reaching
Camden.

Cassandra Kimbrough struggled with an armful of clothes
as she stepped through the front door of Chidester House.
Fanny met her on the porch and said, "I'll take those, Miz
Cassie, an' put 'em in the wagon. Lord knows you done
enough this mornin'." Cassandra smiled in gratitude. She
watched Fanny move cautiously down the steps and wad-
dle across the yard toward their parked wagon.

As Cassie smoothed the loose hair away from her eyes,
she heard a rumble like distant thunder to the west. Spot-
ting Colonel John Chidester standing on the west side of
the house and staring off toward the horizon, she decided
to take a moment and join him. "Hello, Colonel. Is that
noise the sound of thunder?"

John jerked his head around. He had been listening so
intently to the far-off rumblings that he didn't hear her approach. "No, but I wish it were. What you are hearing is
distant artillery fire. I'm afraid that rumble to the west
marks General Steele's progress toward Camden."

"Does our army have any hope of stopping him?"

"I seriously doubt it." Cassandra heard the bitterness in
his voice. "Since General Price stripped Camden of our

troops to defend Washington, there is no one left here to oppose him. If his troops reach Camden, the city will fall."

Cassandra stared for a moment at the colonel and master of the house as she considered his words. He was a powerfully built man, intellectual and influential. As operator of the Chidester-Rapley Stage Line Company, he had kept his stage lines running despite a shortage of drivers and horses. His line was an integral part of the transportation and mail network in this region. He was given the rank of colonel and put in charge of the Confederate mail service in the area due to the significance of his work.

Cassandra said, "Surely General Price will try to oppose Steele's advance. Camden is too important to fall into enemy hands."

"According to the latest dispatches, he has sent generals Shelby and Marmaduke to block Steele's progress. The cannon fire we hear now is from near Poison Springs. I suspect Shelby and Marmaduke are doing their best to stop him, but in the end Steele's superior numbers will push them aside before Price can bring his army into play. Once Steele's army reaches and occupies the fortifications here, it will take the very devil to drive him out." To emphasize his point, John slapped his long, leather gauntlets against the palm of his hand. "Damn, I can't believe we've wasted so much in materials and effort to fortify this city only to leave the trenches and forts empty. Mark my words, the enemy will use it to good advantage against us."

"How much time do you think we have before they reach the city?"

"It's hard to say. I doubt it will be more than a day. You best see to finishing your packing and leaving before they get here. Once the Yankees arrive it will be nearly impossible to leave."

Cassandra remembered how her fiancé, Captain Evan Stryker, and her brothers had begged her to leave Camden and continue their journey to Texas. Even as the brigade marched through town it was common knowledge that the spring would bring a Union campaign against Southwestern Arkansas and Shelby's men would oppose it. She was enjoying her stay in Camden and her family seemed happy in these temporary surroundings, so she had delayed their departure. Now they had waited nearly too long and their journey would be more hazardous.

She still worried about the consequences of falling behind enemy lines. She didn't know if there was an arrest warrant issued for her and her family, or if the dead Yankees near Batesville had ever been found. Yes, she knew it was best they leave, and preparations were already underway. Their wagon and carriage were almost packed and Jethro and Jeremiah were busy hitching the teams. Andrew Covington and his family had decided to flee with them and would arrive at any moment.

In her heart she knew John Chidester was correct. Time was of the essence and they must hurry. "John, I want to thank you again for allowing us to stay here with you in your lovely home."

John smiled and replied, "It has been my pleasure to have so many beautiful ladies around the house. I must confess, I will miss you and your family."

Cassandra blushed a little, embarrassed by his kind remarks. "Thank you, Colonel. I wish you well and hope when this war is over we might meet again."

"It would indeed be a pleasure." John took her hand and, bowing low, kissed the back of her hand lightly. "Have a safe journey."

Cassandra went into the house and inspected the rooms, double-checking to see if they had removed all their personal belongings. Once they were gone, there would be no coming back for anything carelessly left behind. When everything was in order and her family had been gathered outside, she exchanged tearful good-byes with Leah Chidester and her children.

All the women had become close friends during their stay, and Cassandra knew she would miss this house and these people. Camden was a charming city and she would cherish fond memories of her stay here. By two o'clock in the afternoon the little caravan rolled past the city outskirts and away from the advancing Union army. Cassandra wondered about her fiancé and her brothers; she hoped they were safe. It was partly because of her concern for their safety that they had lingered here for so long. A part of her hoped if they stayed in the area they would see one another again. It had not come to pass, and now they were on the run, refugees in an unfamiliar land.

The next morning General Shelby had Collins's battery unlimber in the middle of the road on a large hill. To mask the battery he had his men cut and place a thick screen of brush in front of the artillery. The horses and supply wagons were moved behind the crest of the hill for safety. In the valley below the hill, Shelby placed his dismounted cavalry along the bed of a dry creek.

To bait the trap, two companies were left behind to harass Steele's advance. They retired slowly, letting the Yankees push them down the road. The Yankees set up a mounted battery of four mountain howitzers and began shelling the companies along the road. The two Rebel companies, led by captains Reck Johnson and Will Moorman, passed their fellow soldiers hiding in the creek bed as if there were nothing there.

The unsuspecting Union battery followed and set up in the middle of the road, fewer than fifty feet from the Confederate line. They stood in the middle of the road plainly in sight of Collins's masked battery and fired random shots at the two companies moving in the brush to the right of Collins's position.

Captain Collins trained his entire battery on the unsuspecting Yankees at very close range and fired in battery. The first salvo killed six men and the lieutenant in charge, plus most of the horses. The Rebel skirmishers advanced to capture the howitzers, but Union infantry came to the rescue and recaptured the Yankee guns. Just one salvo had silenced the surprised Union battery.

General Steele now knew that Shelby had somehow gotten ahead of him again. He advanced his artillery and set them to work blasting at the Rebel line, and then ordered his infantry to attack the creek bed. Shelby stiffly resisted, and three times the line was driven back with heavy losses. Finally Steele, seeing the direct attack was failing, sent two columns to flank Shelby's line. Marmaduke's brigade, still held in reserve, moved to meet the threat but were driven back by superior numbers. The Confederates maintained order and withdrew to the right as Steele's army progressed into unprotected and unguarded Camden.

All the men who were to defend the fortifications so carefully constructed around Camden were gone to protect Washington. The Union army marched in unopposed and seized the city. Steele ordered his men to occupy the fortifications and trenches. Confederate-dug trenches now housed and protected Union soldiers.

The Rebel army had Steele bottled up inside the fortifications surrounding Camden. Realizing a frontal assault against the fortifications defended by a larger army was an impossible task, the Rebels decided to starve him out with a state of siege. If they could only keep supplies from reaching the Federals, Steele would be forced to surrender or withdraw.

19

An Old Acquaintance

Jessie Kimbrough lay on the cool ground, gazing up at an azure blue sky. He felt a tug of the reins wrapped around his wrist as Star's Pride nibbled at the grain he had given him. "Just a short rest before we're in the saddle again and charging the enemy," Jessie thought. Although he was exhausted from a month in the saddle and a seemingly endless procession of scouts, skirmishes, and small battles with General Frederick Steele's Union army, he could not sleep. The flow of adrenaline was too strong with yet another engagement perhaps minutes away. It was up to these Rebels to find a way to force the Union army from the captured city of Camden, Arkansas.

Jessie reached up and softly fingered the gold locket Katlin had given him. He thought about the last time he had seen his wife. It had been in March, now more than a month ago. Tears came to his eyes as he opened the locket and lovingly studied the photo neatly tucked away inside. Glen Adam Kimbrough, his son and first child, now shared the locket with a photo of his mother, Katlin Kimbrough.

The time with his family had flown by swiftly, and he and his brothers were called back to duty much sooner than they had wished. In March, newly promoted General Jo Shelby led his troopers to face the advancing Union army of General Frederick Steele and once again Jessie was torn from his young family.

He felt a profound sadness settle upon him as he wished fervently for an end to the war. He longed to hold his son in his arms again and to be there to rock him to sleep. It hurt him to miss so much of those day-to-day experiences with his young child and wife.

"Well, there is little use dwelling on it," he reasoned. "There's only one thing I can do to get home more quickly, and that is to bring a swift end to this conflict."

Despite the brigade's best efforts to stop General Steele's army of fifteen thousand men, they had failed. The Rebel cavalry had managed to slow Steele down and made him pay heavily for his advances, but they could not halt the Union juggernaut.

Just a few days before, Confederate general Marmaduke had captured a large wagon train sent to gather provisions for Steele's Union army at Camden. The second Battle of Poison Springs, fought on April 20, 1864, was a complete success. Marmaduke captured more than two hundred fifty wagons and ambulances, two pieces of rifled artillery, between twelve and fifteen hundred horses and mules, and more than one hundred white prisoners; wounded and killed an equal amount; and left behind uncounted numbers of slaughtered negro infantry. Inside the wagons, the Rebels found items stolen from the people of Arkansas by the Union army, items ranging from every kind of food found on a farm to household goods of every type and nature. General Steele now found himself trapped in the town of Camden, surrounded by Rebels, and lacking food and supplies for his own men and horses. Steele's expedition sent to aid Union general Banks's thirty thousand soldiers for an attack on the Confederate headquarters at Shreveport, Louisiana, was in serious danger of failure.

Jessie recalled the sad day when he had last seen his young family before he had marched off to face Steele's army. He remembered Katlin's tear-streaked face as she held up her young son to watch his father ride past to the sound of a military brass band. He was glad now that Cassandra had decided to take the family on to Texas, away from the fighting here in Arkansas. It would have terrified him to see his family trapped in Camden with the Union army. He wondered if they had reached Texas safely. He didn't know where they were, but he knew they had discussed staying in either Clarksville or Marshall, both considered safe havens for Southern people along the Texas border.

"Soon the orders will come and we'll hit the Yanks hard," Jessie thought. He shifted his weight as he rolled on to his side, supporting his head on his hand.

"Time to mount up, Jess. The scouts have located a large Yankee supply train comin' from Pine Bluff. It's big, I mean real big."

Jessie looked up at the sound of the familiar voice. Standing over him was Captain Gilbert Thomas. Gil was all smiles, for he loved battle almost as much as he loved to tip a bottle.

"We take this train, and there'll be a bunch of starving Yankees trapped inside Camden. Come on, we're burnin' daylight!" Gilbert continued down the line of resting troopers. As he moved he would stop from time to time to toe a slow trooper in the trousers.

Jessie gave Star's Pride an affectionate pat and swung into the saddle. "We've seen hell together before. It's time to do it again."

The column moved out at a walk, then swung into a gallop. They shifted into a line of battle as they broke from the woods and meadow. The sudden attack surprised the Union supply train.

Jessie leaned low in the saddle, his face close to the

neck of Star's Pride as he charged the wagons. Teamsters fought desperately to pull their wagons out of line, but the terrain offered little chance for wagons to maneuver. Other drivers tried to whip their mules and horses into a stampede along an already clogged road. Here and there a small body of Union defenders tried to stand against the onrushing tide of Confederate cavalry.

Jessie rode, pistol in hand, toward the nearest group of black Union soldiers. On both sides of him he felt the comforting motion of other Rebel riders charging with him. He stared almost with a sense of detachment at the puffs of smoke and the whine of minié balls splitting the air around him. He realized the Union soldiers, in their excitement, had fired too high. Star's Pride closed the gap with long, ground-pounding strides, until Jessie was among them.

He leveled his revolver at the nearest soldier as he squeezed the trigger and felt the reassuring kick of the pistol in his hand. As he rode through the haze of the powder smoke from his pistol shot, the action around him blurred. Quick impressions and glimpses filled his senses. Wide, scared eyes set in ebony faces, Union bluecoats, pistol flashes, the clang of steel, and the grunt and snort of plunging horses melded into one terrifying scene. He fired rapidly at point-blank range until one, then another pistol was empty. When the negro soldiers stood, he rode over them; if they broke and ran, he pursued them.

The momentum of the assault and the pursuit had carried him past the train and into the woods beyond. As Jessie rode down two black soldiers, his pistol roared to life again with a will of its own. The shot caught the larger of the two soldiers in the head, somersaulting him to the ground.

The other, a small-framed man, turned and drew a bead on Jessie with a rifled musket that seemed larger than the soldier holding it. Jessie, his gun now empty, waited, expecting at any moment to feel the crushing blow of a minié ball in his chest. In a near-hypnotic trance, as if time were frozen into slow motion, he studied the man. He watched him gently squeeze the trigger and saw the determined eye sight on him. Then slowly, inexplicably, the soldier removed his finger from the trigger without firing and lowered the gun. "Massa Jessie, is that you?"

The voice shook Jessie to his very core as he watched the soldier lower the rifle, stunned by the implications. "Leon! Leon Pepper, is it you?" It never occurred to him he might encounter one of his former slaves in battle. Especially a man he had so trusted at Briarwood Plantation. Jessie spurred his horse alongside Leon and glared down at the small, coffee-colored man.

Leon was wearing a Union uniform that looked to be at least one size too big. Jessie felt the burn of red hot anger flush across his cheeks as he considered Leon's betrayal. He shouted above the roar of battle, "What the hell are you doing in the Yankee army, Leon? How could you turn against us after Cassandra set you free?" Jessie shook his head in frustration. "Didn't we always treat you fairly?"

Leon stood proudly and stared defiantly at Jessie as he leaned on his rifle. "Yes, suh, Massa Jessie. You always treated me good, but I was still a slave until I gots my freedom. Ya'll took good care of me, just like you'd take good care of a fine horse."

Bitterness broke in Jessie's voice. "I thought you were my friend, Leon."

"If I didn't like you, Massa Jessie, you'd be dead now instead of talkin' to me." Leon let his words soak in before he continued. "You were a fair man, Massa Jessie, but I didn't ask to be your friend. You owned me, and I did what I was told out of respect, 'cause a slave knows what happens if he don't. You don't own your friends any more than you can buy 'em."

Leon exhaled slowly before he said, "I was truly glad when Miz Cassie gave me my freedom papers, but if the truth be known I might still be a slave if the Yankees hadn't burned us out. Miz Cassie knew she couldn't take care of us any longer, and who could buy us with the war goin' on and all? Me and the missus are free now, but there's plenty of other slaves still in bondage that haven't been so lucky. I fight so they can be free."

Leon shifted his weight as he slung his musket over his shoulder. Jessie felt the burn of Leon's angry glare as he stared defiantly at his former master, unbowed. "Ain't right for one man to own another like he is some prized horse or bull. It ain't right for a man to tell another who he can marry an' who he can't. Every day you live in fear, wonderin' if the man gonna sell your wife or kids." Leon shook his head. "No suh, it ain't right at all."

Jessie felt his cheeks flush. "We didn't do any of those things at Briarwood. We kept our slave families together. We realized contented slaves would be more loyal and work harder."

"What ya say is true, but we always wondered what would become of us if your father died. Maybe the next massa won't be so kind. You don't know what it's like to be treated like children and have no say over your life. We wasn't free. I ain't sure I know what freedom is yet, but I like it better'n bein' a slave."

"Tell me, Leon, what's changed in your life?" Jessie waved his empty pistol in disgust. "You're in the army now. You have to follow orders, and you belong to them until your enlistment is up. If you desert or run, they'll hunt you down just like you're a runaway slave."

Leon's face looked puzzled before he explained, "You still don't get it do ya, Massa Jessie? It was me that decided to enlist. It was me said, yes, suh, I want to fight against slavery—no one else. I decided. I want my people to be free, and if it's worth havin' it's worth fightin' for. Once the white man gives you a gun an' he makes you a soldier, it becomes nigh impossible to say you ain't earned the right to be free."

Jessie heard the sounds of battle closing in upon them. Like it or not, Leon was his friend and he owed his life to him. He would be dead right now if Leon had pulled the trigger. Jessie heard Rebel yells coming closer to their po-

sition in the woods. Quickly, Jessie stuffed his empty re-
volver in its holster and offered his open hand to the little
Union soldier standing before him. "Give me your hand.
I'll help you up."

"No, suh, Massa Jessie, I ain't gonna surrender. I ain't
gonna be no Rebel prisoner. I know what happens to a nigger soldier if he gets caught by the Rebs."

"Leon, I haven't got time to sit here and argue with you.
Give me your hand before it's too late and I'll get you out
of here."

Leon hesitated as he looked deep into the eyes of his
former master. Something in those eyes told him his trust
wouldn't be betrayed. Jessie pulled the little ex-jockey up
behind him and lay spurs to the big bay horse.

The brush slapped and pulled at them as they raced
through the undergrowth. After about a mile Jessie
stopped, the sounds of battle fading behind them. Leon
swung down to the ground. Leon smiled as he said,
"Thank you, Massa Jessie."

"I couldn't leave you there. I owe you my life."

"You could've taken me prisoner, but ya didn't. Instead
you risked your safety to carry me away from the battle.
I'd say we was even." Leon smiled his toothy grin, and it
brought back memories of a happier time for Jessie.

Jessie offered his hand and Leon took it warmly. "I
wish you luck, Leon. I hope the next time we meet, the
war will be over. You know you're always welcome on
Kimbrough land."

Leon smiled as he released his former master's hand.
"You was born to a slave ownin' family and you never
know'd any other way. Me, I was born a slave. Ain't yer
fault any more than mine. Times is a changin', Massa."

"Thanks, Leon, but you don't have to call me master.
You're a free man now."

"Yes, suh, I call ya Massa outa respect, not because I
have to. You're a good man, Massa Jessie."

Jessie felt a twinge of sadness. "You best head down the
road as fast as you can, Leon. Hide if you hear someone

coming, and don't stop till you reach Camden. This whole area is swarming with our men. Good luck, Leon." Jessie gave his friend a wave as he turned Star's Pride back toward the wagon train.

It took Jessie just a few minutes to retrace his path to the wagons. Already the victorious Confederate cavalry was reorganizing. Dead horses were being cut from the traces, pillaging of the wagons by troopers was halted, and the dead and wounded were being gathered. Jessie watched as men detailed by Gilbert carefully tallied the take of the raid on the Union wagon train. He realized they weren't far from Mark's Mills, which would most likely lend its name to this battle.

Shelby's brigade had attacked from one side, while Fagan and Cabell's brigades struck from the other. It was a near miracle that Jessie had found an open pocket in the lines which had allowed him to help Leon escape. By the time he had returned to the wagons, the hole was closed.

During the battle of Mark's Mills, the Rebels captured three hundred fifty-seven wagons, twenty ambulances, nine pieces of artillery, and 1,325 white prisoners. The Rebels carefully tallied 475 white Union soldiers killed in the attack. Black soldiers were left uncounted and dead where they lay; no blacks were taken as prisoners during the battle. The only survivors were those lucky enough to escape in the woods. The supplies sent from the Union supply depot at Pine Bluff would never reach Steele's army at Camden.

Jessie was sickened by the sight of so many dead. The white Union dead were buried and the prisoners treated well, but there was no mercy for the rest. A full two thirds of the Union troops guarding the train had been wiped out in the bloody confrontation.

The combined battles of Poison Springs and Mark's Mills spelled the end of the Union Red River campaign. With his supplies gone, General Steele could neither hold his position nor advance. Meanwhile, General Banks was defeated in Louisiana, and the Red River Campaign collapsed in failure. General Sterling Price's infantry, fresh from their victory over Banks's army, marched north to link up with the Rebel cavalry near Camden.

Seeing his army was in danger, General Steele abandoned Camden and hurried north toward Little Rock, and the combined Confederate army hotly pursued. They caught Steele's rear guard and smashed it at the battle of Jenkin's Ferry. The rear-guard action did buy the necessary time to save the Union army as the remainder of Steele's forces limped into the fortifications at Little Rock.

Little Rock now stood surrounded on three sides by Confederate forces led by various commanders. On the south and west of the city were the Rebel commands of generals Sterling Price, John Sappington Marmaduke, and James F. Fagan. To the north and in command of Northern Arkansas since May 27, 1864, was Brigadier General Jo Shelby. The Confederate commanders felt that if the supply line to the east could be cut or severely disrupted, just as had been done at Camden, Steele could be forced to abandon Little Rock.

The focus now shifted to finding some way of cutting off the constant flow of food and supplies coming up the Arkansas River to Little Rock. The Union gunboat fleet made it difficult to intercede the river traffic effectively. Confederate pressure would need to be applied to stop supplies from coming up the Little Rock and Memphis railroad line that linked the supply depots at Duvall's Bluff on the White River. Jo Shelby knew he must find a way.

20

To Capture a Queen

Calvin Kimbrough let his eyes wander over the limited view in front of him. Near him rode four brand-new guns pulled by strong horses and brand new caissons of Captain Richard A. Collins's Second Missouri Battery. Trailing behind, ammunition and baggage wagons carried their supplies. Calvin, riding behind the supply wagons, watched with amusement as the youthful Postlewait, the battery's pet black bear, stretched a large paw forward to tap Delmar Pickett on the shoulder.

"Damn it, Postie, leave me alone an' go back to sleep, would ya! Yer breath could stop a train cold."

The black bear ignored his pleas as he roughly nosed Delmar in the back, nearly unseating him from the baggage wagon.

"Dag nab it, ya big, overgrown baby! Only one of us can drive this here wagon, so let me do it," Delmar grumbled.

Postie, bored with the game, rolled over onto his back and quickly slipped into a nap.

Calvin felt Red Rose's uneven gait jar through him as he sat his saddle. Straining to gain some relief, he rose in the stirrups to let his numb fanny regain some blood flow. His eyes studied the line of trail-hardened soldiers stretching before him like a long snake, flowing through every dip and curve in the road before him. The dust wasn't as bad as on other trips—this time they had been plagued with rains and floods. Even now he felt the wet chaffing of his uniform as it rubbed against his body. His mind drifted back over the last few days and the hard miles they had covered since leaving Batesville.

It had seemed so strange to return to Batesville. He remembered how bleak and empty Farnsworth and Covington Manors had looked with the women gone. The houses had been ransacked and now stood forlorn and lonely. Windows were shattered and here and there a door hung askew. He felt depressed when he recalled the happy times he and his family had shared there in the winter of Sixty-three. Now it was June 1864, and a new campaign was underway.

General Shelby began his move to cut the line of supply between Helena and Duvall's Bluff, and intercede navigation of the White River. Traveling with him was his Iron Brigade, which included the First, Fifth, Eleventh, and Twelfth Missouri Cavalry regiments and Captain Richard A. Collins's Second Missouri Artillery Battery of four guns.

General Shelby left the area of Batesville, crossed the White River on a pontoon bridge at Jacksonport, and moved in the direction of Augusta. Heavy and incessant rains delayed him several days in Augusta, but soon they waded Cache Bottom, ferrying over the Cache River, and through the mud and high water to Bayou De View. With much difficulty they crossed this crooked little stream and proceeded toward Clarendon on the White River.

It all made little sense to Calvin or the others in Collins's battery, for it was simply their job to follow orders and stay with the column. They were not privy to the secrets of command and didn't know where they were heading or for what reason.

Ross Kimbrough rode Prince of Heaven briskly along the ditches and fringes of the road. He was already passing the advance units of Shelby's Iron Brigade and he skirted the mounted troopers as quickly as he could. He must hurry to General Shelby with the latest information he and his scouts had gathered near Clarendon. The information he carried could be vital to their mission.

He strained his eyes to recognize familiar faces, ones that would tell him that he had found the headquarters' command. On he rode as Prince slipped and slid from one mud hole to the next.

Finally he spotted Captain Gilbert Thomas riding at the head of the Fifth Missouri Cavalry. Ross sawed hard on the reins as he drew alongside Gilbert. "Good afternoon, Gil. How far back to General Shelby's headquarters?"

"I don't know, Ross. We just stay in line and follow the column until someone says to do otherwise. I haven't dropped behind my company for a spell, but I reckon Jo isn't too far. You know the general likes to be near the front."

Ross snapped off a salute. "You're just a fountain of information, old friend. Thanks a lot, for nothin'." Ross spurred Prince forward.

Gilbert leaned back and shouted after Ross, "Information is your job. Mine is pushin' these raggedy-ass soldiers down this slime hole someone mistakenly called a road." He waved at his friend disappearing down the line. "Good luck!"

Ross continued down the column until he found the lead elements of the headquarters' staff. He saw Evan Stryker and rode toward him. "Good afternoon, Major. Where's the general? I've got some information that might be important."

"Some of our wagons got crossed up at the last stream crossing, maybe a couple of miles back. He went to take a look. He should be back pretty soon. What have ya got?"

"Some information from someone you know. Do you remember Sarah Ann Lightfoot from Clarendon?"

"Sarah Ann? Nah, we aren't close to Clarendon, are we?"

"We're pretty close right now. I'd say less than five miles."

Evan looked puzzled. "Well, I guess it shouldn't surprise me. We've crossed so many streams and made so many turns I've completely loss my sense of direction." He paused as he adjusted the collar on his overcoat.

Evan recalled the days he had stayed at the Lightfoot Plantation after the battle of Oak Hills, or, as the Yankees referred to it, Pea Ridge. While there he had first introduced Valissa Covington to Ross and had met General Shelby. That fortuitous meeting resulted in his eventual transfer to Shelby's brigade. He smiled as he thought about the lovely Sarah Ann Lightfoot. "What did Sarah have to say?"

"She hasn't seen her father for a while. He's serving in the army on the other side of the Big Muddy. She did have some interesting information about the Yankees stationed around Clarendon." Ross paused for a moment, then almost as an afterthought he said, "She asked about Valissa and when I'd last seen her."

"What did she have to tell you that's got you so excited?"

"You'll find out soon enough, Major. I'm holdin' this for General Shelby."

That night, when Shelby's brigade stopped for their nightly encampment, a quickly called staff meeting was held. General Shelby stood rigidly before a roaring fire. He loved to stare into the coals of a good fire and seemed fascinated by the twinkle and glow of the red hot embers.

He stood with his hands behind his back, and when he turned to face his men, the firelight seemed to dance in his eyes. "Gentlemen, I've called you here to plan an important attack. Captain Ross Kimbrough has brought me some exciting news. I'm going to let him tell you what he has told me, then we will proceed from there. Please report, Captain Kimbrough."

Ross stood up from the log where he had been sitting. He turned to face the loose-knit group of officers scattered around the fire. "Earlier today, my scouts and I checked out the town of Clarendon, Arkansas, which is but a few miles distant. There I met a young woman many of you may remember, Miss Sarah Ann Lightfoot of the Lightfoot Plantation. She told me there is a tin-clad called the *Queen City* anchored just offshore, and it's not supported by any ground or naval forces. I have discussed it with General Shelby and he has ordered us to capture it." A loud murmur flowed through the group at this news. "With the capture of the *Queen City* we could disrupt supplies heading for Duvall's Bluff and General Steele's army at Little Rock."

Ross stepped forward dramatically. "One of my men, Sergeant Jonas Starke, rode in with further information a couple of hours ago. He and a couple of men captured an ensign on shore leave from the gunboat. This prisoner gave us some key information. Our boys did their best to make the ensign's disappearance look like he might have deserted, and so far, I don't think the Yankees are aware we're even here." Ross turned toward his old friend. "Sergeant Starke, would you please brief these officers on your information?"

Jonas stood nervously before the officers. It was one thing to face fire from the enemy, and quite another to stand before your commanding officers and give a report. Jonas's voice trembled, and Ross thought he could see Starke's slender knees shake as he stood gaunt and small before the campfire. Jonas nervously cleared his throat.

"Gentlemen, here is what we got outa a fella we caught celebratin' at a local tavern. His name is Ensign Mathews an' he was on shore leave when we caught him. With a little persuasion he got right talkative. He told us the USS *Queen City* was bought in Cincinnati, Ohio, and commissioned in April 1863. She is a side wheeler, weighing two hundred and twelve tons, and has a low water draft of three feet. Her sides have been reinforced with heavy oak and one-and-a-half-inch steel plate over the boilers and paddle wheels. Her armament included a battery of two thirty-pound Parrott rifles, two thirty-two-pounders, four twenty-four-pound howitzers, and one twelve-pound howitzer on a field carriage. She is presently commanded by Acting Master Captain Michael Hickey with a crew of sixty-five men. The ship is anchored near the shore and is alone. There are no other supporting troops in the town of Clarendon."

Colonel Shanks stood. "Pardon me, General, but just how do you expect us to capture a heavily armed gunboat? One good broadside from her could wreak havoc among our troops. Our artillery is no match for the firepower that ship commands."

General Shelby stepped forward holding a hand up to silence his officers. "Sergeant Starke, Captain Kimbrough, you may be seated." Shelby turned to face his company commanders. "What you say is true if we are to take the ship on in battle. It is my plan to sneak in at night and bring our artillery to bear at point-blank range. I intend to surprise the *Queen City* and capture her while her crew is asleep. I admit the task might be difficult, but think of what we might accomplish, gentlemen, if we can pull this off!" The officers looked at one another and nodded in agreement. Jo Shelby continued. "Gentlemen, if this operation is to be successful, then it must have absolute secrecy. You will not reveal our plans until it is time to attack. I want the best riflemen in the brigade to support the artillery on the attack. Select your men carefully and keep them uninformed about our plans until absolutely necessary. Is that clear?" Shelby paused. "Do any of you have any questions?" Again he waited as everyone remained silent. "Captain Collins, I need you to stay here to study my plans. The rest of you are dismissed."

As Calvin Kimbrough and the men of Collins's battery settled into camp, they were unaware of the adventure that awaited them. A strong guard was stationed around the camp to prevent their presence being discovered by the enemy. Orders were given for all to be quiet. The battery remained in camp until about ten o'clock that night, when Captain Collins ordered the men to see that the ammunition chests were filled with solid shot and shells and to be ready for battle in one hour.

"Battle in one hour?" wondered Calvin. "Battle to begin in the middle of night?" Questions bounded between the men as all in the battery tried to make sense of the order. To the best of their knowledge they weren't even close to the enemy. Unanswered questions were on all the cannoneers' lips. "Where are we going? Who can we fight this time of night? Why no grape and canister among our ammunition?" But the men worked feverishly to be ready for action by eleven o'clock.

At the appointed time, Captain Collins gathered the men together, and General Shelby addressed the assembled cannoneers. "Gentlemen, we are about to embark on a special mission. Tonight we will attack a Union gunboat called the *Queen City*, presently anchored near the town of Clarendon."

A loud murmur ran through the gathered artillerymen as they whispered exclamations of astonishment to each other. "A gunboat? How big is it?" they wondered aloud. Collins's battery had faced a gunboat once before, nearly a year ago at the battle of Helena. It had rained down a storm of shot and shell on them from a great distance, and few would forget the menacing, dark shape sending its messengers of death to land among them. None were particularly eager to face that kind of fire-power again. Besides, just one shot from the gunboat would weigh twice as much as a whole volley from their battery of two ten-pound Parrott rifles and two twelve-pound howitzers.

"Gentlemen, please, hold it down and listen up!" The murmuring died down into silence. "The *Queen City* is only a small tin-clad and it is lightly armored. We hope to get within one hundred yards of her before we open fire. If we surprise them, we might catch the crew sleeping. If we can capture her, we can threaten riverboat traffic on the White River for a while."

Calvin felt alternating cold chills and hot blood coursing through his veins as he thought of staring into the dark muzzles of those thirty-two-pounders at a distance of only one hundred yards. He tried to blink the awful picture from his mind. What if the watch spotted them? What would happen if the gunboat opened its full broadside into his battery at close range? Calvin didn't even want to think about the result. He felt the icy fingers of fear crawling up his spine. He looked around him to his friends and fellow crewmen. If they were scared, they tried to hide it. They were a team, and he knew he couldn't fail his friends. If they would stand before the lethal loads of the dark monster, he would stand by them.

At midnight Calvin and the rest of Collins's battery began its three-mile trip to Clarendon to capture the *Queen City*. Calvin knew four hundred hand-picked riflemen from Shelby's brigade would accompany them. Slowly, cautiously, Collins's battery moved forward as quiet as a funeral procession. Every man was on foot except General Shelby and the drivers of the artillery teams. The night was so dark the men could not recognize one another ten feet away except by the sound of their voices.

Calvin felt an involuntary shiver run through him as beads of sweat formed on his brow. He felt his breathing quicken as his pulse began to pound. When they were about a mile from Clarendon, they broke out of the woods and into an open field. There they could see the smoke from the chimneys of the gunboat drifting against the darkened skyline.

General Shelby motioned for them to stop and they began to ready the guns and leave the horses, drivers, and limber chests. They knew they would make too much noise if they tried to take them.

Captain Collins stepped forward and whispered to Calvin's crew. "Try to muffle the wheels of the gun carriages to prevent any possibility of rattling. Take a shirt or a sock and wrap it around the spindles between the hubs and axles." Calvin watched as members of his crew pulled off their shoes and donated their socks.

Danny Dunbar stuffed his worn pair into the hubs. "I figure if this don't work," Danny whispered, "I'm not gonna need 'em come tomorrow, anyhow."

When the socks gave out, Calvin took off his shirt, tore it into strips, and gave them to be used as mufflers. General Shelby stood by and watched. Shelby asked, "How many shirts do you have left?"

"None," replied Calvin.

"I'll see that you get half a dozen when this battle is over."

"I won't need 'em, General. You can bury me without one."

Delmar whispered, "Yeah, Gen'ral, if this don't work you can scrape together what's left of us and fill one good grave!"

They wanted to laugh but they dared not, for it might give away their position. The dark humor did serve its purpose as Calvin and the others felt a loosening of the tension within their bellies. Even in the face of death they could find time to laugh at their predicament. Still, each man secretly thought this could be his last night on earth.

They moved along as quietly as possible. Calvin felt himself occasionally holding his breath, afraid the enemy might hear his breathing. When his lungs began to burn he forced himself to slowly exhale. Darkness and silence were all that could save them from destruction in their advance of a mile across an open field against an enemy whose artillery was ten times their strength. Slowly and silently they inched forward toward the menacing, black superstructure of the USS *Queen City*. Before dawn they would seek their destiny.

21

To Stir a Sleeping Giant

Captain Ross Kimbrough hid in the shadows of a brick home near the waterfront in Clarendon. From his vantage point he had a clear view of the *Queen City* at rest in the White River. He breathed out slowly to ease some of his tension. The Union shore patrol had returned to the ship, and the Yankees were still unaware of their presence. It had been close, much too close for comfort. Just minutes before, the Yankee patrol nearly stumbled onto the hiding Rebels. The Rebel scouts quickly dove into the shadows and narrowly avoided detection. If the patrol had found them, the element of surprise would have been lost and the attack on the *Queen City* doomed.

Ross watched the ship riding at anchor not more than one hundred yards from shore. She had her steam up and a guard at his post, and the big guns appeared loaded and cleared for action. Everything remained quiet on board, suggesting the crew wasn't expecting trouble. Ross sent word by courier to the approaching artillery; everything was proceeding as planned.

As Collins's battery reached the edge of town they found a wide, wooden bridge that must be crossed to reach the *Queen City*. Captain Collins knew the iron wheels rolling across the wooden planks would make so much noise they might be discovered. He ordered his men to gather and cut weeds to throw on the bridge to muffle the sound of their passing. They knew the danger of discovery became more imminent the closer they drew to the gunboat. Close at hand, tall and rank grew great patches of weeds along the road, and Calvin helped in the search for covering to cut and lay on the bridge. Having used up the closest patches of weeds, he extended his search for more. As he crawled along on hands and knees, Calvin parted a thick patch of weeds and came face to face with a ferocious, large dog, disturbed from his sleep by their approach.

Calvin saw a gleam of white as the dog snarled, and he saw the lips twist cruelly back to expose wicked looking fangs. In the weak light cast from a sliver of moon he watched fearfully as the white hairs rose on the back of the dog's neck. Beads of sweat broke across Calvin's forehead and his stomach took a sick twist. He swallowed hard as he slowly eased back the way he had come. The dog walked forward stiff-leggedly, ready to attack at the slightest provocation. He followed Calvin cautiously, all the while maintaining a low and menacing growl. Calvin realized that if he turned his back the dog would attack so he tried to look non-threatening as he retreated ever so slowly. His luck held. The dog had not barked, but he kept up his deep-throated growl as he edged forward, matching Calvin's pace.

Over his shoulder Calvin heard Danny whisper, "What's the holdup, Cal?"

Calvin kept his voice low and steady, afraid if he spoke loudly it would rile the dog. "There's a damn dog over here and he's decided these weeds are his. He has me convinced. Back out of here easy like and we'll look for weeds in another direction."

Once Calvin backed off further, the dog seemed satisfied. He had protected his territory. If they stayed away from his area, the dog would ignore the men. One look at him was enough to ensure that the cannoneers would give him a wide berth.

By two o'clock in the morning, the Confederates had their artillery in position. Two of the big guns were sitting within fifty yards of the *Queen City* and the other two were placed a hundred yards away, near a large brick home directly in front of the tin-clad. One of these guns was manned by Calvin's crew.

From his position, Calvin watched and listened to the Union sentinel walk to and fro on his beat on the upper deck. His steps had a steady rhythm, the leather soles echoing on the deck. The boat was brilliantly lit from inside and, with all artillery gun ports open, the *Queen City* made a tempting and splendid target for night practice.

All the Rebel cannons were loaded with double shot and ready to fire. Captain Collins passed the word down in whispered orders, "Remain quiet and wait. Be ready to fire all four guns simultaneously so the enemy can't count our guns by the number of shots."

Two hours they waited under the guns of the great, armored giant. If the Union crew woke up and discovered them, the ship could blast Collins's battery into eternity at a moment's notice. Ross felt his heart pounding and sensed his pulse as each beat throbbed in his temple. As the seconds turned into minutes and the minutes turned into hours, his nerves drew tighter like an overwound watchspring ready to break. Time seemed to slow down—a minute seemed like an hour and an hour like eternity. Tension, like a giant claw, gripped them tightly. All were afraid the slightest noise would give them away.

So silent had his men moved that Calvin's gun sat fewer than twenty feet from the front door of an occupied dwelling. No one in the house or on the boat knew they were within a hundred miles of the place. The riflemen were also in their places, ready to drive any crew or gunners from their posts once the cannonading began.

As Calvin studied the scene before him, he saw the black, somber outline of the ship cast against the pale moon. Its faint light and that cast from the ship's lanterns reflected in the waters of the river in diffused highlights. On the hour, Calvin listened to the deep peal of the ship's time bell. When they heard it the first time his crew nearly jumped out of their skins, afraid their presence had been discovered.

The steady splash, splash, splash of the waves slapping the *Queen City*'s hull added to his raw and tortured nerves. It further compounded his need to slip away to relieve himself. He fought the urge, afraid if he moved he might be discovered. Slowly, the first faint rays of sunlight began to caress the eastern skies and warned the nervous Rebels of the coming sunrise.

At four o'clock in the morning, General Shelby gave the command to fire, and all four guns blasted into the sleeping gunboat. The riflemen opened fire at the deafening roar of the opening salvo. Long-pent-up emotions exploded from the Rebel gunners as their tension released itself with the first crashing blow. Unrestrained Rebel yells filled the air as the last echoes of the big guns reverberated off the low riverbanks. Never had Calvin felt more alive, or his senses so attuned to all the commotion swirling around him.

Each crew had brought five shots for each gun, and before they had been exhausted the drivers galloped up with the rest of the ammunition in their limber chests. The rest of the brigade then joined the battle.

The cannoneers put five shots through the pilothouse in the opening moments. Somehow they missed hitting the sleeping pilot. Firing as fast as they could reload, the cannoneers sent more than twenty artillery shells crashing through the gun deck of the *Queen City*. The first Union sailor killed was cut in two by a cannonball while asleep in his hammock. The starboard engine of the ship was damaged by an exploding shell passing directly through it. The port engine was damaged by a piece of the same shell cutting the main steam line. Escaping white-hot steam billowed through the gun ports, blinding and scalding crew members on board. Some sailors panicked and abandoned ship, jumping into the river to escape the terrifying and unsuspected attack. Sailors who were not shot before they hit the water swam for the opposite shore, hoping to escape in the dense underbrush on the far riverbank.

Calvin worked at his gun at a furious pace. With every discharge from his cannon, the blast shook the large brick home standing closest to the guns. After the fourth round an elderly lady came tearing out, wringing her hands in fear. Her nightshirt remained partially unbuttoned and gleamed white in the faint rays of early dawn. The strings of her nightcap flew white in the moonshine as she shrieked at every step, "Don't shoot! Don't shoot! There's a gunboat out in the river. Take your gun away, for God's sake, before you wake them. They'll kill us all!"

Calvin looked into the frightened eyes of the old woman. He tried not to laugh, but her pitiful expression and disheveled appearance was too much. The Rebel barrage had lasted for ten minutes or more already. No one could still be asleep through the deafening racket of the artillery attack. Calvin laughed hysterically as the woman stood agape and pressed her trembling hands to her head. When he regained his composure he replied, "Ma'am, we aim to do more than wake up the Yankees, we aim to send 'em straight to hell!" The crew kept to their cannon as the woman made her way to her house with her hands still pressed tightly against her ears.

Amid the continued barrage on the tin-clad by the artillery and the sharpshooters, the panic-stricken pilot ran from the pilothouse waving a white flag. All firing ceased, and General Shelby, who was on horseback, rode forward as near the shore as he could. General Shelby shouted to the pilot, "Are you the commander of the ship?"

The pale-faced pilot replied, "I'm only the pilot, but I'll go and find the captain if you'll hold your fire."

Soon, a partially dressed Captain Hickey came up on

the deck and offered a formal surrender. A boat was
manned and a tow line was brought ashore and tied to a
tree. The ship drifted to the shore near the waiting Rebels.
The entire battle lasted only twenty minutes. Shelby's men
took all those remaining on board as prisoners and confiscated ten thousand dollars in Union greenbacks from
the paymaster. Shelby issued orders to strip the ship of
anything useful. Among the captured items were wearing apparel, medical supplies, food, ammunition, cannon equipment, two twenty-four-pound howitzers, and
a twelve-pound howitzer on a field carriage. The two
twenty-four-pound howitzers were hastily set up as a shore
battery to control the river. The twelve-pounder on the
field carriage was added to Collins's battery.

While the plunder was being gathered from the *Queen
City*, Ross Kimbrough and the other scouts kept their eyes
on the White River. At nine o'clock in the morning Ross
and his men spotted three more gunboats steaming ominously around a riverbend.

Realizing they could not hold the *Queen City* and knowing she was too badly damaged to fight from her, Shelby
made the decision to blow her up. All the men were ordered ashore and a powder train was laid to the powder
magazine by Major Evan Stryker of Shelby's staff. When
the powder was ignited, the gunboat was set adrift. When
the spurting and sizzling fire reached the magazine, the explosion rocked up and down the river, causing trees to
tremble and men to reel from the blast. The dark waters
parted as chunks of wood and splinters of every size and
shape flew into the air. Pieces of the gunboat continued to
fall and drift from the sky for several minutes. The water,
parted by the blast, quickly closed over the sinking remains
of the once proud tin-clad gunboat, the USS *Queen City*.

The casualty report included one killed, one sailor and
one negro drowned, nine wounded, including Captain
Hickey, and twenty Union prisoners captured. Shelby had
not lost a man. The captured Union sailors were hustled

away under guard by a Confederate detail to Helena where they would attempt a prisoner exchange.

The Rebels heard the gunboats approaching long before they could see them. Ross stood on the bank of the river and listened to their snorting, whistling, and bell ringing as they moved around the bend in the river. Great gray-black clouds of cinders and steam billowed above the trees, marking their progress. The Rebels got their first view of the enemy ships as the gunboats rounded the river bend about three hundred yards distant. The Union fleet stormed to the attack against the Rebels just as the *Queen City* was rocked by the fatal explosion.

As the Union fleet came abreast of the Cache River entrance, General Shelby gave the order to fire. Captain Collins echoed the order, and the Confederate cannons roared to life. One of the first shots hit the lead ship in its pilot-house.

Ross recognized the ship in the lead. On those nights when he was particularly restless and he closed his eyes, Ross could still picture the sheets of flames as they danced from the muzzles of the massive cannons on her deck. Like a recurring nightmare he saw that ship again, but this was no dream. In his mind he could still hear the scream of her shells as they cut through the air above him and ripped through the woods and exploded around him. Yes, he recognized this ominous stern-wheeler. It was the *Tyler*, a ship faced nearly a year before at the battle of Helena. There was no mistaking her as she once again stalked the men of Shelby's Iron Brigade like an angry river goddess awakened from her sleep.

Trailing behind the *Tyler* were a second and third ship. Ross thought they looked like three large bullies looking for someone to kick while they were down, but these little guys had a few kicks of their own.

The Yankee ships opened fire as they approached, using their bow guns until their broadsides came to bear. Then they unleashed their combined firepower as sheets of red-and-yellow flames danced from the muzzles of the guns.

The broadsides sounded like a fierce thunderstorm, rolling and echoing their deep-throated rumbles across the water until the sound was hurled back by the riverbanks. On the shore, the Rebels concentrated their principal fire at the lead ship, the *Tyler*.

The second ship was also hit in the early moments of the engagement by twelve-pounder shrapnel—it entered the port shutter of the pilothouse and carried away the bell wires, ringing them relentlessly. Confused by the bells, the engineers aboard stopped the gunboat directly under the Confederate battery. As the second ship came abreast of the Rebel cannons and slid to a stop, Calvin read the name *Fawn* painted brightly on the bow.

In the early broadsides from the *Tyler*, a chance shot hit the two captured guns removed earlier from the *Queen City* that were now set in battery. Many volunteers manning the guns were wounded or killed, and the guns, no longer serviceable, were abandoned. The men servicing them rejoined Collins's battery.

Calvin watched the third ship slide around the *Fawn*, which had stopped dead in the water. He made out the name of the third ship as it passed, barely legible on the side of the ship: *Naumkeag*.

The *Tyler* and the *Naumkeag* continued down the river as the damaged *Fawn* stalled in front of Collins's battery. This gap between the first two gunboats and the *Fawn* put the Confederates in a crossfire.

Ross could not believe the awful firepower of those gunboats. Great geysers of earth and water danced high in the air around them, gouged out of the river and shore by the huge shells fired by the passing gunboats. Ross felt the sting of dirt clods falling around him, and proclaimed it a miracle they survived at all under the *Fawn*'s continued broadsides. He saw a large shell hit a home and explode, sending shards of brick and wood into the air, as if the house had been slapped by the unseen hand of a giant.

Calvin felt his anger rise as the *Fawn* seemed to defy them, stopping directly under their guns. It was as if the

gunboat was challenging his pitiful little battery of field
pieces to take their best shot—if they dared. Months of
drill paid off as the battery poured round after round into
the *Fawn*. Shells that seemed as big as washtubs began to
plow the ground and trim the trees around them, but the
crew stood their ground. How long they kept this up,
Calvin was uncertain. Later he thought it had been only
fifteen minutes, but then it had seemed like hours. White-
gray powder smoke fired from the big guns drifted and
swirled in the light breeze, at times obscuring the target.
Like an evil fog it clung to the riverbanks and climbed silently through the trees.

The Rebels concentrated all their attention on the *Fawn*
and a second shell entered its pilothouse, tearing up the
floor and throwing splinters in every direction. Another
shot came across the hurricane deck and struck the hog-
chain brace. One passed forward between the chimney
stacks, tearing the deck and destroying a harness cask
filled with water. The cask exploded, shooting a column of
water into the air like a fountain. Three shells entered the
casement and exploded on the port side, disabling the
crews of two guns. Shrapnel entered the hull midships,
ranging to the starboard, then passing forward to explode
under the forecastle deck. Two shells entered the stern, one
passing through the blacksmith's forge and bursting back
of the throttle valve, the other exploding over the starboard
engine. Another shell burst on the outside over the starboard crank, cutting in two the remaining hog chain and
brace. During this damaging fire, the *Fawn* began a slug-
gish advance.

By this time the *Tyler* and the *Naumkeag* had drifted
downriver and out of sight. About the time they swung
around to begin another pass, the *Fawn*, badly damaged,
floated past them. She would remain out of the action for
a while.

The *Tyler* and *Naumkeag* moved back into range and
began their second pass on the Confederate positions.
Shelby's men were surprised to see the two gunboats re-

turning, at first believing they intended merely to run the gauntlet past the Rebel position. After seeing the power the gunboats could wield, General Shelby and his staff thought it unwise to continue such an unequal contest. He ordered his dismounted cavalry to give fire support and began to withdraw Collins's battery from the shore.

Calvin heard the shouted orders from Captain Collins— little time was left. Calvin helped limber the guns and then, unnerved by the accuracy of the fire from the gunboats, he began a hasty retreat. Calvin found himself on foot. The artillerymen were whipping the scared and shrieking horses, trying to urge them into the woods. All the while, broadsides continued to rain down death and destruction around them. The horror of the moment only served to hurry their progress as they fled the shore. During the battle Calvin had little time to be afraid, but once he had received the orders to retreat, his fear nearly overpowered him.

His back now to the enemy, his imagination took over. He could picture in his mind those deadly fire-blossoms from the muzzles of the tin-clad guns as the huge shells sought him. Calvin ran and ran some more, and he didn't waste time glancing back. His feet seemed to sprout wings, and he ran with the speed of a jackrabbit. Calvin heard the huge shells from the ship rip through the trees and roar overhead. He didn't stop running until he reached the safety of the supply and ammunition wagons, hidden safely in the woods beyond the reach of the gunboats.

Never in his life had a black bear's face looked so comforting as did Postlewait's, shirking beneath the wagons. Calvin felt better as he dragged the air into his burning lungs. He knew he was safe—Captain Collins always tried to keep his bear away from danger. To Calvin's surprise he realized he had beaten many of the battery's horse-drawn caissons and guns back to the relative safety of the supply wagons.

Delmar Pickett walked up to Calvin with a wide grin on

his face. "Damn, Cal, I believe the way you ran you'd make a jackrabbit die of envy!"

"Hells bells, Delmar! I wasn't scared. I was just afraid if I didn't move pretty damn quick, someone who really was scared might run right over me!"

Because the guns had been disabled so early in the battle, the Confederates were successful in hauling away the damaged twenty-four-pounders taken from the *Queen City*.

As Shelby's men began to withdraw, the *Naumkeag* headed into shore under cover fire from the *Tyler*. The men of the *Naumkeag* recovered the twelve-pound brass howitzer taken from the *Queen City*. The Rebels lacked a spare limber and team to haul away the captured gun and couldn't remove it under such heavy fire. Five wounded Confederate troopers crewing the howitzer were captured. The Yankees also recovered the cutter and the oars from the *Queen City* and much of the captured artillery ammunition.

Ross and his scouts were among the last Rebels to retreat from Clarendon. They were the first in, and now they would be the last out. It hurt Ross to watch the Union sailors recapture the brass howitzer and the wounded crew left behind in the confusion. His disappointment was tempered by the realization that his men were too few to halt the sailors. Although the captives were cavalry troopers who had volunteered to man the howitzer, they had stayed valiantly by their gun. He felt the bitter acid of his disappointment roiling in his stomach and the tears that stung his eyes as he watched them fall into the hands of the enemy.

Although Ross and his scouts had heard the order to retreat, his pride made him stand until the last possible moment, defiantly watching the Union sailors pour ashore. He moved his men back slowly, ever vigilant for news he could bring to his general. When the Confederates had withdrawn from the range of the gunboats, the angry sailors started to burn the buildings close to the river.

His hate for the enemy surged to new heights as helplessly he watched the Yankees burn a large gristmill, a sawmill, and several timber wagons. He clenched his teeth and his fists, his knuckles turned white, as he witnessed the torching of the helpless town. The citizens of Clarendon were not a part of the attack on the *Queen City*, but they would be punished and pay the sacrifice. "Why is it that nearly everywhere the Union army or navy go, black smoke and fire soon follow?" Ross wondered.

From his vantage point, he noticed nearly every tree for a mile along the shore had suffered from the battle. So had the town, from wild shots fired by the Union gunboats. Ross watched the Union ships fire rounds of shrapnel and grapeshot into the homes of citizens of Clarendon, for spite and target practice. Ross slammed his fist into his other hand in exasperation. Now the Yankees made war on innocent women and children.

Ross watched as the Union wounded were transferred to the *Tyler* from the other ships. He saw the *Tyler* slowly steam around the bend and move out of sight in the direction of Duvall's Bluff.

While the *Tyler* was absent, the temporarily repaired *Fawn* and the *Naumkeag* continued to patrol the river along Clarendon. Several times they received musket fire from Shelby's men hidden in the woods. The Union gunboats returned fire from their cannons using shrapnel and canister loads. As night began to close the day, the tinclads anchored a short distance away at the opening of the Cache River.

Ross and his scouts carried the information to General Shelby and his staff. During the night, members of the brigade returned to the riverbank and dug hastily constructed rifle pits and a couple of breastworks. Exhausted from the night attack on the *Queen City* followed by a day of battle with the Union fleet, the men struggled through a second night. They hadn't had time to supply the breastworks with artillery before daylight painted the morning sky.

The *Fawn* and *Naumkeag* steamed downriver and started shelling the Confederate positions from a distance beyond the effective range of the Rebel muskets. Out-gunned and still not prepared, the Rebels withdrew from the river. Neither gunboat suffered damage in this second attack.

On June 26, the *Tyler* returned, escorting three troop transports. Aboard these ships were three thousand infantry and cavalry, accompanied by a battery of artillery under the command of General E. A. Carr. They were unloaded with no opposition at Clarendon. Shelby, who received an excellent count of the enemy he faced from Ross Kimbrough and his scouts, decided he could not stand toe to toe with the enemy backed by the three gunboats. He decided to withdraw beyond gunboat range and see how the Yankees responded.

General Carr immediately attacked the Confederate brigade waiting beyond the town, but met with serious resistance. General Shelby, seeing that his mission to disrupt the supplies along the White River was now futile, fought a slow withdrawal toward Bayou De View on June 26 and 27. General Carr followed very cautiously behind Shelby's retreating force, but soon gave up the chase and returned to Clarendon.

General Shelby was disappointed that his mission had failed. Though he was proud of the attack and capture of the USS *Queen City*. One gunboat had been captured and destroyed in the attack and others were severely damaged by the brilliant attack of one mounted artillery battery backed by a brigade of cavalry. A Union general with a complete brigade had been diverted from service elsewhere to counter the threat to navigation. It hadn't been a wasted effort after all. As Shelby's brigade rode away, the general and his men took comfort in their momentary triumph and knew they had disrupted the enemy, if only for awhile.

22

Clarksville, Texas

Jethro popped a buggy whip in the air above the horses that pulled the lead wagon. "Haw, git up there." The wagon eased off the deck of the ferry and up the sloped riverbank.

Cassandra leaned over the sideboard and looked behind her at the Red River crossing. On the far shore Andrew Covington and his family waited with their wagons. The wooden river ferry on which she and her family had just crossed was already pulling for the opposite shore to retrieve Andrew's party. Cassandra turned as the wagon cleared the slope of the riverbank. In the distance she saw a town that must be Clarksville. She studied the rich bottomland along the river. "So, this is Texas," she thought. She felt the hot sun of early May warm her with its rays. The rocking of the wagon jarred her into her sister, Elizabeth.

"How long do you think it'll take to get Andrew's wagons across?" asked Elizabeth.

"It shouldn't take more than thirty or forty-five minutes. Before you know it, we should be in Clarksville."

Elizabeth smoothed back her strawberry blonde hair. "It won't be too soon for me. I'm tired of riding and I'd love a good hot bath."

Cassandra looked over at her sixteen-year-old sister and realized just how much Elizabeth had matured over the last two years. She had blossomed into a woman with curves to match. "A bath would be nice, but I want a meal at a real table with a tablecloth on it. Can you imagine? It seems so long since we ate indoors."

Katlin left her carriage and walked over to the girls. She held little Glen snuggled warm in her arms. "I heard your dreaming clear over there, girls. A good meal or a hot bath would be nice, but I'm longing for a night in a real bed. Maybe even a featherbed."

Cassandra laughed, then said, "Listen to us. It sounds like we've been on the road for months."

Elizabeth's face turned into a teasing pout. "Okay, we've only been on the road for a few weeks, but it seems longer, doesn't it?"

Cassandra smiled at her sister. "Yes, I guess in some ways it does. Our trip from Camden doesn't seem so bad when you compare it to the trip from Missouri to Batesville."

Katlin said, "I was more worried when we were traveling from Batesville to Camden. Why, everyday I thought the Yankees might find those dead soldiers and have us arrested. The weather was so cold and I had to worry about little Glen getting too chilled. I never was so happy to put the Union lines behind us."

Elizabeth saw their point. "I guess when you compare, this trip has been easy." Liz smiled mischievously. "I'll still be glad to live under a roof again." Elizabeth noticed the far-off look in Cassandra's eyes. "What's the matter, Cassie? What are you thinking so hard about?"

Cassandra was drawn back from thoughts by Elizabeth's question. "Oh, not much, really. I was just thinking about the good times we had in Camden and how much I miss Evan. You know, no matter how hard you try, sometimes you can't help but worry."

Katlin nodded in agreement. "I worry about Jessie and all the boys. You just have to trust in the Lord and pray for their safe return. I'm tired of this war, and I want our men to come home. Sometimes, I wish I could just wake up and discover this was all just a bad dream and find myself at home again in Missouri, the way it was before the war."

"Well, the war won't last much longer. Maybe then we can get back to the old days," said Elizabeth.

A sad expression passed over Cassandra's face. "It will never be like old times, sis. This war has changed everything. If you believe things will ever be like they were before the war, then you'll be sadly disappointed."

"Oh, I know it won't be the same. Nothing can bring Briarwood back, or Ma and Pa, but we could get on with rebuilding our lives. You know, put the war behind us and start over fresh."

"Putting the hate and anger behind you can sometimes be more difficult than fighting the war," Cassandra replied. She looked back at the Red River. "Won't be long and the Covingtons will be across. Let's get ready. I want to get settled into Clarksville as soon as possible and wash off this trail dust."

In an hour, Cassandra, riding in the lead wagon, led the small caravan into the streets of Clarksville. She was impressed by the bustling little community. The town had been treated much more kindly by the war than most of the towns she had passed through in Missouri and Arkansas. People moved briskly along the boardwalks as they tended to their business. Cassandra saw a large, imposing, two-story brick building facing east on the town square. Across the street she saw the courthouse. "Jethro, pull the wagon up in front of the hotel."

"Yes, Miz Cassie."

Cassandra was impressed by the massive brick structure. Large verandas covered both floors of the hotel, and near the entrance stood a tall pole with a large bell at the top of it with a rope near the base. On both the ground floor and second story, wide porches with finished wood floors clearly showed the hotel's quality.

Cassandra, joined by Andrew Covington, entered the lobby at the center of the first floor. Behind a counter in the lobby stood a smiling black man wearing a suit. He watched Andrew and Cassandra enter. "Welcome, suh, to one of the finest hotels in Texas, the Donoho House. May ah be of service, suh?"

Andrew moved to the counter. "I certainly hope so. We are in need of rooms for my family and for Miss Kimbrough's party. Is your master here?"

"Yes, suh, Miz Mary is in her office. I'd be glad to fetch her for ya, but she'll want to know how many rooms you will need, suh."

"I'll need accommodations for my wife and I, and a separate room for my daughter. We also need to quarter three slaves. How about your family, Cassandra?" asked Andrew.

"We need two rooms for ourselves and quarters for four coloreds."

"Yes, ma'am, I'll get Miz Mary for ya right away." Moments later the desk clerk returned, followed by an attractive woman in her mid- to late fifties. She had red hair pulled back tightly in a bun at the nape of her neck. The dress she wore was simple yet attractive and emphasized her slender figure.

She extended her hand to Andrew. "Allow me to introduce myself. My name is Mary Donoho, and I own and operate this hotel. I'd like to welcome you to the Donoho House. Mort, my clerk, said you will need to quarter seven slaves and need four rooms. Is that correct?"

"Yes, that should work out fine, don't you think, Cassandra?"

"I have just one question. What are your facilities like for our coloreds?"

"We don't allow them to sleep in the hotel itself. We

have very nice, clean, comfortable quarters next to our stable. It's right across the alley. I keep a man on duty to watch the stock and property at night."

"May we keep our personal servants in our rooms at night?"

"I'm afraid it is against our hotel policy, but they will be well-looked-after and they may be of assistance to you in your rooms during the day."

"I guess that will be acceptable."

"I'm sure you will enjoy your stay here. The Donoho is one of the finest hotels in Texas."

Cassandra smiled. "So we've been told. We're anxious to get hot baths and to freshen up."

"I'll see to it immediately. How long will you be staying with us?"

"We are uncertain how long we will be in the area. I'm guessing several months, or until the war ends. We would like to find homes for rent if it is possible. We'd like to stay here until other arrangements can be made."

"You might check with our local newspaper, the *Northern Standard*. They might know of homes for rent, or you could place an ad."

Andrew looked stunned. "Did you say your paper is called the *Northern Standard*?"

"Yes I did. It's not a paper of northern sentiment, let me assure you. It was named long before the war, and the paper has retained its name. The owner of the paper is Captain Charles DeMorse of the Twenty-ninth Confederate Cavalry. My son James is off to war with the regiment."

"I'm very pleased to hear that. I thought at first this might be a Union town."

"This town is proudly behind the Confederacy and Texas," Mary Donoho said firmly. She glanced at Cassandra. "You sound like you're from Missouri. Are you?"

"Yes I am, or we were until the Yankees burned us out. We are originally from Lafayette County."

"I thought I recognized your accent. I'm originally from Camden County, Missouri. If you and your family haven't made plans, I'd like to invite you to share supper with me in the dining room."

Cassandra smiled. "Thank you for your kind offer. We would enjoy the pleasure of your company."

"We will ring the bell out front fifteen minutes before dinner is served."

Cassandra nodded. "Until then."

"Of course." Mary turned toward her clerk. "Mort, get Martin and Matilda to help these people to their rooms. Show their servants to their quarters and put away their horses and wagons. Have Matilda prepare hot baths for them."

"Yes, ma'am, I'll see to it right away, Miz Mary." Mary turned and walked to her office.

"We's got some nice rooms on the second floor, if that'll be acceptable, suh."

"Yes, that'll be fine," said Andrew.

Cassandra, Elizabeth, Katlin, and little Glen entered the dining room shortly after hearing the bell ring in front of the hotel. They were led to a table and seated with Mary Donoho and another woman.

"Allow me to introduce my family. This is Elizabeth, Katlin, and her baby, Glen, and I'm Cassandra Kimbrough. This is Mary Donoho, the owner of the hotel."

"Pleased to meet you. I'd like to introduce you to my daughter, Mary Ann Cornelius. Mary lives here in town and spends considerable time helping me while her husband is off to war."

Cassandra looked at Mary Ann. She could easily spot the family resemblance, although the daughter's face was not as thin as her mother's. Cassandra offered the young woman her hand. "I'm pleased to meet you."

The conversation carried past the dinner hour and well after the table was cleared. They talked of Missouri and the war. Cassandra and her family were astonished to hear of Mary Donoho's adventures.

Mary had traveled the Santa Fe Trail with her husband

in 1833. They had settled in Santa Fe and ran a hotel until 1837 when the Mexicans revolted and cut off the head of the local Mexican governor, Albino Perez. Worried that things were getting dangerously out of hand, they fled Santa Fe. Mary was proud to be the first white woman to travel the Santa Fe Trail. Mary Ann, her daughter, had been born while in Santa Fe.

Mary told exciting tales about how her husband had bought white captive women from the Comanche Indians. These women had been captured in Texas by the Indians near the time of the Texas revolution. Santa Anna was invading Texas when the Comanches had taken them prisoners. Rachel Plummer, Mrs. Harris, and Mrs. Sarah Horn were among those bought from the Indians by Mary's husband, William. The women traveled with them over the Santa Fe Trail to Missouri and were reunited with their families. But the former captives died quickly, their spirits broken by their torture and the loss of their children and husbands.

The stories were interesting yet horrifying. It was little wonder the Comanches were so hated and feared in Texas. Cassandra remembered hearing similar stories as a child growing up in Missouri, and listening to Mary Donoho tell her tales of adventure brought those stories to life.

Mary and her husband settled in Clarksville in 1839. Her husband became friendly with a former Santa Fe trader living in Clarksville named William Becknell, better known as the father of the Santa Fe Trail. Becknell, who made his last trip to Santa Fe in 1826, had not known William Donoho during his trading days. Still, they had much in common and had delighted in sharing their adventure stories.

Mary's husband died in 1845, leaving Mary to raise her children and run the hotel with the help of her slaves. Although she had given birth to five daughters and one son, most of them had died. Only James and Mary Ann were still living.

Mary Donoho was proud of what she had accomplished

and proud of Clarksville, which served as an important transportation link to the Confederacy. From Clarksville's Red River ferry crossings to her stage station at the Donoho Hotel, Rebel soldiers spread out across Texas. Hers was an important way station on the route to Arkansas. Supplies for the military flowed through Clarksville heading east, brought north from the Texas ports and Mexico. The *Northern Standard* served as a source of information on the Confederacy's common soldiers and was often distributed to other parts of Texas.

Before supper ended, Mary Donoho promised to help Cassandra find housing for their stay in Clarksville. Cassandra relaxed a little. At least for now they had a place to stay and they were in Confederate territory. She prayed the Yankees would not drive them out.

23

Scuttlebutt

Evan Stryker strolled toward the group of men warming themselves by the fire and smiled as he recognized his old friend, Ross Kimbrough. Weary of the politics and arguing among the commanders at headquarters, Evan sought the companionship only old friends can offer. "Good evening, Capt'n Kimbrough!" shouted Stryker as he approached.

"Well now, bless my soul, if it isn't my favorite scalawag from Texas, Major Evan Stryker! Sit by the fire an' warm yourself." Ross motioned to an empty place on the log beside him. "It isn't soft, but it's better'n standin'." Evan shook Ross's hand heartily as he sat down. Ross gave his friend a smile. "What brings you out this way?"

"Had about all the puffed-up commanders I can stand up at headquarters. I felt like it was time to get away for a while." Evan was fascinated by the red coals glowing and flickering on the burning logs. Somehow, watching red-hot embers twinkling and flickering in a fire always relaxed him.

"I'm glad you're here, Major. I've been wonderin' what's in the wind. You don't get all these officers pow-wowing together and these troops gathered in one army without something big going on." Ross tipped his hat back and scratched his hair. "Scuttlebutt in camp says we're goin' back into Missouri on a raid. Any truth to it?"

"Well, it just goes to show, no matter how hard the generals would like to keep their intentions secret from the soldiers, the veterans always figure it out before the officers do. It's true, a big invasion of Missouri is on the drawing boards."

"Where are we headin', do ya know?"

"From what I've heard, the main thrust of the campaign is to attack the capitol at Jefferson City, then take Saint Louis."

A hush descended on the group as they pondered the dangers of a bold campaign. The battle-hardened veterans knew targets that important would be heavily defended and fortified. The sobering realization of what they could face was not lost on these soldiers.

Jonas Starke was the first to fill the silence. "You don't mean the bigwigs intend to attack ol' St. Loo-ie, do ya?"

"It's General Price's plan, and he thinks he can execute it. You see, with Sherman at the gates of Atlanta and General Lee trapped in Petersburg, the Generals are guessing that the best troops have been stripped from Missouri. Old Pap Price figures we can capture some needed supplies from Saint Louis and get the Feds to pull troops away from General Steele in Little Rock. They might even force the Yankees to bring back troops from Sherman's army in Georgia." Evan reached for a stick to prod the fiery coals. "That's his thinkin', anyway. He feels with the army we have he can pull it off, but I have my doubts."

"What worries you, Evan?" asked Ross.

"Command is my biggest concern. The way I see it, General Kirby Smith is in a fix. Richmond has been insisting he put all his troops across the Mississippi River to help stop Sherman. The general knows he can't do it with the Yankee gunboats patrolin' the river. Be nigh on to impossible to cross troops against the Union navy. Secondly, General Smith knows if he complies with Richmond's request then the Trans-Mississippi region will be defenseless and stripped of its army. Still, he must do something to help those back east, so he agrees to let Price and Shelby invade Missouri, hoping to lure troops and attention away from the war in the east. He has little else he can do."

Ross listened carefully, then nodded his head in agreement. "I think General Smith is right."

"Yes, to a point he is, but I'm still worried. Our past experiences indicate the best way to attack the far-flung forces in Missouri are by rapid, quick-hitting cavalry attacks before the Yankees can gather their armies to stop us. What we need is a large cavalry force led by someone like General Shelby or General Marmaduke. They know how to execute hit-and-run raids."

"That makes sense to me. So what's the problem?"

"General Smith has put the Missouri Expedition under the command of General Sterling Price."

"Ol' Pap Price is a good man. He led well at the battles of Lexington and Oak Hills," shouted Bill Corbin.

"Yes, he did, but it was early in the war. Price has never commanded cavalry operations, only infantry. He had a disaster on his hands at Corinth and wasted many a good man attacking heavily fortified positions. He lost command of the army because of his blunders, and they shipped him back to this side of the river." Evan paused as he scratched his chin. "Look, I know he's a Missourian, but he doesn't know the first thing about moving light or fast." Evan sighed deeply. "That's what scares me."

"I've watched troops pouring into the camps around Pocahontas for days. Looks like we got an army this time. Maybe we'll kick the Yankees' behind like we done early in the war," said Jonas Starke.

"We have roughly twelve thousand troops in this army. General Smith ordered Price to divide our army into three divisions, commanded by generals James Fagan, John

Marmaduke, and Jo Shelby, with General Price in overall command."

"Sounds to me like a good idea to break the army into three divisions. All those generals are good officers, so it ought to work," said Ross.

"It sounds good on paper, but we've got a ton of problems. We've got four thousand new recruits we've rounded up, made up mostly of conscripts and deserters that have avoided service in the past. These men are unarmed until we can capture weapons, and they have damn little training. At every opportunity they'll run for home. We've got over a thousand men that lack horses in our cavalry alone. To make matters worse, they haven't been trained to fight on foot. We've got some of our newly recruited cavalry troops armed with muskets, and you know how useless they are for fighting from the back of a horse. It's like having mounted infantry, except they don't know how to fight as infantry—or cavalry."

Evan watched hot sparks swirl as he poked the fire with his stick while he talked. "Many of the wagons Price wants to take along to haul forage and supplies are worn-out, rickety junk that will never stand up to a tough campaign. We only have fourteen cannons in this army, and most are small caliber and aren't rifled. Collins's battery is by far the best artillery we have."

"We've always been outnumbered and poorly equipped. Ol' Jo will have us take what we need from the enemy, and recruits will flock to our colors once we reach Missouri," Ross replied.

"I hope you're right, Ross. I'd just feel better if we had Jo Shelby leading this whole shootin' match."

"It isn't all so bad. I know we have many new recruits, but we have a solid nucleus of veterans in each division, don't we?"

"I know Jo Shelby's brigade is the strongest of our division and of the entire army. We've got Colonel Shanks commanding Shelby's Iron Brigade and Captain Collins in charge of the battery. Colonel Jackman's brigade is our weakness. Out of his fifteen hundred men only five hundred have guns and, of course, they're new recruits. The good news is they're mounted."

"I've seen them drilling and I think they'll make good soldiers with some experience."

"Maybe so, Ross, but they sure don't look like soldiers. I've seen scarecrows dressed better than most of those men."

"Clothes and equipment don't tell what's inside a man."

"Hard to argue with that, but a man with proper clothes is more likely to stay healthy with fall comin' on."

"Come on, Stryker, we know about our brigade, how about the rest of the army?" asked Fletch in exasperation.

"Okay, you asked for it. I'll give you my opinion and what I've heard around headquarters. First, there's General Fagan's division. General Cabell's Arkansas Brigade is solid with veterans, well-armed and mounted—some of the best west of the Mississippi. Colonel Slemmon's brigade is weak and full of new recruits, as are the brigades of Dobbins and McCray. Other than Cabell's brigade, I'd say his best are Dobbins's men.

"We've fought with General Marmaduke's brigade before, and you know General John Clark is reliable when he's commanding Marmaduke's old brigade. Colonel Freeman's brigade is another story. Again we've got poorly equipped new recruits. Gentlemen, that's what we've got to work with when we hit Missouri."

"So what are you trying to say, Major? Don't you think we should go to Missouri?"

Evan's face looked grim. "We have to go. It's about the only thing we can do in this department that might influence the direction of the war."

"So what's all this about, then?"

"I just think it's a serious mistake to put a cavalry command under an infantry commander who doesn't know how to use what he's got. If old Pap Price screws up, we can be cut to pieces up there."

Ross stood up from his spot on the log and stretched the

kinks out of tired muscles. "Jo Shelby is in command of this division, and as long as he is, I'll trust his judgement to not let some fool general get us slaughtered. I've fought with Jo since this war began. I'd march straight into hell itself and kiss the devil if ol' Jo ordered it! No, sir, when I'm under Shelby's command, I know we got a chance."

Evan Stryker looked at his old friend standing defiantly before him. "I know he's a good officer, the best I've ever seen, Ross, but he isn't God. He's flesh and blood and, most of all, a soldier who has to follow orders just like the rest of us. He isn't like General Lee. Lee has total control and command of his army. He's not got some overaged, overweight fool of an infantry officer telling him what to do. Have you forgotten Pap Price's blunder at Camden? Left the city stripped of defenders and moved them in front of Washington. Steele just waltzed in and took the city and used the forts against us."

"I remember we made an error down there, but it was logical to think Washington would be the route they would take. It doesn't matter, we still stopped Steele and forced him out of Camden back to Little Rock," Ross said in defense of General Price.

"I know what you're saying, but it should never have happened. You haven't heard the worst yet. We've got several Confederate politicians trailing along, hoping to be put back in office when we take Jefferson City. To make a real mess, all a fella has to do is drop a couple of politicians in the middle of the mix." Evan felt his repressed anger boiling to the surface. He rose angrily and stood toe to toe with Ross Kimbrough. "That's why I'm so upset." His words were a challenge, daring Ross Kimbrough to take a stand against his position.

Jonas Starke shoved his way between the two officers. "Whoa, boys, simmer down! I ain't heard this Texan say one bad thing about Gen'ral Shelby. Ain't no need you boys comin' to blows over nothin'."

"Gen'ral Price is from Missouri, and it sounds like

Stryker lacks confidence in our commanders," growled Ross threateningly.

"Here's what I believe," Evan began. "I believe in General Shelby and the commanders leading each division for this expedition. I don't believe there's a decent commander in this whole department above the division level, and that includes General Price and Kirby Smith. All during this war we've been the dumping ground for every worthless commander they couldn't find a use for back east. Anyone that suffered a disaster they sent west to get rid of them.

"From the very beginning the politicians in Richmond have written us off as unimportant. They don't give a damn what happens to us just as long as Richmond is safe. All they ever wanted from us was our money, our equipment, and soldiers to die for them, protecting Richmond and Old Virginny. Now if you don't agree with me, that's fine, you're welcome to your opinion. If you want to take exception to the way I think, here I am!" Evan balled his hands into fists.

Ross Kimbrough found himself looking into the fierce eyes of his Texas friend and although he wanted to be angry, he found himself unable to keep a smile from breaking across his face. "Danged if you don't look just like a banty rooster all ready to defend his part of the yard." Ross let go a laugh, then said, "The worst of it is, I know you're right. We have been saddled with lousy commanders in this region, except ol' Tom Hindman. He did a good job, so naturally they got rid of him."

Jonas was glad to see the tension easing between the two old friends. Even Evan was smiling now. "Let's break out a jug of apple brandy and toast the good ol' Johnny Rebs that do the real fightin'."

"Sounds good to me," said Ross as he good-naturedly slapped his hand on Evan's back. The jug was soon passing freely around the fire and with each circuit, the cares of the world for the moment were lifted. No one there doubted the truthfulness of Major Stryker's words, and each cast wary eyes on the new campaign.

Green Pastures and Clear Streams

alvin took careful aim as he sighted the bore of his cannon at the brick courthouse of Potosi, Missouri. It was as if he were reliving the same scene from the first Missouri raid, when they had faced a similar standoff at the courthouse at Neosho. Again the Yankee troops were holed up in the sturdiest structure in town, which in this case happened to be the courthouse. In his wisdom General Shelby ordered his artillery to remove them.

The order was given and the battery leaped into action. The cannonballs ripped through the structure, tearing big, gaping holes. Columns of dust rose from the shattered building as each succeeding blast pounded away at the courthouse. Mere brick and mortar could not withstand the iron balls from the artillery. This time, when those inside surrendered, Calvin didn't go to look at the results of his work. The memory of the mangled bodies at Neosho was still too fresh on his mind. It was well he didn't—in just eight rounds from three hundred yards, twenty-two men died inside. A white flag flew from an upper window signaling their surrender. Four hundred prisoners were captured in Potosi. While the prisoners were being rounded up and the captured weapons redistributed among the Rebel soldiers lacking weapons, Calvin reflected on the last few days.

They left Pocahontas, Arkansas, on September 19, 1864. When they entered the town of Doniphan near the Missouri border they found it in flames. Yankee soldiers had ridden down from Patterson, Missouri, on a raid and burned the town for spite. Angered by the plight of fire-ravaged Doniphan and the sight of more homeless citizens, Shelby's men pressed hard toward Patterson. Close by, Ross Kimbrough and the lead elements surprised the Yankee raiders asleep in their blankets in camp. They died right where they lay, paying for the sins against an innocent town.

The Rebels pressed on toward Fredrickstown, where seventy Yankees surrendered without firing a shot. Shelby's men waited a day for General Price, who finally arrived on September 24, 1864. Shelby split his division there, sending some toward Farmington and others toward the Iron Mountain Railroad. Shelby's men destroyed the large railroad bridge at Irondale, while Colonel Gordon destroyed the Mineral Point Bridge. Colonel Gordon's men fought a skirmish with men under the command of Yankee general A. J. Smith that had followed the railroad tracks from Saint Louis to stop the Rebs.

General Shelby added his forces to the battle and hit the rail line. Calvin recalled how close they had come to capturing a Union train loaded with Yankee soldiers, but it had outdistanced them. In his anger Shelby ordered his men to destroy the railroad. Soon the men were ripping and heating rails over piles of burning railroad ties. Taking the end of the rails, they twisted the red-hot metal around trees. Mile after mile of telegraph wire was torn out and poles knocked down. Everything wooden was burned— poles, ties, trestles, and bridges. No longer would these rails haul Yankee cargo and troops. Calvin would never forget the sight of those great, dense columns of smoke as they rose to greet the clouds, darkening the air with falling cinders and charred bits of wood.

From there they had dashed on to Potosi to capture the troops in the courthouse. Calvin, already weary, felt grateful for the break.

Shelby didn't let his men rest for long. Soon, the depot, cars, and machine shops were set to the torch. Small units of cavalry were sent out to gather what they could. In a day's time, over twelve hundred Federal militia prisoners were brought into town to join those captured at the courthouse.

They waited for a day for General Price's slow moving column to catch up, but nothing more was heard. Finally General Shelby decided to march back toward Pilot's Knob. He knew General Price intended to travel through, and he had learned from his prisoners that a garrison was located there. He only hoped Price would not be foolish enough to attack the fort. Ross Kimbrough's orders were clear: Ride toward Pilot's Knob until you establish contact with General Price's army. They had ridden south several miles without incident when they crossed tracks left by troops heading north. The tracks weren't plentiful enough though to be General Price's army, and that puzzled Ross. He decided to continue south toward Pilot's Knob.

After traveling several more miles, Ross made contact with Marmaduke's advance. Ross wasn't prepared for what he learned from them. According to the scouts, General Price had decided to attack Fort Davidson at Pilot's Knob. The fort was reputed to have a thousand Union troops protected by high dirt walls and sixteen cannons. The ground around the fort was flat and offered little cover.

The attacks had failed, with heavy losses to the Confederates. To make matters worse, during the night Union General Ewing had blown up his powder magazine and marched his troops north. The Rebels were unaware until daylight that the Yankees were gone. Ross now knew who had made the tracks he had crossed—the Union troops from Fort Davidson.

Not only had much of generals Fagan and Marmaduke's divisions been hurt in the useless attack, but the enemy had escaped. Days had been lost on a futile attack of no importance. Although the Rebels had captured artillery left behind in the fort by the Federals, they had no way to transport it, so it had to be destroyed and abandoned. Shelby's orders were to pursue the Yanks and capture them if possible.

Ross raced back to give General Shelby the orders, and they immediately began pursuit. The enemy had chosen well and, with several hours' head start, were well ahead of the Rebels. The Yankees had taken the road toward Rolla, and the terrain made it nearly impossible to cut them off. The road was too narrow and the terrain too rough to hit them in the flanks. Two more days were wasted in chasing Ewing's Yankees.

When the Confederate forces were finally recalled, they received word that General Price had decided not to attack St. Louis. General A. J. Smith's eight thousand Union veterans now defended the city and its fortifications. Instead, Price's command would attack the state capital at Jefferson City.

Shelby's troopers again took the lead, and at Linn, Missouri, captured one hundred prisoners. Two more days were lost in Linn, waiting for Price and his supply train to catch up. On October 6 Colonel Shanks and his men destroyed the Pacific Railroad bridge that spanned the Osage River, then moved to rejoin General Shelby's division at Westphalia, who had already captured the town, driven out its defenders, and captured more prisoners by the time Shanks joined them. From Westphalia, Shelby ordered Colonel Shanks and his regiment to force a crossing of the Osage River and drive the outlying Union troops into Jefferson City.

* * *

Jessie wheeled Star's Pride into line. It wouldn't be long now till the order to charge would be issued. Jessie had watched Colonel Gordon ride down the line, making his final adjustments. Captain Gilbert Thomas was in his familiar position in front of Jessie's company. It wasn't so long ago that forming into battle line for a charge would have had Jessie as nervous as a cat on a hot stove. Many days in the saddle followed by endless skirmishes had toughened him. Whatever awaited him, he had faced it before. Jessie reached under his shirt and rubbed his hand gently against the gold locket. He felt reassured by the touch of the smooth metal under his fingertips—his good luck charm. Nothing could hurt him if he had Katlin's gold locket.

Jessie knew others might think him foolish. Some might even laugh if he told them he believed the locket could ward off danger. It was just something he believed without question. Maybe it was Katlin's love that protected him, or maybe a guardian angel, he wasn't certain. He just knew that if he wore the locket he would be safe. He believed in its magical powers.

Jessie watched Gilbert Thomas stand in his stirrups and signal the charge by waving his pistol in a circle, then arcing toward the enemy position. Jessie felt the line surge forward as one as the entire regiment moved down the hill at a gallop. Before them flowed the Osage River and the Castle Rock Ford. Blocking their path stood a Union regiment on the far side of the river.

The Rebel troops galloped on. The line narrowed, forced into the smaller opening of the ford where it breached the river. In the swirling crush of men and horses, Jessie slipped behind the first line of troops entering the river. He heard the roaring splash as over a thousand hooves split the water, churning the river instantly into foaming whitewater.

He felt his horse settle in as the cold water closed around his legs. He felt Star's Pride float free, drifting in the current, and begin to swim in the deeper water. As Jessie rode through the splashing foam around him, he heard shots fired and saw the swirling, gray puffs of powder smoke from the guns drifting on the wind. He heard the whine of bullets whirring through the air above him and the cold, flat smack of minié balls striking water. Unconsciously, he leaned farther forward in the saddle, his head inches above Star's neck.

It wasn't much farther now. He could feel Star's Pride as his forelegs found solid purchase and the water level began to slide away. The constant motion blurred around him and the sounds caused by three hundred charging cavalrymen seemed to blunt his senses. As Jessie's horse splashed onto the shore he saw the trooper riding directly in front of him take a solid hit, his head exploding in a blood-red mist. The body tumbled over backward from the saddle and disappeared under the pounding hooves of those who followed.

Jessie felt Star climb as they drove up the far bank of the ford. As they topped the crest of the small ridge Jessie spotted Yankees fleeing on foot and on horseback. He reined in his horse as his eyes searched the lay of the land stretched out before him.

Not all the Yanks were in retreat. About a quarter of a mile away he saw a thin, blue line preparing to make a stand. The power of the charge had carried them this far, as though they were riding the crest of a wave, but now it faltered as the men lost a sense of direction. Captain Thomas broke from the crowd and waved his pistol over his head to show the men where to reform their battle line.

Jessie held the prancing Star's Pride in check beneath him as he watched his old friend Gilbert meticulously organizing his battle line. Jessie watched as Evan Stryker spurred forward to meet Captain Thomas near Jessie's position in line.

"Captain Thomas, congratulations on breaching the ford."

"So, what is it this time, Stryker? I know you didn't ride over here just to give me a pat on the back."

"I'm looking for Colonel Gordon. I have orders for him from General Shelby."

"He was here a minute ago. He ordered us to prepare another charge on the Union line before they can mount a counterattack. You might try the other end of the line, Captain."

Suddenly, Captain Thomas spurred his horse forward alongside Major Stryker and rudely shoved Evan out of the saddle. As the surprised Texan tumbled to the ground, a sharp crack came from the discharge of a Yankee musket. Jessie looked up in time to see a lone Yankee running toward the Union lines after firing a shot at the pair of officers. In a hail of pistol and carbine fire from the Rebel line, the Yankee sniper was thrown around like a broken string puppet before slumping into the dirt. Captain Gil Thomas's horse groaned heavily and moved backward a step or two before rolling over onto his side, spilling Gilbert from his saddle.

In a moment the Rebel line surged around the downed officers, putting themselves between the officers and the enemy. Evan fought desperately to draw air, slammed from him by the hard fall, into his lungs. When he could, he made his way to Gilbert, who now knelt by his downed horse.

A wet gleam of tears trailed down the Missourian's face as he patted the horse one last time. "Now, now, it's gonna be all right, big fella. Nothin' but big green pastures and clear streams will be waitin' for ya." Gilbert slipped his pistol from his holster and fired one shot into the head of the dying horse. The horse's head jumped from the blow and his legs stiffened before the eyes glazed in death. Gilbert looked up in time to see Evan crawling toward him.

"Are you okay, Gil?" the Texan asked.

"I don't know. My leg hurts, but it's probably because of the fall. Damn, I hate to lose that horse. I'd gotten attached to him." Gilbert slid the Colt back into his holster before he began to reel, collapsing to the ground.

Evan moved beside him. "What's the matter, Gil?"

"I don't know. I feel weak and dizzy."

Stryker took a quick look at Gil's leg. Behind the knee he found an artery severed from a passing minié ball—probably the same bullet that had fatally injured Gil's horse. When he pulled off Gil's boot it was full of blood.

With every beat of Gil's heart, the blood flowed from him in ruby red spurts. Evan tried to staunch the flow of blood with pressure from his hand but it welled around his fingertips. Major Stryker whipped his belt off and wrapped it around Gilbert's thigh to slow the loss.

"You can't die on me, Gil Thomas, after savin' my life! I won't have it! Do you hear me?" Evan yelled in desperation.

Gilbert looked at his leg and the pool of blood thickening the dust around him and smiled strangely. It was as if he had just caught the gist of a twisted joke. "I never thought I'd see the day I'd take a bullet to keep you alive, Texas."

"I never thought you would either, Gil. Why did ya do it?"

"I wish I knew. I saw the Yank come out of the brush and level his musket at you, and I knew you couldn't see him. I had to do somethin' pretty damn quick. Damn fool thing to do, now as I look back on it. I lost the best horse I ever had." Gilbert smiled again. "Would ya mind reaching in that saddlebag there? I got a bottle of whiskey I've been savin' for a special occasion. It might ease the pain."

Evan moved toward the dead horse and found a bottle of whiskey in the saddlebag. He gave it to Gil, who immediately took a couple of strong pulls from the bottle.

"Here, Texas, have a drink on me. There's more here than I can drink alone." The Missourian watched as the Texan took a big gulp and then coughed a little as it burned its way down to his belly.

"Stryker, I want to say I'm sorry. I know for a long time there I blamed you for taking Cassandra away from me. It was easier to blame you than to face the truth."

"Don't talk about it now, Gil, just rest."

"I've got to talk about it now. You and I both know I'm bleedin' to death and there isn't a thing we can do about it."

Evan studied Gilbert, already a ghastly white. He knew Thomas was right—he'd known it from the moment he saw the wound. A hole in a major artery would not take too long. Even as Stryker watched, Gilbert began to tremble.

"I'm feelin' the cold more now, Texas." He paused as he swallowed hard. "Anyways, I was sayin', it wasn't you took her away from me. You couldn't take something away from me I never had. Hell, I loved her and I still do, but she never felt the same way about me, and I just couldn't bring myself to face it. I thought given time, she'd learn to love me. Then you came along, and the war, and the time slipped away. I doubt it would have made any difference. I found it easier to hide in a bottle than to face the truth. I've hated you and I've watched you. I tried to lay all my troubles on your shoulders. It never worked, because in countless battles and skirmishes you always stood your ground." He paused. "You'll make her a good husband, Stryker."

Gilbert coughed hoarsely, then took another slug of whiskey. "Good rye I got here. I knew it would come in handy for somethin' special." Gilbert's smile faded as he looked desperately into Evan's eyes. "Promise me, Texas! Promise me you'll take good care of Cassandra. She deserves to be happy."

"I promise, Gil. You know I will."

"You'd be a fool not to marry her. Seldom gonna find a gal with the kind of spunk Cassie's got. Lord, she's a lot of woman." Gilbert's speech was beginning to slur, and the trembling increased. Despite the tourniquet, the blood still oozed in a steady flow from behind the knee.

Gilbert relaxed, using his dead horse for a pillow as he stared off into the blue skies. "Yeah, nothin' but green pastures and clear streams." His expression became puzzled, then it widened into a grin. "Ho, come here, boy.

Let's ride." Gilbert leaned forward stretching his arms out as if reaching for phantom reins, then fell back against his horse. He never regained consciousness, and in a few minutes he was gone.

Evan left Gilbert's body with a soldier from Gilbert's company, then he delivered his orders to Colonel Gordon. The orders were to hit the enemy in the flank after clearing the Castle Rock Ford, while General Shelby assaulted the enemy in front of Jefferson City. The vital attack would begin soon.

25

Assault on Jefferson City

Captain Ross Kimbrough licked his lips in anticipation. A smile creased his face as he realized the trap was about to be sprung on the unsuspecting Yankees. A solid line of cavalry troopers were lined up in front of the ford on the main road to Jefferson City. Behind them, hidden from the enemy, was Collins's battery, fully arrayed for battle.

The cavalry troopers kept up a steady massed fire from their revolvers to keep the Union defenders at bay. So far, the return fire had been lighter than anticipated. The order was given, and the cavalrymen split their formation and uncovered Collins's battery. The four cannons roared as if one huge gun were slamming into the Union defenders at the river crossing. Surprised, the defenders nearest the shore broke and ran. Collins's men fired a second volley into the fleeing enemy to hasten their retreat.

"Charge!" rang out loud and clear, followed by the rousing Rebel yell as a column of Shelby's troopers galloped into the river. Ross rode near the front of the column as his mount dashed into the water. The water splashing up from the horses plunging into the river beside him formed a wall of spray that showered down in a drenching, wet rain. The icy water made him gasp for air as it doused him. He felt a shiver course through him as his horse's hooves dug into the muddy bank on the far side of the river. The water drained away, and he was on land once more. Ross swung out of line and urged those behind to close their ranks.

His scouts, riding with the men of the Twelfth Missouri Cavalry for the charge, joined in as the regiment formed into a line of battle. Ross helped organize the line, then fell in beside Lieutenant William Gregg and Billy Cahill. Ross watched with anticipation as Colonel Shanks rode before the line and led the charge at a gallop. As Shank's Twelfth Missouri reached the skirmish line, they drove past the Rebel skirmishers who were slowly being forced back. The advancing Yankee infantry were startled by the fresh ranks of screaming Rebels with pistols blazing riding down on them.

At first the Union line staggered and fell back slowly before the onslaught. The Union lines stiffened and the battle raged with neither side able to move the other. Colonel Shanks led his troops against the enemy as he rallied the Rebels and urged them to form new ranks and follow him.

Over the last three years Ross had often seen this fine and brave officer snatch victory out of near disaster. Shanks was never afraid and led by example, often putting himself in the very front of his men. Ross felt his pride swell as he saw the colonel boldly facing the enemy. Inspired by Shanks's reckless courage, Ross rose in his stirrups as he reached for another loaded pistol from his belt. He waved the revolver over his head. "Come on, men, follow the colonel!"

Ross felt his heart pounding with excitement and the adrenaline pouring through his veins as he spurred his mount forward to the attack. The enemy stood, started to waver, then fell back in retreat before the new charge. Ross tried to stay near Colonel Shanks, and as he rode he saw the colonel knocked from the saddle as if he had ridden into an invisible wire. Ross felt his breath catch in his throat as Colonel Shanks tumbled from the saddle like a dropped sack of potatoes. Immediately, Ross reined in Prince of Heaven, dismounted, and rushed to the colonel's side.

Ross gently rolled the colonel over on his back. "Where ya hit, Colonel?"

"I think I took one in the chest." The intense pain racked Colonel Shanks's body.

"Take it easy, Colonel. I'll take a look at it." Ross began unbuttoning the overcoat, then the field jacket. A wide, ruby-red stain was already spreading over his shirt. Ross tore the shirt loose to get a better look at the wound. The minié ball had torn a jagged hole in the Colonel's chest.

"It hurts like hell. How bad does it look, Captain?"

"I'm afraid it's pretty serious, sir."

"It feels like it. Every breath I take hurts."

By now, one of Colonel Shanks's aides had joined them. "Is there anything I can do for you, Colonel?"

"Yes, Jim. You better find General Shelby. Tell him he's going to need a new brigade commander." The colonel paused as a wave of pain passed through him. He bit his lip and fought to maintain his composure. "You'd better arrange to have me removed from the field. I'll need an ambulance or a wagon."

"Yes, Colonel, I'll be back."

"Tell me, Ross, how is the attack going?"

"Looks like the men are driving them, sir." Ross bit back his tears. "They would follow you anywhere."

"If any brigade in this war could do the job, it'd be my boys. I . . ." Colonel Shanks lost consciousness in midsentence.

Ross pulled the blanket roll from behind his saddle, covering the colonel and fashioning a pillow from the colonel's field jacket.

In a few minutes, Colonel Shanks regained consciousness. He was awake when General Jo Shelby arrived at his side. Colonel Shanks's features, wan and worn with pain, lit up with tenderness and joy as he looked up into the face of his commander and old friend.

General Shelby, nearly overcome with grief, could not at first speak. He was afraid by doing so he might lose control and weep in front of his old friend.

Colonel Shanks sensed how badly his general was affected by seeing him in this condition. He gripped his old friend's arm and gave it a weak squeeze. "Don't fret, Jo. It isn't too painful."

Jo Shelby's lip began to quiver as he said gently, "A few months' rest, David, an' you'll be good as new. Don't worry, we'll get you out of here. I've got the division surgeon and an ambulance comin' to take care of you."

"Jo, I don't want you trying to take me with you. Find me some Southern family and leave me there. I'm hurt too bad to travel very far, and I don't want to slow down our column."

"I can't leave you. The Yanks will take you prisoner."

"I'll die anyway if you try to take me with you. You know how it has to be and so do I."

General Shelby looked away as he blinked hot tears from his eyes. Despite the general's best efforts tears slid down his bearded cheeks. He hugged his dear friend and held him for several long minutes. Even the most battle-hardened veterans standing nearby were deeply touched by the tender good-bye. As Jo Shelby rose to his feet he said, "God be with you, David. I wish you a speedy recovery. I won't find another capable of filling your position. We'll just have to do the best we can."

Colonel Shanks seemed comforted by his general's kind words. He smiled faintly. "Give 'em hell, Jo!"

General Shelby walked to his sorrel and swung into the saddle. He waved at his old friend one last time, then turned his horse. Ross watched the general ride away, head bowed and shoulders slumped forward.

Soon the ambulance came and Colonel David Shanks was gently loaded into the wagon. With the doctor in attendance and followed by one of Colonel Shanks's devoted aides, Lute McKinney, they bore him from the field of battle. The men under Colonel Gordon who had crossed at Castle Rock Ford drove on the right flank of the enemy and captured three Federal companies trapped between them and Shanks's Rebels.

Ross knew they had fought for the last time under Colonel Shanks, and he realized it was a severe loss to the old Iron Brigade. Because of Shanks's leadership, the Federals had been driven from the river crossing and forced back into the fortifications of Jefferson City. Nightfall brought a blessed end to the day's battle.

General Price, who had been notified of the capture of the fords across the Osage River, advanced during the night. General Shelby's men camped in line of battle just six miles from Jefferson City.

During Shelby's engagement, General Cabell's brigade burned the river bridge at Franklin that spanned the Merrimac River and held off a brigade of Union general A. J. Smith's corps from St. Louis. On October 4, General Marmaduke burned the bridge over the Gasconade and captured a large supply train loaded with arms and ammunition on the Pacific Railroad.

Early on the morning of October 7, General Fagan's division, with Cabell's brigade in the advance, attacked Jefferson City and again pushed the Federals into the capital city. Again the fortifications caused heavy losses to the Confederates, with little progress to show for it.

As darkness brought an end to the day, Jessie Kimbrough studied the huge capital dome of Missouri, the Stars and Stripes flying defiantly above it. Jessie felt sure, as did the men around him, that the morning would bring orders for a fresh assault.

Jessie lay down to troubled sleep under a sky twinkling with a billion stars. The air was crisp and the ground cold as he wrapped himself into his blankets. There could be no fire to warm him this night camping this close to the enemy.

Morning came clear and bright, but still no attack was ordered. Around ten o'clock in the morning orders were given to march westward. There were to be no more useless attacks on the fortifications of Jefferson City. The common Confederate soldiers in the ranks felt relieved they would not be ordered to a certain slaughter against the embattlements. Finally, Marmaduke and Shelby had talked General Price out of the attack.

Major Stryker, as a member of General Jo Shelby's staff, heard the relief in Shelby's voice when he shared the news. He recalled the general's bitter complaints at the slow movement of the army. Since leaving Pocahontas, Arkansas, they never covered more than fifteen miles a day; General Shelby normally expected to cover thirty to thirty-five miles on a cavalry raid. If they would have traveled light and fast and bypassed Pilot's Knob, they could have captured Jefferson City before it had been garrisoned.

The Yankees had known for weeks that the Rebels were coming, yet they had not placed troops into the Jefferson City forts and trenches until just days before the attack. A swift movement might even have taken St. Louis before General Smith's troops arrived to protect that vital city, just days before the Confederate's ridiculous assault on Pilot's Knob.

Major Stryker's concerns were proving true. Led by General Sterling Price, an infantry commander with no experience at rapid movement, the army had lost the initiative and surprise factor. The huge baggage train slowed the march considerably. To compound his errors, Price made the same mistake he had made at Corinth: He attacked Union troops in heavily fortified forts and trenches and wasted much of his army. Several days were lost in the attack on a fort of no significant importance. The delay caused by the battle certainly ended all real hope of capturing St. Louis or Jefferson City, as it had allowed the Yankees time to rush reinforcements to the potential targets of the Rebel raid. If only Jo Shelby had led the column, Major Stryker thought, things would have been far different. As they left the outskirts of Jefferson City Evan had time to ponder these grievous errors.

Once again, General Shelby's division separated from the main body of the army and captured the town of California, Missouri, where they burned the railroad depot and all the rolling stock on the line nearby. The men of Gilbert's company paused briefly to see Gilbert Thomas laid to rest in the California cemetery. Then they galloped on to Boonville, Missouri, with the rest of the command.

Things at Boonville had changed considerably in little more than a year. The courthouse, defended by four hundred state militia, was well fortified surrounded by a stockade, and the streets leading to the courthouse were barricaded. The walls of the stockade were lined with loopholes for the soldiers to shoot through. Shelby knew too well the cost of a frontal attack on fortifications, so he placed his artillery to bombard the courthouse into submission.

Before the bombardment began, Shelby offered the Yankees a chance to surrender. After the Union commander discussed it, he accepted Shelby's terms. For the second time in a little over a year, Boonville was in Shelby's hands without firing a shot.

A steamboat tied up at the docks was captured along with the city. Soon the boat would be used to transport Rebel troops back and forth across the Missouri River. The next day General Price arrived at Boonville with his ponderous baggage train in tow.

26

Knights of the Bush

I f Boonville was surprised to see General Shelby march in followed by General Price's army, they were stunned when the Knights of the Bush joined the Rebel army.

Bloody Bill Anderson, fresh from his massacre of Union troops at Centralia, rode in under the famous black flag with his army of three hundred guerrillas. Among those riding with him were members of nearly every famous group of Bushwackers left in the state of Missouri. William Clarke Quantrill was there, although no longer the leader of anything but a small band. George Todd, David Poole, Clifton Holtzclaw, Arch Clements, and John Thrailkill all brought their guerrilla bands under Anderson's banner to talk with General Sterling Price.

Lieutenant William Gregg and Billy Cahill took advantage of the opportunity to visit their old comrades. Always flamboyant, the old band was easy to find. As the two men stepped into the bar that had become the unofficial headquarters for the guerrillas, they recognized an old friend sitting at a table near the door.

Bill Gregg was the first to speak. "How ya doin', Frank? Long time no see."

"Well if it ain't Bill Gregg and Billy Cahill. I figured you two was dead and buried by now."

"Not hardly, Frank. Leastways if we are, they plum forgot to let us in on it."

Frank James chuckled and motioned for the men to have a seat. "Heard you boys joined the regular army, but I wasn't inclined to believe it. Hard to make money fightin' in the real army."

Billy Cahill sat next to Bill Gregg and studied the famous guerrilla. Frank James was tall and lanky with piercing blue eyes. He looked thinner than Billy remembered him. Seated to Frank's right was his younger brother, Jesse, who had grown considerably since Billy had seen him last. Like Frank, he was thin, but looked more powerful than his brother. His eyes were a cold, pale blue, and he was strikingly handsome. He had a large black plume stuck in his hat and the side was pinned up for a rakish effect. Pistols were strung all over him, and Billy wondered if the weight of them didn't tire him out. Just a boy when Billy first met him, Jesse didn't look so innocent now. They'd nicknamed him Dingus.

Bill Gregg said, "Never was in the war to make money, Frank. I was fighting to kill Yankees and Jennison's Jayhawkers. I killed all of Jennison's boys I could find."

"Well, we've done a sight of that along the way, ain't we, boys?" Frank smiled. Then he leaned forward in his chair. "What are you boys after?"

"We ain't after nothin', Frank." A hurt expression passed over William Gregg's face. "You ought to know us by now. We heard you boys were in town, so we decided to drop by to visit old friends and catch up on the news."

"You boys care for a drink?"

"Be proud to join ya over a glass, Frank," Billy responded.

"Barkeep! Bring a pair of glasses and another bottle of bourbon over here for my friends. Bring the good stuff if ya don't want to suck on the end of a gun barrel."

Frank looked back at Billy and Bill. "Ain't nothin' too good for old friends, huh, boys?"

"Thanks, Frank, you're mighty kind. So, fill us in on the goin's on in Missouri."

"Been a plenty boys, and that's the truth." The bartender came to the table and left a bottle and two more glasses as Frank James continued. "You boys recall ol' Andy Blunt?" Bill and Billy both nodded. "General Brown's Feds caught up with him in April and killed him and a couple of others. They didn't even bury him, just left him to rot. They caught Dick Yeager in June and killed him, too. Fletch Taylor caught a blast from a shotgun this summer and had to have his arm cut off. The damned old rascal survived it. Don't know how he kept from bleedin' to death."

"Sounds like the Yankees have been turnin' up the heat on the boys since last fall." Bill Gregg filled their glasses.

Jesse said, "I don't think it's been any different. You're always gonna lose some men in any fightin' outfit."

"One thing is for sure, we've been givin' 'em fits," pronounced Frank James. "We hit a twelve-wagon military supply train in September near Rocheport. We captured eighteen thousand rounds of ammunition, a wagonload of new Yankee uniforms, a thousand rations, and, best of all, we killed twelve Yankees."

Jesse James leaned forward eagerly. "Tell 'em about Centralia, Frank."

"Yeah, I betcha they'd enjoy that. Boys, ya shoulda seen Bloody Bill there."

Billy Cahill said, "We've heard some rumors floatin' around about Centralia. Didn't know how much of 'em to believe."

Frank James rocked his chair back, crossed his legs at the ankles, and let his boots rest on the top of the table. He leaned his head against the wall and took another swallow of whiskey as he started his tale. "Ol' Bloody Bill led us to this little whistlestop of a town sittin' on the tracks of the North Missouri Railroad. The locals called it Centralia. We got in there an' we set about gettin' the locals to fix us some breakfast. Then some of the boys found a barrel of whiskey an' several cases of new boots down at the depot. Word got around an' we all helped ourselves."

"Yeah, that whiskey was smooth, an' best of all, it was free. Bunch of the boys got near fallin' down drunk on the stuff and was usin' new boots for glasses," Jesse added.

"Dingus is right. See these boots I'm wearin'?" Frank pointed at his boots resting on the table. "I got these boots right there in Centralia."

"Nice lookin' pair of boots, Frank. Wish I had a pair like those," said Bill Gregg. "Centralia isn't a big deal just cause ya got a new pair of boots, is it?"

"Nah, that was just the beginnin'. A stage came in about eleven and we cleaned out the passengers. Then about noon a train came rollin' into town. We made all the passengers leave the train. We put the civilians on one side an' the soldiers on the other. All the soldiers were on furlough, and some were wounded. Most of them were on leave from Sherman's army in Georgia. Bloody Bill personally shot two of them that refused to leave the train.

"Well, ol' Bloody Bill lined up them soldiers and explained to them how the Feds had been killin' his men an' not taking any prisoners. He told 'em, 'I'm gonna do the same to the Yankees. From now on, I don't take any prisoners either.' Some of the blue bellies tried to tell him they were with Sherman's army and had nothin' to do with killin' his men, but Bloody Bill told 'em they was all Yankees an' just as bad. Next he had them all take off their uniforms at gunpoint. They was a sight standin' there in their longjohns and underwear. A bunch of us lined up and on Anderson's orders we mowed 'em down where they was a standin', except for one sergeant that Bloody Bill let go later."

Billy glanced away, thinking of those unarmed soldiers being shot down like stray dogs. He swallowed hard, then took another sip of bourbon. He knew this was the wrong place and time to say anything against the slaughter. He bit his tongue and kept his thoughts private. Now he was more glad than ever he had left the Bushwackers with Bill Gregg.

Frank continued with his story as his guests listened. "We burned the depot down, set the train on fire, and sent it rollin' down the track with the throttle tied open. Soon a freight train pulled in an' we killed the crew and plundered the cars. Then we mounted up an' rode back to our camp where George Todd, Quantrill, and some of the others were waitin'.

"After a while, we got word that a Yankee column was a-comin', so Todd told the boys to get ready for a big fight.

"We rode on out there, an' there they was—a group of mounted militia with rifles. The damn fools dismounted and prepared to fight us on foot."

Frank stopped and took another sip from his glass before continuing. "At two hundred yards, Bloody Bill gave the order to charge. The Yanks fired one volley that killed three of our men an' wounded a few others. Then they turned an' ran in panic, some of 'em even throwin' away their rifles. Well, it wasn't nothin' more than a big turkey shoot. We rode 'em down and pistoled them at close range. A few that were left back with the horses got mounted, but we tracked most of them down an' killed them, too. In all we killed their commander an' one hundred and twenty-four of his soldiers."

"We heard ya killed a bunch of Missouri Federal Militia, but we heard you boys mutilated a bunch of the bodies. That isn't true, is it, Frank?"

"That's the part I ain't proud of, it's true. Arch Clements, Bloody Bill, David Poole, an' several of the others were roarin' drunk. They thought it was fun to cut up the bodies and switch some of the heads around. They even put some heads on fence posts. Jesse an' I didn't have anything to do with cuttin' up the bodies. We were both in

Centralia chasin' after the Yanks that tried to run away. We stayed in town and got drunk."

Bill Gregg's eyes hardened. "I hope you're tellin' me the truth, Frank. I left this outfit for the same kind of stuff at Baxter Springs. It's one thing to kill a man if he's your enemy, but it takes someone real sick to get pleasure out of cuttin' up dead bodies for a lark."

Frank James saw the disgust clearly in Gregg's and Cahill's faces. Wishing to distance himself from the atrocities, he replied, "I swear to ya, Bill, we didn't do any of it. Jesse shot the officer that led them, an' we both killed all the soldiers we could catch, but we didn't do anything else." Frank paused. "Quantrill didn't do any of it, either. He more or less kept to himself when the fightin' was over. Him an' Bloody Bill is at odds with one another. I think Capt'n Billy is afraid of Bloody Bill, if ya want my opinion."

"Can't say as I blame him much. I wouldn't want to get crosswise of Bill Anderson myself," said Bill Gregg quietly.

Moments later two guerrilla leaders walked in through the front door. Billy recognized them immediately— Bloody Bill Anderson and George Todd. The two men were so involved in their own conversation they didn't acknowledge the men at the table as they continued on to the bar at the back of the building.

Billy watched them pass. Bloody Bill was more flamboyant than ever. His black beard was full and bushy. He wore a black hat with a silver star that pinned the floppy brim to the crown in the front. His long, dark curls hung thickly from around the hat, but it was the eyes that Billy remembered. Those eyes—the color steel blue, with a wildness in them. Few could dispute his youthful good looks or challenge his leadership. George Todd, walking beside him, was a study in contrasts. Todd stood much taller than Anderson. He was ruggedly built, with wide, strong shoulders. He had blond hair that was cut short, and he was clean shaven.

The conversation at the table stopped as the men watched the two guerrilla leaders pass.

Jesse James was the first to speak. "I've had enough of this rotgut. Billy, would ya mind gettin' me a glass of beer? I'm kinda stuck back here in the corner."

"Sure, Jess, I'll get it for ya." Billy shoved his chair back and made his way to the bar.

As he elbowed his way in where he could yell at the bartender, he heard a familiar voice. "That you, Cahill?"

Billy turned to look, but he knew who it was. "Yeah, it's me. How ya doin', Riley?"

"Didn't think you'd care. Thought you was too good for the likes of me an' the boys."

"I never felt I was better'n you. I just wanted to fight in the regular army is all."

"You hoped it'd get ya closer to that Kimbrough bitch, is the way I figured it."

Anger flared in Billy like a flash flood. His eyes narrowed to dangerous slits as he stared threateningly at Riley Crawford. "Riley, I'm only gonna tell you once. Leave Elizabeth Kimbrough out of this."

Riley laughed at the anger he read on Billy's face, amused at how easy it was to get to Billy. He knew he'd found the key to hurting him. "Oh, I'm sorry if I insulted you. Didn't know you felt so much for the little whore." He smiled wickedly at Billy, taunting him.

Billy turned to the bar, as if to ignore him. With a motion as smooth and fast as a flash of lightning, Billy landed a right hook square on Riley's nose. The blow caught Riley by surprise and his head snapped back. He staggered a couple of steps as his hands went to his face. Billy stepped in with a second punch that landed in Riley's belly, pumping the air out of him. Riley doubled over, gripping his stomach.

"I warned you, Riley, leave the girl out of it. You got a problem, I'm right here." When there was no response from Riley, who was busy gasping for breath, Billy turned toward the bar. The men there had grown silent; the hard eyes of men accustomed to fighting and death watched closely. "Barkeep, I need a couple of beers down here, pronto."

The beers arrived, and Billy paid for them. Suddenly, Billy was startled by the crash of shattered glass. He looked over his shoulder and saw Riley holding the neck of a busted bottle in his hand. Spilled booze and broken glass littered the edge of the bar. Riley's nose was slanted to one side and bloody streaks ran down his chin. He waved the jagged glass slowly in front of him. "Nobody hits me with a sucker punch and gets away with it, Cahill. I'm gonna cut your face into ribbons so that gal won't even recognize ya."

Billy backed up slowly, his hands low in front of him for balance. Riley stepped forward, slashing the air in front of him with the bottle. Twice he jabbed the jagged glass at Billy, but Billy dodged. They danced across the floor for another minute before Riley made another thrust at Billy. Billy sidestepped him, spinning his back to Riley and grabbing the hand that held the bottle. Billy slammed his elbow into Riley's ribs and stomped his boot on Riley's instep. Crawford let out a roar of pain and Billy twisted him toward the bar. In one smooth motion, he pulled Riley's arm behind his back and slammed him hard into the bar, wrenching the wrist of the hand holding the bottle upward until he felt the bone crack. He twisted it further as Riley cried in pain. The broken bottle fell to the floor.

"Damn it, Billy, ya broke my wrist."

"You're lucky I didn't kill ya, Crawford. Next time, watch who you try to push around." Billy let go of the Bushwacker and stepped over to retrieve the beers. He turned his back on the bar and started toward the table.

He only made a few steps when behind him he heard a scuffle and the unmistakable click of a revolver hammer being thumbed back. He turned slowly to face the bar.

"Nah, you ain't gonna shoot him in the back, Riley. He beat you fair an' square, and the way I see it, you was lookin' for trouble an' ya darn sure found it." The voice belonged to George Todd who held a cocked revolver to Riley Crawford's temple. In his good hand Riley held a Navy Colt revolver which he let drop to the floor.

George Todd looked up at Billy. "Billy, it was nice to see you work, but I think it's time you and Bill Gregg get on back to your soldier boys. We'll take good care of Riley here an' see he gets his wrist fixed. I'll see if I can calm him down a mite, but I'm afraid you've riled him some."

"Thanks, George, I'm beholden to ya." Billy turned toward the table and set the beers down. "Here Frank, Jesse, the beers are on me."

Frank and Jesse smiled. "Take care, Billy, hope to see ya again sometime."

William Gregg and Billy slipped out the door cautiously and walked toward camp. "Guess I'll know better than to let you get the beer next time, Billy boy." William Gregg slapped his hand on Billy's back.

"Next time, Dingus can get it himself," Billy replied.

27

A Man of Destiny

Major Benton Bartok spun the last number of the combination on the safe in his office. With a satisfying click the tumbler fell in place. Benton grabbed the handle and gave it a twist, and the door swung open to reveal his money. He glanced at it for only a moment before he began filling his waiting saddlebags.

The cash was a pitifully small amount compared to the currency he had amassed and sent to his brother, Jacob, before Quantrill raided Lawrence. He never thought the guerrillas would have the audacity to attack the Jayhawker stronghold and was stunned when they hit Lawrence. In their wake, his fortune was gone and his brother dead.

The loss of his brother hit him harder than he expected, but it was the loss of his money that haunted him. Sometimes he would wake up in the middle of the night in a cold sweat, dreaming of piles of money burning before his eyes. Try as he might, he couldn't put out the fire.

Early in the war, the pickings had been easy. He felt like a man of destiny, the whole war preordained for his benefit. He could confiscate large numbers of livestock and horses, diverting them for his own gains and for those working with him. Money was easy to obtain before he had drained most of the wealthy Southerners dry. All it took was the burning of a few plantations—make an example of a few while enjoying the bounty of stripping and stealing their wealth so the others would make their payments. Those payments were supposed to protect them and their families from the Jayhawkers, but only delayed the inevitable. When Bartok had wrung all he could get from them by playing on their fears, he took what he wanted anyway.

Then there was what he prized more than the wealth he stole—sex. Those who couldn't meet the financial quotas for his benevolent protection could save themselves with a few personal favors. He was always willing to cut a deal if the family had an attractive daughter willing to be cooperative.

Even the most stubborn women could be had if a man was skillful and cunning. You could even get them to pretend they enjoyed it if you were clever. Benton Bartok loved the power he wielded over these women. They would do his bidding no matter how wretched or distasteful. They would submit to his every wicked desire or they would pay. Pay with the loss of their homes, their property, or their family.

If all else failed, he simply arrested a member of the family and threatened to let them rot in prison. If this still didn't get the coveted woman's cooperation, he threatened to have the imprisoned family member executed.

He found this sense of control exhilarating. He loved to imagine himself a Roman emperor and the women his slaves, here for his pleasure. They must fulfill his wishes for he was in power and for as long as the war lasted, Lafayette County was his empire. He could take what he wanted when he wanted—and he had.

He would have been set for life with riches beyond his wildest dreams if not for the Bushwacker raid on Lawrence. Money had become scarce in Lafayette County over the last year. He had nearly milked the county dry. Benton was even forced to steal from those who supported the Union.

He remembered with some satisfaction an old German couple living in the southwest corner of the county. Benton heard that the old man was loaded but he was a Union man. He knew there was a way to get to the old man's money if he put his head to it. One night he led a few of his most trusted soldiers to the home. He enjoyed forcing the old German to talk by beating his wife, whom he would have raped had she not been so old and ugly. He smiled as he placed her gold wedding band in his bag and remembered how he had outwitted them. After the old man gave him the money, Bartok had them both killed, making the killing look like the work of Bloody Bill's Bushwackers.

The way Benton saw it, they just beat the Bushwackers to the money. If he hadn't taken it, they most likely would have. Those damn Krauts should have stayed in Germany anyway. What right did they have coming to this country and making good money off the land? Hell, they could hardly understand English, let alone speak it.

Benton finished closing the saddlebags. Just a little over twenty thousand in Federal greenbacks was all he could scrape together in the time since his brother's death. It would have to do. A man has to buy loyalty from his men if he wants to make a buck, and Benton knew it was a fact of life. If it hadn't been for the payoffs he would have had much more, but that was the price of doing business.

At least General Kessington was gone. He had been promoted and sent to Sherman's army. Kessington had repeatedly blocked Benton's promotion to colonel. When the previous colonel commanding the Third Kansas regiment had died, Major Bartok took over.

General Kessington never forgave Benton for the time he fled Lafayette County in search of phantom guerrillas in the next county just as Jo Shelby arrived to recruit a

Confederate brigade. Benton wasn't stupid enough to stick around with the Lafayette County cavalry coming to town. Not after all the things he had done. Only a fool would have stayed, and Major Benton Bartok was nobody's fool. Still, it made him wonder if he was the only major in the army to command a regiment for this long without reaching the rank of colonel.

The war was supposed to be winding down. Leastways that's what the eastern papers seemed to think. Lee's Rebel army was trapped in Petersburg, and General Sherman was deep in Georgia. Just a matter of time they said, but someone forgot to tell General Price and his Rebel army currently terrorizing central Missouri.

Even now, Shelby's men were closing in. Benton had heard they were already in Waverly, maybe even in Dover by now. If they caught Bartok in Lexington he would be lucky to see the next sunrise. Luckily General Curtis, in command of Kansas troops and the army of the border, had ordered Benton Bartok and his Third Kansas Cavalry to fall back on the crossings of the Little Blue River and join the Second Brigade under the command of Colonel Thomas Moonlight.

It was fortunate Benton had been ordered to leave his post, for he had no intention of staying to fight for Lexington by himself. If necessary, he would have left as he had done before—in the search for phantom guerrillas. Facing Jo Shelby and his men offered no easy profit, and Benton saw little benefit from the endeavor. He didn't mind a little danger if the money was right, but he wasn't interested in risking his neck unless the prize was substantial and the risk minimal. Besides, Shelby's men were dangerously tough fighters from Lafayette County, and they would be anxious for revenge. They intimidated him almost as much as Quantrill's men had.

Benton stood with the heavy saddlebags in his hand and swung the safe door closed. After the raid on Lawrence, Bartok had convinced the proprietor of a local hardware store to give him his safe and the combination in exchange for allowing the man to keep his store. After all, in these volatile times a fire could occur at any time, or the goods could be confiscated for the use of the army. The man was happy to make the deal, but it left Bartok with another ticklish problem—Benton didn't relish the idea of the storekeeper having the combination to his new safe. The solution was simple: He had the man killed in a fake robbery and the store looted by his Jayhawkers. It had worked out even better than he hoped; he gained a new safe and still got all he wanted from the store.

The heavy safe on its four iron wheels was a perfect addition to his headquarters. Benton made sure someone was always posted on guard, day or night, to safeguard his money. It comforted him to know his money was so close at hand and the safe was large and heavy enough that no one would easily take it.

Benton patted the safe like he was saying good-bye to a faithful old dog to whom he had grown attached. He looked once more around his headquarters, where for the last few years he had wielded his power over the county. He felt sad leaving his throne of power, even if it was only for a little while. With any luck, he would return when the Rebels left.

Benton turned and walked out the door and swung into the saddle of his mount, held for him by his orderly, Sergeant Adderly. He had done his best to use every opportunity that came his way. In that light he took a small measure of pride in his accomplishments. Who knew what tomorrow might bring? Maybe new and better things awaited beyond the horizon for a cunning, talented man of vision like himself.

28

Sad Duty

Jessie rode along the familiar path leading to River-view Plantation, Katlin's childhood home. The line of mighty oaks and maples along the familiar lane near Dover, Missouri, gave him a sense of homecoming. He spotted his first glimpse of the stately home from a high rise in the road before he had entered the lane. It was still there and he sighed with relief, glad Riverview had escaped Briarwood's fate.

On his eleven-mile ride from Waverly, where Price's army was camped, he had plenty of time to think. His thoughts turned to Briarwood Plantation, and the day that Major Benton Bartok and his Jayhawkers killed his father and burned his home to the ground, leaving his sisters and mother homeless. On the long journey south, his mother caught pneumonia and died. He lost both of his parents and his home to the Jayhawkers.

During the last Missouri raid when he stood by his father's grave, the finality and cruelty of the war struck home for the first time. Hate raged in Jessie like a fiery inferno. When he returned to war he did so with renewed purpose and hateful passion. It was only his love for Katlin and little Glen that gave him more than hate to keep him going. Jessie vowed someday he would see Briarwood rise anew from the ashes.

His attention turned from his private thoughts as he considered this sad duty. He felt an urgent sense of responsibility to ride on and tell Harlan and Caroline Thomas about the death of their son, Gilbert. Jessie was family now, and they deserved to learn about their loss firsthand. Accompanying him rode Major Stryker, who had asked if he could come along. Since Gilbert Thomas saved his life, Evan wanted to be there to tell the parents of their son's final brave moments at the attack on Jefferson City. With the army staying in Waverly for a day they had time to pay their respects.

Jessie studied the solemn-faced major. He knew what Evan was thinking, for no one looks forward to breaking the news of a loved one's death. But the loss the Kimbroughs had suffered was not theirs alone to share. Many from Lafayette County paid the price for their loyalty to the South.

General Jo Shelby's home on Mount Rucker lay in ashes. It had been burned by the Yankees just this year. The smell of burnt wood was fresh, lingering among the haunting remains of the brick chimneys, still standing like mute headstones on a black grave. First Shelby's businesses had been burned. His factory where the locally grown hemp had been turned into rope was destroyed, then later followed by his sawmill. Both had been early casualties of the war. The burning of his home was further punishment for his service to the Confederacy.

Jessie remembered seeing the agony in the general's face and identified with it. He knew firsthand the feeling of loss at the hands of a hated enemy. Yet nothing could restore what had been lost. All that was gained was resolve in battle to make the enemy pay in additional blood.

Jessie's mind snapped back to the task at hand when

they turned into the curved drive leading to the house. Riverview had changed dramatically. Rank weeds, now dead from the fall chill, stood in stark contrast against the great house. The paint on the mansion was peeling and fading and gave the appearance of poor upkeep.

Harlan Thomas had always been very particular about his home. He made sure his slaves kept it spotless. The present condition of Riverview was an abrupt reminder of the harshness of the war on the locals. As they rode, Jessie noticed the slaves' quarters, empty and abandoned.

They tied the horses to a railing near the steps leading to the front door of the large home. A few quick steps and Jessie was knocking on the door.

After a short wait, he was greeted by a tired looking lady with gray hair. Jessie had to look twice to recognize Caroline Thomas. "Hello, Caroline, is Harlan home?"

Caroline's eyes were dull and lifeless. Slowly, her eyes began to focus and a glimmer of recognition lit her face. "Jessie? Jessie Kimbrough, is that you?"

"Yes, Caroline, it's me."

Caroline smiled excitedly and ran into Jessie's arms. Her embrace was surprisingly strong for one who looked so frail. She screamed loudly over her shoulder. "Harlan! Harlan, come quick! The boys are home!" She pulled back from Jessie and looked in his eyes. "Where's Gilbert? Is he with you?"

She knew the answer by the look on his face. "No, I'm sorry, Gilbert isn't with us."

A look of concern crossed her face. "Will he be here soon?"

"No, I'm afraid not."

Before he could say more, Harlan approached. "Jessie, my boy! My God let me take at look at you." Harlan glanced over at Evan Stryker who was standing nervously in the doorway, crushing his hat in his hands. "Who did you bring with you, Jessie?"

"I'd like to introduce Major Evan Stryker. He's engaged to my sister Cassandra."

Harlan stepped forward and shook Evan's hand firmly. "Sure, I remember him now. Aren't you from Texas?"

"Yes, sir," responded Evan.

"Well, Evan, you're welcome in my home anytime and welcome to share what we have left. I'm sorry to say, in these days and times it is very little."

"Thank you, sir."

"Please, call me Harlan. This is my wife, Caroline." As the two exchanged greetings, Harlan turned to look at Jessie. "I don't believe I've ever seen you wear a beard before, Jessie. I hardly recognized ya."

Jessie blushed. "I didn't intend to grow one, Harlan. I just haven't had an opportunity to shave lately. If I meant to keep it, I'd trim it better."

"Well, if ya want to shave, boy, we can heat up some water an' lend you a razor." A look of hope lit Harlan's face. "Well, son, is Gilbert with you?"

"No, sir, he isn't." Jessie paused, then continued uncomfortably. "You'd better sit down. I have some bad news."

Harlan stiffened and Caroline's eyes widened in fear. "Is it Gilbert? Has something happened to him?" Caroline's voice trembled.

Jessie saw that neither one of them were making any move to sit down. They weren't going anywhere until they got some answers. "I don't know any easy way of sayin' it, so I'll just say it outright. Gilbert was killed in the attack on Jefferson City a little over a week ago. We buried him in the city cemetery at California, Missouri."

Caroline's eyes rolled and she slumped to the floor as she passed out from shock. Jessie tried to catch her, but he missed. He scooped her up and carried her into the family room where he laid her gently on the davenport. Harlan followed and stood, head down in front of a window with his back to his guests. Jessie watched the old man's shoulders shudder in sorrow. After a few minutes he regained control of his composure. He walked back to stand near his wife and face Jessie. "How did it happen?"

Evan stepped forward. "Sir, if you don't mind, I could tell you more about it. I was there when your son died."

Harlan looked at Evan. "Please tell me."

"We'd just driven the Yankees away from the river ford we were ordered to capture. A lone Yankee soldier in hiding took a shot at us. I had my back to the Yank and couldn't see what was happening. Gil moved forward and knocked me out of the path of danger. He saved my life, but he took a shot in the leg. The bullet severed an artery. We tried to stop the bleeding, but it was hopeless. He bled to death."

Harlan, his eyes still wet and red from crying, asked, "Was he in much pain?"

"No, sir, he didn't suffer. He got the chills, then passed out before he died. His last thoughts were of you and home." Evan lied about Gilbert's final thoughts. He didn't want to tell them Gilbert's final words had really been about Cassandra. It would make it worse if they knew, and he wanted to ease their sorrow.

Caroline regained consciousness and sat up slowly. She'd heard Evan's story. Her sobs built into a torrent as Harlan stepped forward and held his wife in his arms. Embarrassed, not knowing what they should say or do, Evan and Jessie stood uncomfortably. After a few minutes Caroline held out her hand for Jessie.

"Jessie, now we've lost our son, you and Katlin are all we have. Only one letter has gotten through to us since January. Katlin told us she had a son she named Glen Adam. Have you had a chance to see him yet?"

Jessie smiled. Even in this time of sorrow there was joyful news to share. "Yes, I've seen him and he's a fine healthy boy. I haven't seen them for several months, but when we were in Camden I did have a photographer make images for us. We had a set made for you. Did you receive them?"

Disappointment showed clearly on her face. "No, we haven't received any letters except the one just after she had the baby. I know it's not her fault. I'm sure she's writ-

ten us often, but I think the Union men in the postal service make special effort to make sure the mail doesn't get
through to Southern families."

Jessie could see the eagerness in the faces of his in-
laws. He reached behind his neck and pulled the gold
locket over his head. He bent down on one knee and
handed the open locket to Caroline.

She sighed with pleasure as she saw the photograph of
her grandson for the first time. "Look, Harlan, doesn't little Glen look like Katlin did when she was a baby? He has
her eyes." Tears began to run down her cheeks again as
she studied the small photos. "I wish I could hold him."

Harlan sat beside her and studied the photos. Jessie
could see he was deeply touched by his daughter and
grandson. "I wish we could have these. It would be comforting to see Kat and the baby." He paused. "It's been so
long since we've seen her." He looked at Jessie. "If it
hadn't been for the war I would have thrown a celebration
for the two of you the likes of which this valley has never
seen before. This damn war has ruined everything."

"We didn't want to get married without you being there,
but we just couldn't wait, with the war an' all. I hope
you'll forgive us."

"Of course, Jessie, I'd already given my approval before
you left for the war. I'm proud to have you in the family."

"General Shelby intends to stay in the area for at least
a day. Would you mind if we stay here with you?"

"Of course, I insist. I'd never forgive you if you didn't
stay."

"We left our horses out front. We should put them away.
Might be trouble if anyone sees them and knows you have
company."

"Yes, of course, I should have suggested it earlier. We
don't have slaves anymore, but I'll be glad to help you put
the horses in the stables. The darkies that didn't run off
were ordered off by Major Bartok and his boys. Follow
me."

Jessie was glad to get Harlan away from Caroline. The

news he had for him would be best revealed in privacy. The three men led the horses to the stables. When the horses were unsaddled, rubbed down, and fed what meager rations were available, Jessie asked Evan to give them a few minutes alone.

"Harlan, I'm not good at beatin' around the bush. Kat read the letters you gave her to be read after you died. She shouldn't have done it, but she was homesick and curious and she read them. She has told Becca you're her father. Becca has been given her freedom, and Katlin and Becca have grown closer because of it. It was quite a shock at first for both of them."

Harlan stiffened at the news; the revelation had caught him offguard. "I suppose it had to come out sooner or later, but I'd preferred it to be after my death. I never intended to hurt Caroline. I suppose I should have faced up to it myself." Harlan looked pale and shaken. "I hope you don't hate me for what I've done, or blame Katlin."

"I'm in no position to judge any man, Harlan. All I know is I love your daughter. Kat and my son are the only things that really matter. I'm not going to lie to you. I was shocked when Kat told me Becca was her half sister, but I've had time to get used to the idea."

"How long have you known?"

"Kat told me when we were together at Camden, Arkansas. That's when we had the pictures taken."

"I suppose everyone knows about my indiscretions now."

"I'm not planning on tellin' anyone, and as far as I know, only Katlin, Becca, and myself know. I don't think anyone else does."

"How did Becca take the news?"

"At first she was angry. She made a deal to keep it a secret if Kat would help her buy the freedom of a slave in Arkansas. It seems Becca fell in love with this darky she met down there. He is a good fellow and treats her well."

"She still plans to live with a slave when she knows she's a Thomas?"

"She's never thought of herself as anything but a slave. It's only natural for her to love one of her kind. Besides, you loved a slave, didn't you? I suppose it isn't any of my business, but she isn't doing anything you haven't done."

Harlan looked startled. "Yes, I suppose you're right. I guess I shouldn't expect her to change how she feels about herself overnight." They walked on quietly for awhile, then Harlan said, "I know what I did was wrong. I think Caroline knows where I was and what I was doin' and I think she just ignored it. She's a fine lady, but she never enjoyed making love. I suppose she chose to look the other way. She's never said so, but I'm sure she knew Callie's kids were mine. I guess a real lady like her would never mention it. It just wasn't the way she was raised." Harlan kicked at a stone in the path. The rock skittered away.

"I guess not."

"I always treated Becca special. I couldn't help it. I often wondered what others thought about her light skin. No one ever said nothin' about it to me."

"I think people noticed it, but it's not such an uncommon thing. I know many Southern men bought slaves for their pleasures. A good-lookin' slave girl always brings high prices. I think Southerners just expect it. You're not the only slave owner to father his slaves—we both know it's happened before. It's kind of funny we seldom talk about it. I suppose we hope by ignoring it, it will just go away. We are all just human after all and share our human weaknesses, but I guess it's just something gentlemen don't normally discuss."

"God help me, Jessie. I love Becca, just as much as I love Katlin and Gilbert. It was hard not to recognize her publicly, but I couldn't hurt the rest of my family. The truth is, I was afraid of what others might think of me."

"You've taken an unusual step, Harlan. It is one thing to admit fathering children by your slaves. It is another thing to accept them as your children and not your property." Jessie stopped walking and looked Harlan in the eyes. "I just thought you should know, Harlan. I'm not judging you."

"Thanks, Jessie. We'd better get back to the house before Caroline gets worried. She's gonna need me even more with Gilbert gone." They walked along quietly for a few steps. "After the war, I want to bring Gil home. I want him buried on Thomas land."

"I'll help you bring him back if I can." The two men retraced their steps to the barn, rejoined Evan Stryker, and returned to the house.

Caroline was still crying on the sofa. She clasped the locket firmly in her hands. Jessie felt her sorrow. He thought how much it would hurt him to hear of little Glen's death, though he had spent only a little time with his son. How hard must it be after loving and caring for a son, watching him grow up, then finding out he was killed. Jessie silently prayed he would never have to suffer the loss of one of his children.

Caroline looked up at them as the men entered the room. "I'm glad you brought the locket, Jessie. It's been so lonely here with both of our children gone. Day after day, I wondered how they were doing and if they were all right. You don't know how much it means to me to see our grandchild and our daughter. Would you let me keep the locket?"

Jessie felt a sinking feeling inside, as if someone had dumped ice inside him. Give up his locket? How could he give up something so important to him? It was his habit to touch the locket whenever he was lonely. He spent time every day looking at the photographs of his wife and son. How could he go on not having that little bit of comfort to carry him through all the loneliness and danger? That locket had become his personal luck, his charm to ward off danger. Jessie couldn't explain it, but somehow he felt protected from harm when he wore it. Call it superstition or faith, but it was something he believed in deeply.

Everything within him wanted to scream out, "No! No, you can't have it, it's mine!" But when he saw the sorrow

on Caroline's tear-streaked face and the pleading in her
eyes, he couldn't force himself to hurt her further. Here
was a chance for him to do something important for
Katlin's family and, despite his needs, he couldn't refuse
her.

Jessie stepped forward and put his hand over hers. "This
locket was given to me by Katlin. I've worn it all the time
I've been in the brigade and through every battle and skirmish. Somehow, I've always believed it has brought me
luck." He looked deeply into her eyes. "I think Kat will
understand if I gave it to you. You should be able to see
your grandson."

"What about you? Are these the only pictures you have
of them?"

"Yes, it's all I have, but I've spent time with them more
recently than you have. I've gotten to hold my son, and
I'm grateful to you for such a wonderful daughter. She's
made me very happy. You keep the locket, and when I see
you again you can return it to me."

Caroline pulled Jessie to her and gave him a long, firm
hug. "Thank you, thank you so much, Jessie." She sobbed
softly.

Major Evan Stryker spurred his horse forward along the
broken and trampled stocks of a former cornfield. Any
ears that might have been missed in harvest had been
picked clean by the passing of a moving and hungry Confederate army. Evan kept to the fields. More than five hundred wagons of every description and condition crowded
the road, and beside the wagons marched nearly five thousand new recruits, untrained and lacking weapons, and
moving in a haphazard fashion.

Evan could never remember seeing a more ragtag bunch
of stragglers in his life. They wore clothing of every type
and description; some rode horses, but most walked.

Added to the strange mix were families of Southern refugees joining the army out of desperation. Many were in
the most wretched of conditions with nearly broken-down

wagons and sorry looking draft animals. Most things of value they might have owned had long ago been taken from them. Children, many hungry and dressed in little more than rags, rode with their mothers or, if they were old enough, walked alongside.

At the fringes of this moving circus of despair were the former slaves set free with no idea of how to take care of themselves and with no place to go. Many of these lost souls joined the route in hopes of receiving care from former masters. The mass of humanity plugged the roads and slowed the column which, since they had left Boonville, seemed to have a mind of its own. To Evan's way of thinking, this was no way to run a raid.

Evan felt satisfied with General Shelby's replacement for Colonel Shanks. Shelby had selected M. Jeff Thompson, the famous swamp fox of Southeast Missouri, to take his place. Officers as good as David Shanks were hard to find, but Jeff Thompson was a man capable of filling his shoes.

General Rosecrans had the Union cavalry under General Pleasonton pressing the rear of the Confederate army from the moment the Rebels left Boonville. Before them, Shelby's brigade was running into stiffened resistance from Union armies led by General Blunt and General Sam Curtis.

Shelby's men had driven Blunt's scouts through Lexington, and Evan had been assigned to find Marmaduke's brigade and bring them to the front to relieve Shelby's command. The Iron Brigade could use a little break from the action.

The guerrilla bands under Bloody Bill Anderson, Quantrill, and all the others except George Todd's had left the army. Price had assigned them to attack railroad lines and then rejoin the army. Only George Todd had followed the general's orders and stayed with the Rebel army. The rest of the Bushwackers disappeared into the Missouri landscape.

Evan thought back wistfully to the night he had spent at

Riverview Plantation. Even though their mission had been a sad one, he had slept in a real bed again. He had forgotten how nice it felt to lie in clean sheets and a soft bed. It seemed so funny now, the way he'd always taken such pleasures for granted before the war. Now easing into a real bed was a memorable experience. The one-day stay was a refreshing break from the war.

As he rounded the bend Evan saw the familiar banners of Marmaduke's veterans. With a sigh of relief he spurred his horse forward to deliver the orders he was carrying.

29

A Time of Reckoning

For Ross Kimbrough the day had been a long and hard one. In the early morning hours Marmaduke's division had moved into the lead. Shelby's veterans were tired and low on ammunition; they had fought skirmishes constantly since leaving the Dover-Waverly area. Resistance continually stiffened the farther west the army marched. As they neared the town of Independence, Missouri, movement was nearly stalled.

The Yankees, determined to slow the advance, had made a stand at the crossing of the Little Blue River. Marmaduke's brigade briskly attacked the mix of Blunt's Kansas and Colorado troopers, but the Union defenders had chosen their battlefield wisely. The banks of the Little Blue River were steep and narrow. The soldiers took advantage of a series of rock fences, using them for shelter to fight the Rebels. The volume of fire from the Union soldiers, armed with the latest in repeating arms, was terrific. The Southerners had little previous experience facing this type of firepower. Soon the orders came for Shelby's division to rejoin the battle.

When Shelby's command entered the conflict, the Yankees were forced away from the river and retreated to the crest of the ridge beyond the banks. Shelby's men forded the shallows of the Little Blue and moved to the left against the Eleventh Kansas and Bartok's Third Kansas Cavalries.

Once in the front lines, Shelby's men charged the exposed artillery battery of the Eleventh Kansas Cavalry. The Union troops, realizing their battery was in jeopardy, met the Rebels with a cavalry charge. Union troopers of the Eleventh Kansas, Third Kansas, and the Second Colorado Cavalries rushed to intercept the Rebels before they reached the Union battery. The cavalry columns slammed together like two waves crashing. The battle turned immediately into desperate, one-on-one combat. Yankee sabers met Rebel revolvers in a swirling, bloody affair.

Ross found himself in the midst of the fighting. Around him he heard the screams of horses shot and sabered, the raging curses of men, and the rattle of sabers mixed with the pop of revolvers. The action blurred as he dodged, fired, and kicked his way through the deadly tempest. Ross emptied the saddles of two Yankee mounts with shots from Double Twelve. In the milling collage of battle he emptied two more pistols.

The Union troopers slowed the Rebels long enough to cover the retreat of the artillery and fought a steady withdrawal. The Southerners continued to press the attack, but Blunt's boys made stubborn stands at Massey's farm two miles east of the Little Blue and a second one at Saunders's farm three miles west of Massey's farm.

For Ross, the day passed in a daze, jumbled in his mind. It was now nearly four o'clock on this fall-shortened October day. Again the Yankees were forced to withdraw toward Independence, Missouri. Ross and the scouts found themselves detached from the main body of the Confederate army as they pursued stragglers. Finally, near a bend in the road beside a wooded grove, Ross called a halt and waited for his men to gather.

As he waited, Ross and Rube Anderson reloaded their weapons. The men were so scattered that only the old scouts that had been with Ross from the beginning joined them. They were a close-knit group and generally fought together in battle. First to ride in was Fletch Taylor.

Bill Corbin and Sergeant Jonas Starke came in next, bringing a captured Union officer wearing a dusty, sweat-stained uniform. The prisoner rode a fine gray gelding. Ross saw by the way the man sat his saddle that he was pompous and arrogant. He seemed indignant to find himself a prisoner in the hands of these poorly uniformed Rebels. As the officer rode forward, Ross noticed the flapping cover of his revolver holster and the empty cavalry scabbard bouncing at his side. Jonas had disarmed the officer and now followed him with revolver drawn.

The officer rode directly before Ross and reined in. "See here, are you the officer in charge of this rabble?"

"I'd be damned careful who you're callin' rabble, soldier. After all, you're the prisoner here." Ross smiled with contempt. "I'm in command of these men." The captain studied the man with care. He looked very familiar and Ross had a sense this prisoner was special. He tried hard to place him, and yet couldn't quite recall where he had seen him before.

The officer ignored Ross's comments. "You look to be a reasonable man. I'll make it well worth your while if you'd let me go. No one will ever know. You and your men can make some money, and I can go on my way." The man smiled nervously. "How about it?"

Ross fixed eyes as hard as blue steel on the officer. "It seems to me you're in a damn poor position to be negotiating your release. While you're busy shooting off your mouth, how about tellin' me who you are." Suddenly it came to Ross. Of course he knew his prisoner. He had ridden north in 1863 with the intention of killing this man and he thought he had gotten the job done. It was only af-

ter he returned to Jo Shelby's command that he found out
this man had somehow survived. Ross felt his cheeks flush
with red and felt his temper edge toward the boiling point.

The officer hesitated, as if he were nervous about telling
them. He saw the intent look on the Rebel officer's face
and the change in temperament. Finally, the Yankee made
up his mind. "My name is Major Benton Bartok of the
Third Kansas Cavalry. I'm an officer in the United States
Army and I demand to be treated with the respect due to
an officer being held as a prisoner of war."

Ross's eyes flashed with fire. Just inches away from
him sat the man responsible for his father's death, the
burning of his home, and the ruthless rule over Lafayette
County. He was almost certain before, and now he was
convinced of this man's identity. "Did you say your name
is Benton Bartok?"

Bartok was exasperated. "Do I have to repeat myself?
My name is Benton . . . Bartok," he said slowly and sar-
castically, as if speaking to someone mentally inferior.
"My rank is major. Now, if we could just get on with it,
maybe we can make a deal."

Anger and resentment held for far too long raged like a
wind-propelled forest fire inside Ross Kimbrough. This
was the man he had dreamed of killing, the man who had
filled him with dreams of revenge. The hate for Bartok
gnawed at his mind like a dose of rattlesnake venom.

Like a coiled spring unleashed, Ross threw a hard,
straight left punch to Bartok's face, slamming home on the
bridge of Bartok's nose. Ross felt the satisfying, solid impact of his fist as the Union officer's nose smashed from
the blow. The momentum of the punch pitched Bartok
backward out of the saddle. He clawed desperately at the
empty air, trying to break his fall. Bartok slammed to the
ground, flat on his back. The wind whooshed out of him
as a small cloud of dust rose about him. The gray gelding,
startled by the sudden movement of the falling rider, skittered sideways. Jonas grabbed the reins of the snorting animal as the horse reared, pawing the air.   .

Ross swung quickly out of the saddle and grabbed Bartok by the shirt front, hauling him to his feet. "You rotten son-of-a-bitch. Do you know who I am?"

Bartok stood shaken; his nose canted peculiarly to the left and blood ran rich and red down his teeth and lips. He wheezed out, "I've never laid eyes on you before. How should I know or care who the hell you are?"

"When you kill a man you ought to take time to find out who's gonna come lookin' for ya." Ross threw a punch to Bartok's stomach that doubled the Yankee over in pain. He followed with a knee to Bartok's face that straightened him, then flung him once more onto his back in the dust.

Rube Anderson was the first to reach Ross. He grabbed his arms and held him away from Bartok. "Hold on there, Capt'n. You're gonna kill the poor son-of-a-bitch."

Ross fought against the restraint. Everything within him wanted to kill Bartok. "Let me go, Rube! That bastard needs killin', and by God I'm gonna do it." Ross in his fury kicked dirt toward Bartok, who slowly rolled onto his face. Anger raged in Ross like a fire run amuck. "Bartok! You had my father killed and you burned out my family, now you're gonna pay for it."

Bartok hurt all over. He could barely breathe. Blood, irony and salty tasting, filled his mouth. He ran his tongue over his shattered and jagged teeth and a swollen lip. He spit blood into the dust just inches in front of his face. He stuttered out, "I . . . I don't know what the hell you're talking about."

The denial only served to inflame Ross Kimbrough's anger. "I'll spell it out for ya, Jayhawker. Do you remember Glen Kimbrough and Briarwood Plantation? Do you remember stealin' everything my father worked for his whole life? You and your men killed him when he tried to stop you, you bastard!"

Bartok's voice was muffled by the dirt. "I didn't shoot Kimbrough. The man came at us with a shotgun. He killed one of my sergeants. My men had to shoot him. It was self defense. The old man was out of his mind." Bartok slowly closed his hand, collecting a handful of loose dirt in his palm as he came up to his knees. "Who the hell are you, anyway? I never saw you there."

"I'm Ross Kimbrough, Glen's oldest son. I was off fightin' in this stinking war while you were busy filling your pockets with stolen goods. That wasn't good enough, was it, Bartok? No, you killed my dad and you burned out my family." Ross's voice lowered into a dangerous growl. "Now I'm gonna even the score."

Ross broke loose from Rube and moved toward Bartok. Still on his knees, Bartok threw the handful of dirt into Ross's eyes. Ross clutched as his face, his eyes burning and blinded. In a moment Benton was rushing Ross, landing a wicked uppercut to Ross Kimbrough's chin. The blow staggered the Rebel captain backward into the arms of Rube Anderson. Bartok followed closely and grabbed the butt of the revolver stuck in the gun belt Ross was wearing. He swung the gun clear and stepped back as he thumbed the hammer. "Any of you move and I'll blow your captain into the next world."

Ross's eyes teared heavily as he fought to clear the dirt away. He had felt the tug at his belt as Bartok cleared the revolver. He fought to focus, but his eyes still burned.

The other scouts around the two men were stunned by the sudden reversal. They stood tensed, but afraid to attack for fear of getting Ross killed. Bartok wasn't stupid. He knew if he shot Kimbrough his own life was worthless. His only hole card was to keep the Rebels at bay for fear of killing their captain. "Kimbrough, you better pray these men like you, 'cause if one of them tries anything you're a dead man." He waved the gun, motioning those around him to move behind Ross and Rube. The only man to stay put was Jonas Starke, still mounted and holding the Union officer's horse.

"You'll never make it, Bartok. I'll hunt ya down and kill you."

Bartok wiped the back of his hand across his bloody mouth. He spat a glob of blood with a piece of tooth at

Ross's feet. "Don't tempt me, Kimbrough. I owe you for this. You know the only thing I regret about burning that plantation of yours? I should've had my way with your sister. She's a fine lookin' bitch. If I ever find her again I'll correct that little error."

Bartok walked backward, keeping the gun on the Rebel soldiers, until he reached the gray gelding. "Hold him steady, soldier." Bartok looked down to spot the stirrup. As he placed his foot into it and prepared to swing aboard, his eyes and the gun swung off Ross Kimbrough and the men standing behind him.

Jonas yelled loudly, "Haw! Get up there, boy!" as he slapped his slough hat down on the hindquarters of the gray gelding. Bartok, caught by surprise, staggered and stumbled out of the stirrup as he fought to maintain his footing. In that instant, Ross reached behind his neck and slid Double Twelve out of its special holster. As Ross slung the barrels down to level he thumbed back both hammers of the deadly sawed-off, double-barreled shotgun. A moment too late Bartok swung his revolver toward Ross.

Ross pulled the first trigger and Double Twelve leapt in his hands. Bartok's gun hand and forearm exploded in a shower of red mist as a load of double-ought buck nearly severed his limb. Bartok, stunned, stared down at the bloody, ragged remnants of his right arm. The gun slipped uncontrollably from his shattered hand, and he glanced from his hand to Ross's shotgun. Fire and smoke belched from the second barrel as Ross pulled the last trigger. The boom of the blast ringing in his ears was the last thing Benton Bartok heard. A second deadly load of buckshot hit him full in the chest and flung him back like a string puppet, sprawling in the dirt.

Ross stepped forward with his smoking shotgun and stood over Benton Bartok's dying body. He looked down on the dirty Union blue tunic filled with even, round holes, blood oozing from nearly every one. He watched as Benton rattled his last breath, his body trembling and jerk-

ing in his death throes. Ross lowered his gun as he looked
at the bloody face of his enemy. Bartok's glazed eyes
stood open, staring into nothingness. Ross spit on the face
of the corpse lying still at his feet. "Rot in hell, you son-
of-a-bitch!"

The anger began to drain away as the weariness of the
day came crashing down upon him. He walked over and
leaned against a nearby tree, his still-smoking gun hanging
by his side.

"Holy Jeez-us!" yelled Jonas. "These saddlebags are
stuffed plum full of money!" To prove his statement, Jonas
held a fistful up for the scouts to see. Ross jerked his head
up as he heard Jonas yell.

The men swarmed around the gray gelding as they
stared at Jonas. Rube Anderson opened the other saddlebag on his side. "This one is full, too! Looks like it's
mostly Union greenbacks and a little gold coin."

Ross stood upright, stuffed Double Twelve in his back
holster, and joined the group. "It doesn't surprise me,
boys. Bartok and his thievin' Jayhawkers have been
stealin' from the people of Lafayette County since before
we even formed the brigade back in Sixty-two. I didn't
think he'd leave without taking his loot."

The men gathered around their trusted leader. "Boys, I
know this is a lot of money, and there isn't any way to
know who it belongs to for sure. All we know is it comes
from Lafayette County. I don't know about you, but it
seems to me we got as much right to it as anyone. I think
we ought to split this money between us when the war is
over. Is it agreed?"

The men looked at each other. Each soldier in turn nodded in agreement. "Who's gonna take charge of it until it's
time to split the money?" asked Jonas.

"If you boys will trust me, I'll carry it until it's time. If
something happens to me, it will fall to Sergeant Starke,
then to Rube Anderson. When this war ends we split it
five ways, agreed?"

They all nodded in agreement. "Then, boys, let's shake

on it." The men exchanged handshakes. "I expect each of you to keep it to yourself. Lordy, the problems we could have if others know about this money. Generals would likely try to take it away. It isn't much for all we've suffered through, but when this is all over, it'll give us a fresh start." He looked around the circle of four men gathered around him. "Let's saddle up and get out of here." Ross took charge of the saddlebags after Jonas replaced the money. He tied the saddle wallet securely to Prince of Heaven.

Jonas yelled over to him. "Hey, Ross, you mind if I take the gray gelding? He seems all right—looks like you missed him with your shotgun. My horse is near broke down. She's been limping on her hind leg all day and is nearly lame."

"Go ahead and take her, Sergeant. Bartok won't have any further need for her."

Ross swung into his saddle, and Rube Anderson rode up beside him. He handed Ross the revolver Benton Bartok had slipped from his belt. Then he handed Ross a wallet, a gold band, a watch, a pocket knife, several fine cigars in a battered case, some matches, and a handful of loose coins. "I found these on the Yank's body. The watch has a ding in it from one of your buckshot. Still seems to work fine."

"Thanks, Rube, I'll add this stuff to the money later. You better get mounted. If I know Shelby he'll want to press the Yankees until it's dark." As they rode away Ross somehow felt his soul lighten a little, as if a great weight had been lifted from his shoulders. Bartok was dead, and he knew he would sleep better just knowing that.

30

Grim Reaper's Harvest

The Yankees fell back to Independence, Missouri, where again they made a stand. Colonel Walker and the Union Eleventh Kansas Cavalry covered General Blunt's retreat to the Big Blue. A mean skirmish was fought through the town as dusk fell. When the dust settled the Rebels held Independence.

Earlier in the afternoon, as the Rebels were approaching Independence, George Todd, the leader of the guerrillas, was killed by a Yankee sharpshooter. Todd was scouting ahead with his men when he was shot through the throat by a minié ball. The ball shattered his spine and ripped his throat out causing instant death. He was buried that night in the city cemetery at Independence.

Saturday morning, October 22, 1864 dawned cold and windy. The air, pushed by a stiff cold breeze from the northeast, penetrated the thin blankets and coats of the Rebel soldiers. The Southerners were up and on the road by nine o'clock in the morning. The Confederates didn't travel far before they struck a strong Union defensive line along the Big Blue River. The Union army hoped the Rebels would make a frontal assault across the river's natural defensive position. Shelby realized such an attack would be disastrous. He ordered Jackman's brigade to make a noisy demonstration in front of the Union lines, while he sent most of the brigade against the right of the line to search for fords where they could cross and flank the Union line.

General M. Jeff Thompson, now the commander of Shanks's old brigade, moved upstream probing the right until they reached Byram's Ford. It was now eleven in the morning and General Shelby decided to attack. Colonel Jackman, having crossed the main ford at Independence, joined Shelby at Byram's Ford. Once in place, he began to pressure Colonel Jennison's hated Jayhawkers on the other side of the ford.

Meanwhile, Colonel Frank B. Gordon with the Fifth Missouri Cavalry crossed upstream and Lieutenant Colonel Alonzo Slayback's Missouri Cavalry Battalion crossed downstream. Slayback's Confederates found an unguarded crossing at Hinkle's Ford and attacked the exposed flank of Jennison's Jayhawkers.

The surprise assault on their flank while they fought off Jackman's troops was too much for the Kansans, who buckled and retreated. The infamous Jayhawker and his Kansas Red Leg thieves were now in full flight to the west. Byram's Ford lay open to the Rebel army. After stopping to clear the ford of felled trees, the Confederates rumbled across the Big Blue River.

The Union forces tried to make a brief stand at the Mockabee farm under General M. S. Grant. He lacked the skills of the more famous Union general U. S. Grant, and the stand was short and costly.

Colonels Jackman and Gordon formed their Rebel commands and artillery for an all-out charge. Down the line the old Rebel yell broke the stillness of the cold autumn day. The prairie beneath them shook with the pounding

hooves of hundreds of charging horses. They rode like a
wave of thunder rolling across a storm-tossed sky. The
rebels rode over the Yankee defenders as if they were only
a mild hindrance.

More than one hundred Kansas farmers soon lay dead in
the dust. A larger number were wounded, and one hundred
and two were taken as prisoners. Dead horses littered the
ground. The Rebels regrouped, and General Marmaduke
placed the rear guard in the very same positions guarding
Byram's Ford that Union general Jennison's troops had occupied earlier.

During the night the Rebel supply train of six hundred
wagons and more than three thousand head of cattle
moved south toward Little Santa Fe and the military road
leading to Fort Scott, Kansas. Protecting the supply train
were General Cabell's brigade and the unarmed, ragtag recruits.

The situation was now critical for the Confederates.
General Price found himself sandwiched between two Union armies. Undaunted, he ordered General Marmaduke to
hold the crossing at Byram's Ford against the Union army
chasing him, led by General Pleasonton. Union general
Curtis, now at his new headquarters, decided during the
night to stand and fight at Westport. He ordered his men
into defensive positions along Brush Creek. During the
night General Price ordered Jo Shelby's and Fagan's divisions to attack. The stage was now set for a decisive battle.

Jessie Kimbrough, mounted and waiting in line, pulled
his jacket collar up around his neck to shield against the
cold. Out of habit, he felt for his good luck charm and realized it was gone—he had left the locket with Katlin's
parents. Jessie had always felt protected when he wore
Katlin's locket, and now that it was missing he suddenly
felt vulnerable. He felt the cold fingers of fear playing
with the back of his neck as a heavy sense of dread descended over him. Would this be his last battle? He felt a

cold premonition that it would be. He wished desperately he had kept the locket.

The air felt cold and damp and Jessie strained his eyes to see through the white, swirling mist surrounding them. The enemy was out there somewhere, hidden in the fog. It was like facing a phantom army. At times he heard them as horses moved and cannons rolled into place. His fears multiplied their numbers. In that moment, Jessie realized how much easier it is to face what you can see, rather than what you imagine.

Jessie thought he saw flickers of slow movement—or was it his imagination toying with him? Sounds became more distinct, and finally, like ghosts out of the rolling mist, the Union soldiers became visible. Dull lights dimmed by the fog erupted before him like the flashes of giant fireflies. Jessie heard the Rebel yell as the Southern line moved out at a trot, the Confederate line answering the Union barrage with a broken ripple of fire winding its way down the line. Before him, Jessie heard the heavy thump of Union artillery and the shells passing through the lines, sounding like the shrieking of banshees.

The Rebel lines held firm and slowly advanced, driving back the Union soldiers before them. The continuous din of battle rose to a steady, rattling crescendo as the assault stretched nearly two hours before the last of the Yankees splashed into the icy waters of Brush Creek. The Federals didn't rout and instead took positions in the heavily timbered crest on the north side of the creek. Jessie dismounted, left his horse with a holder, and took cover with his brigade along a rock wall amid a stand of blackjack trees.

Despite their success, the Southerners were unable to exploit their power. General Shelby was forced to halt his men while ammunition was replenished. The wait took an hour and the Rebs' advantage disappeared as Union troops moved to fill the gap and strengthen their line. The battle became an artillery duel across Brush Creek. Again the Union army advanced, and once more they were driven back. As noon passed, Jessie was beginning to feel better about his chances of survival.

Suddenly, from the west behind their lines, artillery fire burst upon the Confederates. The Rebel line had been flanked by a hidden gully and the Union Ninth Wisconsin Artillery was now firing down the length of the exposed Southern line. Jessie hastily left his position in the stand of blackjack trees, rushed to the soldier holding his horse, and remounted. The Rebel line wavered under the brutal flanking fire and fell back from Brush Creek to the other side of the little South Valley, a short distance to the rear.

Calvin Kimbrough helped roll his cannon forward. His toes dug into the dirt as he strained to push the piece into position. Captain Richard Collins had seen the Wisconsin battery open up on the exposed Rebel line and he ordered his battery forward to the attack. Above the roar of battle Calvin heard his captain bellow out his orders. "Concentrate your fire on the Yankee battery flanking our line! Fire on my command!"

As one, the four Parrott guns of Collins's battery roared to life. Calvin heard the Rebels' cheer in response to the shots fired at the Yankees while his crew hastily reloaded. Two mountain howitzers were wheeled into line to join the Union artillery battery. More Union batteries on other parts of the field joined the duel.

The Union line again crossed the ice-fringed waters of Brush Creek and reached the rock walls on the south side recently vacated by the retreating Confederates. The Union line edged past the safety of the rock fence and inched forward across the valley. Twice the Rebel line bowed back around Collins's battery before driving the Union army back to the stone fence.

If it hadn't been for a bold flanking move by Colonel Gordon and the Fifth Missouri Cavalry that wrecked the second Union attack, Collins's battery would have been overrun. Calvin knew Jessie was in the thick of the battle and prayed he still survived. Again the Yankees retreated.

During both attacks the artillery fire never slackened. For over an hour, more than forty artillery pieces tore at each other and the charging uniformed lines on the battlefield.

Calvin became a machine, falling into the routine of aiming and firing the cannon. Concentrate on the job. . . . Shut out all the deadly missiles hurling around you. . . . Concentrate on firing the cannon over and over, as fast as you can. Destroy the enemy before he gets you. . . . Keep it steady, consistent, and accurate.

Geysers of dirt erupted around them, and the bone-jarring thumping of their guns dulled their senses even more. The mist of morning was gone now, replaced by acrid gray clouds of burned black powder smoke. The smoke swirled and eddied about them, half concealing them with choking tendrils.

The artillery duel raged on; the barrel of their cannon became so hot Calvin could blister a hand simply by touching it. Heat waves shimmered along the length of the barrel and made his aiming more difficult. When the wet sponge rammer slid down the length of the bore after each fired round, steam hissed from the red-hot metal in little white clouds. As the heat built, the danger increased. With each exploding shell loaded into the muzzle, Calvin prayed the overheated bore wouldn't prematurely ignite a fused shell. In such an event the shell could explode inside the cannon's breech or shortly after leaving the muzzle, doing serious damage to the crew.

Moments later, the cannon on the far side of the battery had a premature fuse ignition. The shell exploded not more than ten feet out of the barrel, showering its crew with deadly shrapnel. Out of the corner of his eye, Calvin saw Rebel crewmen ripped apart. Calvin thanked his lucky stars it wasn't his crew, though it was a sign of the increasing danger and should have been a warning. A cannoneer must take his chances when the outcome of a battle depends on the fire support from his battery.

Ten minutes later, Calvin Kimbrough's cannon exploded at the breech from a premature lit round. Calvin's last order was to load. Moments later, a tearing, ripping explosion lifted him from the ground and hurled him through the air as the cannon barrel disintegrated. Calvin felt the stunning shock of the explosion and the sensation of flying before his consciousness slipped into the dark pool of death. He was dead before his torn body hit the ground, his chest full of jagged shrapnel.

By noon the Union line pushed forward and drove the Rebels back to a series of stone fences just north of the Wornall house. Collins's battery had been reduced to one gun. The remaining cannon moved into the new line with Captain Collins still in command.

Jessie heard the sounds of battle building in a new direction as the Iron Brigade fought for every inch in a slow withdrawal. He heard the rumblings grow stronger behind them and to the east in the direction of Byram's Ford. Jessie knew the Union soldiers were pressing their attack. General Pleasonton's Union army was attacking from the east. It didn't take Jessie long to figure out that Yankees were now to the north, west, and east of their position. If they came from the south there would be no escape. He was dismayed to see Colonel Jackman's brigade withdrawn from the line and heading to the rear. Now only Shelby's Iron Brigade stood against the might of General Curtis's army.

Jessie looked out across the battlefield. In every direction lay the twisted and mangled bodies of the dead and dying. He heard shrieks of pain and cries for help from the wounded lying where they fell. The grim reaper was taking a bountiful harvest.

The Yankees also heard the firing from the east and, observing the weakened Confederate line, began an assault. The charging waves of blue-clad cavalrymen swept down toward the Iron Brigade. The two cavalry units slammed together in a bloody hand-to-hand affair. Jessie rode to the front, determined to do his part. He found himself surrounded by a swirling mass of blue and gray. Swords flickered in the sunlight and sliced deep into flesh. Pistols spoke deadly messages at close range. Jessie fired until his pistols were empty, and still the blue riders fought. Jessie switched to a Bowie knife, slashing and stabbing his way through three more Jayhawkers that got too close. Many men were unhorsed and on foot. There were too many bluecoats. Men began to break in panic and run from the fight. Collins's remaining gun was already withdrawn and heading for the rear.

Generals Thompson and Shelby waded in among the men, shouting encouragement and urging them to stand. Small knots of Rebels gathered, trying to resist the relentless pressure. From the east, one of Pleasonton's Union batteries opened from Hinkle's Grove and ripped into the milling Confederates from yet another angle. Fire from that direction could mean only one thing—Marmaduke's division must have been driven from the field.

All around him, men fell dead or dying. Jessie knew if he stayed, all was lost. He turned his horse to the rear; around him, others of the brigade were running for their lives while the Yankees hotly pursued them.

Jessie, riding low over his saddle as one Union cavalryman pressed him closely from behind, turned to see if the enemy was closing. One glance and Jessie felt fear steal his breath. His guns were empty, and he watched as the Union trooper drew a bead on him. Helplessly, he watched the flash from the muzzle and felt a sudden stab of pain as he lurched forward in his saddle. Jessie desperately clung to the saddle with both hands, holding on for dear life as the chase continued.

Jessie glanced back again to see a familiar rider gaining on the Union cavalryman. Jessie watched over his shoulder as Billy Cahill rode alongside the Yankee and fired his revolver point-blank into the blue-coated cavalryman. The Yankee rolled out of the saddle and sprawled lifeless into the dust.

Billy grinned wide as he rode alongside Jessie. "Ya better hurry, Jess. I ain't got time to wait. I don't wanna get run over by the stampede."

Jessie felt sharp pains in his side; the pain was spreading. Each jar of Star's Pride's hooves extended the circle of pain and wetness. They galloped on until they reached a line of stone fences where the Rebels turned to make a stand. The survivors of Shelby's brigade rallied again around the proud and tattered banner of the Stars and Bars.

General Shelby had lost his plumed hat during the retreat and his sandy locks flowed in the wind. "Hold 'em here, boys, or we'll lose the whole army."

Jessie knew they must buy time—time for Marmaduke and Fagan to escape, time for the supply train to get away. He took a handkerchief from his haversack and covered his wound. The pain made him cringe as he plugged the hole in his side.

He reloaded his guns with his bloodstained hands as he sat with his back to the wall. His thoughts were on Katlin and little Glen as he fought against the aching in his side. They withstood another charge before Jessie felt his world begin to spin. Moments later, he felt himself sinking into a dark, spinning vortex. Jessie's knees buckled as he slid to the ground. The black void of unconsciousness swept over him.

31

A Visitor

Cassandra Kimbrough heard a knock at the door. She was lying on her bed reading a book when she heard Fanny's familiar voice. "Miz Cassie! Miz Cassie, you got company. Miz Valissa Covington is here to see ya."

Cassandra sat up quickly and moved from the bed. She smoothed her dress and looked at herself in the mirror. Her hair was in order. She looked quickly around the upstairs room as a gentle breeze lifted the curtains at the open window. It was late August and in a few short hours the sweltering heat would increase and the cool, gentle breezes of morning would be gone.

This house was small compared to other homes they had lived in, but at least it was a home and away from the bustle of the Donoho Hotel. Their stay at the Donoho had been comfortable and pleasant, but the cost of the rooms ate into their limited budget. No one was sure how long the war would last, and even when it was over, money would be hard to come by. With Mary Donoho's help they

found this house, which Cassandra felt sure they could
rent until the end of the war. After one last glance around
the room, Cassandra turned and walked down the short
hall leading to the stairs to the living room.

Valissa arose from her chair as Cassandra entered the
room. "I apologize for dropping by so early. I hope I
didn't catch you at a bad time."

Cassandra smiled. "No, not at all, I was just lying in
bed reading. I'm usually an early riser. It's the best part of
the day, before the heat has time to build. The upstairs becomes nearly unbearable by afternoon." She smiled as she
looked Val over from head to toe. "I'm glad to see you
again."

"I wouldn't have stopped by so early except I needed to
finish my packing before we leave tomorrow."

Cassandra looked surprised. "I didn't know you were
planning a trip. Where are you going?"

"Father says we are going to the coast to meet Joseph
Farnsworth. We received word yesterday that Joseph has
run the blockade and is waiting to discuss business with
Father. Ever since we arrived in Texas Father has sent telegrams to all the different Texas ports in hopes of contact-
ing Mr. Farnsworth. If he couldn't reach him personally he
hoped he could catch one of his captains when they ran a
load through the blockade. Finally, after weeks of trying,
he received an answer. Joseph Farnsworth is here in Texas.
He said he would wait for us to reach him."

"So you want to go with your father?" Cassandra asked.

"I don't really want to leave. I keep hoping we'll hear
from our boys, especially Ross. I want to see him again."

"I'm afraid we won't see them for awhile. After all, it's
still summer and the army will be busy with the summer
and fall campaigns. Unless the war ends suddenly, I don't
expect to see them until late fall or winter."

"That's what Father said. He said he'd feel better if I
traveled with them. He would worry too much about me if
I stayed behind while he was away. I really don't want to
go, but Father can be very persistent."

"I understand how he must feel, but it is a shame you must go on the road again."

"Believe me, I'm not looking forward to the trip."

"Traveling takes time, and the war only seems to slow things down even more. Valissa, would you care for some tea? I'll have Fanny bring us some if you'd like."

"Yes, that would be fine. I am a little dry this morning."

Cassandra turned and shouted toward the kitchen. "Fanny, would you fix us a pot of tea?"

"Yes, Miz Cassie, but it's gonna take me a while. You can't heat water instantly, ya know. Land sakes alive, you shoulda given me more warnin'.." Fanny continued to grumble as she moved around the small kitchen. "She must think I can just pluck hot tea right outa the air at the snap of my fingers. Lor . . . dy!"

"Fanny is her old self this morning," said Valissa with a slight smile on her face.

"Yes, she's as feisty as ever. It wouldn't be Fanny if she wasn't." Cassandra looked thoughtful. "Why does your father want to meet with Joseph Farnsworth?"

"He says he wants to talk to him about their shipping business and their investments in Europe. Father is quite pleased with Joseph and their business dealings you know."

"Yes, I know Andrew has a great admiration for his partner. How do you feel about him?"

"I'm glad he's doing so well for my father. I believe his work greatly benefits the cause, if that's what you mean."

"No, I wasn't talking about your father's business dealings with Farnsworth. I meant how do you feel about Mr. Farnsworth personally?"

Valissa looked down at her hands. "Joseph is a gifted businessman. He's handsome, I suppose, in his own way, but he's in his thirties."

"Thirties isn't so old, is it?"

Valissa looked up at Cassandra. "No, I suppose not. Farnsworth does have considerable power and wealth, and this war has only made him wealthier. He can handle him-

290 Randal L. Greenwood

self, but he doesn't fire my passion, like Ross does. No one I have ever met excites me the way your brother does."

Cassandra smiled. "I was worried you might be interested in Mr. Farnsworth."

"Oh to be sure, Mr. Farnsworth has shown interest in me. Daddy has done his best to push us together, but you don't have to worry. I don't love Joseph. If I love anyone, it is Ross."

Cassandra felt more relaxed. "I'm glad to hear it. Ross loves you more than he loves life itself. You are his world. I can see it in his eyes and in his every action whenever he is near you. To tell you the truth, I was surprised when you didn't marry him in Camden. Didn't he ask you?"

"Yes, he did ask at Batesville and at Camden, but I turned down his request. I just don't want to be married until the war is over."

Cassandra looked puzzled. "Why not?"

"I'm afraid of becoming a young widow and I couldn't manage that. Besides, being married might detract from his concentration. If he didn't do his duty, or got hurt because he was worried about my safety . . . well, I'd feel responsible."

"Detract from his concentration? My Lord, Val, having him uncertain about your relationship will be more of a concern. It would have been a great comfort knowing you were here waiting for him."

"He should know anyway. Besides, it's too late to change anything now. At the time I felt it was the right decision. Nothing has happened to make me change my opinion."

"I suppose it's useless to worry about the past. I only have one question, Val. Are you sure you love him?"

Before she could answer Fanny entered carrying a tray with a pot of tea and china cups. She sat the tray down and poured the tea. "If'n you want sugar for your tea, you're done outa luck. We ain't got any," Fanny said matter-of-factly.

"Thank you, Fanny. I'm sure we'll be just fine. Sugar has been in short supply for so long I doubt I could get used to drinking it with tea again anyway."

"Is there anything else I can get for ya?"

"No, thank you, Fanny. I believe that will be all for now."

"Thank you, Miz Cassie, Miz Val. If you don't mind, I'll get back to cleanin' my kitchen." Fanny waddled out of the room.

Valissa smiled as she gingerly blew into the cup before carefully sipping her tea. "I swear Fanny and Etta are cut from the same mold. Both of them have absolutely no fear about talking their minds. Why is it we put up with them?"

Cassandra smiled. "I suppose we do it because, even though they are spirited, we know they love us as much as we love them. No one could do a better job of taking care of us. I'm not sure she would be Fanny if she didn't speak her mind."

"I suppose you're right." Valissa finished her cup. "I guess I'd better go and finish my packing." She paused. "In answer to your question, Cassie, I think I love Ross. I know I'm strongly attracted to him. Sometimes, I'm not sure if I really know what love is. All I know is I want to be with him and I miss him. If it's not love then it is as close as I've come." Valissa rose to her feet. "I'm glad we had this talk, Cassandra. I'll be back from the coast as soon as I can." Valissa sat her cup and saucer down and gave Cassandra a hug. "No need to see me to the door, I know my way out."

"Have a safe trip."

When Valissa Covington left, Cassandra felt uneasy. She wondered if she would ever see her friend again.

Retreat

Shelby's last stand at the stone wall saved the remnants of Price's defeated Confederate army. Their stubborn fight along the moss-and-ivy-covered wall allowed the army to reorganize and bought time for the supply train to work its way south. The Yankees, almost as battered by the rugged fight as the Rebels, pursued cautiously. The Southerners used the time wisely and retreated south down the state line road.

Once sure the Union advance was not going to be aggressive, General Price ordered Major General John Sappington Marmaduke to assume the rear guard with his cavalry division. Major General Sterling Price then ordered Brigadier General Joseph O. Shelby to move his battered division to the front of the column and command the advance. The Rebel army followed the state line road south for fifty-six miles toward Mound City and Fort Scott. Price fully expected to encounter Union troops, the bulk from Fort Scott, attempting to block his escape to the south. Anxious to save the plunder captured from the Yankees during the expedition, he wanted his most dependable fighters in the lead.

General Shelby took the point, but before he left, he pleaded with Price to destroy most of the baggage train, which was slowing down the army. But Price would not hear of abandoning any of the more than five hundred wagons filled with goods. The sheer mass of the train—the herd of five thousand cattle, extra horses, ambulances carrying the wounded, the large group of Union prisoners, and hundreds of refugees and unarmed new recruits— hopelessly tangled the muddy roads.

Seeing his arguments fall on deaf ears, Shelby marched to the front. They camped for the night near a place in Kansas called Trading Post, just across the border from Missouri. Cattle from the supply train were slaughtered to feed the men, and soldiers set to work grinding grain at two local mills. The weary, hard-marching soldiers, tired from countless battles, were nearly starved. They eagerly welcomed the chance to rest and eat again. As night fell the glow of many fires across the prairie sparkled like flights of dancing fireflies. The camps completely encircled the little village of Trading Post. The food in their bellies eased the disappointment in their defeat at Westport. Heartily, the men ate the fresh meat roasted on sticks over the open fires.

Ross Kimbrough used the pause in the action to look for his brothers. In all the confusion of battle and the mad flight away from Westport, the brigade had become scattered and jumbled. He knew Shelby's brigade was to take the lead in the morning, and he rounded up his scouts to prepare them. Once he issued his orders, he began his search.

He looked first for Collins's battery, moving slowly from campfire to campfire in the darkness. Finally, he found a fatigued Captain Collins sitting on a log near a meagre fire. One look around the camp and Ross's heart sank. Only one artillery piece and its caisson sat near the camp alongside a supply wagon.

Captain Collins looked up wearily as he saw a figure striding in out of the darkness. "Hello, Dick, you look exhausted."

A melancholy expression crossed Captain Richard Collins's face as he recognized the approaching soldier. "Captain Kimbrough," he said with a heavy voice. "I've been dreading this moment. Please"—he paused briefly—"be seated."

This unexpected response took Ross by surprise. He knew something was wrong, dreadfully wrong. He sat heavily on a log facing Captain Collins. "It's Calvin, isn't it? Has something happened to him?"

Captain Collins stared at his boots. He glanced up slowly and looked deep in Ross Kimbrough's eyes. "We lost Calvin at Westport. He was killed when the breech of his gun exploded from a premature ignition of a fused shell. He was a good soldier and did his duty to the last." Collins saw the hurt in Captain Kimbrough's face, and it pained him to witness it. He averted his eyes and stared into the dying coals of the campfire. "I wish there was something I could do to change things, Ross, but there's nothing. We lost too many good men in that fight."

The words struck Ross like a Bowie knife through his heart. A cold shudder hit him. He tried to fight against the tears forming in the corner of his eyes, but they spilled down his cheeks despite his efforts. He clenched his jaw, fighting for control of his voice. He wanted desperately to remain calm. "Where's Calvin's body? I want to see him buried properly."

Captain Collins kept his eyes on the fire. "We don't have his body, Ross. We had to leave him on the battlefield."

Rage burned inside Ross as he realized he wouldn't even have the chance to bury his brother. In one smooth movement he was on his feet. He jerked Captain Collins roughly to his feet, twisting his uniform lapels and pulling him to within inches of his angry face. "Why in God's name, Captain, did you leave my brother behind in the hands of the enemy?"

Captain Collins responded quickly as he yanked himself free of Ross's grip and stood toe to toe with Ross. "Damn it, Ross, do you think I had any choice? The whole line collapsed and we had to run for our lives. I lost two artillery pieces to enemy fire, your brother's cannon exploded in our faces, and I lost half my men. All I have left of my battery is right here in front of you. I left over half my men dead or dying on that battlefield, most of my supplies, and even our mascot. I had to leave behind many of my wounded. I couldn't waste time retrieving dead men when there were so many living that needed my help." Collins stood trembling from a mixture of remorse and anger. Defiantly, he held his ground.

As they stared each other down, Ross studied Collins and noticed Dick was visibly shaken. Captain Collins's eyes began to cloud with tears glistening in the firelight. He settled back wearily on his log, as if suddenly overcome with fatigue. His hands fell limply to his sides. "I did what I could."

Ross knew in that moment how wrong he'd been to accuse his friend of neglect. Ross had fought and lived through that battle and knew Captain Collins had done his duty. Whatever may have occurred was not Dick's fault. Ross Kimbrough's anger began to drain out of him, replaced by an aching sense of loss and despair. "Are you sure he was dead, Richard? Maybe he was wounded and they took him prisoner?"

Captain Collins shook his head. "I checked him personally, Ross. His chest was full of shrapnel and he was dead before he hit the ground. Danny Dunbar was his rammer at the time of the explosion, and he was killed, too. Most of his crew went down, except Delmar Pickett. Your brother's body shielded him from the blast. You might say he saved Delmar's life."

The last bit of hope drained away from Ross as he heard

this news. He bowed his head. "Thanks, Captain, I'm sorry for my behavior."

"I'd have reacted the same way if I were in your shoes. Don't worry about it." Before Captain Collins finished his sentence, Ross had faded into the night.

Ross set out to locate Jessie. He wanted to break the news of Calvin's death himself before Jessie heard of it from a stranger. Moving from fire to fire, he searched for his brother for several hours. With Captain Gilbert Thomas gone it would be harder to locate Jessie's company. No one seemed to know where they were until he stumbled into Billy Cahill's camp. Billy recognized Ross immediately. "Hey, Ross, are you lookin' for your brother Jessie?"

"Yes, do you know where I can find him? I found out Calvin died at Westport and I must tell Jessie."

Billy saw the weariness and grief etched on Ross's features. He realized suddenly that Ross didn't know about Jessie. "You won't find Jessie in any of the camps, Ross. When we all hightailed it out of there at Westport I saw your brother near to being ridden down by a Yankee trooper. He was out of ammunition and helpless. Luckily the Yankee was so busy concentrating on trying to kill Jessie, he didn't see me. I blew the bluebelly away, and Jessie and I dashed for the stone wall.

"I was with him when we made the stand at the wall with General Shelby. By the time the fight was over, your brother went down. Jessie was shot through the side and I think he passed out from loss of blood. I threw him over a saddle, tied him down, and took him to the supply train. I found an ambulance wagon and stopped it. The driver had a dead soldier on board and we dumped the dead man and put Jessie in his place. After that I returned to my company."

Ross's expression bordered on panic. "Was he alive when you last saw him?"

"Yeah, he was unconscious, but his breathing was more

even. I used a hanky to staunch his bleeding. It had nearly stopped by the time we put him on the stretcher."

"Thanks, Billy. Thanks for saving Jessie and getting him to a wagon. I won't forget it."

"No need to thank me, Ross, I was just doing my duty. Besides, Jessie and I have become good buddies. I wasn't about to leave him there." Billy turned and started walking back to the fire as he talked. "Liz would never forgive me if I didn't help her brother." He expected Ross to follow him, but instead Ross slipped away in the darkness. Billy wanted to question him about Calvin's death, but Ross was already gone. Billy stared into the darkness and shook his head in amazement. "Now, where in the hell did he go?"

Before dawn General Shelby called Major Evan Stryker to his side. "Major Stryker, as you know, we've been ordered to take the lead with my division. General Marmaduke is in charge of the rear of the army. I want to maintain communication with General Marmaduke so we can coordinate our movements. If we separate too far it might prove disastrous.

"I want you to take Lieutenant Jacobee and join Marmaduke's staff. Keep me informed of what is going on back there. General Marmaduke is a good commander, but I expect the Yankees to push us hard. They're fresh from a victory at Westport and should be anxious to exploit their advantage. Do you understand?"

"Yes, sir," Major Stryker replied. "I'll keep in touch, General. If there is anything you should know, I'll send Jacobee with the news."

General Shelby nodded in satisfaction and saluted briskly. "Godspeed, Major, and give General Marmaduke my regards." Evan wheeled his charger and sought out the boyish Lieutenant Jacobee. In minutes the two officers were spurring north toward the rear of the army.

The supply train stretched out for eight miles, more than five hundred wagons rolling and slipping from one muddy hole to the next. The tramping of soldiers' feet, the passing of the cavalry, and the large cattle herd quickly turned the road into a quagmire. The road was congested and movement often came to a complete halt as the wagons became stuck in the muddy morass. It took them longer than they thought to cover the distance to the rear of the army.

The two officers finally reached the south bank of the Mine Creek Ford. Evan wasn't prepared for the sight that greeted him. Water from the creek had been splashed up the south bank by the wagons and horses as the supply train made its crossing. The bank was badly rutted, slick, and muddy. More than one hundred wagons of Price's train still needed to cross, but the civilians who had made a late start from the camps around Trading Post were converging on the ford.

The crossing was narrow, and a civilian wagon was overturned in the middle of the ford. Old men and young boys worked frantically to right the wagon, while others crowded in panic into the water. Unwilling to wait for the obstacle to be cleared from the ford, they edged forward, further blocking their only route of escape. The water ran deep, swelled by the rains from the night before, making the narrow defile even more hazardous. Each wagon had to be pushed up the muddy bank and over the slippery ground. Evan recognized Colonel Tyler at the ford, trying with little success to untangle the mess and restore some kind of order.

Whips cracked as horses and mules grunted and strained against their tangled harnesses. Shouts and curses of frustration filled the air. Ross heard a beautiful young woman's cries as she pleaded to those around her to help her save her animals and carriage. Chaos reigned as panic swept through the crowd like an electric jolt. The fear was so palpable Ross could nearly taste it in the air. Beyond the ford, Ross saw General Marmaduke's soldiers drawn up in line of battle. Trapped on the north side of the creek was Marmaduke's division, all the artillery except Collins's battery, and Cabell's brigade.

Even more ominous, Ross saw long ranks of Union cavalry forming on the plain a short distance beyond Marmaduke's defensive line. Feeling a sense of urgency, the two officers moved above the ford and swam their horses across Mine Creek. Once on the far bank they rejoined the Fort Scott Road.

Ross expected to find the Confederate cavalry dismounted. Unlike Shelby's brigade, most of these troopers were armed with single-shot Enfield rifled muskets. To be effective the soldiers must be dismounted and fight on foot in order to reload. In effect, they were mounted infantry. He had seen the Yankees make this mistake repeatedly and the sight made him feel uneasy. To top it off, he noticed that Freeman's brigade was stationed in the center of the line along the Fort Scott Road. Freeman's was a new brigade recruited from conscripts and deserters rounded up in Arkansas just before the Missouri Expedition. They had been used sparingly then, and having them anchor the center of the line was discomfiting. Four artillery pieces—three from Harris's battery and one from Hughey's battery—were set squarely on Fort Scott Road; to their right was General John B. Clark Jr.'s Missouri Brigade. Two ten-pounder Parrott rifles of Hynson's Texas Battery were placed on the extreme right of Clark's brigade.

Sixty yards directly behind Freeman's brigade and extending far to the left stood General William Cabell's brigade. Two cannons belonging to Blocher's Arkansas battery were placed to the left of Cabell's position on a small hillock. Three brigades belonging to Fagan's division extended the line to the west. Slemmon's and Dobbins's brigades were placed in line with Anderson's battalion in reserve. The Third Missouri Cavalry under the command of Colonel Colton Greene was held in reserve eighty yards behind Harris's battery, beyond the flank of Cabell's brigade.

As Evan studied the troops in line of battle he estimated the Confederate strength at six thousand men and eight artillery pieces. He knew the names of each unit by their banners and regimental colors. He knew General Marma-

duke and General Cabell were both West Point graduates
and commanded two of the strongest brigades in Price's
army, yet he was frightened by what he saw. General Marmaduke clearly had his back to the wall. If he needed to
retreat his path was blocked by the swiftly flowing Mine
Creek. The soldiers remained mounted, and Freeman's brigade stood squarely in the middle of the line. Obviously
the line had been thrown together hastily. If this position
remained temporary and the Yankees didn't attack in force,
they might survive this day. If the Yankees made a determined effort, the day could turn catastrophic.

With these thoughts fresh in his mind, Major Evan
Stryker joined General John Marmaduke and his staff.
"Good morning, General Marmaduke, General Shelby
sends his warmest regards. He has asked me to accompany
your staff and keep him informed of your operations. He
hopes you will understand the need for cooperation to coordinate the advance of the army."

General Marmaduke returned Evan's salute and listened
carefully. The general had a long, thin face with a long but
scraggly and thin beard. His nose was prominent and his
eyes shone with intelligence. Always a slim officer, he carried himself well with the military bearing only West Point
training can give. He looked every bit the soldier.

"General Shelby's staff officers are always welcome at
my headquarters, Major. When you see General Shelby,
please give him my regards." General Marmaduke hastily
finished scribbling a written order and handed it to one of
his orderlies. "Take this dispatch to General Fagan. Make
sure he understands that I want him to set up the remainder of his division on the south side of Mine Creek on the
hillock near the Palmer House." The junior officer saluted
briskly and rode off to the west.

Major Stryker watched quietly as the general dispatched
his orders. When Marmaduke was done, Evan said, "General, don't you think we should dismount the men?"

"Nonsense, Major, I have them prepared to charge, and
to dismount them would only be a waste of time. All we

must do is keep the enemy off balance long enough to get the rest of the supply train and civilians across the river. We'll withdraw soon and take better positions on the south bank of the river. From there we can delay the Union advance long enough to let generals Shelby and Price capture Fort Scott." The weariness in Marmaduke's eyes was evident and Major Stryker thought better of second-guessing a major general. He did the wise thing and nodded his head in agreement while remaining silent.

Evan let his eyes sweep cautiously over the horizon to the north at the ever-growing amount of Union blue as Federal cavalry rode into view. These were not the ill-equipped and timid cavalry they had fought against in Arkansas. These were not Steele's weak-willed and often defeated troopers.

These men forming on the prairie just a short distance away were Philip's Brigade of the Missouri State Militia Cavalry. They had been recruited from Union sympathizers and trained and equipped especially to fight against Missouri guerrillas. Many of Philip's Yankees were armed with Henry repeating rifles, lever-operated weapons shooting the newly invented brass cartridges. They chambered twelve rounds in the magazine and thus could be fired twelve times before reloading. They could be fired as fast as a man could pump the lever. These Henry rifles were accurate and offered deadly firepower unlike anything the Rebels had ever faced before. Each Union trooper in his brigade also carried a revolver and a cavalry saber, making them extremely well-armed and deadly.

The Union brigade of Lieutenant Colonel Frederick Benteen came up on Philip's left. This was also a veteran brigade of troops from Missouri and Iowa who had served for some time east of the Mississippi River. These men were armed with carbines, revolvers, and sabers.

The Fourth Iowa was armed with the seven-shot Spencer repeating carbines and six-shot Navy Colt revolvers. Other units in the brigade were armed with Sharp's breech-loading carbines, Gallagher's carbines, and Hall's carbines. These veteran Union brigades were armed to the teeth with the most advanced weapons available. Finally, the Union cavalry had learned from their many defeats at the hands of the guerrillas and Confederate cavalry. It had taken time, but they learned of the need for superior fire-power at close range the hard way. These Yankees were specially equipped and anxious to test their weaponry against the Confederate cavalry.

As General Marmaduke and his staff watched calmly from their position near Mine Creek, they were unaware of the danger they faced. If the Yankees found some back-bone and attacked while Marmaduke's position remained precarious, Price's army could be dealt a deadly blow.

33

Action at Mine Creek

Major Evan Stryker stayed with General Marmaduke and his staff. He watched as the two Union brigades across the prairie aligned themselves in columns as if to prepare for a charge. Nearly a thousand yards of open prairie sloped toward Mine Creek separated the two armies.

Quickly Ross tallied his estimates of the Union troop strengths. He counted their regimental flags and estimated they faced approximately twenty-five hundred Union troopers divided between two brigades. As he glanced down the Rebel lines he felt more confident. If the Yankees did attempt an attack, the Rebels should easily outnumber them by better than two to one.

Evan saw the sunlight glint and shine on the drawn sabers of the Union brigade on the right. Off in the distance he heard the Union soldiers yell as bugles blared across the field, issuing the order to charge. In magnificent order the Union cavalry started forward at a walk, switched to a trot, and finally to a gallop. The sound of more than fifty buglers blowing charge echoed across the land.

The sight of those resplendent troopers mixed with the sound of the buglers and the pounding of a thousand hooves rolling across the grassland made the hair rise on Evan's arms. He felt a tingle at the back of his neck as he shifted nervously in the saddle. The Yankee soldiers were silent as they charged across the field. Evan flinched as the Rebel artillery boomed defiantly.

The Rebel gunners fired canister shot, turning their cannons into giant shotguns with the same telling effect. The case shot whistled and ripped through the air, mowing gaps in the Union line. Horses and riders went down sprawling and cartwheeling in the grass. Many saddles were emptied from the first artillery salvo. The men of McCray's brigade opened up on the Yankees with their long-range musket fire from the high banks of the south side of Mine Creek.

Benteen's Union brigade thundered on, aimed directly at Marmaduke's Rebel veterans. Evan felt his stomach tighten. He had faced battle often during the war, but this was the first time he had to face an enemy cavalry charge of this magnitude. He wondered if the Rebel line would stand. The soldiers of Price's army were demoralized after their defeat at Westport and had suffered heavy losses at Pilot's Knob and the battle of Big Blue. He knew he would be more confident if Shelby's brigade were here. Would these men be up to the challenge?

Philip's Union brigade on the left joined the charge, bearing right to keep from running over Benteen's men. This slight shift in direction sent them directly at Freeman's brigade in the center of the Rebel line. Twenty-five hundred splendidly equipped and uniformed Union cavalrymen provided a magnificent and frightening spectacle to the ragged Rebels waiting to receive the attack. The Rebels didn't realize at the time that they were facing one of the largest single cavalry charges of the war.

Evan watched the onrushing charge sweeping at the

Confederate lines. It seemed as if every saber, every pistol was thrust forward and aimed at the Rebels. The distance closed to within three hundred yards as the Yankee buglers sounded charge above the rolling thunder of the attack. The Union troopers began picking up speed for the final effort. The Rebels shifted nervously in line as they readied themselves for the assault. Another hundred yards passed and the Yankee troopers began to realize the Confederate line was standing firm. Benteen's lead regiment, the Tenth Missouri, saw that the Rebel line was not wavering and froze with fear. The Union Tenth Missouri stopped dead in their tracks. The troopers of the regiments directly behind them piled into the Tenth, totally disorganizing the attack of Benteen's column.

Evan felt relief as he watched the attacking column on the right shudder to a halt. He watched with amusement as Lieutenant Colonel Benteen rode out within pistol shot of the Rebel lines and tried to rally his men. Above the roar of battle he heard the bugles blare and the steady stream of cuss words as the officer berated his men for their cowardice, while artillery fire poured into the Union position. At Benteen's urgings, the Union line advanced just enough to let the other Union regiments in the rear reorganize and untangle themselves.

Philip's brigade came to a halt when they saw their brethren stop about three hundred yards from the Rebel line. Philip's lead regiment dismounted and began to fire on the Confederate line with their breech-loading and muzzle-loading carbines. Philip's men issued a withering fire on Harris's battery and Freeman's brigade. Benteen's men held their ground but did not fire at the Rebels.

Major Stryker knew then the Rebels had a great opportunity within their grasp. If the Rebel line would only charge down on the stalled Union columns only a few hundred yards away, they could annihilate them. The other Rebel commanders realized it too and prepared their men for a charge. A feeble and half-hearted Rebel yell rippled weakly down the Confederate line while artillery continued to rake the Union position. The commanders urged their men forward, but the line stayed in place. General Marmaduke cussed vilely as his demoralized Rebel soldiers refused to respond. Evan, as an observer, could do nothing but watch.

Suddenly a Union regiment swept out from behind the Union Tenth Missouri and rode to the left of the stalled Yankee regiment. Once clear, the major leading the charge ordered a column right, trot, then gallop. Even from where Evan sat astride his horse, he could hear the brave officer in blue yell to his men, "Follow me!" His bugler sounded charge as the Union major waved his large dragoon saber over his head, a regimental banner of the Fourth Iowa fluttering behind him.

The charge continued and thundered through the Rebel line near Hynson's Texas Battery. Colonel Burbridge's Confederate Fourth Missouri Cavalry of Clark's brigade took the brunt of the attack and were driven back in panic. Carried by the momentum of their charge, the Union Fourth Iowa Cavalry rode through the hole, circled to the right, and hit the remainder of Clark's brigade from the rear. The rest of Benteen's brigade, encouraged by what they saw, charged the Rebel line and hit Clark's brigade from the front.

Philip's Union brigade in the center witnessed the charge made by the Fourth Iowa and, invigorated, charged Freeman's Rebel brigade in the center of the line. Freeman's brigade—filled with new recruits, conscripts, and deserters—bolted before Philip's Yankees even reached them. Many threw away their weapons in panic as they turned tail and ran. As the mob of cowards fled the field they swept through the right of Cabell's brigade, disrupting their lines and spreading panic. Some of Cabell's men joined the rout and poured toward the rear. As they did, they struck Colton Greene's Third Missouri Cavalry being held in reserve, scattering and trampling them. Seeing the disaster left by the gaping hole left in the line,

Colton Greene moved a regiment diagonally to protect the remainder of Cabell's flank.

Philip's brigade swept through the void left by the running Rebels of Freeman's brigade. They charged over the unprotected guns of Harris's battery. In a matter of minutes, the Rebel battery was silenced as the men were sabered and shot down by pistol fire. Captain Harris fought to save his battery, so rudely abandoned by Freeman's flight, ordering two of his artillery pieces removed to the rear. His gunners bravely rolled them away by hand until they reached the bank at the Mine Creek Ford.

Philip's Union brigade captured the crowded ford and blocked the main escape route. Seventy-one teamsters still waiting to cross were captured with their wagons. The ford was utter chaos as panicked Rebel cavalrymen stampeded for the safety of the south side of the creek. Union troopers followed closely on their heels, raking them with pistol fire. The remainder of Harris's battery surrendered near the ford.

General Marmaduke witnessed the collapse of his line and turned to face Evan. "Major, I fear we are in serious danger. Ride immediately and tell General Price and General Shelby of our situation. Have General Fagan set up a line on the south bank. I want him to fight a holding action so we can withdraw. Hurry, we haven't got much time."

Understanding the urgency of the situation, Major Stryker and Lieutenant Jacobee rode for the creek directly behind their position. Philip's brigade, having reached the river, swept to the right against Cabell's brigade. As they did so, some of his troopers rode along the creek in the opposite direction to seal off escaping troopers from Marmaduke's and Clark's commands.

As Stryker and Jacobee crested a rise, two Union troopers loomed in their path. Leaning low in the saddle, Evan fired his revolver and a Union soldier tumbled from his horse. The other, still blocking their way, fired his revolver and the shot struck Jacobee in the head, and the young

Rebel cartwheeled from his horse. Evan saw him go down out of the corner of his eye, but his attention was on the trooper blocking his way. He fired at the same instant the Union soldier opened up on him.

Stryker heard a soft smack as the bullet struck horseflesh. He felt his mount shudder and stumble as they neared the enemy horse and rider. His bullet struck home and the Union soldier slumped forward on the neck of his charger. The Yankee let his revolver slip from his fingers as the two horses collided. The blow unseated the wounded Yankee, hurling him beneath Evan's own dying horse. Evan dove for the saddle of the enemy horse and managed to drag himself partway aboard as the horse reeled away from the collision. Desperately, Evan hung on as the horse stumbled along, and he managed to swing his leg over the saddle. He leaned far forward on the horse's neck and retrieved the reins.

Evan wheeled the captured black mare and glanced over his shoulder. His horse was down and the Yankee soldier, who had been riding the mount only moments before, was pinned beneath Evan's dying horse. One look at Jacobee and Evan knew he was dead. He wanted to return for his carbine and blanket roll, but one look to his left discouraged the idea.

Union troopers were charging toward him, firing their pistols. He felt a pistol ball rip through his coattails. Without further hesitation he spurred forward toward the rapid-running waters of Mine Creek. The horse beneath him was strong and powerful and her strides were long. Encouraged by the whine of pistol balls slicing through the air around him, Evan urged the black horse into a full gallop.

He saw the creek bank approaching and gritted his teeth while hanging on to the saddle for dear life. He pressed his legs tightly against the mare. She jumped off the lip of the dirt bank, launching herself and her rider into the air. It seemed to Evan as though they hung in the air for a long time before plunging into the cold waters of the creek. Their momentum carried them better than halfway across the creek when they splashed heavily into the water. The impact and the shock of the cold water nearly stole his breath away.

The violent impact of their striking the water sent sparkling water drops flying through the air in a glittering spray. He felt the horse swimming as the current pushed them downstream. Pistol balls smacked the water around him, sending little geysers skyward. He felt his horse's hooves grip the creek bottom as she found purchase. Evan felt the water shed away as they scrambled up the south creek bank.

Bullets whacked and thudded into the dirt as Evan spurred onward. They crested the ridge safely and he wheeled toward the Fort Scott Road and General Fagan's position. It only took moments for him to reach the general. Already Fagan was forming his line along the hillock, carefully leaving gaps as escapes for the routed soldiers.

"General Fagan, my compliments. General Marmaduke requests you to form your men and make a stand to cover the withdrawal of Marmaduke's command."

"I'm doing the best I can, Major, but the boys are spooked by the way our men are turnin' tail and runnin'. Half my division is north of the creek with Marmaduke. I'll do my best."

Evan gave the harried officer a salute and he said, "I must inform generals Price and Shelby of the situation here, General."

"Yes, it is imperative they are aware of this disaster. Godspeed, Major." Before he left the high ground and its splendid view of the battlefield, Evan took one last look. The Confederate line had melted away like snow on a hot summer day. Here and there a small group made a stand as Yankees attacked. Other Rebels rode up and down the creek, desperately seeking a point to cross. Still others made the attempt, their horses coming up short and falling into the river. Some were shot down in the attempt. Soldiers, wide-eyed and panicked, fled the field, many without their weapons. Large groups of soldiers surrendered and were being grouped and sent to the Union rear. In less than fifteen minutes the Rebel command had been turned from a formidable force into a routed army.

Evan looked back to where he had last seen General Marmaduke and saw him being led away as a Union prisoner. Angrily, he slammed his fist into his leg as he realized the importance of this fiasco. He wheeled his horse and galloped south.

As he rode, Evan noticed that in their panic the soldiers were discarding anything that might weigh them down. Guns, blankets, canteens, and everything else a soldier might need littered the road. Wagons were overturned and abandoned. Here and there, a trooper who had been wounded and could travel no farther lay beside the road awaiting capture. Troopers flailing away at their mounts unmercifully pushed them far too hard as they sped past him. If they kept up this rapid pace as they tried to distance themselves from the enemy, he knew they would kill their horses. His yells and cries went unheeded as they ignored his orders.

Evan rode on. His captured horse was strong and kept a steady pace. He finally found General Price eight miles south of Mine Creek camped on the south side of the Little Osage River where they had halted to eat.

Evan was taken immediately to General Price to make his report. Because of his ill health and immense size, Price was using a carriage for his transportation most of the time. Evan bravely faced the gray-haired, rotund general. "General Price, General Fagan sends his regards. General Marmaduke and possibly General Cabell have been captured by the enemy. They hit us on the north side of Mine Creek. Our supply train was jammed up at the ford. We lost at least seventy supply wagons and all eight pieces of artillery. We've taken heavy casualties, and our army has suffered a rout. General Fagan requests immediate assistance. He will try to hold off the enemy pursuit as long as possible."

General Price's face went ashen. His eyes looked

stunned as his jaw hung open in shock. There was a long pause. Only moments before he had worked on his plans to capture Fort Scott. Taking the unfortified post and its vast stores of military supplies and weapons would have eased the pain of his defeat at Westport. In mere seconds his hopes and dreams of recovering some hope from his expedition had been shattered.

General Price realized what he must do. "Major Stryker, find General Shelby. Tell him the planned attack on Fort Scott has been canceled. My new orders are for him to gather all the men he can and march to the rear. Tell him only he can save our army."

"Yes, sir, I'll give him your orders personally." Evan knew his horse was jaded and he didn't want to kill her. She had made the ride with courage and he admired the horse's stamina. When he rode into the encampment he noticed Shelby's regimental flag and knew he was but a short distance away. It took him only fifteen minutes to reach Shelby and relay his new orders. Meanwhile, General Sterling Price left his rig, mounted his white charger, and rode north toward his army while the wagon train continued to work south along the road.

While changing out the black mare for another, Ross went through the saddle and equipment he had captured. To his immense surprise he slid a strange new weapon out of the scabbard. The rifle had a brass blocked receiver and what appeared to be two barrels, one above the other. A lever was attached below the trigger. Evan slipped his hand through the lever. It fit his hand well as he operated it. He ducked involuntarily as an unfired brass cartridge flew out at him. With the breech open he slid the lever closed slowly and watched in amazement as a new bullet and cartridge was inserted in the chamber. The action of cocking the weapon had the hammer pulled back and ready to fire.

Curious, he lifted the newfangled rifle to his shoulder and aimed at a distant tree. He squeezed the trigger and felt a mild buck against his shoulder. He hit the target squarely. He pushed the lever once more and ejected the spent cartridge. He looked at it closely and noticed the rim was dented by the hammer and it caused the cartridge to fire. He was amazed at the efficiency of the weapon and the speed at which he could reload. He examined the weapon more closely. Stamped on the gun he found NEW HAVEN, CONNECTICUT. In another place he read HENRY REPEATING RIFLE. He turned the rifle over and realized the bottom barrel was actually a spring-fed magazine. Excitedly he searched through the saddle wallets and found one pouch full of the new style brass cartridges. He took a few out, loaded the weapon, and found the gun held twelve rounds. He estimated them to be forty-four caliber.

Running through them swiftly without firing, Evan found he could clear the entire magazine in less than thirty seconds. He was quick to realize the impressive nature and devastating firepower represented in this Henry rifle. He smiled smugly, happy as a boy on Christmas morning as he slid the new weapon back into the scabbard. He would protect this with his life.

He switched the saddle, scabbard, and saddle wallets to a fresh horse while leaving his captured mount with the wagon train. He promised to reclaim her come nightfall.

General Shelby gathered his men and began a countermarch to the north. Soon the first elements of Marmaduke's and Cabell's brigades came streaming toward the rear. General Price and other officers tried hopelessly to rally the fleeing troops. Fortunately, Fagan's stand on the south bank of Mine Creek bought them a little time.

Shelby made his first stand along the Little Osage River. Driven from there by a determined force, he fell back to the Marmaton River crossing, six miles east of Fort Scott. There the supply train was again struggling to make a river crossing. Shelby moved his men north of the river and positioned them to make a stand. By now the panic in the fleeing troopers had eased. Remnants of Colton Greene's regiment, Clark's brigade, and Freeman's men formed up behind Shelby's division. Dobbins's brigade

had escaped pretty much intact and swung into line.
Fagan's troopers also joined the battle line. Altogether
nearly eight thousand Confederate troopers formed on
Charlot Prairie, though only about three thousand were
still armed.

The Yankees were disorganized by the pursuit. Many
were dispatched to see to the prisoners and take care of the
captured weapons at Mine Creek earlier in the morning.
Not realizing that most of the men they faced were unarmed, they hesitated to attack such a large force with their
dwindling numbers. Serious skirmishing continued until
nightfall, with small charges made across the field. The
Rebels withdrew in the night and crossed the Marmaton
River.

As night fell, General Price finally realized the expedition had turned into a horrible fiasco because of the cum-
bersome and awkward supply train. Realizing he could
lose his entire army if he couldn't march at a faster rate,
he decided to rid himself of the train. If he had only done
this at Trading Post he might have kept his army intact. Instead nearly six hundred men had been captured, three
hundred killed, and two hundred more wounded. His artillery had been decimated, losing eight cannons in the battle
of Mine Creek. Now at last he ordered the supply train
burned.

The order irked many Rebels who had fought so hard
and watched men die to defend it. It was the last tangible
sign of their success on the expedition. Still, most realized
only more lives would be lost if they continued to defend
the train. Orders were given, and the train was set on fire
by General Jackman's brigade.

Many horses and mules too jaded to continue were scattered and left behind the retreating army. The wagons
burned bright as the flames seared the canvas covers, lu-
ridly lighting the night. Captured goods, uniforms, food,
weapons, and ammunition not hauled away by the troopers
went up in smoke. The ammunition in the wagons began
to cook off and explode, sending burning bits of wagons

hurling high into the air in a deadly spectacle. Fused shells soared into the night skies and exploded like Fourth of July fireworks, adding to the fearsome sight visible even from the Union lines.

Evan Stryker watched dejectedly as the wagon train was given to the flames. As he watched this fiery inferno consume the hopes of an army, he felt a little bit of himself die in the whirling smoke that eddied and swirled among the dancing fires. He realized as he stared into those burning wagons that Confederate hopes for victory were just as elusive as the smoke that curled from the conflagration.

34

Butcher Wagons

Jessie's eyes popped open as a sharp pain shot through his side. He strained his eyes, but all he saw above him looked like dirty, blurred canvas. He tried to sit up, but the pain made him think better of it. His teeth clattered together as the wagon slammed into another rut in the road. He heard the driver yell, "Ho, mules, git up thar, mules!"

Jessie turned his head and studied his surroundings. At first he hadn't been certain, but now he knew he was in a wagon. What he didn't know was how he got here and where he was going. He hoped by studying the wagon's contents he might get some answers.

He looked over at two cots stacked in racks to his left, one above the other. In the top one he saw a young soldier. The boy had a bloody bandage on his head. Tufts of dirty blond hair stuck out from beneath it. Jessie noticed the boy wore a sling around his arm, and his face was covered in beads of sweat, even though Jessie felt the cold. Jessie pulled the blanket tighter around his neck.

The young soldier on the bottom cot was a bearded
man. His eyes were open, staring vacantly at Jessie. Jessie
kept waiting for the man to blink those wide, black eyes.
He wondered if he saw him would he speak. He noticed
the man's mouth was hanging open, but not a word was
spoken. Crimson blood seeped through the man's blanket
and fell drop by drop, pooling slowly on the floor beneath
his cot. As Jessie stared in fascination, the man's head
lolled back and forth with the movement of the wagon. Directly beneath Jessie's own cot, he heard low groans.

The boy on the top cot beside him finally spoke. "Good
to see ya awake. You ain't opened your eyes enough to
know what's been goin' on since they loaded ya in here
six days ago. I figured ya was a goner for sure."

"Where the hell am I?" asked Jessie.

"I figured the way you was staring at everything you
knew. This here is a hospital wagon."

Jessie studied him with a worried expression. "Whose?"

"Can't ya tell?" asked the blond boy. Finally, with a dis-
gusted look he replied, "General Price's raggedy-assed
ambulance corps. If the damn Yankee bullets don't kill ya,
ridin' in one of these butcher wagons will for sure."

"How did I get in here?"

"Right after that mean fight at Westport, a rider brought
you in draped over a horse. He asked us if we had room.
We happened to have an opening on account of a death in
the wagon. We'd stopped because Hank wanted to leave
the dead feller by the side of the road. Hank is our driver,
and he hates to ride with the dead. Kinda makes him
spooky. You never really woke up. Once in a while you'd
moan and groan. Hank spooned a little broth into you and
a few sips of water now and again. Young feller brought
you in said ya lost a lot of blood. I thought you'd die for
sure."

"Did you catch the name of the man that brought me
here? Did he say what his name was?"

"If he did I didn't hear it. Hell, I've had plenty of my

own problems, so I didn't worry too much about you, no how."

The rough bouncing of the wagon sent a fresh surge of pain through Jessie. His side hurt something awful. He tried to look beneath his blanket, but a dark circle of dried blood showed through an old bandage that covered his wound.

The young blond soldier next to him said, "Hank took a look at your hole when we stopped for a spell. He put another bandage on ya. He said the bullet went clean through and didn't reckon it hit anything vital. Hank says if ya hadn't lost so much blood, you'd be fit as a fiddle."

Jessie's head still felt like it wanted to spin. He felt weak but alive. "I hurt too much to be dead," he thought. Jessie glanced at the blond soldier. "What's your name?"

"William Gaskill, but you can call me Bill."

"Mine's Jessie Kimbrough, of Company E, Fifth Missouri Cavalry of the Iron Brigade, attached to Jo Shelby's division. Glad to make your acquaintance. Which outfit you with?"

"I was a part of Colton Greene's Third Missouri Cavalry, Company D, 'fore I caught these lead souvenirs. Funny thing is we ain't too far from my home. I'm from Wright County, which is over yonder. We have us a little farm in Pleasant Valley near Mansfield, Missouri."

Bill noticed Jessie staring at the soldier on the cot beneath him. "Don't need to worry about that feller. He died round an hour ago, best as I can figure. If Hank finds out at the next stop we make, he'll set him beside the road. Boy died real slow. Took a plum mean gut shot. They say that's the worst way to die."

Jessie looked up from the dead man and studied Gaskill. His mind couldn't block out the memory of the face of the dead soldier, but he wanted to, desperately. "Isn't the Third Missouri Cavalry under General Marmaduke's command?"

"Yes sirree Bob, it sure enuff is. General John B. Clark is our brigade commander."

"What the hell happened? You boys were supposed to guard Byram's Ford. Next thing we know the Yankees are behind us, cutting us to pieces. We had to run like the very devil was after us. It was every man for himself. That's when I took this bullet in my side."

Bill looked surprised. "We were in a real mean fight there at the ford when the Yankees up an' hit us in the flank. Some of their boys must have crossed the river upstream somewhere. Anyway, they rolled up our flank fast and we had a wild run ourselves. I didn't turn tail an' run till I got these wounds. When you're outnumbered and flanked it's hard to make a stand."

Jessie sucked in a breath as another wave of pain hit him. He laid back. "I didn't mean it was your fault. We can't win 'em all, I guess."

"Be a sight better if we could win a few more, I reckon."

William noticed Jessie was in pain. "You better get some rest. We'll stop again after a while, an' we can talk more then."

It was later that night when Ross Kimbrough finally located Jessie. It had taken him quite some time to find his brother. The wounded Rebel soldiers had been removed from the wagon and placed near a campfire for the night. They had already eaten their scant rations by the time Ross found them.

Ross Kimbrough looked relieved. "Jess! By God, it's good to see you alive. I thought sure you would die on us."

"I wouldn't dare, big brother. Katlin would never forgive me if I died and left her to raise little Glen by herself." Jessie gave him a weak smile. "I still feel a mite under the weather, though. How's everyone else?"

Ross's smile faded as his expression turned grim. "A lot has happened since you were wounded, Jess. You sure you're up to it?"

Jessie felt a cold chill go through him. Bad news must

be waiting if Ross needed to question his health first. "What is it, Ross? Tell me!"

Ross studied the fire, unable to look directly at Jessie while telling him. His voice quivered slightly with emotion. "I talked to Captain Collins and he said Calvin was killed at Westport."

The words stung Jessie like a hard slap in the face. In disbelief he asked, "What do you mean, he's dead? Are you sure?"

Ross looked at Jessie and blinked away tears. "I didn't see him myself, but Dick Collins said the breech exploded on Calvin's cannon and killed him. Collins said he checked him out personally before they pulled out and there's no doubt he's dead. Calvin's chest was full of shrapnel from the breech and Dick couldn't find a sign of life."

"Did they bring him out?"

"They didn't have time to save half the wounded, much less the dead. Collins's battery only had one gun left after they pulled back."

"You left him there?"

Anger flashed in Ross's eyes as his face contorted in rage. "Damn it, Jess, I was kind of busy at the time! Hell, I didn't know he was dead any more than you did." Ross bent down and grabbed a twig, tossing it into the fire. "What was I supposed to do? We'd fought all day in a running retreat before I found out he was dead. I couldn't go get his body in the middle of the whole Union army."

Jessie said, "Sorry, Ross. I didn't mean anything by it. I guess there isn't anything anyone could have done." He paused for a moment as his mind raced. "Are you sure he's dead?"

"Don't you think I've wondered about it ever since I found out he was hit? I didn't see him with my own eyes, so it's hard to believe he's gone. I talked to everyone I could find in the battery. They're all sure he was dead. I have to believe they know what they're talking about."

"What do you suppose they did with his body?"

Harsh words snapped hard off Ross's tongue. "Hell, how am I suppose to know? Damn it, Jessie! I'm not in the Yankee army."

"Ross, stop cussing at me. I know you don't know exactly what they did with him. I just wanted you to guess."

The reply stiffened Ross. He let out a big sigh. "I'm sorry, little brother. I don't mean to take it out on you. It's just that I feel like I should've done *something*."

"When it's your time to go, I don't suppose there's anything anyone can do to prevent it."

"I imagine by now the Yank burial details have gathered the bodies and thrown them in a mass grave somewhere on the battlefield. They never bury our men proper. Only their soldiers get individual graves. Most likely he was buried in an unmarked grave with other Johnny Rebs. I don't like knowing he's out there somewhere lying under the sod in some unmarked grave, known only to God."

"He's in a far better place than we are."

"I hope you're right."

"So, what else has been happening since I passed out?"

"It's been nothin' but one fiasco after another. Two days after we left Westport, our rear guard got hit at Mine Creek. Our supply train blocked up the ford. The Yankees hit us hard and before we knew it the Yankees captured Marmaduke and Cabell, at least five hundred of their men, and eight pieces of artillery. All told we lost over a thousand men—killed, wounded, or captured. Marmaduke's and Cabell's men that weren't captured were in a complete panic. We couldn't get them to stand and fight. Many had thrown away their guns and were running like the devil himself was after them."

"Sounds like things have gone from bad to worse."

"It ain't the half of it. Price finally decided to do something about our supply train. He ordered Jackman's boys to burn any wagons in bad shape or with poor teams. When they were done they had torched over a third of the train that wasn't captured at Mine Creek. All night we saw the shells going up and heard the explosions in the burning wagons behind us. It was a good decision and it should've been done sooner. We moved much faster after leaving them behind. On October 28, the Yankee advance led by General Blunt caught us just south of Newtonia. We weren't far from the old battlefield. Our division went into line, and after a hard fight we drove them from the field. I don't think the Yanks will chase us any farther."

"I didn't know I'd missed so much."

"I lost Bill Corbin at Newtonia, too. He's been scouting with me since the brigade was formed. I miss him already." Ross glanced back at the fire. "He caught a bullet in the head just above his left eye. I've still got some of his blood on my pants." Ross threw a pebble into the darkness of the night and continued his story. "The poor devil never knew what hit him."

"Where are we now?"

"We were in Arkansas along the border yesterday. I'd guess we're in Indian Territory by now. We're still heading south for Texas." Ross rose from the ground. "I'm sorry about jumping all over you, Jess. I'm glad to see you alive. You better get some rest. We'll be moving out at first light. I'll look in on you again later." He turned to go.

"Ross, thanks for everything. I'm sorry about Calvin."

"Yeah, we all are, little brother. Good night."

Jessie tried hard to sleep after Ross left, but he couldn't. All night his thoughts were on memories of Calvin. Jessie's eyes, red-rimmed and aching, stared into the star-filled skies. He finally drifted off to sleep long after midnight.

35

A Long Way to Texas

Ross felt the shivers rack his body as he wiped cold rain from his face. His stomach convulsed as still another hunger pain tightened his belly. He hardly noticed the soldiers around him as he continued onward in a sea of misery. Movement was slowed as they slid in the cold, clinging mud. The men were now too tired to cuss and far too hungry to care.

Only one thing kept Ross from surrendering to the misery: his thoughts of Valissa Covington. Winter was closing on them, and once they reached Texas they would go into winter camp. He hoped he would be near Valissa.

The war had taken so much from him. First his home, then his mother and father. Now, his brother Calvin was dead, and Jessie was struggling to survive to reach his wife and child. Waves of anger, mixed with bouts of remorse over the war, alternately flowed through him. Hadn't they given their all? Why in God's name were the Yankees always coming out ahead? He didn't understand it, and the pain filled his soul to overflowing. Well, what did it matter? He was just one small flyspeck tossed around in the waves and currents of a seemingly senseless war. Only survival mattered now—survival so he could again be with Valissa. She was the only thing that seemed to make any sense to him and, except for his family, the only thing that mattered anymore.

On November 7 they had crossed the Arkansas River about thirty miles west of Fort Smith, Arkansas. Just before they crossed, General Price detached the brigades of Freeman, McCray, and Dobbins to their home areas in Arkansas to collect the absentees and deserters. Their orders were to rejoin the army in December. Shortly after crossing the river, General Price furloughed what was left of General Cabell's and General Slemmon's brigades.

General Price knew he might as well let them go. A large number of them had been captured at the battles of Westport and Mine Creek, and those still remaining had lost faith and hope. All along the route the ranks thinned as men, disheartened and tired of war, slipped away into the brush during the march. Others left at night in small groups or individually. All they wanted was to go home. Many believed the war was beyond hope. Who among them wanted to be the last to die for a lost cause?

Still, among the grumbling veterans there were those who remained steadfast. They were not ready to abandon all hope. They had suffered severely and witnessed the death of many a friend. How could they now turn their backs on those sacrifices? For these men, there could be no surrender, no deserting the cause.

Shelby's Iron Brigade was not immune to those who would turn their backs on the army, but they were losing far fewer men than the rest of the army. Shelby's men were discouraged, but they had not lost faith in Jo Shelby or in the Confederacy. As long as General Lee held on in Virginia and Shelby led their brigade, they would stay the course.

What was left of General Price's battered army continued first through the Cherokee, then the Choctaw Nations of Indian Territory. Winter cold and starvation maintained a tight grip on the beleaguered army. Grain and pasture were in short supply, and horses began to die by the hundreds. Worn out by constant campaigning and insufficient food, they collapsed on the road beneath their riders never to rise again. Wagons had to be abandoned for lack of animals to pull them. Only those carrying the wounded were kept.

Major Evan Stryker, tired of traveling with the staff officers, wanted to break the monotony of the march. Hoping for adventure, he requested permission to ride with Captain Ross Kimbrough and his scouts. Shelby granted permission, and Evan joined the scouts as they rode ahead of the column.

Evan rode the large mare he had named Shadow, because she was so black. Her right foreleg had a small white patch just above her hoof, giving her the appearance of wearing one white sock.

Sometimes they visited as they rode, and at other times they were silent, lost in their misery. As they neared the Canadian River, the land began to look more abundant. Their spirits began to rise.

As Ross and Evan turned one twist in the trail, an explosion of action blurred around them. A group of ragged riders rode from the brush to block their path. Ross was caught off guard, embarrassed by this slip. His fatigue and hunger had allowed him to lose his edge, and now the two men had ridden into a trap. A red hot blush climbed his cheeks. He studied the riders surrounding him as he lifted his hands in surrender.

A familiar sounding voice said, "Gettin' kind of careless aren't ya, Ross?"

Ross snapped his head around and stared into the eyes of one of his captors, an old acquaintance, Samual McKerrow. Sam was a mixed breed, the son of a white trader named John McKerrow and a Cherokee mother named Minnehaha. Ross had seen him for a few brief moments before the battle of Prairie Grove in 1862, but it was during the time that Douglas H. Cooper's Indian brigade had joined Earl Van Dorn's command around Pea Ridge, Arkansas, that the two had become friends.

During the encampment near Elkhorn Tavern, Sam had taken Ross aside and, using his Cherokee heritage, trained Ross in the subtleties of tracking and scouting. After the battle of Elkhorn Tavern, the Indian brigade had returned to the Indian Territory, while Van Dorn's army went to Mississippi. Except for the brief encounter at Prairie Grove in December 1862, Ross hadn't seen his friend since. He was glad to see Sam alive, but he wished it weren't under such embarrassing circumstances.

Chagrined, Ross smiled weakly. "It's been a long time, Sam. I'm glad to see you're still alive."

Sam McKerrow laughed heartily at his old friend's discomfort. "Yeah, I'm still kickin', but it makes me wonder how you've managed to last so long, ridin' in a daze like you are." Sam glanced over at Evan. "Who's your friend?"

Ross lowered his hands and twisted in his saddle. "I'd like to introduce Major Evan Stryker of General Shelby's staff. He's a Texan, so you'll have to forgive his nature. Evan, I'd like you to meet Sam McKerrow." Evan spurred forward, and the two men shook hands. Ross said, "Are you still with the First Cherokee Mounted Rifles, Sam?"

"Yes, I'm a lieutenant now. We're on a scout through Choctaw territory. We heard there was a column passing through here, and we decided to check it out." He studied Ross Kimbrough's uniform. "I can tell from the looks of your collar you've moved up in the world."

"Thanks to what I learned from you, I made chief of scouts for Jo Shelby's brigade." He studied his friend. Samual McKerrow had deep, dark eyes, spaced wide over high cheekbones. His nose seemed a little large for his face but helped to balance his square jaw, and his thin lips often turned into a smile. Dark hair hung from his slough hat and was pulled into a tight ponytail at the nape of his neck. He wore a ragged and holed Rebel jacket over captured and dirty Union sky-blue wool pants. Although his uniform looked worn, his leather goods and weapons shone with care. He rode a strongly built chestnut gelding.

Ross Kimbrough looked at the other troopers gathered around them. All were well armed and uniformed in a hodgepodge of mixed uniforms ranging from civilian dress, captured bits of Union uniforms, and well-worn Rebel uniforms. Most looked less taciturn than they had earlier. Two of them were smiling, apparently amused at catching this scout of Jo Shelby's famous Iron Brigade.

Sam's words brought him back from his observations. "You won't make major if you let the Yankees slip up on you like this."

"Sam, we've been on a raid of more than fourteen hundred miles in two months and fought over forty skirmishes and engagements during the raid. We've lived through a couple of tough losses, and we're tired and hungry. I know it's no excuse, but it's the best I've got."

Sam lowered his revolver as if just remembering he still had it drawn. He slipped it into his holster. "That column passing through here must be your boys, then."

"Yes, we have Shelby's division and some of Price's command. We left several of our regiments in Arkansas. Say, you boys wouldn't know where we can get some food, would you? Our men and horses are starving."

"Supplies are tight, but you might find something at Boggy Depot." His expression changed as if he just had an idea. "Game is plentiful along the Canadian River. There's plenty of deer, wild turkey, and a few longhorns in the area. I'd try camping there and sending out some of your men to hunt. Grass is good along there for your horses and mules, too."

Ross turned to Evan. "If you are ever up this way or in Cherokee country, check in with Sam McKerrow. He's honest, fair, and dependable and a hell of a man to back you in a fight."

Evan replied, "I'll keep it in mind."

Sam said, "Come on, Ross, you're makin' me blush. I'm liable to get a bigger head than I already got if you keep talkin' that way." His smile faded. "I haven't forgotten what you did for me either, Ross. He wouldn't tell anyone, because he's not that kind, but he saved my life. I bet he's never mentioned it, has he?" Sam was looking directly at Evan Stryker.

Evan looked earnestly at Ross, studying his friend. "No, I can't recall him ever mentioning it."

Sam McKerrow smiled, pleased he was reading his friend right. "He did. I got into a poker game one night with a drunken Missourian built like an ox. I won fair and square, but when I had my back turned, the son-of-a-bitch pulled an Arkansas toothpick on me. He'd have run that blade clean through my back if Ross hadn't leveled him with a blow to the head with his revolver. Knocked him out cold and it saved my life. That's how we became friends. I taught him some tips on scouting in return. I still owe you."

"You can pay me back by not mentioning how you caught me dozing. It's plain embarrassing."

Sam gave a hearty laugh as his thin lips lifted into a smile. He seemed like a man who enjoyed a good laugh. "I'll try to keep it quiet, but it's hard to give up talkin' about something like this." His expression sobered. "I still feel I'm in your debt, Ross, and someday I'll make it right."

"Your friendship has always been payment enough."

"Well, I need to return and report to Major Parks and General Watie, and you need to get your column south. I wish there was some food I could give you, but this area has been hit hard by the war. We just don't have anything to spare."

Ross knew his friend was being truthful. If he hadn't known the man's nature he could have seen it in the painfully thin condition of McKerrow and his men. "We appreciate the advice. I'll talk to General Shelby. Maybe we can rest along the Canadian for awhile. I'll see you around, Sam. You take care of yourself."

"You too, Ross. Stay awake and keep your powder dry."

The scouts of the First Cherokee Mounted Rifles melted into the woods like ghosts in the night.

Ross wheeled his horse and spurred for the column. Evan kept pace. "Did you say those men were Indians? I've seen a Comanche or two, but they didn't look nothing like that."

"The Cherokees are one of the civilized tribes. They were originally from the mountain country of North Carolina, Georgia, and Alabama. The United States government took their homes and land and forced them to move to Indian Territory in what is known as the Trail of Tears. Many people died during this terrible journey. Sam told me about it once.

"They are called the civilized tribes because many of them live and dress like white men. They have their written language and publish their own newspapers in Cherokee and English. Some of them own slaves and have Southern-style mansions."

They rode on in silence until they reached the column. They made their report to General Shelby. Realizing his men must have food and rest, General Shelby requested permission from General Sterling Price for his men to stop for a week along the banks of the Canadian River. General Price reluctantly agreed, and Shelby's command halted along the riverbanks while Price's men continued their journey.

Here the grass was plentiful, and wild cattle, deer, and turkey roamed the woods. Those men who still had horses formed them into skirmish lines and began driving game. Guns used recently against Yankees now fired on the wild animals.

Within a short while Shelby's men were gorging themselves on wild beef, venison, and turkey. They ate until they couldn't eat anymore, then slept. When they awoke they ate again. Leftover beef was dried and jerked. A week of good water and good grass saved what few horses remained. Soon Shelby's brigade was on the march again.

But Nature wasn't finished torturing them yet. Cold,

driving rains continued, followed by blinding snowstorms. Finally when the men were weakest, a wave of smallpox hit the straggling army. Hundreds more soldiers died along the march. Most of those lost were wounded and weakened by the struggle. Heaviest hit were the mostly unarmed new recruits who had been gathered on the expedition through Missouri. Unused to the rigors of outdoor living, this extreme weather took a heavy toll among them. Weakened by exposure, they were easy prey for the disease that ran rampant through the column.

The army left those who died along the trail where they fell. The soldiers didn't want to leave their comrades and friends for the coyotes and wolves to feast on, but the ground was too frozen to dig graves, and those still living were too weak to dig them. The precious few spaces left in the remaining wagons were needed for those still fighting for life.

Through it all, Jessie Kimbrough managed to survive. His strength increased slowly. Star's Pride died before they reached the Canadian River. Reduced to skin and bone from the hard campaign, he collapsed on the march, too weak to rise. A bullet ended his misery. The cavalryman who had borrowed him to ride died of smallpox two weeks later.

Although Jessie was recovering, he was unable to walk strongly enough to keep up, and horses were in very short supply. Even General Shelby's horse had died. He refused the offers from his men to take their mounts, and as an example to those on foot, he walked with them the rest of the way to Bonham, Texas. Jessie still rode most of the time in the ambulance, though the recovering William Gaskill gave up his place in the ambulance and walked alongside so others more sickly could ride.

Finally Shelby's brigade made it to the Red River. General Shelby was presented with a powerful, milk-white stallion by a local Texas commander, Captain Collins. The horse cost the patriotic Texan five thousand dollars at a time when both money and horses were rare.

Ross, Jessie, Evan, and Billy were pleased to learn Shelby's brigade was being ordered to Clarksville, Texas, to set up winter camp. Even before the campaign of 1864 had begun, General Shelby had mentioned wintering in the Northeast Texas region, and the Kimbrough men had suggested to the women last winter while at Camden that they should try to live either in Clarksville or Marshall, Texas. They hoped the women had chosen Clarksville. If they had, they would soon be reunited.

36

Bitter Homecoming

Ross rapped lightly on the door of the modest, white frame house. As the man in charge of Shelby's scouts it had been easy for him to get to Clarksville before the rest of the command, and by making various inquiries, he was given directions to the house wherein he would find his family.

Fanny answered the door, and her eyes opened wide in surprise to find Ross standing there. Before she could say anything, Ross signaled her to be quiet. Fanny rushed into his arms and nearly squeezed the life from him. With aching ribs he separated himself gently and walked into the living room. He found Cassandra sitting in a rocking chair reading a book, her back to him.

Ross moved beside her chair and squatted down beside her. "Is it a pretty good book, little sis?"

Startled, Cassandra looked up quickly into the twinkling blue eyes and blond-bearded face of her brother Ross. "How did you get here?" she exclaimed.

Ross laughed at his sister's shocked expression. "On a horse. It was much easier than walking."

She turned and slapped playfully at his shoulder. "Ross, you haven't changed a bit. Still full of the ol' nick, aren't you?"

"Well, don't just sit there. Haven't you got a big hug for your brother?"

Cassandra dropped the book to the floor and embraced Ross tightly. She pulled back from him after a bit so she could see him better. "Are any of the others with you?"

"Now who do you suppose you might be interested in seeing again? It couldn't be a certain Texan, could it?"

Cassandra slapped his arm again because of his teasing. "Well, you know I want to see my brothers, but yes, I've missed Evan. Is he with you?" Her eyes filled with hope.

"No, but he'll be here soon. The whole brigade is heading for Clarksville to set up camp for the winter." Ross paused for a moment, his expression worried. "Are the Covingtons in town? I asked about them and I was told they were here for a while, then left. Are they staying in Marshall?"

Cassandra's smile faded from her face. "No, they aren't here, Ross, and they aren't in Marshall either. They left in June and went somewhere along the coast to meet Joe Farnsworth. Andrew never really said where they were going, and they never returned. In August I received a letter from Andrew Covington. Wait here a moment and I'll get it for you." She could see the shock at the news on Ross's face.

He sank into a chair as she turned and walked to the stairs. She climbed them swiftly and entered her room where she removed the letter from one of the trunks where she had stored it for safe keeping. From the day she had received the letter she dreaded the day she would have to show it to her brother. She knew the news inside would hurt him deeply. She turned with a heavy sigh and returned to Ross in the living room.

"Here it is. I'm afraid it's not good news. I wish there were some way I could change it."

Ross took the letter and looked at it with rising fear in his heart. He felt a cold chill and pulled out the letter, unfolded it, and began to read with trembling hands.

> *Dear Cassandra,*
>
> *We have made our trip safely and met with Joseph Farnsworth. He has offered to take us to Europe on his ship and, in view of how badly the war is going, we have decided to accept his kind offer. It's time I took a more active role in supervising my interests with Farnsworth in our shipping business.*
>
> *Valissa is going with me, and please tell your brother it is over between them. As you are probably aware, I have been opposed to their relationship from the beginning. A man like Joseph Farnsworth has more to offer her than does your brother. After all, your family has lost everything, or at least that is my understanding. Besides, it is doubtful your brother will survive the war in one piece. I have discussed this with Ross before at Covington Manor, and he knows how I feel about it, so I won't go into any more detail about it here.*
>
> *Please tell him good-bye for Valissa and ask him to forget her. I am greatly pleased to say Valissa has found Joseph Farnsworth a most attractive and attentive man. I don't intend to return to Arkansas to settle my affairs until the war is resolved. By then I'm sure Valissa will be Mrs. Farnsworth.*
>
> *I want to thank you for guiding us to Texas and for helping arrange our temporary quarters in Clarksville. We are sailing with the tide on the morrow. Best wishes for you and your family.*
>
> > *My regards,*
> > *Andrew Covington*

Ross felt anger and hurt build within him as he read. Finishing the letter, he crumpled it in his hands until it was a ball, then flung it to the floor. "How could she do this to me?" he bellowed. "How could she turn her back on me like this?" Ross turned and looked at Cassandra as he rose to his feet. Tears rimmed his eyes. "I thought she loved me as much as I love her."

Cassandra moved to her brother, hoping to comfort him. He shoved her away and walked to the fireplace where he laid his head on his arm resting on the mantle. "I thought she was waiting for me. Now I understand why she refused to marry me at Batesville and Camden. She really loved Farnsworth all along and was just using me to amuse herself in his absence."

"Ross, surely you don't believe that. I spent a great deal of time with her after you were gone. She even came here just before she left and told me she loved you. I know women, and I'm sure she told me the truth."

"If she loved me, then why did she leave for Europe with Farnsworth?"

Cassandra looked thoughtful. "I don't know, only she does. Remember, Ross, the letter was written by her father. Maybe she doesn't even know he sent it. Her father might have forced her to go against her will."

Ross was bursting with pent-up anger. All reason fled as he seethed like a bubbling cauldron. "Well, thanks a lot, Cassandra, for the great news. She's gone and there's nothing I can do about it." His jaw was tight and his face flushed. "Well, I've got a job to do. Jo Shelby is waiting for a report on conditions here at Clarksville. I'd better ride."

Cassandra tried to stop him, but he brushed her aside and stormed out of the house. She followed him, trying to get him to listen to her. "Ross, please don't leave here like this! I know it hurts and you're angry, but we love you and we're family. Please stay a while," Cassandra pleaded.

Ross, angry beyond words, flung himself into his saddle after untying the reins of his horse from the hitching rail. His face was a mask of contorted rage. "I'll be back in a little while with the rest of the command. You'll see your precious Evan. At least someone will be happy."

His words stung her with sarcasm. This was a new Ross, an indication of the deep hurt he was suffering. She watched as he spun his horse around and galloped down the street out of sight. Then she turned and walked back in the house.

Fanny was just walking in the living room with a tray of drinks and food. "Where did Massa Ross go?"

"I told him about Valissa. I'm afraid he didn't take the news very well."

"Oh, Lordy, I knew it was gonna be trouble. Did he say how long till the rest of the boys come home, Miz Cassie?"

Cassandra walked past Fanny and over to the balled-up letter on the floor. She carefully began to unroll it and tried to stretch out the creases left in the paper. She thought there might be a time when he wasn't so angry that Ross might regret throwing away the letter. She would keep it for him until then.

She turned to look at Fanny. "Ross said they would be here shortly. How long have Elizabeth and Jethro been gone after groceries?"

"It's been nearly an hour, I'd reckon, Miz Cassie. They should be gettin' back real soon. Lordy, Miz Elizabeth gonna be happy to hear the news."

"I'll be sure to tell her when she gets back. Why don't you slip down to Katlin's house and tell her Jessie is coming home. If Ross can recover from his grief, it will be great to have our family together again."

Fanny smiled as she turned to take the tray back into the kitchen. "Yes, Miz Cassie, it's gonna be like ol' times. I'll hustle right over an' give Miz Katlin and the baby the news. Daddy's comin' home again."

Ross rode Prince of Heaven hard as Clarksville faded behind him. Gradually, he realized he was pushing Prince too harshly and slowed first to a gallop and then to a walk as he let Prince regain his wind.

Ross had never known such confusion. His head was

filled to bursting with a maelstrom of anger, resentment, and grief. The emotions flowed from one into another, then melded in a strange, explosive mix. The pressure within him built until he could contain it no longer. He screamed his pain to the cold night skies in a wail of anger-filled vindictives. His shrieks of pure rage and pain lasted until his voice was gone. Prince sidestepped nervously, the howls roaring about his ears. The horse had never seen or heard his master carry on this way before, and it made him skittish.

Bit by bit, Ross felt his anger slowly subside as his temper spent itself. The yelling rage had vented his wrath, leaving him drained. As his anger diminished, remorse took its place. Remorse for losing the one thing that gave his life hope and direction. Remorse for the loss of his dreams for the future, now broken and shattered. Remorse for the way he had treated his sister and Prince of Heaven.

None of this was Cassandra's fault. She had become a victim of his anger; just a handy target for his pain. Waves of regret filled him now as he resolved to set things right when he saw her again. He had acted like a spoiled child who hadn't got his way. It was not an act worthy of a battle-hardened veteran of Shelby's brigade. He was just glad none of his fellow soldiers or officers had seen his childish display.

Then there was Prince. The poor horse had nothing to do with his present misery and had served him faithfully. He had mistreated him when the horse was worn and tired from months of hard campaigning. He rubbed and patted Prince as he apologized to him. Then tears came quickly and unstoppably, flowing freely as he buried his face into Prince's neck. They came in blurry torrents as he felt the grief and pain released from his body in racking sobs. He was, after all, only human; a man pushed beyond his emotional limit.

This damn war had taken so much from him. He had lost his parents and his home. He had lost his brother and many friends. Now he had lost the girl he loved. He had done all the right things, hadn't he? He had served faithfully and well, always doing his duty. The whole brigade had fought like tigers time and time again, yet victory in the war was slipping through their fingers. It seemed for every Yankee they killed, two more took his place. He had seen them, always well-equipped and uniformed. For the Rebel army, supply was doubtful and always a struggle.

Each Confederate soldier lost was irreplaceable. The ranks were filled with old men and young boys as the South began to scrape the bottom of the barrel. All those brave soldiers—like Calvin—dead and gone, no one left to fill their shoes.

He remembered their march through Indian Territory. Visions filled his memory—visions of tired, starvation-thin soldiers straggling along in rags and bits and pieces of captured Union blues, and horses and draft animals with every rib showing for lack of forage. Death stalked the army like a hunter, making kills here and there and leaving the victims where they fell.

It wasn't fair. The war was being fought in defense of states' rights, for the right to choose the form of government the Southerners wanted. Wasn't it the second American revolution? For Ross it was much more than that. Like so many others, he fought to defend his state and his home. Wasn't it worth fighting for? Hadn't they made the sacrifices and fought the noble fight? The Union had sent troops and they had ravaged and persecuted the people, destroyed his home among countless thousands of others. What had gone wrong? Why had God turned his back on them?

Inside he knew the war was lost. Yet he found he had nothing left but the war. Fighting was all he knew, the only time he felt truly alive. Why couldn't he have been among the brave souls who had died on one of those many battlefields? He envied the dead and felt they were the lucky ones. He would change places with Calvin in a minute if it were only possible. He didn't have to face the pain of admitting they were beaten, of living with surrender.

Ross knew he must draw on some forgotten inner strength. "I can't give up. If I do, then all the lives, all the suffering will have been for nothing. I won't give up! I'll fight to the end, and I'll take every stinkin' Yankee with me that I can," Ross resolved. Eyes aching and red and his voice gone, he rode on to find his army and lead them home.

37

Texas Wedding

Ross rocked the chair up on its back legs, stared up into the early evening skies, and rested his feet on the porch rail. A cool evening breeze flowed over him. The stars were just coming out as he sipped the steaming cup of coffee, its heat comforting him and warming his hands. He enjoyed the satisfying rich taste, warm and wonderful, as it traced its way down his throat and began to warm his belly.

Real coffee. It had been so long since he had enjoyed a cup, but Cassandra had managed to track down the elusive beans. This particular bag had made its way north from Mexico as part of the bustling border trade supplying the Confederacy. In the South, coffee was as scarce as hen's teeth and had been for a long time. Its rarity only enhanced his pleasure.

Ross realized how hard Cassandra and Elizabeth had worked to make their weddings the best they could. Cassandra had gathered the material and lace for the dresses, and with Fanny's help, they had made their wedding gowns.

Tomorrow would be Cassandra and Elizabeth's big day and Ross would walk the two of them down the aisle before friends and family. Tomorrow Cassandra would become Mrs. Evan Stryker and Elizabeth, Mrs. Billy Cahill.

Ross had grown to respect the Texan and considered Evan a brother. He knew from experience Evan was a good man to have protecting your back in a bad situation. He realized Evan loved Cassandra and would do his best to make her a good husband, and the knowledge eased Ross's mind. He contemplated who else he'd rather see Cassandra marry, and only one name came to mind—the one man he respected above all others, Jo Shelby. Since General Shelby was already a married man, Evan Stryker would just have to do. Ross smiled to himself as he thought how silly it was for him even to entertain such ideas. He knew Cassandra was a strong woman and would never allow Ross, or anyone, to make decisions for her in such important matters of the heart.

Ross felt less secure when his thoughts turned to Elizabeth's pending marriage to Billy Cahill. Ross felt Elizabeth was too young to marry, but his opinion had mattered little to her. She argued that many girls much younger than she were getting married all the time. Reluctantly Ross had to admit it was true. Indeed, at age sixteen many Texas and Missouri girls were already married and had children. For those raised in the more genteel climate of plantation life, the age tended to be a little older, but the war was changing many things.

Ross had counseled her to wait a while, but Liz remained adamant. She loved Billy and he loved her, and that was all that mattered. At a tender age, they had survived ordeals young people should never have to face and had stood the test. The hormones of youth run strong, and both were determined, with or without family support, to be together. Ross knew that nothing he could say would discourage them. As the eldest member of his family, he eventually agreed and gave his blessings.

It still concerned Ross when he considered Billy's time with Quantrill. Anger and hatred for Jennison's Jayhawkers and Yankees in general had changed Billy into a calloused killer. Quick of temper and quicker still with a gun, Billy had been trained to fight and kill by the most skilled and cold-blooded killers Ross had ever met.

Billy Cahill was tough and self reliant well beyond his age. Still, in the back of Ross's mind, the worries lingered. Would Billy be the kind of man that could readjust to a peaceful life after killing and raiding had become second-nature to him? Ross smiled. For that matter, he wondered the same about himself. Despite his misgivings, Ross accepted the inevitable.

So tomorrow there would be a double wedding, with Cassandra and Elizabeth sharing each other's big day. The wedding would be at four, with a reception and dance following in the evening at the Donoho Hotel. The wedding ceremonies would be held in the simple chapel on the town square.

"Well, I guess January is as good as any month to tie the knot. At least they'll have a good start to a new year," he thought.

Ross heard the door swing open as Cassandra came out onto the porch. She pulled her shawl tight around her arms as she sat on the porch rail beside him. "It's a beautiful evening, isn't it?"

Ross looked over at her. "Made all the better by this coffee. Thanks, sis."

Cassandra smiled and her expression became more thoughtful. "Ross, are you sure you want me to keep the money?"

"Yes, I want you to have it. You know I don't have any need for it." Ross rocked the chair down on all four legs as he leaned forward and took her hand. "I would like to think it's someplace where it will do some good. Besides, it'll be better protected here than it would be with me."

"I'm glad you killed Bartok. If ever a man more deserved to die, I haven't met him yet. The money is a fine gift. I know it will be a big help. I know Elizabeth and Jessie appreciate their shares, too, but do you really think we should keep it? It was taken from the people of Lafayette County, and it really doesn't belong to us."

"If we hadn't taken it from Bartok, it still wouldn't have been returned to its rightful owners. There's no way we can identify to whom it originally belonged. I only know Bartok burned and robbed our home, and even if we kept the entire amount, it wouldn't replace the value of Briarwood."

"I suppose you're right, but it really belongs to you."

Ross released Cassandra's hand and sat back in the chair. "I don't need it, and the three of you are married, or will be after tomorrow. Consider the money a wedding present to my brother and sisters. Just keep my extra three hundred with you until I need it. I figure the hundred I'm carrying will keep me going for a while."

"Well, you know you're always welcome at San Marcos."

"So you've decided to stay in Texas when the war is over?"

"Yes, Evan has family land there and Jessie will want to return home. I'm not sure I could face seeing Briarwood in ashes again anyway." Cassandra sighed. "Evan has talked so much about San Marcos and how beautiful it is. He even has me dreamin' about a fresh start in a new land. I can take Jethro and Fanny with me, and they've already said they would go."

"He's probably right, sis. When the war is over there will still be hard feelings in Missouri for a long time to come."

Cassandra felt a shiver as the cool evening air worked its way through her shawl. "Let's go in the house where it's warmer. I think Fanny just finished baking a fresh cake. Maybe we could talk her out of a piece and another cup of coffee."

Ross stood and stretched the kinks out of his legs. "It's

too cool out here anyway, and I'd like a piece of cake." Cassandra smiled as she turned and entered the house. Ross followed her.

Cassandra heard the lilting notes of the pump organ as she stood with Ross and Elizabeth at the back of the church. The organist entertained the waiting guests. Cassandra tightened her grip on Ross's arm as she looked up into her brother's eyes. "You know, for the first time I feel like this isn't just a dream. I'm really getting married!"

Ross smiled. "I hope so. I'd hate to think we were doing all this for nothin'." He paused as he looked more concerned. "You're not havin' second thoughts, are you, Cassie?"

"Of course not! I've just waited so long to marry Evan and dreamed so long about my wedding day. It just seemed as if the day would never come. Do you know what I mean?"

"I guess so. Sometimes when you want something with all your heart, you worry about it not coming true. You're not the only one who's nervous. When I saw Evan this morning he was as jumpy as a father of triplets. He's wanting this even more than you are. Don't worry, Cassie, it'll be all right."

Elizabeth said, "I know how Cassandra feels. I've wanted to marry Billy for months, and now it's finally here." She gave Ross a kiss on the cheek. "Thanks, Ross, for giving us your blessing and walking me down the aisle."

Ross smiled at his youngest sister. "My pleasure, Liz." He looked from one sister to the other. "Just remember if you ever need me, just holler and I'll come running. The whole world might turn their backs on you, but family should still be there when all others turn away. Dad always said that's what families do—care for each other through thick and thin. Just remember you can count on me."

Both sisters hugged Ross tightly as the first notes of the wedding march sounded. The cue for their entrance was given as the organist increased her volume on the pump organ. "Wait till Evan and Billy see your wedding dresses. They'll never see anything more beautiful than my sisters if they live to be a hundred."

Cassandra felt her heart pounding as she gripped tightly on her brother's arm. "Here we go," she whispered.

Cassandra, Ross, and Elizabeth paused for a moment in the doorway. Cassandra's eyes locked on Evan as he caught his first glimpse of her in her gown. She vaguely felt the presence of her guests as they entered the aisle and approached the minister and their two grooms, Billy and Evan.

Evan looked stunning in the new major's uniform he had purchased specially for the wedding. Billy Cahill, a wide grin on his face, looked a little outclassed as he stood in his new private's uniform on the other side of the minister.

Cassandra didn't take her eyes off Evan until he stood beside her. She locked all consciousness of those around her from her mind, and for a moment there was only Evan. For today and for always, she would be his. Cassandra was jarred from her thoughts when she heard the minister say, "Who gives Cassandra and Elizabeth Kimbrough to be married to these men?"

Ross Kimbrough said proudly, "I do, on behalf of their family." He turned and took his seat in the front pew.

Ross felt happy for his sisters, but he found himself struggling with envy. His mind cried out, "Why did you leave me, Valissa? I could have made you happy, if I'd only had the chance."

The marriage ceremony passed swiftly, and the two couples kissed. As they walked down the aisle, the congregation exploded into applause. Ross rejoined the newlyweds in the foyer to congratulate the couples. Cassandra rushed to him and held him close for a long moment. "I love you, Ross," she whispered to him.

"I know you do, sis, and I love you, too. Don't forget, if you need me . . ." He let the words trail off silently.

Before Cassandra could reply, Elizabeth pulled him away and took her turn. "Thank you, Ross. I've never felt so wonderful."

"I hope you always feel this happy when you recall this day," he replied.

Billy shook hands with him while he still held Elizabeth in his arms. While Ross shook Billy's hand, Evan pounded him on the back with joy. Ross felt relieved when he stepped aside, allowing Jessie and Katlin to congratulate the newlyweds.

Ross noticed Becca holding little Glen in the alcove near the door. Becca seemed more settled and secure since he had seen her last. Ross attributed the change to her marriage to Jeremiah shortly after the group had arrived in Clarksville. The couple had talked of returning with Jessie to Missouri when the war was over. He envied them—at least they had a plan. All he had was the war.

As the couples greeted their guests on the steps of the church, Ross hurried to the Donoho Hotel. The wedding was more difficult than he had imagined. Right now all Ross wanted was a stiff drink to soothe his aching heart.

Ross sat with his back to the wall with a slightly stupid grin on his face. It had been a hell of a night, though it was far from over. The beer and wine flowed freely at the wedding reception and dance. Ross had made a special effort to get his fair share. The fine bourbon filled him with a numb, warm glow. Ross couldn't recall when he had last escaped the searing pangs of his lost love, but he intended to revel in it and pay the consequences later. After all, it wasn't often a fella married off his two sisters on the same day.

He watched Billy and Elizabeth lead off another waltz. Those two were pure poetry in motion. Ross knew he was a fair dancer, but even he had to admit he didn't hold a candle to the two of them. They flowed around the floor as if they were one person.

Cassandra and Evan had slipped away early from their

guests. Ross smiled slyly. He knew Evan was anxious to begin his honeymoon. "Hell, I don't blame him," he thought. "I'd be in a hurry too if it were my wedding day with a war still going on. Enjoy your time together while you have it, for who knows how long you'll have." With that thought still fresh in his mind, Ross realized he was holding an empty glass—a problem that definitely needed rectifying. He would see to it at once. As he wove his way across the dance floor he bumped into General Shelby and his lovely wife, Betty. "Excuse me, General."

"Good evening, Ross. This is a wonderful dance and reception. I can't recall when I've enjoyed myself more."

"Funny thing, General, I was just thinkin' that myself."

"Your sisters looked just lovely today, and the grooms looked so handsome," Mrs. Shelby said. "It brought back memories of our wedding day. We held our dance on a riverboat while it steamed up and down the Missouri River. It seems like such a long time ago." Her wistful words trailed off.

Ross felt a sudden urge to get on with his quest for another drink. "Thank you, Mrs. Shelby, I'm glad you have enjoyed the day. If you'll excuse me, I should see to our guests." He bowed and stepped away.

"Especially any standing near the bar," Ross said to himself under his breath as he walked away from General Shelby and his wife. Today at least the pain within him was temporarily drowned. When he sobered up he would face reality. Tomorrow . . . perhaps tomorrow.

38

Chaff on the Wind

Two months after General Shelby had established winter camp in Clarksville, Texas, orders came from General Kirby Smith ordering Shelby to march his division to Fulton, Arkansas. General Fagan was organizing an expedition against Little Rock, and General Shelby's division would accompany them. Again tearful good-byes were said as the men left wives and families.

Jessie Kimbrough had just finished eating the last bite of his supper of hardtack and bacon when he spotted Major Stryker walking toward him. Jessie shouted, "How's it goin' at headquarters, Major? Any word when we're headin' for Little Rock?"

As Evan entered the circle of light cast by the fire, Jessie saw the dead serious expression on the face of his brother-in-law. "I've got some news for you, Jess, but it's not about Little Rock. We've heard the rumors for a week, but now it's confirmed. General Lee has surrendered his army and Richmond has fallen."

Jessie looked confused as he tried to decide if this was

some kind of joke Major Stryker was trying to play on him. He half smiled as he tried to play along. "Yeah, and I suppose the King of England has taken over Washington."

"I'm not making a joke, Jessie. General Lee has surrendered his army, Richmond has fallen, and Jefferson Davis and the Confederate congress have scattered like chaff on the wind."

The news hit Jessie like a locomotive. His mind tried to comprehend the news, to grasp its implications, but he just sat there, stunned.

After a moment Evan continued. "I understand they offered generous terms and let our soldiers go home. General Lee wasn't even arrested."

Finally Jessie recovered. "Well, what happens now? Is the war over?"

"I really don't know, Jess. The war isn't over here, not yet anyway. We still haven't heard the fate of the other Confederate armies. Last we heard, General Johnston still had an army in North Carolina."

"What will happen next?"

"I don't know. Ol' Jo went into a rage when he heard about the surrender. He swears up and down he'll never surrender to the Yankees and will fight to the death if need be. He wants to meet with the governors of the Trans-Mississippi region and other field officers to discuss a plan of action. He says they plan to meet at Marshall, Texas, or Shreveport, Louisiana."

Jessie noticed how tired and worn Major Stryker looked. The news had obviously taken the starch out of him. "Do you think the war is lost?" Jessie watched as Evan's eyes watered. A single tear broke away and streaked down his cheek as Evan blinked it away.

He sighed deeply. "It doesn't look good. With the East falling apart, the Union forces will be concentrated on us. To be honest, I don't see how we can win. The best we can do is hope to drag the war out a year, maybe two. In the end, we'll still fail. I just don't see how we can compete with their supplies or numbers."

A heavy gloom settled over Jessie. He thought of all he had been through—the battles, the nights sleeping in the snow, the long separations from family. His brother Calvin was dead, and many friends had been buried along the way; Briarwood was only a memory, and his parents were gone. What had it accomplished? Had all the sacrifice been for nothing? Suddenly he felt very tired. "Why don't we just surrender then and get on with our lives? I'm sick of the killing, the fighting, and living by the side of a campfire. I've had nearly all I can stand. Sometimes I can't even remember why it all started. More and more I realize the only thing that matters is my wife, son, and family. I'd just like to try and put all this misery behind us and start over. How about you?"

Evan nodded grimly. "Yeah, I know, Jess. It nearly ripped my heart out to leave Cassandra again. A man doesn't mind a good fight if you have a chance to win, but I don't want to die for a lost cause."

"Don't let Ross hear you say that. I don't think he'll give up till they bury him."

"I reckon you're right there. Well, I'd better get on back to headquarters. I'm not sure where we're headed yet, but ol' Jo wants me to accompany him to meet with the bigwigs. Take it easy, Jess." Stryker turned to go.

"Yeah, be careful, Major." As Jessie watched Evan disappear into the darkness of night, his emotions rolled over the edge. His face contorted in agony as tears flooded from his eyes in torrents. "Why, Lord, have you forsaken us?" Jessie whispered. "It isn't right we should suffer so much and still lose the war." He buried his head in his crossed arms.

The news of Lee's surrender struck the Rebel army like a thunderbolt. Many refused to believe the reports when they first heard the news. Morale, already at an all-time low, collapsed in most of the army.

The next morning, General Shelby ordered his men to

form in ranks and offered an emotional plea to refuse surrender. He appealed to their bravery, suffering, and pride. They would stand and fight to the last, rather than surrender to the Yankees. If everyone else surrendered, they would gather the loyal Confederates on the Rio Grande and join with Maximilian in carving out a new empire in Mexico. When he was finished with his speech, his old veterans rallied to their commander. Cheers rolled off the surrounding hills. As long as they still had hope, these Missourians would stand with their general.

Ross had been away on a scout when the news broke in camp, and he returned after Jo Shelby had left for the conference. Once in camp he couldn't believe what he was hearing. Talk of surrender was rampant among other segments of the army. Only Shelby's division, for the most part, stood steadfast in their belief in the cause and their commander. Ross could understand why soldiers were discouraged and tired of war, but he couldn't understand how they could even consider surrender. Better to go into the hills and fight until the bitter end than admit defeat to the enemy!

For the moment the division stood by their commander, and General Shelby dispatched Major Lawrence and Major John Thrailkill to Shreveport for additional artillery and ammunition. There they secured a full battery of rifled cannon for Collins's battery. Since Westport they had been reduced to one artillery piece. This would bring them up to full strength.

Ross rode along the riverbank of the great Red River, searching for Billy Cahill. When he found him, Billy was sitting beside a quiet pool, a crude fishing pole in his hands. Ross shouted to him, "Hey, Billy, catchin' anything?"

"Nothin' bitin' but the mosquitoes. How did you know I was here?"

Ross rode near him and swung out of the saddle. "I just got back from around Little Rock. When I got back I started looking for you. Some of the boys said I'd find ya down here fishin'."

"Well, they didn't steer ya wrong." Billy pulled his string in again to check his bait. While he worked at it he talked to Ross. "What brings you clear out here lookin' for me? I don't recall you having any special interest in fishin'."

"Now is that any way to greet your brother-in-law?" Ross tied the reins of his horse to a nearby bush. "Truth is I heard some news while on scout I thought you'd want to know. So I came looking for you."

Billy baited another worm on his improvised hook. When he finished threading the wiggler, he looked up at Ross. "If it's important enough for you to come lookin' for me, I guess you'd better spill it." With a flick of the wrist Billy cast the hook and his wooden float back onto the water and watched as the line settled beneath the surface.

Ross sat beside Billy. "We intercepted Federal telegrams when we tapped into a line near Little Rock. In their reports they passed on some information on guerrilla activities. It seems Federal Missouri Militia killed Bloody Bill Anderson in Ray County, Missouri, on October 26, 1864. The report said he rode through a Union line of mounted cavalry in a desperate charge. He was shot in the back of the head twice as he tried to escape. They found a letter from General Price on his body giving him orders to attack the railroads. Even though he never carried out his orders, the Yanks are using the letter to make us look bad."

Billy continued to stare at the water as he replied. "I knew it would happen someday. Bloody Bill had more guts than sense. I know he'd never let 'em take him alive. Funny thing is the Yankees never realized what a murdering machine they were creating when they messed with his family. They made him the way he was, and a hell of a lot of good men died because of it."

"We also heard they killed Riley Crawford in Cooper County sometime in late 1864. He was shot to death at the age of sixteen. Rumors have Quantrill and a small band of men in Kentucky. Missouri finally got too hot for him. The Feds think other guerrillas are heading to Texas, and a few are still trying to lay low in Missouri."

"You know, there was a time Riley and I was close. As time passed he turned bitter and mean. Ol' Bloody Bill took him under his wing and Riley ate it up. For some reason, I suppose because we were close to the same age, Riley decided to make everything between us a contest. I wouldn't back down to him, and it caused trouble."

"You won't have to worry about him anymore, Billy."

"I know we had some fights, but we had a lot in common. I didn't like the direction he took, but I didn't want to see him die."

"I understand. Once you've fought and camped by another man it makes it personal."

"Yeah, something like that."

"We heard more news. Colonel Shanks died of wounds suffered at Jefferson City. He was in a Yankee hospital at Jefferson City when he died."

"You're just loaded with good news today, aren't you?" Ross threw a rock into the water away from Billy's fishing line. "Colonel Shanks was a good officer. He was one of the most decent and bravest men I've fought under. I didn't think he'd survive his wound, and I think ol' Jo knew it, too. It's hard to replace a man like Colonel Shanks."

"I know."

"Your float bobbed—hook 'em, Billy."

Billy set the hook and a few moments later he pulled in a nice-sized catfish.

"Catch another one, Billy, and I'll stay for supper."

While General Shelby traveled to Marshall, Texas, to get nearer to the commanders, the governors and commanders of the Trans-Mississippi met at Shreveport to consider their course of action. At Shreveport the news was disheartening. General Lee's army had surrendered and disbanded. Jefferson Davis was in flight, and the Confederate Congress was scattered. At the meeting of Trans-Mississippi governors, each in turn stood and resolved to fight on. Texas was full of supplies and perhaps the Rebels from east of the Mississippi would make their way to them to continue the fight. Amid the meetings and patriotic speeches, the Union flag-of-truce boat arrived on the lower Red River with communications for the Confederate commanders. When word reached General Shelby's ears he left immediately for Shreveport to talk with regional commander General Kirby Smith.

For Evan Stryker the day seemed unusually sultry for this time of the year in Shreveport. General Shelby had been almost unbearable since they had left Marshall. Shelby couldn't believe Confederate leaders could even seriously consider surrender, and he was determined to stop them. Bright and early they were at headquarters, waiting to meet with General Smith. Eventually they were ushered into his office. General Shelby marched to General Smith's desk and gave a snappy salute, while Major Stryker did the same from near the door.

General Smith looked up from studying papers scattered on his desk. He returned a casual salute. "Good afternoon, General Shelby. What can I do for you?"

"General Smith, I've heard the Federals have contacted you and asked for our surrender. Is it true, sir?"

General Smith leaned back in his chair while absent-mindedly tugging at his beard as he talked. "The reports you've heard are accurate. I've sent Colonel Flourney down to the lower Red River to meet with them, and I've gone over these reports I've received from him."

"What do they have to say?"

"The news I have received from the Federals is disturbing. They have informed us of the surrender of General Johnston's army in North Carolina and Confederate forces at Mobile Bay. They have asked for our surrender of the Trans-Mississippi region to Federal forces."

"Do you believe them?"

"I've worried about it being some kind of deception, but I've heard similar reports from our own sources."

"General, do you intend to surrender?"

"It seems useless to prolong a hopeless struggle if indeed, the Cis-Mississippi region is in total collapse. However, it is not my intention to surrender this department." General Smith stood and leaned forward on his desk. "If my troops will stand by me, I will fight to the end." He turned and crossed his arms as he stared out the window. "It is nothing more than my supreme duty that I should hold out at least until President Davis reaches this department or I receive some definite orders from him."

General Shelby was visibly relieved. "Then I would like to ask your permission to issue new uniforms to my men and equip them with the latest weapons for battle."

General Smith nodded in agreement. "We are fortunate to be well supplied by the blockade runners and border trade with Mexico. Ever since the Federals seized the Mississippi River and disrupted our trade with our sister states, supplies have built up here." He slammed his fist into his other hand. "If only we had the means to distribute the supplies to our troops." General Smith began to pace. "Most of the Confederate ports east of us have been closed by the blockade, and the blockade runners have brought their surplus to Texas so they can still make their profit. It irks me to see these supplies sitting about idle when they should be put to good use." Smith turned to face Shelby. "General Shelby, I can't think of another brigade or division in this department that deserves it more. I'll sign the orders immediately authorizing you to equip your men from government supplies."

"We'll need additional ammunition, too, sir."

"And you shall have it." General Kirby Smith sat in his chair again. "Jo, I'm calling a meeting of the Confederate governors and commanders at Marshall to discuss the Union demands. We're too close to the enemy here, and conditions are too unsettled. Will you accompany me?"

"Yes, General, it would be my pleasure."

"Then it is settled. I'll make necessary arrangements for the conference, and we'll leave in the morning. You're dismissed, General Shelby." General Smith returned his attention to the paperwork before him.

General Shelby saluted, spun on his heels, and headed for the door, not even waiting for a return salute. Major Stryker followed him out the door.

When Shelby arrived at Marshall he ordered his troops supplied at Pittsburg, Texas, where they had moved from near Fulton, Arkansas. Soon Shelby's old veterans were uniformed in bright, new Confederate uniforms.

Meanwhile General Smith and General Shelby met with the Confederate governors and generals who were able to attend at Marshall, Texas. Disturbed by further discussions with General Smith and the way the meetings were leaning early in the conference, Jo Shelby and most of the important Confederate officers joined in a secret meeting without General Smith's knowledge or presence.

At the meeting Jo Shelby proposed that General Kirby Smith be replaced with General Simon Buckner, military commander of Texas. Shelby also proposed that they confer with leaders of Mexico, concentrate the army on the Brazos River, and fight step by step, if necessary, to the Rio Grande. This would allow time for Confederates from the east to join them and then they could form a new republic or join Maximilian in Mexico. Those attending agreed to the plan.

Evan Stryker accompanied generals Shelby, Hawthorne, and Buckner as they paid a late-evening visit to General Smith. After a short wait, the four were led into General Smith's quarters by his adjutant. "Gentlemen, my adjutant tells me you've come on urgent business. For you to come calling at such a late hour, I assume he's correct."

Shelby, determined and with his course set firmly in his mind, got right to the point. "General Smith, it has become common knowledge you intend to surrender to the Federals. The army has lost confidence in you and demands a change of command. General Buckner has been selected as the proper officer to assume command."

General Smith tried to remain calm in the face of this news, but the emotional impact was too much for him to bear. General Kirby Smith began to cry. His voice cracking with emotion, he replied, "I feel great sorrow that my soldiers, in the last trying hours, should fear my leadership. I have always done my duty to the utmost of my ability." The general quickly wiped his eyes with his sleeve, then said, "It has never been my intention to surrender. I am willing to fight, and ask only for the support of my men."

General Hawthorne, touched by the emotional scene before him, stepped forward and said, "General, not one of us here would doubt for a moment your sincerity and patriotism, but in view of the feelings of the common soldiers and for the almost universal desire for a change in leadership, I hope you will consider this sacrifice for the common good."

Defeat and resignation showed clearly on General Smith's face. He turned warily toward General Buckner. "General Buckner, please issue orders immediately for the concentrating of troops on the Brazos River. I hereby resign my command of the military troops in this region. I will sign the order putting you in command of the troops tonight. I will leave for Shreveport in the morning to see to the rest of my duties as head of the department for non-military matters."

When the meeting ended, Evan Stryker felt sure they had ended any possibility of surrender in the region. He knew feelings in the army ran against General Smith, but Evan had been touched by Smith's reaction to their demands. It had left him uncomfortable and anxious to flee these quarters. General Shelby and Major Stryker returned to the division which in their absence had moved to Stony Point, Texas.

General Kirby Smith, upon returning to Shreveport, found two communications awaiting him. The first was a request from all the governors of the states of Arkansas, Louisiana, and Texas requesting him to give up the struggle and surrender; only the governor of Missouri had refused to sign the document. The second letter was from Union colonel John Sprague demanding the immediate surrender of the armies of the Trans-Mississippi region to General John Pope.

At first General Smith refused to cooperate or meet the Union demands, feeling the terms were too harsh. When General Pope agreed to modify them, Kirby Smith caved in. General Smith then ordered Buckner to surrender, as if Smith had never resigned his command. Meekly, General Buckner complied and, on May 15, 1865, General Smith surrendered his department to Union general Pope at Shreveport. Even though Kirby Smith was no longer commander of the army of the Trans-Mississippi, General Buckner agreed to the surrender, ending forever the official existence of the army of the Trans-Mississippi.

Discouraging news of the collapse of the war in the East spread throughout the region. Soldiers, tired of long years of fighting with no hope for victory, began to drift away. Whole units disbanded and headed home, particularly those calling Texas home. Chaos, followed by anarchy, filled the countryside as entire Texas cavalry squadrons left in the night. Many of those who left plundered all along their line of march. Government stores, warehouses, and manufacturing plants were looted. Treasury offices were raided and supplies stolen or destroyed. Quartermaster supplies and commissary trains were taken over. Private dwellings and stores were robbed of anything of value in the collapse of Confederate control.

Through it all, nearly all Shelby's men remained loyal and stood by their commander. In the areas near his command, General Shelby did all he could to restore order, dispatching his troops to quell the disturbances and protect personal and public property.

During this perilous time, word came of the murder of

President Lincoln, further casting confusion among the Confederates. How would the North react?

It took several days for the orders to reach General Shelby. When they arrived, Major Stryker delivered the message. "General, these orders just arrived from Shreveport. You'd better look at them."

"Thank you, Major. Please remain in case we have to issue orders for a march." Jo opened the order and began to read. As he did, his jaws tightened and his face began to turn red with rage. "Edwards, Stryker, do you know what this is?" Without waiting for a reply from the officers, he continued. "My orders are to march my men to Shreveport to surrender. It says under no circumstances are we to take hostile action against any United States troops. The order is signed by generals Buckner and Smith.

"I knew Kirby Smith was a damn fool, but I thought better of Buckner. This is his fault." Shelby paced in his tent as he wadded the order tightly and threw it on the floor. "How could I ever have been foolish enough to support General Simon Buckner as the leader of this army?"

Major Stryker knew the end of the war was drawing near. The collapse of the war in the east would inevitably bring pressure on the Trans-Mississippi states that they could not withstand. Yet he knew Jo Shelby was far from accepting defeat. Then it came to Stryker—a memory about General Buckner that he had suppressed. Now it would not be denied. "General, if you recall, this isn't the first time Buckner has surrendered a Confederate army. He signed the surrender of nearly twelve hundred Confederates at Fort Donaldson in February 1862, as I recall."

"By heaven, you're right. I'd forgotten it. Now the son-of-a-bitch has betrayed us again. He gave up the first Confederate army to surrender and now the last at Shreveport."

Shelby slammed his fist into the table before him, causing reports and papers to fly in all directions. "Surrender . . . hell, I'll never surrender! Buckner and Smith have turned their back on us, by God, and I'm gonna put a stop to it. Major Edwards, write an address to my troops. I want them to know how these men have betrayed their trust! Tomorrow we march on Shreveport and end this madness! Well ... don't just stand there gawking, Major, get out there and spread the word! I want every regiment ready to march at dawn!"

"Yes, sir, I'll see to it immediately, sir." Never in all his days had Evan seen his commander more angry. There would be hell to pay when they reached Shreveport.

39

Farewell to Comrades in Arms

G eneral Shelby was determined to stop the surrender. After addressing his troops the next morning, the veterans swung into the saddle and began their march on Shreveport. Even with great intentions, nature can play havoc. A great spring storm struck East Texas and turned into a mighty gully-washer. All the bridges between Stony Point and Shreveport were washed away, and normally peaceful little streams became impassable torrents. On the second day of the march, the Missouri division camped in a shallow lake, which the day before had been open prairie.

More days passed before the roads were once again passable. Jo Shelby fussed and fumed at the delays. Every day that passed meant his chances to halt the surrender were slipping through his fingers. Finally, when they could again travel, the Missourians met groups of stragglers on their way home after surrendering.

Shelby and his division were too late. Division after division had marched into Shreveport, stacked arms, been given their paroles, and taken the road for home. Those who refused to suffer the indignity of surrender simply disbanded and headed for home. The army of the Trans-Mississippi had surrendered without so much as firing a shot. Shelby's last battle had been at Newtonia in October, 1864, when they defeated Blunt and ended further pursuit of Price's army. Mother Nature defeated Shelby's veterans where many a Yankee regiment had failed.

Jo Shelby was stunned by the news and his veterans were saddened, but they would not march in to surrender like the rest. Sadly, General Shelby turned the Missouri cavalry division away from Shreveport toward Corsicana, Texas.

The only comfort Jo Shelby found in the reports of the stragglers was that General Kirby Smith had refused to surrender until ordered to do so by the Confederate governors of the Trans-Mississippi. Even then, Smith held out until he could get the best terms. At least they remained at war longer than those surrendering in the East. To his knowledge, only Shelby's Missouri division and General Stand Watie's Cherokee brigade, in Indian Territory, had still not surrendered, but he couldn't be certain, with communications the way they were. Now most of his still-smoldering anger was directed at Buckner. They camped for the last time as a Confederate division on an undulating green plain near Corsicana. Throughout the night Shelby's veterans gathered in small groups to discuss what would happen now and to speculate on what General Shelby would do next. Orders were issued for formation of the division in the morning. Jo Shelby wanted to address his troops.

For the Kimbroughs it was time for a family meeting. Ross called them together around his scouts' campfire. Ross sat staring into the dancing flames as his brothers-in-law and Jessie arrived one at a time. Jessie saw the anguish on Ross's face. The pain and despair were too deep to be hidden. Jessie felt his own hopelessness. They all had suffered, and now it looked as if it had been for nothing. As each man came in, Ross spoke softly and nodded his head in greeting. Each in turn was asked to sit on a log that had been placed around the fire.

When the last one came in, Ross called to Jonas Starke. "Sergeant, I'd like to talk privately with my family. Would you mind taking Rube and the boys somewhere else for a while?"

"No, sir, no problem at all, Captain. A little walk might do the boys good. I'll just air 'em out a mite, if you don't mind. You boys have a good talk, and we'll be back shortly."

"Thanks, Sergeant."

Jonas winked at his captain, then turned to the scouts. "All right you scalawags, get crackin'! Captain wants me to give ya a little air, and by the smell of ya, you sure can use it."

Rube Anderson mumbled under his breath just loud enough for Ross to hear. "If anyone around here smells, it's that damned old scarecrow, Sergeant Starke."

"What was that, Rube?" Jonas asked.

"I didn't say nothin', Sergeant. Must have been my stomach rumblin'." He winked at Ross and followed the sergeant away from the fire.

When they were gone, Ross turned to Evan. "Major, you've been at headquarters. Do you have any idea what's going on? Why has the general called the formation in the morning?"

"Word at headquarters is he's working on a speech with Major Edwards. He'll disband the division in the morning, rather than surrender to the damn Yankees. Those that want to can go with him to Mexico, and those who don't can go home—least that's the rumor floatin' around."

Ross grabbed a small branch from the firewood near him and began prodding the red-hot coals in the fire. "I can't believe it's all come down to this. All these years of fightin', all the suffering for the Confederacy, and now we're just supposed to forgive and forget and let the Yankees have it all." As he talked he jammed the stick harder and harder into the fire until the wood snapped.

Evan said, "We all hurt, Ross, and we've all suffered. There's not a man in this camp who hasn't lost family or friends. We've all seen Missouri, Arkansas, and even parts of Texas laid to waste, but we've done all we can do. We fought a good fight for a just cause, but we're whipped and there isn't any way we can change it."

"The hell we are! The Missouri division isn't whipped. Look around you, Major. This whole outfit is wearing brand-spankin'-new uniforms courtesy of brigade quartermaster Jake Stonestreet. He got us the best for our division. We've never been better equipped or supplied than we are right now. We've had several months to rest our mounts and resupply, and we're going to quit just like that?" Ross stood as he spoke and hurled the stick into the night to punctuate his anger.

"So what's the point, Ross? What good is it gonna do to take on the whole United States Army with one division? We can't whip them by ourselves."

"We shouldn't quit without a fight, either. I say we fight 'em as long as we can, and then we take to the hills and fight 'em some more till they pull out and leave us alone."

Jessie stood toe to toe with his brother. "It won't make any difference, Ross. If every man here dies in the name of the Confederacy, it won't change a thing. Can't you see that? It's not worth it to die for nothin' just because we don't want to admit defeat."

Anger burned brightly in Ross's eyes, smoldering like a raging fire. He clinched his fists tightly at his side. "If we quit, then all we have done will be for nothin'. How do you think Calvin would feel if he were to hear this? Did he die for nothing? What about Mother and Father, and Briarwood? You just gonna forget what happened to them? We can't surrender to those who have destroyed our home and our family. I don't understand how you can turn your back."

The remark hit Jessie like a slap across the face, and he

jabbed his finger briskly into his brother's chest. "I won't ever forget what happened, but there is nothing you or I can do to change it. Killing every damn Yankee won't bring our family back or put one brick of Briarwood back in place. Don't you dare try to tell me what Cal would say if he were here. You know damn well what he would say. Calvin attended college until they closed it. He didn't want nothin' to do with the war until he was forced into it. You want to know what Calvin would say? I'll tell you. He'd say you done your best, but you lost. There isn't any shame in it when you've given it your all. He would say go home. Go home and live in peace, like good, God fearin' men. Get on with your lives and put the killin' behind you. That's what I believe Calvin would say if he were here."

"How can you say that, Jess? Your brother never turned his back to the enemy. He fought like a tiger until the day he died."

"Calvin always did his duty, but he never wanted to go to war. You of all people should know that. How often did you try to talk him into dropping out of college to join the army? I was the one that dreamed of glory, it wasn't Calvin. I was the one who looked up to my big brother and couldn't wait to get in the army and kill Yankees. I thought somehow it would all be grand and glorious and full of pageantry. Well, I damn sure found out different. Somehow Calvin knew, and when he enlisted he did his duty, but he never found pleasure in war. You know in your heart what he'd say—don't sacrifice even one more life if there's no hope of winning."

"So what are ya gonna do, Jess?"

"If General Shelby disbands the division tomorrow, I'll go home to Katlin and my boy. I'll take them back to Missouri. I'll go home to the ashes of Briarwood and see what I can do to reclaim our land. I doubt if I can rebuild her to her former glory, but I don't want anyone but Kimbroughs living on the land where Father died."

"You think you're just gonna walk back in there like

nothing has happened and start over? If you think the Yankees will let Rebels keep their land, you're a bigger fool than I thought you were."

"The terms they've offered say we can return home and live in peace. I aim to try. My wife and son deserve some kind of life. I want more for them than living in constant fear. I refuse to die for a lost cause."

Ross turned to face the others. "Evan, how about you? What will you do?"

Evan Stryker leaned forward, his eyes on the ground before him. He let out a big sigh, then slowly looked up at Ross. "I think Jessie makes sense, Ross. There isn't any point of goin' on with the war anymore. Hell, we don't even have a country left to fight for. If Shelby cuts us loose I'm going to San Marcos. I haven't seen my folks since the war started, and I'm like Jess—I've had enough war to last a lifetime. I want to get back to the land and try to make a living. I want to raise a family. Cassandra deserves a home and I want to give her one, God willin'."

Ross turned to Billy. "What about you, Billy? You've been through more than any of us. Tell them we must fight on." Billy slowly shook his head no.

"Can't do it, Ross. I've had enough, too. I'd like to take Elizabeth and see if I can start over on my father's land."

Jessie smiled at his brother-in-law. "Billy, I hope you and Elizabeth will consider traveling to Missouri with us."

"I was hoping you'd ask. It'd be a pleasure."

Ross couldn't believe his ears. All they had been through, and suddenly they were ready to throw it all away as if it never happened. "I never thought I'd see the day when I'd see Kimbroughs quit." He gave them a bitter look as though he had eaten something that left a foul taste in his mouth. "Well, I refuse to go home with my tail tucked between my legs like some whipped dog. I won't live in the shadows of a Yankee victory. I don't want to hear them gloat how they whipped our tails. I'd rather die first. I'll leave the country before I'll accept defeat. I'll go with General Shelby to Mexico if he'll have me. If he won't, I'll find another way to get out of the country."

"Suit yourself, Ross, but if you change your mind you'll always be welcome in San Marcos," said Major Evan Stryker. "I've been a Texan long enough to know I don't want any part of Mexico. You might have heard of a fella named Santa Anna. He didn't have any problems getting the Mexicans to hate us Anglos, and he slaughtered a bunch of us. I wouldn't trust any Mexican leader, 'cause they're likely to turn on ya at anytime. You'll be just another damn gringo foreigner in their eyes. You'll see what I mean when you find out what it's like to live where you don't savvy the lingo."

"If it's good enough for Jo Shelby, it's good enough for me." Ross softened his expression. "I guess I'd look at things a little different if I had a wife waiting for me. I guess much of what you said makes sense, Jess, but I'm not ready to live in peace with the Yankees. It's gonna take a good long while to settle the hate in me."

"Think it over, Ross. Maybe in the morning, with a good night's sleep, things will look different."

"I wouldn't count on it, little brother." Ross put his hands in his pockets and strolled out beyond the circle of firelight. "I'm gonna find my scouts. Good night."

After Ross left, the others sat quietly around the fire, each not ready to give up this last night of camaraderie.

Jessie knew there would be times he would miss the fellowship of the old Iron Brigade. The adrenaline rush of battle and the thrill of victory had become a way of life and hope had sustained them through the darkest moments. Now all hope of victory was lost, ground away in the crucible of war. It was a strange quirk of war to mix those intense highs, those victorious moments, with the gutwrenching fear of death or dismemberment. Death had been their constant companion, and fear of cowardice under fire in front of his friends had haunted him.

There were those long periods of near starvation, long, miserable marches in horrible weather, and tedious months spent in boring camplife as diseases struck down the weak among them. Somehow by God's grace he had come through it all, and now for the first time he could truly look to the future. The men, one by one, drifted off to their camps before Ross returned.

The next morning, June 2, 1865, dawned bright and clear. Long before the hot summer sun climbed its way onto the distant horizon, Shelby's division formed in ranks on the prairie before their commander.

General Shelby stepped forward and stood in front of his battle-hardened veterans, each outfitted in a new uniform. The general's glance swept down the ranks, falling on familiar faces that had faithfully followed him through endless battles and campaigns without question.

He eyed with pride the proud battle flags, now faded, tattered, and ripped by enemy bullets in engagements too numerous to count. In those stars he had once seen hope for a new nation. Under its bars he had witnessed countless heroes die for Missouri. His eyes glistened a bit as he nervously cleared his throat.

"Gentlemen, you stand before me as the last Confederate division in the field. All others from Virginia, North Carolina, and all points in between have already struck their colors, surrendered, or disbanded and gone home. You alone represent the pride that once was the Confederacy.

"I just want to tell you how proud I am to be the one who had the privilege of leading the best damn cavalry west of the Mississippi into battle. Your brave deeds will be long remembered by those who love Missouri and the South.

"The Confederacy is no more, and the war is over, but when you leave here I want you to stand tall and walk proudly with your heads held high. The South may have lost the war, but you, my brave soldiers, fought to the last until all others had deserted you. You did your best, and I'm damn proud of each and every one of you."

Ross watched General Shelby carefully as he listened to

the general's speech. Shelby's words brought a lump to
Ross's throat and tears to his eyes. He clenched his teeth
tightly together, trying to keep the tears in check, but it
was a losing battle as they coursed their way, wet and
damp down his cheeks. Never had he admired Shelby
more. Jo was the perfect picture of a leader of men: He
was splendidly dressed in an immaculate general's uniform
trimmed in cavalry yellow and gold braid. He wore black,
knee-high cavalry boots. At the general's side swung his
sword, and upon his belt he wore two holstered pistols.
The black plume flowed from the crown of his officer's
hat. They had followed that plume through nearly every
engagement. All the while the general's speech continued.

"They ordered me to march this division to Shreveport
to surrender our arms to the United States government. I
say to hell with them. This division will never surrender
our arms to the enemy.

"However, we still have to face the fact the war is over.
Therefore, those of you who want to go home to your families are free to do so." General Shelby swept the plumed
hat off his head and stood before his men, his chestnut
locks caught in the breeze and fluttering there. "I, for one,
will not submit to the humiliation of accepting defeat at
the hands of our enemies. I am going instead to Mexico
with the hope of joining Maximilian, or if need be, forming our own empire. Those of you who will follow me are
welcome. If you want to join us, remain here tonight. In
the morning we will elect officers and form our command
before we march south."

Before he could say more, one of his veterans bore forward the faded Stars and Bars of his old brigade and
planted the point of the staff in the ground before General
Shelby. As if they were an unstoppable wave rushing toward a shore, his soldiers gathered around their old commander. Some were there to say good-bye and others to
volunteer for Mexico. Jo Shelby couldn't hold his emotions in check any longer, and the tears flowed freely
down his cheeks. His veterans gathered around him to give

their farewell hugs or simply to shake his hand. All seemed to have a universal need to touch the man who had become nearly a father to them and they his children. They had given their all for this man, and they loved him. He had become their symbol of unity and hope, but it was forever over for the Confederacy. Tomorrow Shelby would lead his volunteers to Mexico, but today was for saying final farewells to old comrades in arms.

The hard riding, the burning homes, and the bloody battles were finally done.

About the Author

When you talk to Randal L. Greenwood, his lifelong love for American history comes shining through. He has been fascinated with the American Civil War and western history since the fifth grade. "My mother's family were Missouri Confederates, and all my ancestors on my father's side were Union veterans. For some reason the Rebel in me has always ruled my heart."

Randy has lived most of his life in Hugoton, Kansas, in the southwest corner of the state. He received his B.S. in history from Kansas State University in 1972.

"I've been a full-time professional photographer since 1978. Photography offers a visual creativity to my life, while writing gives me other outlets to express myself. I feel photography helps me visualize." Randy is married to Rebecca Richmeier Greenwood and is the father of three children, Evan, Amber, and Ciara.

His interests include collecting books and novels about western history, the Civil War, and the World War II European theater air war. "My favorite hobby is watching and following Winston Cup stock car racing. I collect the diecast and cards. These guys are my heroes and I follow their careers like other sports fans follow baseball or football teams." Other interests include playing paintball and watching boxing, horse racing, and movies.